I0601083

A DYING SECOND SUN

PETER A. DOWSE

Copyright © 2022 by Peter A. Dowse

All rights reserved. No part of this publication may be reproduced, distributed or transmitted in any form or by any means, without prior written permission.

Publisher's Note: This is a work of fiction. Names, characters, places, and incidents are a product of the author's imagination. Locales and public names are sometimes used for atmospheric purposes. Any resemblance to actual people, living or dead, or to businesses, companies, events, institutions, or locales is completely coincidental.

Serenade Publishing

www.serenadepublishing.com

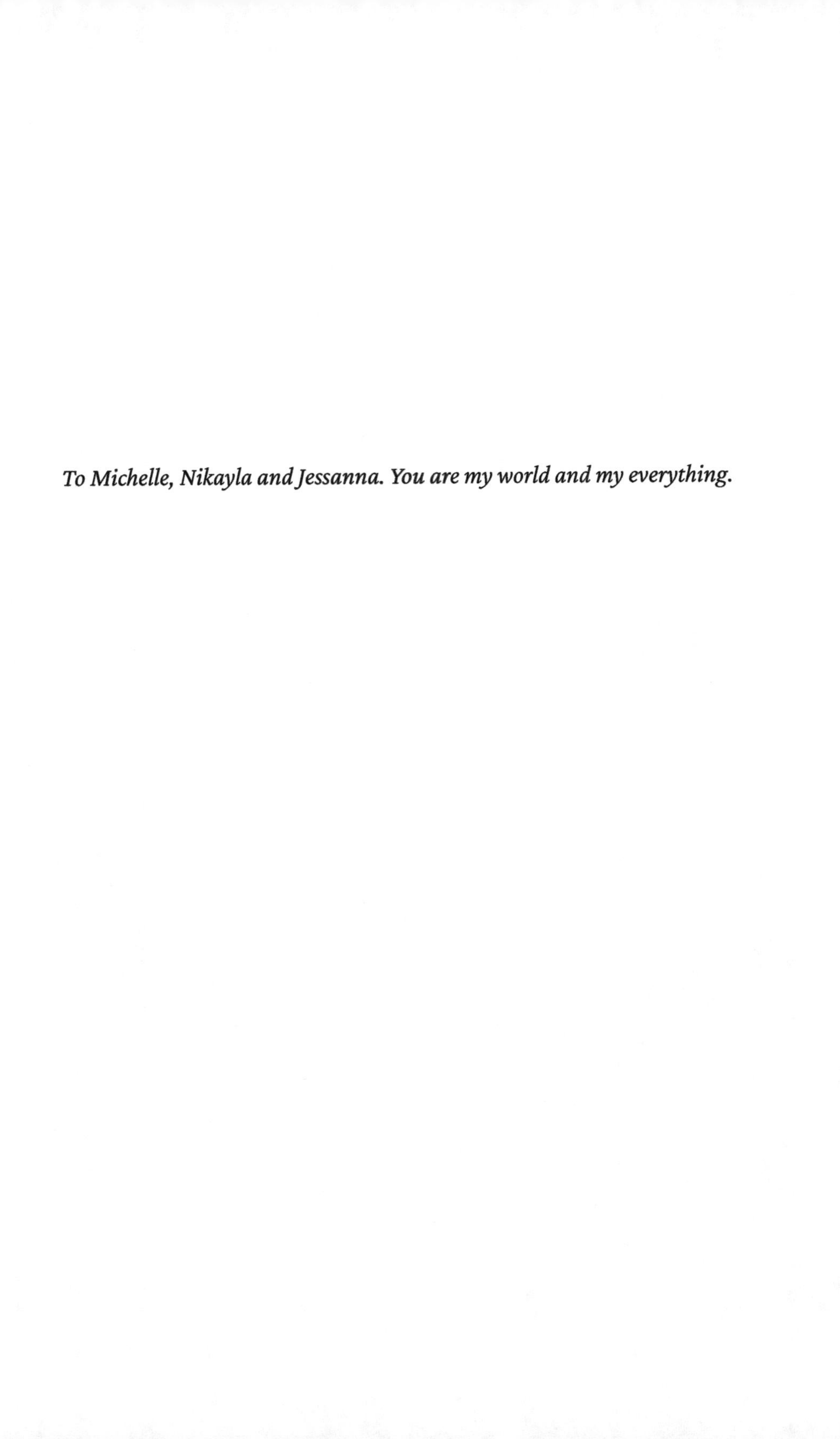

To Michelle, Nikayla and Jessanna. You are my world and my everything.

MORE FROM SERENADE PUBLISHING

Brigadier Station Series

By Sarah Williams:

The Brothers of Brigadier Station

The Sky over Brigadier Station

The Legacies of Brigadier Station

The Outback Governess (A Sweet Outback Novella)

Christmas at Brigadier Station (An Outback Christmas Novella)

Heart of the Hinterland Series

By Sarah Williams:

The Dairy Farmer's Daughter

Their Perfect Blend

Beyond the Barre

A Dying Second Sun

by Peter A. Dowse

Winner Winner Chicken Dinner

by Sarah Jackson

For more information visit:

www.serenadepublishing.com

INTRODUCTION

Fawe is a world in decline. Twin suns grace its skies, but the second glowing orb, which brings summer months and mild weather, is dying. Farmers used to sunshine and surplus wake to find their fields covered in frost and failure. Those who eke out springtime harvests discover their crops are paltry in comparison to years past. Beasts of burden must work harder every year to break frozen ground and traverse the icy roads. Some move to the cities to try their luck. Others sell off possessions just to live. Some become so desperate they indenture their children or resign themselves to a life of servitude for the security of hot meals and warm beds. Many hang a noose from trees in the forests. One final act of defiance and desperation. The only control they have in a world that's growing ever colder.

New and unusual animals arrive in places they'd not lived for centuries. Birds, pyredrakes, spur worms and other flying creatures of the high skies travel farther to find mates and food. The basilisks and leviathans of the deep destroy trading ships regularly, feasting on their unfortunate quarry as precious cargo plunges to the murky depths of the brine. In towns and villages, strangers appear where previously, only family and friends lived peacefully. Soldiers sleep a little closer to fires. Their woollen overcoats don't seem to keep them as warm as they used to. Even in summer, they had to break the ice at the top of their water buckets. Life has grown more arduous for most, and the people of the four kingdoms take little comfort in the chattering of spellbinders languishing in high towers with their maps and charts and theories of why the world is suffering. Smokey taverns fill with stories of witchcraft or enraged deities as the reasons for these troubled times. Some blame kings and khans. Others curse the gods—simple men with simple answers.

OCHOTA MOUNTAI
FIRMALANDS
PYRELANDS
SEMBER
POINT TERRENE
THE GREAT
TUNDRA
THE COLUMNS
SALTPANS

THE BRINE
THADE
THE KINGDOMS OF FAWE

1

STALKING AND SOARING

'If you're unlucky enough to be touched by a spur, you bleed from your eyes and shit your britches as you scream and writhe around on the deck.'

'Really?' said the wide-eyed teenager, tying off the hole he'd just fixed in the rope net he had been repairing.

'Yep. I've heard the pain is so bad, you welcome death.'

'Abe!' shouted Borchin, the ship's burly, bearded captain. 'Stop filling the boy's head with half-truths and falsehoods and get ready at the bow. There are spurworms to be had. I can feel it.'

'That's why they're worth so much,' said Abreeth to the young teenager as he jumped up and clambered to the front of the cloud-cutter. 'Only mad bastards like us hunt them.'

Looking out at the clear afternoon sky below, Abreeth shielded his eyes from the suns and mused, 'I'm not sure we're close yet, Cap?'

'And how would you be knowing if we're close?' enquired Borchin, scratching his red chin whiskers, a hint of amusement in his voice.

'Just a sense,' replied Abreeth, attaching a harpoon to its rope and standing at the front of the craft as it floated through another cloudbank.

'You'll sense my foot in your arse if you miss like last time,' scowled Borchin.

'That wasn't my fault,' complained Abreeth.

'Lightning and storms or not, you still missed,' jibed the captain.

Hefting the unpleasant looking spear used to catch the sky worms, Abreeth investigated the blue horizon painted with clean, white clouds.

'Clear skies this time, Cap. I won't miss.'

Borchin smiled as he spun the wheel and headed for a promising looking cloud formation.

'There's hunting to be had here, boys! I can feel it,' he shouted, sails tight with crisp winds as his craft cut through the skies.

———

Abreeth had worked as a spearman on Borchin's cloudcutter for almost a year and was responsible for hurling the long, heavy spears into the giant flying worms known as spurworms. He was good at it too. Most of the time, he hit the magic spot between two large glands the men called 'ears.' Some crews used ballistas or large crossbows, but not Abreeth.

'I like the feel of the spear in my hands. It gives me more control,' he would say when asked why he preferred the old methods.

If accurate enough, he could hit the sweet spot on the first attempt. When he managed this, the worm was immobilised and no longer able to fly. If a spurworm can't fly, it dies. Even when sleeping, they're on the move. Climbing into the clouds, gently they glide downwards, catching small portions of sleep minutes at a time.

If, however, he missed, that's when things got interesting. An enraged spurworm is not only fast, violent and dangerous; it's unpredictable. Sometimes they take off into the sky, dragging the craft behind them until it's exhausted and the men can reel it in. That's a best-case scenario.

If the worm turns to attack, the captain decides if he's going to cut-and-run or risk his boat, his crew and his livelihood trying to catch the beast with ropes and nets. If the team is lucky, the worm will open itself to a death blow before damaging the boat too severely. It all came down to Abreeth hitting that marvellously exposed nerve behind the first highly poisonous spur.

There were accidents, of course. Deaths were common amongst the spurworm hunters in the highskies. Borchin had captained cloudcutters for fifteen years, and he'd lost only seven men.

The last man to die on his craft was a year ago, just before Abreeth joined his crew. Attempting to reel in a catch, his spearman stood too close when the beast broke free of its bonds. Stabbed by one of the lethal spurs, his blackened and bloated body lay writhing in the corner, blood gushing from his mouth and eyes as he died.

Luckily it rained on the long, sombre journey back to their hometown Arpenta, washing the blood and gore from the decks by the time they returned. Borchin arrived that day with two worms, one less crew member and thrice as many questions from the dead man's wife.

It was dangerous and challenging work, but the rewards were bountiful for those who took the risk of hunting spurworms and lived.

These deadly but majestic animals had been on the move for the past decade, escaping the spears of many crews in the highskies. Still, Borchin somehow always knew where to find them, and his team enjoyed plentiful hunting and the resulting profits under his direction.

Borchin changed tack, steering for a large cloudbank when Morst bellowed, 'Wooooooooorrrrrrrrm! Portside five hundred feet. Hundred feet down.' From his crow's nest, Morst could see for miles, and his job as a spotter had become more critical than ever as their quarry became harder to find. When he wasn't working as the fourth man in Borchin's crew, he often drank himself into a stupor, to the point of hardly being able to walk. But get him on a cloudcutter, and he scaled the mast to the spotter's nest with ease.

Morst scrambled down the rope ladder like a cat with its tail in flames, his soft leather shoes slapping the deck as he called, 'Abe, you got your eye on it?'

'I've got him. And he's a big bastard,' yelled Abe over his shoulder. 'Aft, two notches.'

'Aft, two notches,' Borchin confirmed back, adjusting the wheel slightly.

The craft exploded with activity. Every man knew what he needed to do.

Morst made ready the nets they would use to haul in the worm if Abreeth's aim was true. The teenage boy Dwin grabbed extra spears and carried them to the bow. Borchin, calm as a morning lake in springtime, kept his gloved hands on the tiller steering the red hulled craft towards his prey. Abreeth stood at the bow, spear in hand, his fur-lined cloak pulled tight to stave off the biting wind.

The spurworm floated into a perfect position. The hunters had the suns in their faces, and the worm upwind. Their current position meant they could sail silently behind and above, casting no shadow and hurl a harpoon before it realised what happened. Should they change position, and the craft makes a shadow, it would likely dive straight down into the cover of clouds, and the chase would begin in earnest.

'Total silence from 'ere on in,' growled Borchin quietly. The men knew better than to speak their answer, so nodded in acknowledgment.

Abreeth attached a guide rope to the barb on the end of his spear. Should his spear fly true, the long barb would penetrate almost the length of a man's forearm. Then, giving the rope a sharp heave, he would engage a barb mechanism. This ingenious design detached the spear's shaft whilst simultaneously activating finger length barbs that pierced deep into the flesh of his quarry. The barbs had two uses. First, they helped secure the spear into the animal, making it easier to drag back to the cloudcutter. Second, if Abreeth was unlucky enough to miss the 'sweet spot' these secondary barbs might hit the nerve and take the creature out of action.

Morst moved into position, ready to cast the net when Abreeth hurled a killing blow. Dwin busied himself setting up a second harpoon. Plucky, fearless and a fast learner Dwin quickly became indispensable as a runner. Just turned thirteen, Dwin learned that life on a cloudcutter was not easy. His job involved getting items everyone else needed. Spears, ropes, food, water, shit paper. You name it; he was to fetch it. It was the boat's lowliest position, but it allowed him to watch and learn without being in too much danger. Borchin's sister would never forgive him if something happened to her boy.

Abreeth squeezed the wind from his eyes, locked on the worm gliding its way through the skies two hundred feet in front. The way they moved always amazed him. They flew like liquid through the air, more deadly and vicious than any other creature in all the four kingdoms. The combination of thousands of blade-sharp teeth and hundreds of highly toxic, lethal spurs made them a formidable foe.

Every man on the craft was now acutely aware of the danger they were about to face. Borchin planted both feet solidly to the deck, ready to make minor adjustments. Abreeth sliced three fingers towards the aft side of the craft. Borchin turned the helm with clenched teeth as his floatboat cut through the air, the sound of creaking ropes and timbers the only sounds in the sky.

No matter how many times a spearman launched his harpoon, Borchin always gave a hopeful prayer to Taw, the god of air and sky. The gods didn't always listen to him, but he did it anyway.

Abreeth gave a thumbs-up as they glided into the perfect position. Borchin tensed his arms on the wheel in preparation for Abreeth's throw. It was the moment between breathing in and breathing out. The silence before the strike. A point in time where the hunt balanced on a blade's edge.

Abreeth took his place on the throwing deck. If successful, they could earn enough money to feed themselves for a month. If he missed, they would cross that bridge when they came to it. Morst anxiously picked at a scab on his neck, wiping a bead of cold sweat from his brow as he did. Dwin craned his neck over the side of the craft, trying to get a better look.

Abreeth calmed his breathing and raised his spear. Focusing on the spot he wanted to strike, he thought of nothing else. Drawing back his muscular arm, he let fly. Before the spear had left his hands, he knew he had a direct hit. The harpoon sailed through thirty feet of air and smacked with a wet thud into the sweet spot of the worm's back. He pulled sharply on the guide rope, the comforting feel of barbs ripping their way into thick flesh travelled up the heavy cordage.

Instantly, the worm became limp.

'Bullseye!' shouted Abreeth, pumping his fist in the air, revelling in the thrill and relief that surged through his body after a successful throw. A cheer went up from his crewmates. It was then, a second, unseen spurworm smashed into the bottom of the hull with the power and savagery of an enraged pachyderm.

2

HARKEN BITTER TIDINGS

The cold, dry wind sliced through the mountains like an ice blade. Frozen fingers of chilled air poked and explored every crevice and gap on its path between the snow-capped peaks.

'How far?' asked Deadsun, shielding his eyes from the sun's glare off the snow.

'Three miles, perhaps four,' replied Greeven calculating the distance to Point Terrene, and shaking the snow from his coat.

Cradled in the saddle of the Ochota mountain range it was the farthest outpost from Thade, the largest city in the kingdom; six days of travel in good weather by beast.

'Will this cold ever give up?' complained Greeven, blowing into his hands.

'I don't remember the last time I felt warm,' Deadsun replied flatly, pulling his woollen scarf a little closer around his neck, it did little to elude the needling cold.

'You know, the Spellbinders say this isn't the worst of it. They think ill tidings are ahead of us. More bad weather and more raids,' said Greeven.

'Hmm,' grunted Deadsun, rearranging his backpack and picking his way along the rocky path. 'Usually, I believe the truths spellbinders weave as much as a one-horned horse. In this case, however, it pains me to say, I think they may be right.'

As the glowing suns dragged their way across the sky in the same slow, celestial dance they had taken for millennia, Deadsun and his men pulled on the leads of their donkeys packed with food and weapons for the soldiers patrolling the mountains.

'Stubborn bloody animal,' swore Greeven, his donkey planting its feet and braying in defiance. 'Get moving you cantankerous shit or I'll let the men eat you when we get to camp!' he threatened.

Unperturbed, the donkey snorted and nibbled at the frozen grass on the side of the path.

'It's all about offering the right motivation,' said Deadsun, walking towards the beast and fetching a section of carrot from the folds of his fur overcoat.

'That's why you're the commander,' laughed Greeven. 'You can get both men and beast to bend to your will.'

'Donkeys are easy,' replied Deadsun, holding the delicacy just beyond the animal's nose, coaxing it to walk once more. 'Men need more than just carrots.'

Deadsun enjoyed being on patrol, despite the growing cold. The stuffy, ostentatious environment of royal courts he found distasteful and tedious. He preferred to be outdoors, sleeping by the fire, marching, talking and patrolling with his men. He commanded the several thousand troops of the Lavers Law, the peacekeepers and protectors of Thade and the surrounding kingdom of the Firmalands.

The fact Deadsun still went on patrol was a point of great respect among the lawmen. Those in the courts and castles, however, often looked down their noses at this with pomp and snobbery, but he didn't let that bother him. Although he could justly linger within the safety of the city walls to give orders and proclamations, he chose to be with his men and lead with deeds, not words. He believed in hard work and discipline and thrived in the regimented environment of the Lavers Law. The men respected their commander, and many loved him as a brother.

His was a difficult tenure. Required to patrol greater areas with fewer soldiers meant all men of the Lavers Law, no matter what rank, needed to band together and accomplish more with less. Borderlands required constant patrols against tribes from the Pyrelands across the great tundra on the other side of the mountain range. Attacks grew bolder and more frequent every year. Many farms and villages at the base of the mountain were found burnt to the ground, leaving nothing but ash and misery. Farmers were already struggling to grow crops due to the ever colder weather. Add to this, raids from Pyrelanders and the city of Thade was starting to feel the pinch from lack of supplies.

A creeping sense of despair had snuck its way into the city over the past decade. With such a broad front to protect and the growing boldness of raiders from the west, it sometimes felt like an exercise in futility for Deadsun and his men. Deadsun asked the king for more supplies, more soldiers and more weapons, but his requests were more frequently met with waning approval. Everything in the city was already stretched so thin. Men were needed to act as merce- naries for the merchants who travelled further afield to find the supplies needed to run a prosperous city.

'Greeven! Deadsun!' cried the outer watch. 'We've been expecting you.'

'Then it's a boon we've arrived,' exclaimed Deadsun. 'Are you well, Tombac?' he asked, shaking the massive man's hand in a friendly greeting.

'As well as I can be stuck on this freezing bloody mountain, sir,' laughed Tombac through his beard.

'I swear it gets colder every year. I expect you'll want to speak with Elkstone. He's at the main tent, Commander,' he said, motioning to the large tent up the hill, a grey column of smoke rising from the opening in the apex before being seized by the cold hands of icy winds off the mountain.

'Thank you,' replied Deadsun, making his way towards what he hoped would be a warm fire and soothing tea.

Handing Tombac a skin of wine, Greeven said, 'here, to keep you warm when you're not on watch. And if anyone catches you with it, you didn't get it from me,' he murmured, covering his mouth.

'You know you shouldn't spoil them like that,' exclaimed Deadsun, smirking at his second in command.

'I'm hardly spoiling him,' smiled Greeven. 'I won that skin in a game of dice over a month ago from a grubby looking merchant at the docks. I'm fairly certain he drank the wine and replaced it with horse piss on his way to the city.'

'A game of dice and I wasn't invited?' Asked Deadsun, feigning mock hurt.

'I'm confident you get more than your fair share of games brother. Let us speak with Elkstone and see what news he has,' said Greeven, lifting the flap on the captain's tent.

Deadsun stooped through the tent's entrance and paused, allowing his eyes to adjust to the dim light inside. The adornments in the tent were sparse like a soldier's tent should be. A brazier in the corner provided light and heat, the smell of leather, sweat and wood smoke filled the air.

'Commander,' said Elkstone, grasping his hand in a friendly handshake. His arms were strong from decades of swinging a sword and his beard had the touch of grey a solider gets when he thinks about settling down to grow food and raise a brood on quiet farm-land in an out-of-the-way part of the world. His strong jaw and striking blue eyes framed the face of a leader, one that acted like an older brother, confident and caring. 'It's good to see you, I wasn't expecting you until the morrow. What news from the city?' He moved around the room, clearing maps and papers from chairs around the solid wooden table, then motioned for Deadsun and Greeven to sit.

'It's good to see you too Captain, you look well my friend,' replied Deadsun, resting his tired legs in the offered chair. 'We had kind weather and made good time. As for tidings from the city, good news is scarce these days. More displaced try to enter the city each day and we need to turn away as many as we allow in.'

'I thought as much, and the king?' asked Elkstone, pouring two cups of tea from a pot on the brazier.

'He plays the role of leader as best he can, but many of us can't help thinking we're the custodians of a dying city,' replied Deadsun. 'He spends much time alone in his chambers and seems more sombre with each passing moon.'

'The advisors say we have supplies for eighteen months, twenty at most,' added Greeven. 'And if the rate of refugees we've seen in the past year keeps up, we won't make it past next winter.'

'Bah, what do those bloody advisors know?' scowled Elkstone. 'They're all imbeciles and arse kissers. We live up here for a month with fewer rations than they consume in a week.'

'Even so,' said Deadsun, 'they have a point. Supplies are becoming scarce, and more people enter the city each day. Something needs to be done.'

'Well, luckily that's not a decision we're required to make,' said Elkstone, 'now come, I have something interesting to show you.'

Elkstone stood, grabbing his outer coat and staff.

'But we've just arrived,' said Greeven, gulping down the rest of his tea.

'Trust me. You'll want to see this,' replied Elkstone.

'Apparently Elkstone has a little surprise for us,' said Greeven, opening the tent flap for his commander.

'Let's hope it's some good news for once,' replied Deadsun, making his way into the waning light.

The three men made their way through the camp, soldiers throughout giving them a curt nod as they passed. Some were preparing evening meals to share amongst their brethren, whilst others were sharpening weapons, an ever-persistent endeavour. Greeven narrowed his eyes, spying the donkey he helped haul up the mountain. Watching the animal look up and bray loudly, he was positive its cantankerous bellow was aimed directly at him.

'Attacks are more frequent, but we cope as they're only small raiding parties,' said Elkstone, bringing Greeven's attention back. 'I've heard they're testing our perimeters both north and south of the range.'

'You've heard right,' said Deadsun. 'Nothing we can't handle for the moment, but if they increase in size or frequency, we may have problems.'

They walked a well-trodden path towards what appeared to be a rough-hewn cage, lashed with ropes and nailed tight. Inside were some of the most dejected, unkempt and filthy human beings Deadsun had ever laid eyes upon. Scrappy animal skins covered their emaciated bodies, and their hair was a mat of tangles and mud. Their terrified eyes darted back and forth as they huddled together, their beggarly coverings doing little to keep them warm as they shivered and cowered in the back corner of the cage.

'They have quite the aroma!' said Greeven, holding the back of his hand to his nose. The smell of old gruel, piss, shit and fear wafted from the floor of the cage like marsh gas.

'Mostly that's how we know they're coming,' smiled Elkstone, 'That... and they don't make very good woodsmen. They're noisy, disorderly and have little fight in them after crossing the tundra and making their way up the range.'

Deadsun moved closer to the cage and one of the prisoners clasped him feebly by the sleeve. 'Mercy,' he croaked. Deadsun looked into his eyes, analysing them trying to unearth the motive behind his desperation.

'Get your filthy fucking hands off our commander!' bellowed Elkstone, his staff whistling through the air with precision and force creating a resounding crack as it struck the prisoner's arm. A scream exploded from the detainee, his mangled arm hanging limply by his side. The other prisoners scuffled their way towards the other side of the cage like frightened animals, leaving the injured prisoner howling in pain on the floor.

Deadsun stood calmly, unphased by the violence. 'Elkstone, if you dragged me from a warm tent and hot tea to show me these unfortunate souls, I must say I'm unimpressed.'

'The likes of these, you've seen before. Set to get their punishment tomorrow,' said Elkstone, leaning on his staff. Turning towards the cage he growled, 'Shut your trap or you'll get another,' at the still howling prisoner who quickly diminished his screeching.

'It's the one behind this lot that's well... different,' he said, making his way to a second, smaller cage that held a single female prisoner.

Naked, despite the cold, she rocked back and forth in the dirt mumbling to herself, skinny arms wrapped around her boney knees.

'A patrol picked her up about a week ago,' said Elkstone, squatting on his knees in front of the cage. 'She eats little and seems unphased by the cold. One of our men recognised her. Says she used to work on a farm not far from where he grew up before she disappeared about a year ago.'

'She seems to have rather lost her mind. What's that she's mumbling?' asked Greeven.

'She talks of redemption and something called the menace... naught of which I've heard of or pretend to understand,' said Elkstone. 'But it's this that's got me interested,' he continued, pointing to the back of her neck.

'What is that?' asked Greeven, 'Some sort of jewellery?'

'That's what we thought at first,' replied Elkstone. 'But if you look at it closely, it's grown into her skin.'

The device, shaped like a teardrop with a crystal resting in the middle, had grown into the skin at the back of her neck. Looking at it more closely, Deadsun noticed a thin veil of red running through the middle, pulsing and moving several times a second. He'd seen enough battlefield injuries to know this device was somehow linked to the victim's heartbeat as the line of red behaved like an opened artery. A thin veil of red that ran through the middle, pulsing in time with the prisoner's heartbeat.

'I'm assuming you tried to remove it when you captured her?' asked Deadsun.

'She scratched and bit like an injured wolverine. Gave one of my men a right nasty gash above his eye,' replied Elkstone.

Pulling his cloak around him to try and fend off the cold Deadsun turned to Elkstone and said with authority. 'Execute the other prisoners as planned tomorrow. But keep her alive. We need to learn more about this device and what it does.'

Deadsun heard a pained moan as the naked woman turned from the back of the cage and dragged herself through the dirt to the rough wooden bars. Clawing herself up to standing she rubbed her hands over her breasts toward her crotch. A deranged moan escaped her lips as she babbled in a reedy voice, 'Welltakers ease the pain, but darkness brings redemption,'

'What are these welltakers you speak of?' asked Deadsun, grabbing the woman through the cage roughly by the arms. 'Are they a weapon... a spell?'

The woman's head lolled to one side, as she looked at Deadsun through eyes with a fog of corruption he'd not seen until now.

'Fool,' she purred, 'the menace will come for you.'

She raised her voice to a screech. 'IT WILL COME FOR ALL OF YOU,' she screamed, clawing her face and head. A runner entered camp, sweat pouring off his face from days of constant travel.

'Commander!' he gasped, taking the waterskin offered to him as he ran towards the cage.

'Not now,' said Deadsun.

'Sir?'

'I said not now, can't you see I have business with this prisoner?' he snapped.

'King's orders,' puffed the runner in between heaving breaths. 'It's your brother, sir. He's dying.'

3

SKYFIGHT SPAWNS A SHIFT

The cloudcutter surged upwards, hurling everyone to the deck with crippling force. Crates and weapons flew from their brackets as nets fell onto Morst, tangling him in their bonds. Borchin lost his grip on the helm as he lurched forward, his forehead smashing into the wooden wheel. Blood gushed from an open wound above his right eye as he fell to the deck.

The second spurworm had been tracking them for some time, hidden a hundred feet directly below their craft. When protecting their young, spurworms are particularly aggressive. Abe had killed the male half of a mating pair. The male's mate had laid her eggs a few weeks ago, and the sticky, flexible shells had been travelling on the underside of her body until they hatched, which judging from their appearance was just a few days ago. With babies so young, this was one beast who was rapaciously protective of her babies and the force in which she slammed into the bottom of the boat showed she meant business.

Wood splintered and shook as the spurworm smashed into the hull again. The craft listed dangerously to one side, throwing Abreeth off balance once more.

'Dwin!' he shouted to the young deckhand. 'Get me that harpoon.'

'Yes, Abe,' blubbered Dwin, a look of sheer terror on his young face.

'Morst,' yelled Abreeth, now taking control. 'Get out of those nets and check on Borchin.'

'Abe, look out,' shouted Morst as the spurworm twisted its body and smashed into the side of the craft, tipping it even further.

Both Abreeth and Dwin grabbed the side of the boat and held on for dear life as it came alarmingly close to flipping. Now caught in ropes and rigging, the worm let out an ear-splitting screech, penetrating both sky and skull. Dwin tossed the harpoon he was holding in Abreeth's direction, clasping his hands over his ears and closing his eyes.

Morst struggled with the nets like an insect in a web. Abreeth knew if he didn't do something about this frantic beast soon, they were doomed. If the worm managed to break apart more of the boat, the lightwood that helped make it float would lose its equilibrium and drag them crashing into the Firmalands thousands of feet below. It would be a cruel descent resulting in the death of the entire crew.

'Dwin,' yelled Abreeth, throwing his harpoon on the deck and changing tack. 'Listen to me. We need to cut this worm free or it's going to break up the boat. Understand?'

'Mm-hmm,' said Dwin, nodding his head and wiping tears from his eyes.

'Don't cut the ropes, chop them against the side of the boat... like this,' said Abreeth, taking out his dagger and bringing it down with force on the rope, slicing through it in one swift motion.

'I'm... I... I can't,' stammered Dwin, scared half to death.

'Don't think about it,' Abreeth barked. 'Just fucking do it, or we die.'

Dwin chopped at the rope with his small knife through uncontrolled sobs. Abreeth made his way along the craft cutting ropes tangled in the spurs of the massive beast thrashing and squealing several feet away.

The worm swung its body into the boat again, mauling the red-painted hull, trying to escape with vicious resolve. If any of its deadly spurs touched the men it meant certain death. Each time the beast crashed into the boat, Dwin let out a cry and cut at the ropes ever more frantically.

'You're doing great Dwin,' cried Abreeth from the front of the boat. 'Keep it up, keep chopping,' he shouted.

'I'm scared,' sobbed Dwin, hardly able to hold back tears. 'I don't want to die.'

'I know Dwin. I'm scared too. Only a few more ropes to go,' Abreeth yelled, trying to keep his voice steady.

He had been in some precarious situations in the year he'd worked with Borchin, but nothing compared to the intensity of this attack. The fear surging through his body made his arms shake and his eyes blur. The worm shot upwards a hundred feet above the boat, two ropes still attached to it, pulled taught by the sudden shift in direction. Abreeth knew this was his chance to slash the worm free of its bonds.

Hacking desperately at the second last rope with both hands his exhausted and terror-stricken strikes only cut through half the thick fibre. On what would be his final blow to cut the strings, the worm changed direction and dived straight down towards the ship.

'Abe!' screamed Dwin, but it was too late. He was so focused on cutting the ropes he didn't see the immense beast plunging straight for him, mouth agape with hundreds of blade-sharp teeth bared. Just as the creature was about to smash into him, the craft swerved violently causing the beast to crash into the gunnel instead.

Morst, managing to struggle free from the netting and ropes encasing him, had run towards the helm, grasping the frantically spinning wheel and bringing the ship under some semblence of control once again. Arms straining against the weight of the worm on the gunnel he righted the ship so it wouldn't tip. Abreeth watched as the manoeuvre that saved their craft caused the stunned worm to slide over the edge and disappear below the skyline. A rope, still entangled in its spurs, uncoiled and hissed on the deck like an injured leviathan. Abreeth heard it before he felt it. A crack like a broken femur pierced the air as the heavy cordage snapped tight, slamming into his chest and hurling him through the air.

Time slowed. Abreeth noticed everything in minute detail. Dwin crouched, covering his face with his hands. The drop of dried blood on his arm. The stink of the worm in the back of his throat. A sickening combination of flesh and decay that was more taste than smell.

He looked up at the boat as he fell, noticing the sun's outline making a beautiful silhouette and thinking what a ridiculous thought to have when facing death. The next thing he knew he was lying face down on the back of the worm, blinding pain in his shoulder and wind loud in his ears. He tried grabbing a bunch of the worm's coarse hair but discovered his left arm didn't work.

He still grasped his dagger in his right hand and without thinking, plunged it into the sweet spot of the worm just within reach of where he laid. He felt a shudder as the worm became limp. Letting out a sigh of relief, he rested his head to one side.

Pain surged through his body like fire. He had landed on one of the deadly spurs which was now poking through the back of his shoulder. As he waited for death, the last thing he remembered was Borchin's voice yelling commands and roaring to get him back on the boat. Although he plunged headfirst towards eternal darkness, it was nice to know Borchin was still alive.

———

Thirst. The inside of Abreeth's mouth felt like old parchment, and his lips were desiccated and cracked. An unbelievable drive to wet his throat drove him to speak.

'Wa...,' he croaked, barely audible. 'Water.'

Hearing the sounds of someone stoking the fire in the corner, Abe looked up to see that Dwin was staring at him with a massive grin on his face.

'He's awaaaaake!' he bellowed, running from the room. 'Borchin!' he shouted down the hallway, 'Abe's awake!'

He returned to Abreeth's side. 'You're awake! I knew you weren't going to die, I just knew it,' he said, skipping from one foot to the other like an excited puppy. 'Borchin told me not to get my hopes up, and Morst said you were as good as dead, but I knew you'd pull through Abe. I just knew it!'

'Water,' wheezed Abreeth, once again trying to lift his head.

'Right, sorry. Water,' he said, skipping to the pitcher in the corner of the room and pouring a cup. 'BORCHIN!' he yelled once more, making Abreeth wince. A horrendous headache bashed the inside of his skull like a blacksmith's hammer.

Dwin sat on the bed, holding the cup to Abreeth's mouth. 'Drink slowly,' he said. The water tasted sweet as it trickled into his parched mouth.

'How long?' he asked in a hoarse whisper.

'How long for what?' replied Dwin, blinking at his friend blankly.

'How long have I been out?' Abreeth asked, rubbing his eyes.

'You've not been out. You've been right here the whole time,' said Dwin, looking at Abreeth like he'd lost his senses. Abreeth would have rolled his eyes if they weren't so dry.

'Five days,' said Borchin, standing in the doorway. 'And none of us has hardly slept a wink. It's good to see you alive my boy,' he said, making his way to the side of the bed, a broad grin on his face and relief in his eyes.

'It was touch and go for a while,' he continued, 'the priests and spellweavers who saw you couldn't understand how you were still alive. Dwin here's not left your side the whole time.'

Abreeth tried to sit up but winced as a sharp pain sliced through his shoulder.

'And considering you should be dead, that wound is going to

need time to heal,' said Borchin, motioning towards his injured shoulder.

'What happened?' he asked, lifting the edge of the bandage to inspect his injury. A circular wound, three fingers across sat angry and scabbing in the middle of a large bruise the colour of spilled wine. 'The last thing I remember is falling from the boat.'

'There's plenty of time for stories,' said Borchin. 'First you need to rest and regain your strength. As far as I know, you're the only person who's ever been spiked by a spurworm and lived to tell the tale.'

'I highly recommend avoiding it,' Abreeth replied, relaxing his head back on his pillow. He was surprised at how exhausted he felt by merely talking and drinking some water. In no time at all, he sank back into a deep sleep.

When he woke once more, he wasn't sure how long he'd slept. It felt to him like he'd been absent in the blackness of slumber and strange dreams for days.

As he let out a grunt trying to shuffle himself into a seated position, Dwin was at his side in an instant. 'Careful,' he said, 'you're still weak.'

'I feel like I've been dragged behind a horse and then drowned in a river,' said Abreeth, grimacing. 'In fact, I think that would be preferable to this.' Laying his head back on the bedhead, he gave himself a moment to regain his strength from the immense effort it took just to sit up.

'Here,' said Dwin, gathering up a bowl of broth. 'Borchin says you need to eat this to get your strength back.'

After the first few mouthfuls, Abreeth found he was ravenous.

'You know, I could get used to this,' said Abreeth, between mouthfuls of broth.

'Get used to what?' asked Dwin.

'Having you wait on me hand and foot,' he replied with a grin. 'I quite like the idea of having a manservant,' he continued.

Dwin gently spooned more broth into his mouth, 'Careful, or I might stick you in the other side and give you matching shoulders,' Dwin said smiling. 'It's good to have you back, Abe. I was so worried about you. Borchin has been worried too. He tries not to show it, but I can tell. He's not been anywhere since we got back and he hasn't touched a cup of ale or wine whilst you've been asleep. He says it's because he's busy and has so much to do. I think it's so he could think clearly when you finally woke up.'

Abreeth finished the bowl of soup and asked Dwin to get him some bread to sop up the broth's last morsels.

'I'll be right back,' he said as he ran out of the room towards the kitchen. Resting his head on the pillow, Abreeth wondered how he was still alive. Spurwom hunters knew the risks, and the cemetery outside of town had the graves of hundreds of brave men who'd come off second best against the beasts. Abreeth should be six feet under with the rest of those poor souls, but instead, here he was lying in his bed, very much alive. He was in pain and weak from his ordeal, but had blood in his veins and air in his lungs. He was just contemplating the implications of this when Dwin and Borchin entered the room.

'How are you feeling?' inquired Borchin, making his way to a seat close to the bed.

Dwin broke up the half loaf of bread he'd purloined from the kitchens and handed it to Abreeth so he could sop up the remains of his broth.

'Thanks,' said Abreeth, taking the plate from Dwin. 'I'm feeling better, but this shoulder is killing me.'

'Not surprising,' said Borchin. 'The wound itself is mighty impressive, let alone the fact it was a spur that did it. I'm supposing you want to know what happened then?' he asked, packing some pipeweed into a long wooden pipe and lighting it from a taper in the fire.

'I had been wondering,' said Abreeth through mouthfuls of bread, 'why I'm here and not in the cemetery.'

'That I can't tell you lad,' replied Borchin, puffing on his pipe to get it alight. Retaking a seat in the chair next to Abreeth's bed he said, 'But I can tell you this, you've caused quite the stir amongst the spellbinders and priests. I've never seen them so fizzing with excitement and rumours. They're like a schoolyard full of girls with all their bickering and fighting about what it means.'

'What do you mean, rumours?' asked Abreeth, handing Dwin the finished plate of bread and an empty bowl. Although he was still exhausted and in pain, his energy levels had returned, and he wanted to find out what people were saying about him.

'Oh, you know,' said Borchin, 'the typical stuff. That you're some sort of demon sent here to test us, or that you're part of the old Fawe prophecy. That sort of thing.'

Abreeth snorted in derision, 'The Fawe prophecy. I thought no-one believed in those fairytales anymore?'

'Some of the lads in town are saying you're a Thaumaturge, here to fix the long winters,' said Dwin.

'Bah!' grunted Borchin, 'Full of flight and fancy those boys you hang around. They wouldn't know their arses from their elbows, let alone a warlock if they saw one.'

'I'm not saying I believe it,' said Dwin, trying to preserve some of his honour. 'It's just what they say, is all.'

'You were about to tell me what happened after I fell off the craft,' said Abreeth, gently reminding Borchin to help fill in the gaps of his memory.

'Right, yes,' said Borchin, taking another draw from his pipe before he began.

'Well, when that second worm hit, sneaky bloody harpy that she was hiding in the clouds like that, I got thrown into the helm. Got me a nice little cut to remember it by too,' he said, pointing at the large scab above his eye. 'I wasn't knocked out cold, but I took a pretty good hit that made me eyes blur, and feet wobble. The next thing I know, Morst is standing over the top of me, hands on the helm. That's when he swerved to stop you from becoming lunch.'

'Speaking of Morst, where is that devil?' asked Abreeth.

'He's got a couple of weeks off and a pocket full of gold. He's gone to see his brother three day's sail to the north of here. He took off yesterday with another crew.'

'If he's got gold, we must have managed to get a worm back then?' asked Abreeth, whose interest suddenly peaked at the chance of a payout.

'We'll get to that in a minute,' chuckled Borchin. 'And don't worry, even though you were a useless sack of meat for the trip back, you've more than earned your share.'

'I bought a new knife with some of my gold,' said Dwin. In his excitement to show Abreeth, he pulled the blade out a little too quickly from its sheath, and it clattered to the floor with a metallic ring that made Abreeth and Borchin both wince.

'It won't be new for very long if you keep dropping it like that,' scorned Borchin. 'I think maybe the lad decided that tiny pig sticker he had wasn't large or sharp enough after he struggled to cut through those ropes,' he said, slapping the boy on his shoulders.

'Well, I wasn't to know we'd have to be cutting through ropes, was I?' Dwin cried. 'But next time, I'll be ready.'

'You're keen!' said Abreeth in surprise, looking at Borchin with a smile. 'Already talking about the next time!'

'It'll be a good while till we get a next time in that boat,' said Borchin with a hint of sadness in his eyes. 'She took a mighty walloping. She'll be out of commission for at least a few weeks.'

'I wish there was more I could have done,' said Abreeth, feeling a sting of guilt about the part he played in the destruction of Borchin's pride and joy.

'Bah! Don't worry about that, my boy. Thanks to you we managed to bring back two worms, which will more than cover the cost of repairs.'

'We brought both back?' exclaimed Abreeth, eyes wide.

'Not only that,' said Borchin proudly, 'the female you killed is the largest caught for over fifteen seasons anywhere in the whole of the Welkinpeaks.'

Abreeth shook his head in disbelief.

'That's the other thing that's driving all this talk about you,' Borchin continued. 'Not only did you live when you got that spur through you, but you also managed to kill two worms in the one hunt, *and* it was a record-breaker. You've caused quite the stir here in Arpenta. Lots of other skyports know about it too. It wouldn't surprise me if word of this hadn't already made it to Roda Codex or even Thade.'

'I remember feeling a pain in my chest and my ribs hurt like I'd done ten rounds in a tavern prizefight,' said Abreeth, rubbing them tentatively.

'That's from the rope,' offered Dwin. 'It caught you on the chest as the worm fell from the boat. That's what hurled you over the side. I looked up just as you were going over. There was nothing I could do Abe. I'm really sorry. I ran to the side, but it was too late, you were flung over, and I couldn't get to you. If I could have, I would have grabbed you or thrown a rope to you or something, but it all happened so quickly.'

'Dwin,' said Abreeth gently, 'there's nothing you could have done and there isn't a single thing you should be sorry about.'

'When you landed on the back of that worm, I thought you were dead,' said Dwin, trying unsuccessfully to hide the mist gathered in his eyes. 'You laid there for the longest time not moving. Then I saw your arm move, and you stabbed that worm right in the back of its fucking head.'

Dwin's head leapt forward as Borchin slapped the back of it. 'Language,' he growled, giving the boy a stern look of disapproval.

'Sorry,' said Dwin as he turned to smirk at Abreeth. Abreeth smiled and gave him a wink.

'When we pulled the worm up,' continued Borchin, 'we thought you were dead. We saw you'd been stuck through the shoulder with a spur, which as you know means death. It was Dwin here that noticed blood oozing out with every heartbeat. Strange blood too, black-looking, thick.'

'You should have seen it when we pulled you off the spur,' said Dwin with a boy's enthusiasm for all things objectionable. 'I could've put my hand through the hole... oh, and the smell!' he said, pinching his nose for extra emphasis.

'That's when you groaned, and we knew you were still alive,' continued Borchin, 'then we managed to tie both worms to either side of the craft and limp back to port. Took us twice as long as usual.'

'All the other crews couldn't believe it when we sailed in with two worms, Abe. Two worms!' cried Dwin as he jigged a little dance.

'And not to mention a man that should've been dead,' added Borchin, a steady stream of smoke floating from his mouth after a long draw on his pipe.

'Well,' said Borchin with finality, 'I think Abe has had more than enough excitement for one day. It's time we let him rest. Come Dwin, you and I have other places to be.'

'Yes, Borchin,' said Dwin, starting to tidy up.

Borchin stood at the doorway and looked back at Abreeth.

'I'm glad you didn't die,' he said simply, then made his way down the hall.

'Abe?' said Dwin quietly after Borchin had left. 'I need to show you something.'

'Is it another knife?' asked Abreeth. 'Because I don't want to be accidentally stabbed if it is.'

'No, it's not a knife,' said Dwin in a hushed tone. 'It's... well... I don't really know how to explain it. I have to show you. I was fixing one of your pillows the other day when a feather came loose, and that's when it happened.'

'What happened?' asked Abreeth, not wanting to play boys games in his exhaustion. 'If this is another of your jokes or silly games,' he said, starting to get slightly irritated.

'It's not Abe, I swear. Just look,' said Dwin, grabbing a feather from inside the pillow and moving toward the bed.

'Lie still and hold your hand out.'

He held the feather above Abreeth's hand and let it go. The feather should have gracefully swayed back and forth on its way to the floor, but this feather didn't. It stayed right where it was, slowly turning on its axis.

Abreeth stared at the feather in confusion, then eyed Dwin with a suspicious look.

'This is a trick feather, isn't it?' he asked the boy. 'You've tied it with a hair and you're trying to fool me whilst my head is muddled,' he said as he grabbed at the feather.

'Nope,' said Dwin, looking at Abreeth with a no-nonsense face, 'it's not a joke. Why would I joke about something like this?' he asked. 'Look, I'll do it with another feather,' he said as he ruffled in Abreeth's pillow, pulled out another, larger feather and placed it above his hand once again. Once more, the feather didn't move towards the ground or dance onto his bed as it should have. It just hovered like it was caught in time, slowly turning but not losing any height.

Abreeth didn't know what to think. So much had happened in the past week his head was swimming. He knew this was important. Things didn't typically hover over people like that, but he had no idea what it meant. He'd heard of people being able to control things like elements or energy, even other people's minds, but they were stories from ages long past.

'How many people know about this?' asked Abreeth, giving Dwin a hard, sober look.

'Just you and me,' he answered.

'Good,' he replied, 'let's keep it that way.'

4
SANDS OF CHANGE MOVE ETERNAL

Deadsun had never pushed his mounts or his men so hard. What was usually a three-day trek to the bottom of the mountain range, he'd completed in a little over twenty hours. The thought of seeing his dying brother alive kept his legs moving when his mind screamed for him to stop. Many of his men fell behind, unable to keep up with the blistering pace. Even Greeven, his closest confidante, struggled to match the measure of his step. He clenched his jaw, doggedly hung his head, and forged ahead in the steady pace of a forced march from a determined commander. They had eaten little on the way down and rested for only 30 minutes every four hours in a cold camp. No fires, no hot tea.

It was brisk, but not the same biting chill they found high in the mountains. If they weren't marching under such bitter tidings, it would be a beautiful day, but it was no such day for Deadsun. He'd pushed himself and his men to the limit of their endurance in the hope he would be able to spend some time with his brother before he passed. The cold, stark reality of never seeing him again hit him like a rockslide. There were memories he wanted to share and much to discuss, but would he get that chance?

'Look,' said Greeven, pointing into the distance, 'Horsemen.'

'Good,' said Deadsun, more determined now than ever to keep up the pace.

The group approached riding hard, their grim faces painting a worrisome story.

'Commander,' said the leader of the relief team, 'we left to meet you as soon as we heard about your brother. I'm sorry we weren't able to come sooner, there was...,' he looked to one of the other men, 'an issue with the horses.'

'My brother?' enquired Deadsun softly, although he could see the answer on their faces.

'Sir, I'm sorry, but he passed a few hours ago.'

'I see,' said Deadsun, 'excuse me.' He stepped off the trail into the woods, dropped his pack and unbuckled his sword. A rage-fueled roar exploded from his throat as he snapped a sapling the size of a man's arm and started beating the other trees with it.

He'd managed to clear several metres of trees and bushes around him when he fell exhausted to his knees. Breathing raggedly, he pushed his sap covered fists into the earth, hung his head and squeezed his eyes together as his chest heaved up and down.

Greeven approached, kneeling beside Deadsun, offering him a waterskin. He shook his head, not ready to quench his thirst or his rage just yet. When it came time he would let it flow out of his body like snowmelt in a stream, but he wanted to hold onto it a little longer. He tried to embrace the hurt and loss, for he knew that once he returned to the city, he would need to don the mask of the sombre, grieving brother.

Deadsun looked at Greeven. 'I should have been there,' he said through heavy breaths. 'I should have been there for him at the end.'

'You weren't to know, brother,' replied Greeven, placing a hand on his friend's shoulder. 'None of us could have known.'

'He'd been sick for so long,' spoke Deadsun quietly. 'I didn't think much about it. If I did, I would never have been able to go out on patrol or do what's required to protect the city.'

'He was an amazing man. One you can stand proud to call your blood,' said Greeven, standing and extending his hand to Deadsun.

'Come, let's wash our faces and hands in the stream. We should make for the city. There's much to do.'

Deadsun took Greeven's hand and stood, embracing him in a bear hug.

'He may have been my blood,' he said, pushing Greeven back, holding him by both shoulders and looking him in the eyes, 'but I count you as a brother also.'

They both turned towards the stream where the waiting men suddenly had feet to look at and pebbles to push around with their boots.

'You!' shouted Deadsun, pointing at the lead horseman, 'you said there was a problem with the horses. What problem?'

'I... well... it's just... ' stammered the man, trying to look anywhere but Deadsun's icy stare.

'I suggest you spit it out, and quickly,' hissed Greeven through clenched teeth.

'I'm sorry, sir. When we got to the stables, there was an order that no horses were to leave without the king's blessing. He said they were needed for merchant protection.'

'Who said?' asked Deadsun, trying to keep his temper in check.

'Bailur, sir. The King's Steward.'

'That good for noth...,' Deadsun stopped himself before he said something he may regret in front of his men.

Bailur was everything Deadsun hated about the men who lingered in the royal courts toying in the game of politics like a chess match. Small in stature and effeminate in nature, he had an obsessive thirst for power and luxury with a velvet tongue that could innocently draw you in, then flay you in the next breath. He was a boyhood friend of the king, which was how he became a steward for the royal family. He ensured every move they made was thought out, planned and executed with the least amount of risk to the king, and himself, of course. This kind of self-preservation made for a measured approach to the advice he gave the king, but his slender fingers were in many pies throughout the kingdom.

Any man who became an inconvenience quickly found themselves at the bottom of a river or lying in a back alley with a crossbow bolt through his bloody chest. There were rumours he'd even had children and pregnant women 'taken care of' in the past. It seemed there was no moral quandary dark enough to make him shy away from delivering a blow he perceived as a requirement for the kingdom. Deadsun didn't like the man. He would go so far as to say he despised him but was also acutely aware he could be a powerful and cunning enemy. Bailur had spies everywhere throughout the kingdom, which led him to err on the side of caution in what he said about him.

After some calming breaths, Deadsun continued, 'You said Bailur stopped the horses, yet you stand in front of me with four of them?'

'Yes sir. We were stopped at the west gate, closest to here, so we made our way to the north gate where my cousin runs the stable. That's how we managed to get away with these four. We weren't going to let no tool nibbler tell us we weren't getting horses to you, sir. Not when your brother was deathly sick and all. That's why it took us longer to get here.' He finished and looked at his feet, waiting for his commander to respond.

'What's your name son?' asked Deadsun with a softness to his voice after hearing what this young man had done for him.

'Dillek, sir,' he said, looking up.

'What you did was admirable, Dillek. Stupid, but admirable and I appreciate the risk you took getting these horses to me,' said Deadsun.

'Thank you, sir,' said Dillek, a smile flashing across his face at the praise he just received.

'Oh, and Dillek?' said Deadsun lightly.

'Yes, sir?' he answered.

Deadsun's tone became deadly serious, 'If I ever hear you speak ill of a member of the royal court like that again, I'll have you flayed in the market square. Am I clear?' Deadsun spun on his heel and strode to pick up his pack and sword in preparation for the ride back to the city.

'Yes, sir,' called Dillek, his smile quickly fading.

———

Deadsun and Greeven rode through the outlying towns on their way to the city as children laughed and played in the streets, oblivious to the turmoil raging in Deadsun's mind. Greeven turned to his commander and said, 'Your brother was a good man. I'm going to miss him. I didn't speak with him often, but when I did get the opportunity, he always struck me as someone who knew a great deal about many things.'

Deadsun drank from his water-skin, wiping his mouth with the back of his hand and answered, 'When we were children, and we didn't know about his condition, many people said he had a weak fortitude. The other children teased him because he couldn't run fast or fully draw the string of a bow. They used to call him Ashaar the Almost. He tried so hard at so many things the other boys could do, but could never manage them.' Deadsun shook his head at the painful memory.

'I think that's why he was so smart. He wasn't able to keep up with the other boys physically, so he used the only thing he had. His mind.'

'He was lucky to have an older brother like you,' said Greeven.

'There were many that felt a fist in their face when I overheard them making fun of him,' replied Deadsun, smiling.

'You know,' Deadsun continued, turning in his saddle, 'I almost drowned once and he was the one that saved me.'

'I didn't know that!' said Greeven in surprise.

'We were playing near a riverbank, and there had been much rain that summer, so the rivers were swollen. There was a group of us; myself, Ashaar, a boy who lived next door and two sisters from the other side of the farm we lived on as children. The older sister had just turned sixteen. Her hair was a crown of red curls and her skin the colour of the white quartz they mine in the north. She was the most beautiful girl I'd ever seen, well, for the fifteen years I'd been alive at least. I remember showing off, walking over a log across the river. I don't know if it was the affections of a beautiful girl or the leftover snow that made me slip, but I remember hitting my head on a rock as I fell into the stream.'

'What happened next?' asked Greeven.

'I was swept away by the current. It wasn't a wide river, thirty feet perhaps, but the water was running so fast, and cold. I managed to grab onto a fallen tree that had been lodged in some rocks in the middle of the river. There was no way I would be able to swim to the bank without being swept away again, so I was stuck on that damned log. Soaking wet, bleeding, freezing and thinking I was going to die. Ashaar followed me down the river and shouted at me to stay where I was and don't do anything stupid, like try to swim back to the bank. Then he disappeared.'

'He left you there?' asked Greeven, raising an eyebrow.

'Yes. But he came back with a pack mule and a length of rope. He knew exactly what to do,' continued Deadsun, tapping the side of his head. 'He tied a sturdy branch around one end of the rope, the other to the mule and got the boy from next door to swing the branch around his head and throw it to me in the middle of the river. It took a few goes for me to catch it because my hands were freezing, but once I did, he and that mule pulled me out of that river. I would never have thought of something that ingenious.'

'Nor I,' said Greeven, 'particularly at that age.'

'Twelve years old and already rescuing his big brother,' said Deadsun. 'These days we're lucky to have any twelve-year-olds that know which end of a donkey to feed and which to avoid, let alone how to rescue someone with it!'

'Now I know where you get your love of redheads, respect for mules and dislike of rivers!'

They rode in companionable silence, remembering Ashaar as they took the road leading to the city of Thade.

———

The guards on duty saluted their commander as he entered the hustle and bustle of the outer region of Thade. It was late afternoon when Deadsun and Greeven made their way through the outskirts towards the royal stables. The shadows had grown long on the cobblestones but children were still playing. The smell of evening meals reminded them both just how tired and hungry they were.

It had been a long journey down the mountain, with little sleep and minimal stops for rest. As they made their way to the royal stables, a merchant stopped them.

'I'm sorry about your brother, Commander,' he said, bowing his head.

'Thank you,' said Deadsun simply.

'Word travels quickly in the city,' he said as they turned down the alley leading to the royal stables. 'It seems your brother will be missed by more than those he collaborated with in the courts,'

'He was known and loved by many. Not only for his mind but also his kindness,' replied Deadsun. 'He contributed to many feasts and festivals.'

'He did love his parties, didn't he?' said Greeven, dismounting his horse as they approached the stables.

A squire came running towards them. 'Commander, Greeven,' he nodded, taking both their horses. They crossed the square as Deadsun recognised a figure sweeping down the stairs of the keep.

'Bailur,' he growled to Greeven as the king's steward floated gracefully towards them in a golden silk gown with silver cuffs and a decorative belt cinching it in the middle.

'Deadsun,' Bailur purred with his silky tongue, 'I'm glad to see you safely back, we have much to talk about.'

'Yes, we do Bailur. Unfortunately, it seems I was too late to see my brother alive,' he said coldly. Looking directly into Bailur's eyes as he spoke, trying to detect any kind of remorse for shattering his chances of seeing his brother alive.

'Yes. It's a terrible loss and we're all deeply saddened,' he said with a look of chagrin on his face.

'Here,' said Bailur, handing Deadsun a wooden box, beautifully made with a carving of a winged woman on the lid.

'What's this?' asked Deadun, trying not to let the suspicion in his voice sound obvious.

'Not for now. You have more important matters to attend. We shall talk about it at a later time. For the moment the king is in your brother's quarters expecting you. I suggest you be on your way, and quickly,' he said, motioning his arms flamboyantly towards the main keep.

'As you wish,' said Deadsun, giving Greeven a confused look as they made their way towards the castle's main keep.

When he turned, he saw Bailur striding away to some other matter. He looked at the wooden box as they walked the stairs to the keep's main entrance before the household's head stopped them.

'Commander, I'm so terribly sorry for your loss. Let me take your things and have them delivered to a room we have waiting for you,' he said with practised ease.

'Thank you, Oben,' said Deadsun, unbuckling his sword, taking off his pack and handing the older balding gentleman his items along with the box Bailur had just given him.

'I trust my brother is in his usual quarters?' inquired Deadsun.

He was suddenly struck by how mundane that question seemed. It's a question he'd asked hundreds of times when he checked up on him, or visited whilst in an audience with the king. Today would be the last time he asked this.

Just days from now, Ashaar's body would be taken through the city in a state procession and buried in a plot he had arranged for himself years earlier. Ashaar was like that. Always thinking ahead.

Always pondering and figuring out better, smarter ways of doing things.

'Yes, Commander, his usual quarters. Is there anything I can do for you? Anything I can get?' asked Oben in the competent manner of someone used to playing host.

'Some food and hot water to wash would be greatly appreciated,' said Deadsun, putting his hand on the older man's shoulder and giving him a tired smile.

'Certainly, Commander. I will have it brought to your brother's room as I suspect you will want to have some time with him before... the arrangements are made.'

'Thank you. You're very kind,' said Deadsun, making his way to his brother's quarters for the last time.

———

Deadsun stood, staring at the door he'd walked through thousands of times. He'd never noticed the detail in the wood grain, the slight dent on the right panel or the rust starting to accumulate on the hinge. It was a door with character and age. It was a door that his brother had walked through every day. Now, however, he was just on the other side of it. Cold. Gone. Dead.

'Are you OK?' asked Greeven. 'We can come back a little later if you need some time.'

'I'm fine,' said Deadsun, breathing slowly. His palm touched the wood of the door, his hand lingering above the handle. He pushed and entered the room to a group who looked up as he walked in. The room was heavy with incense to hide the smell of death. At the end of Ashaar's bed, a priest chanted death rites as chambermaids fussed over his body, cleaning and covering him in white linen. The king made his way towards the two men, arms open, a royal blue robe flowing behind him.

'Deadsun, you're here,' he said.

'My King,' replied Deadsun, kneeling and taking the king's hand, kissing it.

'Please, stand,' said the king, taking his hand back quickly. 'You've lost a brother. There will be plenty of time for formalities later.'

Deadsun stood and walked to Ashaar's body lying on the bed. He looked peaceful. In no pain at all. The opposite of the life he lived battling the condition that ate at his muscles and deformed his body. Seeing him lie straight without pain was something Deadsun hadn't seen for many years. His brother often wore flowing robes to hide his disfigurements, but seeing his half-naked body like this, Deadsun was acutely aware of the terrible toll his brother's condition had taken on his physical body.

'He wasn't in any pain towards the end,' said the king, standing close to Deadsun.

'You were with him?' Deadsun asked.

'Yes,' the king replied, looking morosely at Ashaar's bent and crippled frame, 'he was given mandrake to help ease his transition into the next life.'

The fatigue and exertion of the past few days had finally caught up with Deadsun. He fell to his knees beside the bed. Exhausted both physically and mentally, he took his brother's hand and pressed it against his forehead.

'I'm sorry I wasn't here for you, brother,' said Deadsun, choking on the last word. 'I'm so sorry.'

The priest stopped his death rites and quietly departed with the chambermaids leaving only the king, Greeven, Deadsun and Ashaar in the room.

'You've nothing to be sorry for Deadsun,' said the king kindly. 'No man knows the time of his ending or can stop it when it comes for him. He spoke of you towards the end. Told us of your time together as children. About your adventures as young men. His love for you and yours for him. Don't hold onto memories of what could or should have been. Look forward and honour your brother. Honour him for all of us and yourself, but most importantly, for the man he was.'

'Thank you, my Lord. Those are kind words,' said Deadsun, standing and covering his brother's body up to the neck with the sheet. They all stood for a moment looking over Ashaar's serene face thinking about the man who only just yesterday was alive and able to converse with a pained smile. A quiet knock at the door brought them out of their thoughts as a serving girl delivered food and warm water.

'I think I'd prefer to wash and sup in my chambers,' said Deadsun.

'As you wish, Commander,' replied the girl. 'If you'd like to follow me, I'd be happy to show you to your room.'

Deadsun turned to his king, 'If my liege permits?'

'Go,' said the king, 'your trip was long and arduous no doubt. I will post sentries at the door to make sure your brother's body is not disturbed. We can deal with formalities on the morrow. Go, refresh yourself and get some sleep.'

'My thanks,' replied Deadsun, following the chambermaid through the door, Greeven not far behind him.

'This way, Commander,' said the young girl, taking Deadsun and Greeven down the corridor towards chambers usually reserved for royal guests. For once, Deadsun was glad he didn't have to go back to the barracks on the other side of the castle. As much as he loved lodging with his men, he didn't feel much like facing other people right now.

'Commander, if you'd like to take this room. Captain Greeven, I have you a few doors down.' The girl pushed the door open, placing the jug of hot water and a tray of meat, cheese and bread deftly on the side table.

'You'll be OK?' asked Greeven, looking at his exhausted commander.

'Thank you Greeven, I'll be fine,' replied Deadsun. 'I haven't thanked you for today. I know it's not easy being by my side sometimes, but it's days like today that show me you truly are a brother.'

'It's nothing,' said Greeven, putting his hand on Deadsun's shoulder. 'You're the one who's suffering, not me. Go eat, wash and get some sleep. I'll see you in the morning.'

Deadsun walked into his room and closed the door behind him, thankful for the solitude. He took off his leather jerkin and under-shirt, stepped out of his travelling pants and washed himself down with hot water and cloth. The water was lightly scented with essential oils and felt pleasing to his dry skin. Rubbing the grime from his body reminded him just how weary he was.

He sat on his bed staring at the floor, eating the food left for him, but not really tasting it. He felt he was in a dream. Not knowing if this was real, or something he would wake from at any moment, discovering it was all a nightmare. Forcing down more food, he stood to blow out the candles when he noticed his pack and sword in the corner. On top was the elaborate wooden box Bailur had pushed into his hand earlier that afternoon. Picking up the box, he turned it over in his hands. He could feel something rattling inside. Walking to his bed he sat, contemplating the box before opening it. The wood was soft and sanded to a smooth finish. Inside was a piece of folded leather which he unwrapped, showing a tear-dropped piece of metal with a black crystal in the middle. He'd seen this before. His mind flashed back to the naked prisoner in the mountains realising he was holding the same thing she'd had on the back of her neck. The device he held was slightly different. Like the fangs of an adder, two small spines poked out from this device's top and bottom. He gently ran his fingers over the needles, feeling the potential of their sting.

'What is Bailur up to?' he wondered to himself, wrapping up the device and putting it back in its box. He realised he was too tired to care and laid on his bed for some much-needed, but troubled sleep.

5

A REMARKABLE DISCOVERY

It had been five days since Abreeth had woken to discover he was still very much alive. His appetite returned quickly, and he was getting stronger every day. He'd even managed to make it out of bed on day three, weaving his way to the door using Dwin as support. Borchin commented he'd never seen a wound heal so fast. In his forced recuperation, Abreeth found himself spending time in the shipyards visiting Yonex, the head shipwright to discuss the repairs on Borchin's craft.

'When do you think we'll be back in the air?' Abreeth asked, nibbling on an apricot turnover he'd pilfered from the kitchens.

'I'd say at least another four weeks,' said Yonex, wiping his dirt-covered hands on his leather apron. Stout and strong, he had a friendly smile constantly etched on his bearded face. 'I've spliced the bottom of the ship to the ground, so the lightwood starts growing again. In a couple of days I'll be able to start training it through the holes the beast made.'

Even though lightwood was fast-growing, it still required skill and patience to train the branches in and out of each other to create a tight fit for the hull's shape.

'That worm certainly had fun with your ship,' chuckled Yonex. 'A few more hits and I think it might have broken apart. I've had to get six other lightwoods from my rootstock just to plug the holes.'

The shipyards were more like a colossal greenhouse than a factory – home to multiple rows of lightwood plants at different growth stages. The demand for ships had grown over the past hundred years, and Yonex's family were famous for making the best cloudcutters in all the Welkinpeaks.

Abreeth drifted lazily towards a smaller boat when something unusual caught his eye. The ship was only big enough to hold a handful of people, but it was the pair of wings on either side that piqued his interest.

'What's this?' he asked, 'I've never seen anything like it. Are they sails made to look like wings? The artistry is amazing. They look so real.'

'That is the culmination of over fifteen years of trial and error,' replied Yonex, proudly running his hand down the wood of the craft. 'What you're looking at is a hybrid system I've been working on for a long, long time.'

Abreeth reached out to touch the sails. They stretched and flapped with a mind of their own. Abreeth leapt back, knocking a table with tools and cuttings as he gasped. He looked at Yonex, who laughed at his surprise. 'They... they moved!' he said.

'They did,' smiled Yonex.

'I... I don't understand. They moved like they're alive,' said Abreeth, edging a little closer.

Yonex chuckled, 'That's because they are alive, my friend. It's quite safe. They won't hurt you,' he said, picking up a wingtip, sliding his hands over the skin. 'They react to touch, just like when they're on the animal. I'm still fiddling with the nerve endings to give a captain more control. They're the first set I've managed to keep alive and working for more than a month.'

'You mean to say, these are wings... real wings from an animal?' asked Abreeth in amazement.

'A pyredrake,' answered Yonex. 'She was injured in a fight with a much larger animal and wasn't going to make it. Luckily she was brought to me before she died and I was able to keep her alive long enough to splice her wings onto the lightwood to combine the two into the living craft you see here. Don't worry. She didn't feel any pain,' said Yonex, at the look of discomfort on Abreeth's face.

'How do you keep them alive?' asked Abreeth in pure wonder after he'd gotten over the initial shock of realising there was a pair of actual, real wings attached to a floatboat.

'That's the tricky part, my friend,' said Yonex, making his way around the side of the boat. 'I've discovered you need to get the animal while it's still alive. I refuse to hunt pyredrakes just for their wings, so I've only ever taken injured animals, which is why it's taken me so long to try different things. Every time I've successfully spliced a pair of wings to lightwood, they've always withered and died after a few weeks. The wings draw their energy from the lightwood. I could get them to live a little longer by splicing the lightwood and putting it back in the ground, but that's no good for a floatboat as you would have to come back into port every few days and splice your lightwood into the ground to nourish the wings. Hardly a sustainable solution.'

Yonex lifted out a small box that had been placed snugly into a space inside the deck, 'Then I came up with this. I call it a gutbucket,' he said, opening up the box.

Abreeth gagged. 'That smells awful,' he said, holding his hand to his nose.

'I should think so my friend. Pyredrakes aren't known for their clean diets,' laughed Yonex, closing the lid.

'That smell is what powers these wings. I managed to get the lining of the stomach and grow a box around the gut. I'm hoping to keep them alive for as long as possible. I've been feeding it rats and lizards, a few other scraps and even a chunk of spurworm flesh. So far it's been exactly six weeks and... three days,' he said, doing the mental calculations.

'Yonex, this is remarkable.'

'Yes, my friend… it is quite remarkable, isn't it?' he replied, smiling to himself.

'This will allow us to hunt further afield and go faster to hunt bigger worms! How long before you could get these onto a proper boat instead of this little skiff?' asked Abreeth, his excitement at this new development clearly showing.

'Slow down there, my friend,' replied Yonex. 'Let's keep these wings alive for a while longer before we get into large scale experiments. I haven't even taken this into the air yet. There's work to be done on the nerves and tendons that make the wings move and open. I've got to figure out the right amount to feed the gutbox for growth and how much just to maintain the wings. Then there's the question of placement, wingspan and a whole other bag of things that need organising.'

'Now I see why it's taken you so long to get to this point,' said Abreeth, putting his good hand on the living skin of the wing, feeling its smooth texture and the power within its muscles.

'Taking a break, I see?' announced Borchin, good in humour as he walked through the shipyard door. 'And here I was thinking I was paying you to repair my boat! How goes it, Yonex?' he asked, slapping his friend on the shoulder.

'Slowly,' said Yonex, 'but as you know, these things can't be rushed.'

'I see you've shown Abe our little experiment,' said Borchin, walking to the boat, looking it over with a captain's eye. 'Have there been any issues with the gutbucket?'

'So far it's looking good. There have been no problems with the wings. In fact, it looks like they're actually growing,' said Yonex, puffing out his chest a little.

'Excellent,' said Borchin, 'it's been a long time coming, friend, but it looks like we might have cracked it this time. If we get this to work, it means not only can we outfit our ships to hunt further, but we can sell winged boats for a mighty profit and stand to make a fortune!'

'Let's not get ahead of ourselves,' replied Yonex. 'I want to test them on an appropriately sized boat and keep them alive before we start having dreams of selling them to other crews.'

'Now, speaking of crews, how long before I can get mine out again?' asked Borchin, clearly itching to get back out and start hunting.

'I was just saying to Abe here. It's going to be at least four weeks, perhaps more. I've got extra lightwood in the ground to fill the gaps the spurworm made as quickly as possible, but if you want it done properly, it's four weeks I'm afraid,' said Yonex, looking apologetically at Borchin.

'No matter,' replied Borchin, 'I have another assignment for young Abe here that will keep him busy.'

'You do?' said Abreeth in surprise.

'Don't worry, nothing too strenuous,' replied Borchin, 'I need you to travel with Dwin. He's due to go and see his mother, Grenda. She lives about four days ride from here.'

'So a babysitting job?' said Abreeth, his shoulders slumping.

'If you'd like to look at it that way, yes, a babysitting job. But you'll do it, understood? Besides, it will give your arm some time to heal. In any case, I wanted my sister to look over your wound. She's a damned good healer and knows everything there is to know about herbal lore, elixirs, venoms and such. Plus, she hasn't seen her son for well over six months now. It's about time the boy saw his mother. I've arranged three donkeys. One for you and Dwin and another to carry your supplies and a few items to go to Grenda's.'

'Fine,' sighed Abreeth, 'but when we get back, I want to get right back out there and finish up the season with some more catches.'

'You see,' said Borchin, smiling at Yonex, 'this is why I like the boy, he wants to get right back out there hunting again!'

'There's many a man that would have thrown in his bones and called it quits after what you went through my friend and personally, I wouldn't blame them,' said Yonex.

'It's good you want to get back out there. That shows real character. Now, before you take off and get ready for your trip, there are a few items I would like you to take to Grenda,' continued Yonex as he rummaged through boxes and bags.

'Do I really need to go with Dwin?' asked Abreeth, trying to get out of what sounded like a dreadfully dull assignment.

'It'll do you good to have a break. We've been hunting hard the past few months and with your arm out of action along with my boat,' Borchin looked sadly at his beloved cloudcutter and sighed, 'we're a month away from hunting proper. Look on the bright side. You can meet my little sister, spend time with Dwin and get to know him a little better. I want him to grow into a great captain one day, and I value your opinion of him,' said Borchin, stroking Abreeth's ego, hoping to make this babysitting job a less bitter pill to swallow.

'Here,' said Borchin, pulling out a pouch and jiggling it in front of Abreeth's face, 'this is your share of our last hunt,' he declared, tossing the bag to Abreeth who caught it with his good arm.

'By gods it's heavy!' said Abreeth, smiling from ear to ear.

'Two worms, twice the pay,' said Borchin, 'You did well Abe, you're a damned good spearman, and I'm glad to have you on my crew.'

Abreeth smiled at both the compliment and the weight of the pouch in his hand.

Yonex arrived with a small box and some papers which he handed to Abreeth.

'I'll leave you two to finish up,' said Borchin, 'Abe, come and see me after you're packed. You leave at first light tomorrow,' he continued, patting Abreeth on the shoulder and leading Yonex to the shipyard's exit. Yonex spoke quietly with Borchin as he walked him to the doorway. Abreeth guessed they were talking specifics about the winged experiment.

Looking at the wooden box, he ran his fingers over the wood. Constructed of pine and smooth to the touch, on the front was a small latch with a piece of leather tied around it fixed with wax. Yonex made his way back and stood opposite Abreeth.

'Now my friend, listen to me because this is important,' he said, looking him in the eyes. His smile had gone, and a look of deadly seriousness washed over his face. 'Whatever you do, that box is not to be opened by anyone except Dwin's mother Grenda, is that understood?'

Abe nodded.

'Good, and the contents of that box is for her eyes only, got it?' Yonex continued.

'Don't open the box and give it only to Grenda. Got it,' said Abreeth.

'Good lad,' said Yonex, the smile returning to his face. 'Now you'd best be off if you're to pack for your trip tomorrow.'

———

The early morning suns made their way slowly over the horizon, throwing a pink hue across the clouds and doing little to warm the cold morning air. Abreeth and Dwin stood beside three donkeys, two with saddles and one packed with supplies.

'Abe, travel safe and I'll see you when you get back,' said Borchin, clasping him by his good hand and giving it a fatherly shake.

'Don't worry, Cap,' replied Abreeth, 'We'll be back before you know it, then we take to the skies to catch three worms,' he said dramatically.

'Three!' cried Dwin, 'We almost died with two, and you want to hunt three!'

Borchin and Abreeth both laughed as they made their final inspections of their gear.

'Travel well,' said Borchin as he waved them off.

Soon all three donkeys were keeping a steady pace through a small wooded area just outside of Arpenta where they met crossroads and turned east. Abreeth and Dwin travelled in companionable silence for a few hours when Dwin declared, 'I think you'll like my mother.'

'Is that so?' replied Abreeth.

'Yes,' said Dwin, 'she knows so much about plants and potions. She once got asked to brew an elixir for the king's cousin, you know?' he continued proudly. 'And she knows how to read. She's got loads of books and scrolls in one of her rooms. It's like a library. That's where I learnt to read. I'm not as good as my mother, but I know all of my letters and numbers. I get stuck sometimes on some of the big words. Do you know how to read, Abe?'

'Yes, Dwin, I can read,' replied Abreeth.

'Who taught you to read then?' asked Dwin with the curiosity of the banal only a thirteen-year-old boy could muster.

'My father,' he answered.

'Was he a teacher or a scribe or something?' probed Dwin.

'No, nothing like that,' laughed Abreeth. 'When he was young he was in a hunting accident. He was shot in the face with a crossbow bolt. Shattered his jaw and knocked out most of his teeth on one side.'

'Ow, that's awful,' said Dwin, holding his hands to his face, thinking about a bolt destroying the bones and teeth in his face.

'It nearly killed him, but when he got better, he wasn't able to speak, so letters were the only way he was able to talk. Since he was so young when it happened, he didn't really know any better, so that's just the way he grew up. We used to have a bag of runes made from bone and antler he would arrange to make sentences. That's how he used to talk to me, so naturally, I got pretty good at reading.'

'Did he have a scar?' asked Dwin.

'Yeah, a big one,' said Abreeth as he pointed to a small stream just off the path. 'Let's stop over there for lunch. You hungry?'

'I'm starving!' said Dwin with youthful exaggeration.

'You're always starving,' said Abreeth, smiling at his young travelling companion. 'C'mon, let's eat.'

———————

The days rolled on as Abreeth and Dwin travelled the hilly lands of the Welkinpeaks, passing fellow travellers and swapping news as they followed the roads east. That night they camped on the side of the road around the warmth of a welcome fire.

The next morning, with mist on his breath, Abreeth jabbed his young companion in the ribs and pulled down his cloak, 'Dwin... wake up. We need to break camp and be on our way.'

'Mmmmhhpphh,' complained Dwin, dragging his cloak over his head once more.

'C'mon, the last thing I want to be is in your mother's bad books because I delivered you a day late... up!' Abreeth said, nudging him with his foot repeatedly.

'OK, OK, I'm getting up,' groaned Dwin, rubbing his eyes and trying to stretch out the fatigue from sleeping on the ground.

'How far are we from your mother's cottage?' asked Abreeth, pouring two cups of tea and warming his feet by the fire in the early morning sunlight.

'Thanks,' said Dwin, taking the tea offered to him. 'About half a day's ride from here.'

'Are you sure?' asked Abreeth, chewing on a leg from last night's pheasant they had managed to snare and cook for their evening meal.

'Positive. I had a friend who used to live just over there,' he replied, pointing to a rocky outcrop to the south of where they camped. 'He was a year older than me and went to work with his uncle in Roda Codex as a tanner in one of the worm houses near the docks.'

'Well, if we want to be lunching with your mother, we'd best break camp and be on our way,' said Abreeth standing up, swirling the rest of his tea around his cup and throwing it on the fire.

They were soon packed and back on their donkeys, making their way through a series of small creeks with ice gathered at the edges and waterfowl in the reeds. The donkeys weren't bothered by the cold and happily walked across the chilly streams whilst Dwin and Abreeth sat thankfully on their steeds with dry boots and warm feet.

Dwin took them down a small track around midday that led to the edge of a lightly wooded area, dappled sunlight filtering through the treetops. The grey and green of bark and leaf gave the woods a ghostly appearance. Whilst the thick carpet of leaves hid the typical sounds they'd been used to on the paths and fields they'd followed for days, making the forest seem mysterious and strange to the ear.

'This way,' said Dwin, taking them deeper into the woods.

'Your mother lives in these woods?' asked Abreeth, looking around at the damp, dark woodlands with a slight sense of foreboding.

'Yep. Just over there,' Dwin said, pointing to a copse of trees, 'is where I shot my first deer with a bow Borchin gave me for my tenth birthday.'

'Impressive,' said Abreeth, 'I should like to see this bow, and you shoot it.'

Dwin looked at his hands and said, 'I... I don't have it anymore. I left it outside, and an animal chewed on the wood and ruined it,' he looked at Abreeth. 'I didn't mean for it to get eaten and I didn't leave it outside on purpose, I just... forget things sometimes.'

'We all forget things sometimes. I wouldn't worry about it. One time before you were part of our crew, would you believe I forgot to pack a spare pair of pants. I spilled an entire bowl of soup on myself our first night out. Five days later we pulled into port with me smelling like the inside of a spurworm.'

Dwin laughed, the dimples in his cheeks reminding Abreeth of just how young he was.

'We're not far,' said Dwin. 'Just over this hill and we're there.'

———

The donkeys kept a steady pace on the pathway through the dim forest as the trees started to thin and change. Abreeth noticed they had more uniformity, looking as though they had been deliberately planted in rows. As he looked closer, he could see nuts and fruit hanging from them, along with vines of pumpkins and passion fruit growing in between rows of trees on wires between the food-laden shrubs. Dwin leant over and plucked an apple from a tree and bit into it, visibly savouring the flesh.

'Want one?' he asked, leaning over and plucking another, which he tossed to Abreeth.

'Thanks,' Abreeth replied, taking a bite. The sweet juice made the back of his tongue tingle.

They soon came to a clearing with a small cottage made from stone, mud and wood. A thatched roof sat atop the structure and smoke rose lazily from the chimney. A small stream meandered its way past, as a water wheel turned slowly to the water's currents and eddies. Plush gardens surrounded the entire area with many herbs, shrubs and colourful flower beds planted.

Abreeth was pulled out of his reverie by the barking of the largest dog he'd seen in his life.

'Murphy!' cried Dwin, dismounting his donkey and running towards the massive canine. They both met with a crash as Dwin grabbed him by the jowls, letting him lick his face with his enormous, slobbery tongue.

'Oh, I've missed you too, boy, how are you? Who's a good boy? Abreeth, come and meet my dog,' said Dwin as he scratched the delighted animal behind his ears, making his tail wag even more fervently.

'Are you sure he won't eat me?' asked Abreeth, eyeing off the hound with suspicion.

Dwin laughed as his face lit up in a boyish smile, 'Don't be silly Abe, he won't eat you. He's a good boy, aren't you Murphy. Yes, you're such a good boy,' he continued, rolling around with the massive hound in the grass.

Abreeth cautiously walked towards the dog and let him smell his hand. Murphy jumped up and placed both of his massive paws on Abreeth's shoulders and proceeded to lick his face.

'That means he likes you,' said Dwin, giggling at the sight of Abreeth struggling under his weight whilst being subjected to sloppy kisses.

'I'm glad you're enjoying yourself. Get him off me!' cried Abreeth.

'Murphy! Down!' said Dwin in sharp command.

Dropping to all fours the hound looked at him and wagged its tail.

'Where's Mother?' Dwin asked.

Murphy bounded off through a pasture, full of what looked like peas, with great enthusiasm.

'We'd better find Mother and let her know we've arrived,' said Dwin, wandering off in the direction of his four-legged companion.

Murphy bounded up to a woman wearing a blue dress and fur jacket, crouched over planting new seedlings at the other end of the pasture. The hound barked with enthusiasm, causing her to look up from her work. She was in her late thirties, slim and attractive. Her blond curly hair had been tied back in a rough ponytail, and loose strands had fallen during her work, framing her face.

'Dwin!' she squealed, hitching up her skirt and running straight over the top of the seedlings she had just planted.

'Hello Mother,' called Dwin, happily waving and making his way towards his excited mother.

'Oh, my boy!' she cried, enveloping him in a loving embrace that only a mother can give. 'How I've missed you,' she continued, kissing him over his face and head whilst he squirmed and tried to escape.

'Mother!' cried Dwin, embarrassed, 'not in front of company!'

'Oh,' said Grenda, looking at Abreeth with a cheeky smile and a quick wink, 'incredibly sorry, won't happen again.'

She then proceeded to grab him even harder and blow a raspberry on his cheek.

'Who's your friend?' asked Grenda, ruffling Dwin's hair and pulling him close again.

Dwin was trying his best not to look flustered, but wasn't able to rid his face of the smile his mother had induced.

'This is Abe,' he said.

'Pleased to meet you, Abe. I'm Grenda,' said Dwin's mother, embracing him in a warm hug. 'Welcome to my little patch of paradise.'

Abreeth was a little taken aback. Not used to such easy affection. He took an instant liking to Grenda and her effortless nature.

'It's nice to meet you. Dwin's told me a lot about you,' replied Abreeth, smiling as he absentmindedly scratched Murphy behind the ear.

'I see you've met Murphy. I'd go crazy if I didn't have him for company, well crazier than I already am,' she laughed, walking towards her cottage slapping the dirt from her hands.

'You two must be hungry from your travels,' she called, 'Come, let us have some lunch together and catch up on what's new in the world. What happened to your arm, Abreeth?' she gestured to his sling.

'A spurworm injury,' replied Abreeth simply.

'Well,' said Grenda, 'That sounds like a story I must hear. Let's get some food, and you can tell me all about it.'

The inside of Grenda's home was warm, snug and filled to the brim with herbs, pots, cuttings and plants. Her furniture was a mish-mash of wooden chairs and furs strewn on the floor. It had a comfortable, worn-in look to it that made Abreeth instantly feel at ease. In the middle of the well-lit kitchen stood a small table with two chairs and a wooden stool retrieved from a back room.

'Now,' said Grenda, rubbing her hands together after putting down some bread and three bowls of corn chowder. 'How long do you two plan to stay?'

'We were hoping it would be OK to stay for four or five nights,' said Abreeth, taking a bite of broken bread dipped in the chowder. He closed his eyes and savoured the flavour of the expertly prepared food.

'Of course!' said Grenda, raising her eyebrows. 'You can stay as long as you like! It's nice to have company to be honest. Usually, I'm stuck chatting to that lump,' she continued, motioning to Murphy who was gnawing happily on a bone in the corner of the room.

'Now tell me, Abreeth, what's happening in the world out there. The last I heard there were some troubles in Roda Codex and Thade. Lots of people were streaming into the city.'

'We don't get much news where we are, unfortunately,' replied Abreeth. 'As far as I know, the problems are growing steadily worse because of the creeping winter. We had a crew come in from the south a few weeks ago talking about gangs in Roda Codex causing trouble – not stealing anything, just wrecking stuff and hurting people.'

'One of the older boys in town said there were people whose eyes were all funny, and they felt no pain,' said Dwin, adding to the conversation. 'He said that some city guards attacked them and cut one of their arms off and they didn't even flinch, just kept trying to attack them with blood squirting out everywhere and then he...,'

'Dwin, sweetheart, we're eating lunch,' Grenda gently reminded her excited son.

'Oh, right... sorry Mother,' he replied, looking down and shovelling a spoonful of chowder into his mouth.

'Now, Abreeth,' said Grenda, 'tell me about this spurworm wound.'

Abreeth recalled the story of his experience with the two spurworms to the amazement of Dwin's mother. After he'd finished telling his tale, Grenda commented, 'Abreeth, this is unprecedented. I've never heard of anyone surviving a spurworm injury. You were lucky to get out of that alive.'

Dwin chimed in, 'You should see what he can do with a feather.'

Abreeth kicked him under the table. He caught Grenda cocking her head to one side and looking at her son quizzically, like she knew there was a secret in there somewhere, but she seemed to let it go. He was fully expecting her to bring it up later once they'd all gotten a little more comfortable.

After lunch, they sat on the small front porch where they shared cooled tea made from mint and camomile, sweetened with honey from a hive closeby. Abreeth played absently with the new bandage Grenda had wrapped his shoulder in, the smell of herbs and ash from the poultice she applied to his wound wafting to his nostrils on the light breeze.

'Tell me something, Abe,' Grenda said as she leaned back in her chair, 'why do you think you were spared from the clutches of death?'

'I've thought about that,' replied Abreeth. 'Part of me thinks it's just some strange stroke of luck. I was spared because the spur went in a certain way or it was injured and couldn't inject the venom properly.'

'You know,' said Grenda, topping up Abreeth's tea from a pitcher, 'there's an ancient tale that tells of a black rider called Lager Velho who brought misery and destruction to every enemy he encountered. It's said he sat upon a pyredrake made of molten rock, had a sword of pure fire and drank the venom of snakes, spurworms and seawater to get his powers.'

'That sounds a little like a fairytale to me,' said Abreeth, somewhat doubtful about ancient stories and prophecies.

'Well, perhaps it is, but there tends to be some truth in stories that endure for thousands of years. I'm sure there have been embellishments added to the story over the years, but you'd be surprised how many old fables have some element of truth to them,' said Grenda.

'Dwin told me you have an amazing library. I would love to see it,' said Abreeth, changing the topic.

'You read?' asked Grenda, surprised.

'His father taught him. Did you know his father was hurt in a hunting accident when he was a child? He got shot in the face with a crossbow and had it half ripped off.'

'Well, not quite, you certainly know how to embellish a story though!' said Abreeth, rolling his eyes and smiling.

Grenda gave him a knowing grin.

'He was injured as a child and couldn't talk, so reading and writing was the only way he could communicate,' corrected Abreeth.

'Now,' said Grenda, 'do you see how easy it is for stories to become greater than they are, but still have a core of truth to them?'

'You're right,' smiled Abreeth, 'I hadn't noticed that!'

'Come,' said Grenda, standing up, 'let's take a look over some books and scrolls to kill some time before our evening meal.'

The rest of the afternoon the trio lounged in the living room of the cottage with piles of books, sharing exciting stories of strange and wondrous adventures, fallen heroes and feats of bravery from the texts from Grenda's library. As the suns made their way behind the treeline, the temperature cooled. Grenda built up the fire in the cottage to warm the room a little more.

Their evening meal comprised of salad made from freshly picked herbs, leaves and nuts from the gardens surrounding the cabin, garnished with boiled eggs and a dash of vinegar dressing and a bottle of wine.

'I've been saving this for a special occasion,' smiled Grenda, showing them both the bottle, 'and tonight seems like as good a night as any to open it.'

'Tell me,' Abreeth asked Grenda after they'd finished their meal and sat in front of the fire, sipping wine and eating sugar plums, 'do you really live here all by yourself?'

'I have Murphy for company, but yes. Since Dwin left to work with my brother, I'm here by myself,' she said.

'You care for all these trees and gardens, and grow all your own food?' asked Abreeth, fascinated by this attractive woman who lived by herself in the woods.

'I even kill my own chickens when I need the meat,' she replied proudly. 'There's no one else here to do it for me, so it's up to me, although Murphy's been known to kill the odd chicken here and there, haven't you, you naughty boy,' she continued, giving Murphy a scratch behind the ears when he lifted his head at the mention of his name.

'You are quite remarkable,' stated Abreeth.

'Thank you, but if there's anyone in this cottage that's remarkable, I think it might be you, Abe. You've told me about your injury and how you got it, but you still haven't shown me what you can do with a feather,' said Grenda, looking at Abreeth directly as she said it.

Abreeth shot a black look at Dwin, who busied himself straightening cushions and animal skins on his pallet. Abreeth sighed. Perhaps it was the wine, their secluded lodgings, or Grenda's friendly and warm nature, but he thought if there was one person he could trust telling and maybe learn about his anomaly, it was Grenda.

'It was Dwin that discovered it,' Abreeth finally replied.

'Is that so?' said Grenda in surprise.

'It was entirely by accident,' said Dwin, 'I happened to be moving Abe's pillow around and a feather floated down over his hand, that's when I saw it happening.'

'Show me what you mean by 'it',' said Grenda.

'Do you happen to have a feather of any sort?' asked Abreeth.

'Yes, I have a quill around here somewhere. I think it's in the back room with all the books,' she said, getting up and making her way into the room.

Dwin looked at Abreeth. 'Don't worry,' he said, 'you can trust Mother. She knows loads about this type of stuff.'

'What type of stuff?' asked Grenda, walking back into the room holding a quill.

'You know, weird stuff,' said Dwin.

'I can't argue with that,' Grenda, handed Abreeth the feather. 'I've always been fascinated with the strange and unusual. Now, what's this trick I've heard so much about but haven't seen?'

'I'm not quite sure what to make of it, or if it means anything, but after being injured by the spurworm I found I could do this,' replied

Abreeth, holding the feather above his hand where it floated in mid-air, spinning on its axis.

Grenda stared at the feather for a long time before Abreeth asked, 'What do you think it means?'

Grenda stood and walked towards Abreeth, taking his hands, flipping them over in her own and examining them in great detail.

Dwin asked, 'What do you think it...'

'Shhhhh,' hushed Grenda, 'I'm thinking.' She closed her eyes and seemed to look into Abreeth's soul with the touch of her hands.

She rocked back and forth like she was trying to conjure a spirit as a look of concentration settled on her face. Suddenly her eyes opened wide, and she let go of Abreeth's hands.

'What is it?' he asked.

Grenda got up and walked into her book room calling out, 'I have a scroll somewhere in here that talks about floating feathers.'

Abreeth and Dwin could hear books being shuffled and piles being moved when they heard, 'Aha, here it is!'

Grenda walked out with a wooden box and laid it on the floor, opening it to sort through the scrolls within.

'That reminds me,' said Abreeth, looking at the box, 'Yonex gave me a similar box to give to you. Dwin, could you get it from my things?'

Grenda rummaged through the scrolls inside the box, muttering to herself and dropping the ones she didn't need beside her.

'List of those killed in the battle Keegon. Treaty of peace in the seventh realm. Oh, a recipe for a spinach tart! I shall make that tomorrow,' she chirped, as she slid that particular scroll onto the kitchen table. 'Ah, here we are, chapter five of the Fawe proclamation,' she said, looking pleased with herself. Rolling the scroll out on the floor and recited:-

Darkened veins and echoed heart, the victor rises twice.
When feathers float and water beads, the black demands a price.
The earth will move, the flames won't burn, to tarry is certain death.

The time will come to face despair and triumph over wrath.

They all sat in silence for a moment, trying to take in what they'd just heard and make sense of it.

'Darkened veins are easy,' said Dwin, 'when we pulled you off the worm, the veins around your shoulder were all black.'

'Yes, and they're still not quite back to the right colour; in fact, I'm not sure they will go back,' agreed Abreeth.

'You know what I think,' said Grenda. 'I think some of that venom made its way into your body and is pumping around your blood now.'

'Possible,' said Abreeth, 'but that doesn't explain the next part about the echoed heart.'

'Echoed heart,' mused Grenda, pacing around the living room. 'Echoed heart. What could that mean?'

'Perhaps it's about someone Abreeth cares for,' offered Dwin, 'you know, like two hearts become one?'

'That's a possibility I suppose,' said Grenda, lifting her eyebrow. 'Abreeth? Is there anyone who could be said to have your heart?'

Abreeth looked down, finding a chip on his fingernail thoroughly fascinating.

'I'll take that as a yes,' smiled Grenda. 'Men only make those stupid faces when they're trying to get out of work they wish not to do and when they're in love. What was her name?'

Abreeth sighed, knowing he wasn't going to get out of this without spilling some details.

'Her name was Prue. She was the Duke of Roda Codex's daughter.' Abreeth let the words tumble out and sit in the room uncomfortably.

'Really!' sniggered Dwin excitedly. 'How'd you get to know a girl like that?' he asked.

'That's a long story I'd prefer not to get into right now,' said Abreeth, trying with all his might not to blush.

'Awww, c'mon. I bet it's a great story,' said Dwin, rubbing his hands together.

'Dwin, Abe said he doesn't want to tell it so he shan't. Let's move on,' said Grenda.

Dwin's face fell at the prospect of missing out on a colourful story about a beautiful young woman and forbidden love.

'Abe, come here for a moment,' said Grenda, motioning to the spot beside her.

He got up and sat next to her. She smelled of lavender and apples. A homely scent that made him feel at ease. Everything about her; her house, her gardens, her presence, made him feel at ease, like everything was going to be OK, no matter what happened.

Grenda put her head to his chest and wrapped her arms around him. Abreeth didn't quite know what to do. At first, he thought she was hugging him, so he started to put his arms around her.

'That's very kind, Abe, but I'd like to listen to your heart.'

'Right. Yes, of course,' Abreeth said, removing his arms and going from feeling completely at ease, to incredibly embarrassed quicker than a lightning strike.

'Hmm, interesting,' she said, sliding her hands up to his neck and pushing two fingers against his carotid artery.

Abreeth concluded he had no idea what was going on, but was thoroughly enjoying being so close to this humble, attractive woman, so he just went along with it.

'Abe, did you know you have an irregular heartbeat?' she asked.

'No. I don't even know what that means,' said Abreeth, trying not to seem too confused. 'Is it dangerous?'

Grenda smiled, 'No, you're not in any danger. As far as I know, it's not life-threatening and shouldn't affect you. You probably haven't noticed because you can't tell by taking your pulse, you have to listen to the heart, which is impossible to do by yourself. I've heard those that look after animals say it's common in dogs. They call it a heart murmur,' she said.

'So I've got a dog's heart?' said Abreeth, looking confused.

'That would explain the fleas in your room,' laughed Dwin.

Grenda tried hard to stifle a smirk but failed and accidentally snorted. Abreeth opened his mouth in mock insult and threw a cushion at Dwin's head.

'I'm lucky I don't have a dog's nose, or those favourite shoes of yours would have made me ill a long time ago!' Abreeth fired back.

'They smell, but they're comfortable!' said Dwin, still laughing. 'And besides, I don't have to impress any duke's daughters!' Abreeth made for another cushion.

'Alright boys, that's enough,' Grenda said in good humour.

'A heart murmur,' continued Grenda, 'is also known as a heart echo, and it seems you have one,' she said, listening to his chest once again.

'That would explain the second part of the proclamation,' said Abreeth.

Dwin offered, 'And victor rises twice could be talking about you. You should be dead after that spurworm hurt you, Abe, but you lived. It's like you got a second life.'

'He's got a point,' said Abreeth, 'and the feather part seems pretty self-explanatory. What about the beading water?' he asked.

'Let's try,' said Grenda, walking towards the kitchen.

'Try what?' asked Abreeth, watching her come back with a cup of water.

'This,' she said, as she gently held his still injured arm and pulled it towards her. 'Hold out your hand.'

She poured the contents of the cup into his hands. Instead of flowing through his fingers as water should, it collected into a ball in his palm and sat in his hand, defying gravity.

'Woah!' cried Dwin, jumping up to get a closer look. 'That's amazing!'

Abreeth sat and stared at the orb of water in his hand for a long time. Even though none of the liquid was touching his hand, he could 'feel' the water in a way that was hard to explain. He felt the shape and temperature of the liquid in his mind, like it had always been a part of him.

'Remarkable,' said Grenda, looking at the ball from all angles. She poked the ball, and it wobbled, but still held its shape, then slowly became smooth again, like ripples in a pond eventually becoming still.

'It's like magic,' said Dwin.

'It is magic,' replied his mother. 'Potent magic. Abe, how many people know about this?' she asked, a serious tone in her voice.

'Just you, me and Dwin,' replied Abreeth.

'Let's keep it that way for the moment, shall we?' she said. 'There are many people in this kingdom, the next and several others who would do terrible, terrible things to you if they knew you had this power.'

'What do you mean?' asked Abreeth, suddenly feeling like his life had taken a turn that was ultimately out of his control.

'Who? What kind of things? I don't like this at all. I didn't ask for this. All I can do is float a stupid feather on my hand. Why would people want to hurt me for that?' His voice took on a tone of panic.

'It's alright, Abe,' said Grenda, cradling his hand in comfort. 'Nothing's going to happen to you. Only the three of us know about this so, until that changes, there's nothing to worry about, OK?'

'OK,' said Abreeth, calming a little. 'You said this is potent magic, what did you mean by that? How do you know about all this?'

'I had my suspicions as you were telling me your story about the spurworm, but didn't want to say anything until it was confirmed,' said Grenda.

'Until what was confirmed?' asked Abreeth.

'This,' said Grenda, grasping Abreeth's wrist whilst simultaneously grabbing a nearby candle and holding it under his hand.

'Hey,' yelped Abreeth as he tried to yank his hand back reflexively. 'What are you doing?' he shouted as he struggled to move his hand away from the flame.

'Abe, stop struggling,' said Grenda in a loud voice, which made him snap to attention and stare into her calm blue eyes. 'The flame doesn't burn,' she said.

Abreeth stopped struggling and looked at his hand, realising he felt no pain.

'Abe,' said Grenda, letting go of his hand and putting the candle back in its place, 'you can weave the Bind.'

'Weave the Bind?' asked Abreeth, knowing little of what she was saying.

'Let us pour another wine before I explain,' she said, heading into the kitchen. 'You're going to need it.'

6

A DROP OF BLACK TO TAKE YOUR MIND

The long, stately procession wound its way slowly through the streets, like a snake coiled around its prey. Deadsun rode at its head, along with the king and several of the royal family in their finest ceremonial garb. He wore a fine black tunic with elaborate, yet subtle patterns, woven into the fabric. A helm of silver decorated with black feathers adorned his head, as a mark of respect for the dead. Sitting atop a massive warhorse fitted out in full regalia, he looked every bit as intimidating as his reputation.

Behind him rode a group of twenty of his finest guards, decked out in the ceremonial dress reserved for state funerals. Next was the carriage that bore Ashaar's body, pulled by four white mares and surrounded by foot soldiers of the Lavers Lawmen.

As the caravan made its way through the city, men, women and children from all walks of life attached themselves to the end of the procession to mark their respects to a man that was well known and liked throughout the city. Ashaar had given much to the people in his years of service to the kingdom. He had been an excellent mathematician, who assisted with the kingdom's clerks to estimate yields, stores and taxes. He even invented a large sundial that stood in the middle of the market square, helping everyone in the city know the time.

He was also responsible for modifications to the gutter and sewer systems that helped lead waste away from the city, helping to keep it clean and relatively disease-free. He'd studied the skies every night and had thousands of scrolls with star charts and readings that helped many areas of the kingdom, from merchants who navigate via the stars, to farmers deciding when to plant and harvest their crops. He could even predict the time and date of celestial events like eclipses, which the king used to his political advantage by organising important appearances around them. A 'sign' from the gods at the right point in his speech helped secure the love, support and superstitious fear of his subjects.

A mile outside the city gates stood the ornamental wrought iron entrance of the cemetery. The plot Ashaar had purchased for himself was in a prime position overlooking the city, not that he would need the view in his eternal slumber. Gravediggers had already done the difficult job of shovelling through the cold, semi-frozen earth to burrow six feet down. The long procession moved around the grave, leaving room for the stewards that carried Ashaar's body on a bier from the carriage to the graveside. Wrapped in white, with freshly cut flowers scattered around it, his lifeless form was placed with care next to the gravesite.

The ceremony passed in a blur of incense smoke, drawn-out prayers and the occasional sniffle or wail from someone in the crowd. Deadsun stood stoic through the entire event, shutting out the noise from the priest's speeches as he thought fondly of past times with his brother. Incredibly close growing up, they'd drifted apart in their early twenties, when Deadsun travelled to many lands as a soldier and Ashaar expanded his education by visiting the many mages, shamans and intellectuals throughout the four corners of the kingdom. With Deadsun spending more time in Thade and Ashaar being on the king's council, they had grown closer again in the last five years. They often spoke into the night about a great variety of topics from military strategy, philosophy, making beer, drinking beer, wooing women and everything in between.

Now that was all gone—a memory. There was nothing he could do except grieve and watch his brother's body be swallowed by the earth. Many of the mourners had left by the time the last patch of dirt had been shovelled. Now the process of celebrating his life would begin with drinking and merriment in the taverns and alehouses throughout the city. A night of revelry where citizens would recount stories of a time they met, or had dealings with, the dearly departed. As the night grew later, the stories would become more ribald and elaborate until it was difficult to tell apart fact from fanciful fiction. There would be many sore heads and sandy eyes in the morning. Deadsun would not be joining them. He was acutely aware that the courtiers, court officials, office-bearers, wealthy merchants and others who play the game of politics would already be moving to conserve or advance their power within the kingdom.

He was deep in thought when a steward politely coughed, pulling him from his thoughts. 'I'm ever so sorry to disturb you, sir,' said the steward. 'At your earliest convenience Bailur, the king's steward, has requested an audience with you. Here are the details.' He handed Deadsun a scroll with the personal seal of Bailur stamped in red wax, a peacock with a snake in its claws.

'Thankyou,' he answered, taking the scroll and putting it inside his tunic.

The steward nodded and turned on his heel to leave, then stopped and turned back momentarily. 'I'm sorry about your brother, sir. He was always very kind to me.'

———

Deadsun stood outside Bailur's door, imagining him at his desk, surrounded by papers and scrolls related to the running of the city. His slender fingers would be adorned with rings topped with emeralds and other precious gems, the one on his middle finger bearing his personal mark.

Deadsun was not particularly looking forward to this meeting and had taken time in his room to collect his thoughts after he returned from the funeral.

'You wanted to see me,' he stated as the steward showed him in. He stood looking at Bailur with a cold, reptilian stare that divulged neither enmity nor fondness. 'I assume it's about the box you handed me yesterday?' he asked, placing it on the table.

'Yes, in part,' replied Bailur, offering Deadsun a tankard of cool water, 'and may I say thank you for coming to see me so quickly. I was not expecting you until tomorrow, given the day you've had. Can I offer you something to eat, some cheese or fruit perhaps?'

'Thank you, but no,' replied Deadsun, wanting to get this engagement over with as quickly as possible.

'Now, before we talk about this box and the device in it,' said Bailur, motioning to the ornately carved box on the table, 'I would like to talk to you about the place in which we met yesterday.'

'Where we met?' exclaimed Deadsun in surprise. 'I don't understand what that has to do with this box or the device in it?' he continued.

'It doesn't,' said Bailur, looking at Deadsun with keen eyes, as if trying to evaluate as much as possible without having to ask questions.

'As you were making your way out of the royal stables, and given the time it took you to get to the castle, I can only assume you acquired horses for a portion of your trip from the mountain, correct?'

'Yes,' said Deadsun cautiously.

'And one can only assume that since you were able to acquire horses from the royal stables, word of the order that no horses were to leave without the king's blessing met your ears. No doubt you made the connection that this was a proclamation I was likely to have ordered?' questioned Bailur.

Deadsun sat for a moment trying to assess his next move.

'We met on the way to the keep,' he replied slowly. 'How can you be sure we were coming from the royal stables, or that we were riding the king's horses? We may have acquired horses in one of the villages on the way back to the city,' said Deadsun, not wanting to make it easy for Bailur to get the information he wanted.

'Yes, I suppose that's entirely possible, but that's not what happened, is it?' Bailur replied, leaning back in his chair and resting his hands on his lap. 'Deadsun, I realise there's been a level of... shall we say, coolness between us over the years, and that is something I would like to attempt to abate. We might never thoroughly warm to each other, but it's in the best interest of the kingdom for us to at least try to work together, given the growing difficulties we face and recent developments.'

'What recent developments might they be?' asked Deadsun.

'We shall get to that in good time, Commander. Before we do, I would like to offer you an apology.'

'An apology?' said Deadsun, raising his eyebrows. Bailur was not known for his good nature or kindness. An apology was the last thing Deadsun was expecting from this meeting.

'Yes, an apology,' replied Bailur. 'I indeed gave the order for no horses to leave the royal stables under the guise they were needed for the protection of merchants, but the truth is Deadsun, I was trying to protect you.'

'Protect me!' exclaimed Deadsun incredulously. 'And how do you suppose stopping me from seeing my dying brother helped protect me?' he asked, attempting to abate his anger, but doing a poor job of it.

Bailur put both his hands up in supplication, 'I understand your acrimony, and sitting where you are now, given the information you have, I might just feel the same way, but hear me out.'

'Continue,' replied Deadsun, shooting him an icy stare.

'When I was a younger man, a much younger man, in fact, I also had a brother,' started Bailur.

'Had?' asked Deadsun. 'What happened to him?'

'You do like to get straight to the point, don't you?' said Bailur smiling.

'I find when a fellow combatant is swinging his sword at your head, there's little time for inquisition or levity,' replied Deadsun cooly.

'Of course,' said Bailur, resting his hands in his lap again. 'I sometimes forget men of action don't have the luxury of time and conversation. Something we in the court, have an excess of at times.' Bailur looked at the ceiling and steadied himself. 'Forgive me as I find this... somewhat difficult to talk about,' he said with a slight shake in his voice. 'My brother's name was Eshera, and he suffered from a condition also. Whilst his disfigurement was worse than your brother's, it didn't seem to affect him in terms of pain. You see when he was born, there was another baby, a twin if you will. His twin, however, wasn't born separately as is usually the case. They were born connected, you see, but there weren't two of them, just... how would you put it, extra parts attached to his body. The people in my hometown called him an abomination and a curse of the gods. He saw seven summers before he wandered to the dark realms.'

Bailur took a sip of water from his tankard, his hand slightly shaking, and continued, 'You see Deadsun, when he died, it was not with dignity or grace. His was a painful rite of passage that saw his bodily functions expire whilst his mind was fully aware of the ramifications. I can still see the fear and supplication in his eyes.'

Bailur lowered his head and looked Deadsun in the eyes. 'Deadsun, I don't see any point in lying to you. Your brother's death was a harrowing experience, not only for himself, but for others in the room with him. It was this experience that I've had to live through, from which I was trying to protect you. You're the city's commander, Deadsun, and now more than ever we need you to take on the complications of our ever-expanding problems with the clearest of minds and the best of intentions. I'm not pretending that what I did was right, but it was logical. I'm hoping that if you look deep into your soul, you will find it in yourself, perhaps not to agree with me, but to at least forgive me for this thinking.'

At first, as Deadsun listened to Bailur's story, he was askance in his evaluation of its authenticity, thinking perhaps Bailur was manoeuvring after being found out about the order with the horses. But as his tale continued, Deadsun could see the physical discomfort Bailur experienced in talking about this subject, and knew then he was telling the truth.

Perhaps Bailur was even a little sorry. Not as sorry as his flowery apology tried to portray, but there was an acknowledgement in his eyes and a truth to his tongue that toppled Deadsun's defences. Deadsun thought for a long time. His answer came slowly, as there was much to consider in his response.

'Bailur, it's true, you and I haven't seen eye to eye, but we are both, I believe, the king's men. For this I respect you. On the matter of my brother, this was not your decision to make, and you denied me the opportunity to see my brother whilst he was still alive. I admit your intentions might have been admirable, but they have caused me great pain. Know this.'

Bailur nodded, waiting for Deadsun to continue.

'Like you, I serve the realm. I understand your decision was for the advancement of the city, the people and the kingdom, and it's difficult for me to find fault in your choice, however,' Deadsun continued, making his voice deadly serious, 'I can see past this... indiscretion on your part and forgive you. However, if your courtier's fingers find their way into my personal matters again, I shall pursue you without end, or mercy. There is no haven you can hide or lands you can run to. And when I find you, you'll wake up, clawing with broken fingers at the ceiling of your grave. Is that clear?'

'Understood. I would expect no less from a man such as yourself, Commander. Now, can we put this behind us and move on, or is there something more you wish to discuss on the matter?' asked Bailur, transitioning back to his usual velvet tongue.

'Let's move on,' said Deadsun, feeling fatigued.

'Good,' replied Bailur. 'Before we discuss what's inside that box, can I offer you a cup of sweet tea?' he asked.

'Yes, I think I will.' Deadsun took the cup and drank the warm liquid.

Bailur picked up the box from Deadsun's side of the table and asked, 'Now, what do you know about the device inside this box?'

'I've seen one other like it. On a prisoner at Point Terrene a few days ago,' answered Deadsun.

'Did you notice anything different about this prisoner?' pressed Bailur, obviously wanting Deadsun to expand on his experience with the device.

'Yes,' said Deadsun, 'she was naked by choice, when a woman of her allure had no reason to be in a camp full of men in such cold conditions. She also struck me as being quite mad.'

'In what way?' asked Bailur thoughtfully.

'Well, every other prisoner in that place looked fearful about what was going to happen to them, but she was not phased in the slightest.'

'Do you remember anything else she said, or something about her behaviour?' pushed Bailur.

Deadsun thought for a moment. 'She spoke of darkness bringing redemption. She also talked of the Menace. Her behaviour was like those I've seen in a sanitorium or a prisoner who's mad after spending too much time in solitary cells. She didn't appear normal, put it that way,' finished Deadsun.

'Yes, it would appear so,' said Bailur as he opened the box, carefully taking out the teardrop device from the leather wrap and holding it to the firelight so it glinted like a jewel in sunlight.

'Tell me, Bailur,' asked Deadsun, 'what do you know about this device? How did you come about it?'

'This is not the first one of its kind I've seen, but it's certainly the most beautifully engineered version,' said Bailur, slowly turning the device in his hands.

'Version?' inquired Deadsun. 'So you've seen different types?'

'Yes, it's not uncommon amongst the acolytes of Stardark to use them to see beyond the realms of the living, to help them become closer with the gods. I imagine they are like the device your prisoner was wearing.'

'Wearing,' scoffed Deadsun. 'It looked more like it had grown into her skin. So you know what these devices are and what they do?' he asked.

'To an extent, yes. The Stardark acolytes only use them as a temporary measure. It had grown into her skin, you say?' asked Bailur.

'Yes,' answered Deadsun, 'and she put up a hell of a fight when my men tried to remove it. Gave one of them a nasty gash.'

'Well, it's a good thing they didn't remove it,' replied Bailur, 'because every person who's had one removed by us has died a painful, horrible death as soon as it was detached. And dead prisoners can't talk.'

'What does it do? What use is it if you perish once you take it off?' asked Deadsun.

'Both excellent questions,' replied Bailur. 'As for what it does, we're still trying to get to the bottom of that. As far as we can tell it's a device to give and also take away aspects of the human condition.'

'I'm not sure I follow?' said Deadsun.

'When a welltaker is bound to a person's nape, it seems they lose some of their inhibitions around pain, particularly delivering and receiving it. It seems to deaden any pain felt, or remorse inflicting it. They also gain a certain collective thought process that seems to echo through others that share a device of the same nature.'

'They can read each other's minds?' asked Deadsun incredulously.

'No, nothing as sophisticated as that,' replied Bailur quickly. 'But we've seen similar behaviour, particularly violent behaviour, being mimicked when there's more than one person with this device on their back. Whilst you were on patrol, we had an incident in the eastern wing of the city. A group of young men had a little too much to drink and decided it would be a good idea to test their mettle against another man in the street. They were no doubt expecting a typical drunken encounter, with insults and wild swings traded, but that wasn't to happen this night. The man wearing this device killed three of the drunkards in a frenzied attack and, like your bare-skinned captive, he seemed unphased about his actions when dragged into the dungeons.

'By Gods,' said Deadsun in surprise.

'That's not the worst of it,' said Bailur.

'There's more?'

'Apparently, around the same time of night, several other attacks happened throughout the city. Men and women behaving like wild animals, attacking people, all of them wearing a device like this. They attacked innocents with no provocation on the part of the victims. It's almost like something snapped within them, and they shared a collective unbalancing of their mind. In all, eleven people were killed,' said Bailur, shaking his head.

'Why am I only hearing of this now?' asked Deadsun, delivering a steely gaze in Bailur's direction.

'As you can appreciate, I considered telling you as soon as you returned to the city. Given the circumstances, I thought it better to give you a few days to collect yourself after such a grievous loss. As much as it pains me to admit, we're still in the process of scrutinising what we're dealing with. I think it prudent we tell only those that need to know at this point. Since you're the Commander of the Lavers Law, and responsible for keeping the city and its people safe, it's imperative you and I work together to understand what these devices are, how they work and where they're coming from.'

'Understood,' said Deadsun. 'We should increase the night guard.'

'I've taken the liberty of approving the additional funds required to ensure we have extra men available,' said Bailur.

'My thanks to you,' said Deadsun, raising his eyebrows, surprised at Bailur's goodwill.

'Think nothing of it. Now, as for discovering what these well-taker devices are, this is what we know. Somehow they're attached to the skin on the back of the neck. How that's done, we have some ideas, but nothing is certain at this point. I have a group of mages and priests working on different theories and an assembly of shamans and physicians on their way north to visit the acolytes of Stardark to find out as much as we can from their senior priests. As far as we can tell the spines at each end are inserted into the skin to allow the victim's blood to flow through the crystal in the middle of the device. It's this crystal that seems to hold all the power over the wearer.'

'Where do you think they are coming from?' asked Deadsun.

'Our best guess is from the Pyrelands,' answered Bailur.

'Makes sense,' said Deadsun. 'That naked prisoner was found with a lot that came across the tundra. They were attacking villages, stealing food and killing a bunch of livestock to take back to the Pyrelands. Bastards,' growled Deadsun.

'Yes, it seems many that make their way across the expanse go out of their way to make themselves unsavoury,' replied Bailur.

A knock at the door interrupted their conversation. A man in a robe of deep purple and a short, cropped beard that showed the greys of advanced age opened the door.

'Ah, Ashnam,' said Bailur, 'it's good to see you. I don't believe you've met our city watch commander, Deadsun.'

'Hello,' said Ashnam in a squeaky voice, looking very uncomfortable at the prospect of talking to the mountain of a man.

'Greetings,' said Deadsun simply.

'What brings you to my quarters at this time of the evening, Ashnam? A report of progress I hope,' said Bailur, standing up and walking toward the robed man. 'Don't worry, you can speak freely. Deadsun has been brought up to speed. Now, what news?'

'Well, sir,' said Ashnam nervously, 'we have made something of a breakthrough,' he continued, wringing his hands.

'Excellent!' said Bailur excitedly. 'Please, come in and tell us all about it.'

'I think it better if we show you, m' lord,' he replied.

'Even better!' said Bailur, delightedly rubbing his hands together. 'A demonstration! Lead the way my good man.'

Deadsun and Bailur followed Ashnam through the castle for several minutes, weaving in and out of narrow pathways, hallways and thoroughfares lit with candles and torches.

'This way, please,' said Ashnam, guiding them down a staircase, into the bowels of the castle. Deadsun felt a distinct change in the temperature and pulled his coat around him. From the cold, he knew they were well below ground level, into a part of the castle few ever ventured.

Ashnam led them to a door with a carving of a pyredrake on it. Red garnets decorated its eyes and it was guarded by four men that were not castle soldiers. Deadsun recognised this, and scrutinised them with an experienced eye.

'Don't worry,' said Bailur, catching his look, 'they're not from your stock. They're used to guard, shall we say, some of the more unknown rooms throughout the castle.'

Deadsun simply nodded.

Ashnam opened the door and took them through a corridor that had hallways leading left and right into rooms and dark spaces beyond. Deadsun caught a glimpse of storage boxes and medical devices in the first room. In the next, he spied three prisoners chained to the wall.

'Tell me, what is it you do down here, Ashnam?' asked Deadsun as they continued down the hallway.

'Many things,' replied Ashnam, shuffling his feet and leading the way, 'but mostly what Lord Bailur asks of us.'

'And what would that be at this particular time?' Deadsun could only imagine the fetid experiments and grim tasks Bailur would be conducting in the depths of the castle's secret corridors.

'This,' replied Ashnam as they entered a well-lit room with rows of pallets lining each wall in neat order.

Every bed had a prisoner laying face down. Deadsun counted twenty bodies in total, all with welltakers attached. All in various states of dying. Several appeared to have been dead for some time, their limp bodies no longer groaning or begging for mercy like the others.

'This,' said Bailur, sweeping his arms in a grand motion around the room, 'is where we've been trying to make headway into understanding how these welltakers work. We know, for example, the needles at each end enter the body, but are yet to discover how they melt their way into the skin to change the personality of the victim.'

'That's what I wanted to show you, sir,' offered Ashnam. 'I think we may have figured that part out.'

'Lead the way,' replied Bailur, smiling broadly. 'Let's see what you've come up with, shall we?'

'This way gentlemen,' replied Ashnam, leading them to a room just off the main chamber.

Inside was a table with an assortment of what looked like medical devices, sharp knives, pokers and other implements that would do just as well in the torturer's den. In the middle of the room sat a metal-framed bed with leather restraints for a victim's head, hands and feet. Two assistants led a prisoner into the room and laid him flat on the bed, face down.

'We've tried putting this device onto fifty-three prisoners so far,' said Ashnam, looking at his feet.

'The first few, we tried just inserting the needles into their skin, but the wounds soon went septic, and they passed after a few days. Then we tried different methods of putting the needles in, heating them with fire first. Freezing them. Boiling them. Getting them to the same temperature as the body, but that didn't work either. From there, we moved onto incorporating different elements into that crystal you see in the middle. We've tried many herbs and elixirs.

Even liquid metals and blood from a range of animals, but nothing has worked. Until now.'

Ashnam opened a box and chose a welltaker from several that sat inside and deftly placed the device on the back of the prisoner's neck. The man stiffened as the cold metal touched his skin. The mage put on a pair of gloves and carefully opened a glass vial, dipping the top of a sharpened feather into the inky, viscous liquid inside.

'Is that what I think it is?' asked Deadsun, taking a step back.

Never taking his eyes off the feather, Ashnam answered, 'If you think this is spurworm venom, then you'd be correct. Now excuse me whilst I concentrate. This liquid is incredibly deadly, and expensive.'

Ashnam handed the vial to his gloved assistant, who put it back in its place amongst the other elixirs, poisons and venoms he had stacked in a rack at the back of the room. Ashnam hovered the feather over the welltaker device, making sure the tip of the feather lined up with the crystal in the middle of the device. Gently, he touched the crystal with the feather tip, and for a moment, nothing happened.

Then, as if the device were alive, the needles whipped through the air like an injured snake and injected themselves into the prisoner's body, causing him to scream and violently arch his back. Ashnam observed with a steady, unflinching gaze as the man struggled with such force; Deadsun thought he would surely break his bones, the restraints or both. As his muscles tensed and shook, the skin around the welltaker bubbled and bled as reddish smoke rose from his flesh. Within a few moments, the device had grown into his nape, giving the appearance it had always been there. The man had gone limp and began to mumble incoherently.

'Fascinating. What's he saying?' asked Bailur, inspecting the device.

'It's the same for all of them, m' lord,' replied Ashnam, 'Darkness brings redemption, that's all they say again and again, over and over.'

The assistants unshackled the prisoner and turned him over so he could sit. Deadsun and Bailur looked at the man and saw a different face to the one they witnessed being led into the room only moments before. This man's eyes were opaque and colourless. His features had slackened to give him the appearance of someone that was both dead and living at the same time.

The prisoner looked directly at Deadsun with those soulless eyes and spat, 'Darkness brings redemption,' as he lurched off the bed, hands clawing at Deadsun's throat, a wail escaped from his throat.

Deadsun stepped back, drew his short sword in one swift motion and brought the blade down, taking the prisoner's head off at the neck.

Bailur, Ashnam and the two assistants stood, their mouths agape as the body fell to the floor, blood spurting from the stump at the shoulders as the prisoner's head rolled to a stop at their feet.

'Well,' said Deadsun, wiping his blade clean on the prisoner's tattered pants, 'at least we know how to kill them.'

7

LOVE LOST AND DEAD HEARTH

'The Bind,' explained Grenda, taking another sip of wine from her wooden cup, 'is everything and nothing at the same time. It is the moment between breathing in and out, that tiny flash of breathing as well as not breathing.'

'So, holding your breath?' asked Abreeth, confused.

'Not really, let me expand,' replied Grenda, shifting her weight on the cushion.

Abreeth got the feeling this was going to be a long night with a lot of explanation and discovery.

'The Bind is what holds everything together, but it's also the gaps in between everything that exists. It's light and dark. Cold and heat. Life and death. Man and woman. Good and evil. But it's also much more than that. If, for example, you take a rock of a certain size and break it down into dust with a hammer, that rock no longer takes up the same amount of space. Even though the rock appears solid, there's space inside it. The Bind is energy and understanding, all at once and not at all. The Bind is everything between your comprehension of what is and isn't. Take this cup, for example,' continued Grenda, holding up her wooden vessel. 'It holds its shape, no matter what liquid I put in there, hot or cold. If however, I was to throw it in the fire, it would soon burn and disappear to ash. That ash will make its way into my garden and return to the earth from which it originally came. So that cup is a tree, a cup and ash all at once and not at all. I know this must seem very confusing for you Abreeth, so let me put it simply for you.'

Abreeth sat with a face halfway between utter confusion and complete ineptitude.

'As I'm talking to you, you hear me, yes?' asked Grenda.

Abreeth nodded, not trusting himself to talk.

'So you would agree the words I'm saying right at this moment exist?'

'I suppose so,' said Abreeth.

'What about now?' asked Grenda.

'What do you mean?' asked Abreeth, feeling even more confused.

'Would you agree that the words I just uttered a few sentences ago still exist?' she asked again.

'Well, yes,' said Abreeth, trying to think his way through the question, 'and no. They *did* exist, but they don't right now.'

'I think you're getting the idea,' said Grenda with a pleased smile. 'The concept that something can exist and not exist at the same time is difficult for many people to grasp, but we do it all the time. Those words lived in space just a few moments ago, but now they only exist in the past, or perhaps in your mind when you conjure a vision of me saying them. A cup can exist inside a tree, or a statue in a piece of stone. A sword lives in ore from the ground. They both exist and don't at the same time. They're just waiting for someone to sculpt them and move elements around to make this out of that. The ability to control the Bind is just like being able to craft a statue out of stone, but with the elements of the world; fire, air, water and earth. That's why you can keep that feather floating and hold water in your hand Abreeth, don't you see? You are remarkable. There's been only a handful of people in the history of the four kingdoms that have been able to control the Bind, possibly more that we don't know about, but Abreeth, this is something that will change your life forever, perhaps the course of history as we know it.'

'Hold on, hold on,' said Abreeth, rubbing his eyes. 'So you're saying I can control elements? How do you know all this and what good will it do me, anyway? So what if I can hold a cup of water in my hand? That's no use to anyone.'

Dwin snorted, 'Abe, fire doesn't burn you. That's pretty amazing if you ask me.'

'Well, yes... that could come in handy, but it still... I just think I'm... Bah!' he shouted, throwing his hands in the air in frustration.

Grenda took Abreeth's hand in her own, 'I know this is a lot to take in right now, and it's getting late. Why don't we finish our wine, get some sleep and hopefully things will be much clearer in the morning.'

'I think that's a fantastic idea,' yawned Dwin, stretching and wrapping a blanket around himself.

'Before we do, I'm supposed to give you this,' said Abreeth, handing over the box that Dwin had retrieved earlier.

'Oh yes, the box from Yonex. I'd quite forgotten about that with all the excitement. I hope he was able to get me what I asked for,' she said, opening the box and pulling out a small glass vial with a black, inky liquid inside.

'What's that?' asked Dwin with curiosity.

'This, my dear boy is lament, or as you would call it, spurworm venom, but it's been distilled into a very deadly elixir by a series of processes known to only but a few people in all four kingdoms.' Abreeth and Dwin's eyes grew wide at the sight of something so deadly.

'What?' Grenda said, at the boys' look of fear. 'I use it for my black nasturtiums.'

Dwin and Abreeth looked at each other and shrugged.

'And what do we have here?' Grenda said as she pulled out a scroll of red paper. 'I haven't seen one of these for years!'

'What is it?' asked Dwin, still full of questions even at this late hour.

'This is a fire scroll,' replied Grenda.

'I've heard of those,' said Abreeth. 'You can only see the writing if you hold the scroll up with firelight as the backdrop.'

'Excellent, Abe,' said Grenda, 'but not just any fire, there are different types of fire scrolls and unless you know what you're looking at, to the average person, it seems like a blank scroll. Look,' she continued, pointing to the wooden handle, 'do you see these twin olive branches? That's the alchemy sign for copper, so this is indeed a fire scroll, but will only work when read by a fire that's also burning copper. Oh, and look, Yonex has been kind enough to send me a small parcel of copper filings.'

She walked to the fire and threw the filings into the flames, quickly unrolling the scroll and holding it to the light.

'Nothing's happening,' said Dwin.

'Patience, my dear,' replied Grenda.

The copper finally caught alight and raised bluish-green flames from the hearth. A series of symbols, diagrams and instructions took shape upon the scroll.

Abreeth recognised some familiar-looking images that appeared on the document. There was a pyredrake and a boat that looked like it had wings. To the side of the drawings was a column of written instructions and what looked like ingredients and tools.

'By the old gods, he's done it. He's actually done it,' said Grenda in wonder.

'Done what?' asked Dwin.

'Are they instructions on how to build a boat with wings?' asked Abreeth.

'How intuitive of you, Abreeth. Yes, that's exactly what they are. How on earth did you know?'

'Because I've seen one,' replied Abreeth.

'You've seen these instructions before?' queried Grenda. 'Did Yonex show them to you?'

'No,' said Abreeth, smiling, 'I've seen his boat, with wings. Real live wings that move and look like they can fly. Yonex and Borchin said they had been working on it for years, and they'd finally gotten it to work, at least mostly, I think.'

Grenda's mouth was agape, then it suddenly turned into a broad grin. 'He did it!' she squealed, 'You mean, he really did it? You've seen it?' she asked, full of excitement.

'With my own two eyes,' said Abreeth.

'Oh,' said Grenda, pacing back and forth across the room, 'Oh my, my. This changes everything. I can't believe he's done it. He did it. We did it!'

Grenda squealed and danced on the spot, then kissed the scroll she was holding in her hands. She stooped down slightly and kissed Dwin on the top of his head then turned to Abreeth, grabbed him by surprise and kissed him fully on the lips.

Grenda looked from the scroll to the two young men, 'We pack tonight and leave tomorrow. I have to see this with my own eyes.'

'But we've only just got here!' cried Dwin, through his sagging eyelids.

'Yes, of course, I'm getting ahead of myself,' replied Grenda. 'You've had a long journey and I have things to organise before we go. We shall leave the day after tomorrow then. Right, we have a big day tomorrow, let's all get some sleep.'

'Finally!' said Dwin with dramatic flair, flopping down on the blankets, 'Good night Mother, good night Abe.'

'Good night Dwin,' said both Grenda and Abreeth at the same time.

They looked at each other and smiled.

'Good night Abreeth. We shall talk more in the morning,' said Grenda, dancing to her bedroom and shutting the door.

Abreeth stepped over Murphy and laid his tired bones on the comfortable pallet stuffed with fresh straw and grasses. He lay for several hours trying to make sense of everything he'd learnt that night before eventually drifting off into a sleep filled with wonderful and strange dreams.

———

Abreeth was woken, what felt like five minutes later, by Grenda buzzing around the kitchen making breakfast, banging pots and pans, boiling water for tea and humming a merry tune to herself. Abreeth sat up and yawned, stretched and gave Murphy a scratch behind his ear, making his back leg flicker and jump.

'Good morning, lazy bones,' sang Grenda.

Early morning sunlight filtered through a window behind her, giving her the look of a breakfast-making angel.

'Good morning,' replied Abreeth, rubbing the back of his neck and groaning as he got up. 'My arm is feeling a lot better. Whatever that poultice was you put on my shoulder, it seems to have worked wonders.'

'That's good. Here, drink this,' said Grenda, holding out a cup of steaming hot liquid. 'It's peppermint and rosemary. Should give you a little pick-me-up after your long journey.'

'Not to mention all that wine,' said Abreeth, shielding his eyes from the light as he walked into the kitchen, taking the mug of tea from Grenda.

'I suppose you don't get to have a drink that often being in Borchin's crew. He always was a stickler for being professional on his boats. He never drank much as a young man either. He preferred to tinker with things like harpoons, and designs for new sails and such,' said Grenda as she put three plates upon the small kitchen table.

'Dwin!' she sang loudly. Abreeth winced at the sudden loud noise. 'It's time to get up! Breakfast. Now.'

A groan and some rustling came from Dwin's pallet, and a shabby, yawning figure with crazed hair stumbled into the kitchen and sat, zombie-like, at the table to start eating.

'Good morning to you too,' said Grenda.

'Sorry,' said Dwin, plastering a big, fake, cheesy smile on his face. 'Good morning Mother, good morning Abreeth. How are you both on this fine morning?' he said, all feigned cheerfulness and bright eyes.

'Oh, gods,' laughed Grenda, 'I think that's worse! Eat up, boys. We have a lot to organise today. I need to make preparations to be away for at least a few weeks, as I want to spend some time with Yonex and Borchin on our wingships.'

'Wingships. Is that what they're called?' asked Abreeth.

'That's what I'm calling them. Or at least what I will be calling them when we get them working properly. Eat up. Eat up. I'll need your help in the gardens today. I'm putting netting up to stop my crops from getting butchered whilst we're away. Dwin, I'll need you to cut down some bamboo for irrigation. You still remember how, don't you?'

'Mmmm,' grunted Dwin through a mouthful of sausage and bread.

'Good. Abreeth, I was wondering if I could ask a favour of you,' said Grenda, refilling his cup with more tea.

'Thanks,' said Abreeth, holding up his cup. 'Of course, name it and consider it done.'

'Could you take your clothes off and give them to me?'

Abreeth nearly spat out his tea, 'Excuse me?'

'I've no travelling clothes you see. Last winter a family of mice got into them, and since I hadn't planned on going anywhere I never really got around to sewing more. So, if it's not too much trouble and since we're around the same size, I was hoping I could borrow a pair of pants and maybe a tunic from you?'

'Of course,' said Abreeth with a sigh of relief, 'I have fresh clothes in my pack you're more than welcome to try on.'

'That would be wonderful,' said Grenda, 'Thank you, Abe.'

'Given the rumours of trouble in some towns, it's probably best you keep a low profile, anyway. Pretty women in bright dresses are sure to attract unwanted attention,' said Abreeth.

Grenda glossed over the compliment and gave Abreeth a coy smile. 'Did you experience any trouble on your way here?' she asked.

'Nothing too out of the ordinary,' responded Abreeth, 'a few dust-ups at a local alehouse and the usual pickpockets around town, but nothing we weren't able to handle.'

'It's good to know I'll have two strapping young lads with me for protection and company,' said Grenda, squeezing Abreeth's arm and letting her touch linger. Abreeth stood quickly, picked up his plate and walked to the bench where he dumped it in the bucket of water used to clean the dishes.

'Right,' he said 'We ahh... we need to... Dwin, we need to do that thing.'

'What thing?' asked Dwin, shoving the last mouthful of breakfast into his face, totally unaware of the interaction between his friend and his mother.

'That thing. With the donkeys, to get them ready for tomorrow,' said Abreeth hurriedly.

'I've no idea what you're talking about,' said Dwin, looking at his friend like he'd grown a second head.

'Just come with me,' said Abreeth, dragging Dwin away from the table.

———

A cool had settled over the small glade as the twin suns sank slowly below the treeline.

'Do you get lonely living here on your own?' asked Abreeth, peeling potatoes and putting them into a pot of water.

'Sometimes,' answered Grenda, 'but then again, it's nice to have the animals as my only companions. They don't judge or get too drunk to walk up the stairs and be useless the next day. I have my books, and the gardens certainly keep me busy in the warmer months. Winter is when I miss people the most. I go a little stir crazy being cooped up in the cottage for weeks at a time. That's why I try to go into town or make the journey to Arpenta after the snow melts enough for me to get through.'

'How is it you're helping Yonex and Borchin with their flying boats?' asked Abreeth.

'I've always had a fascination with plants. Ever since I was a little girl. I was drawn to anything that grew from the ground,' Grenda starred off into space for a minute, then smiled. 'My father used to call me Grenda the Ground Ghoul. I was always in the dirt planting something or other. When I was around nineteen, I started experimenting and discovered you could graft one plant onto another.'

'I've heard about that, but never really understood what it meant, or how it works,' said Abreeth, hoping she would expand. He enjoyed seeing her eyes light up when she spoke of the things that drove her passions.

'Imagine for a moment you've hurt your finger,' explained Grenda, moving next to Abreeth and taking his hand in hers. 'The cut is deep, so there's a slice running down your finger,' she continued, lightly brushing her finger along the length of his, causing the hair on the back of his neck to stand on end and goose pimples to raise on his arms.

'Imagine my finger has a similar cut. Now, imagine each of our fingers is a different type of plant, like a peach and nectarine or lemon and lime. If you're careful and do it the right way, you can combine those two plants, so they heal together and make one tree,' she continued, putting her finger next to his and squeezing both together.

'So two become one?' asked Abreeth in wonder.

'Technically they're two trees joined together, but yes, I suppose you could categorise that as one tree.'

Abreeth tried not to let his disappointment show when Grenda let go of his hands.

'So how does that help Yonex and Borchin build a boat with wings?' asked Abreeth, forcing himself to return to the topic at hand.

'Not many people know this, but there are certain animal parts that can grow into, around and alongside lightwood. I discovered this when I was on a trip about ten years ago, to find some rare herbs that only grow far to the north. On one of my daily walks, I noticed a copse of lightwood trees that had grown over a large colony of land coral. I didn't think anything of it at first, but as I looked a little closer, I discovered that the coral and the lightwood had combined and were living together. That got me thinking, perhaps other things could live if they were combined or grafted together. So, I started experimenting with all sorts of things. First, I tried different types of plants, then butterfly eggs and silkworms, then some reptiles and so on. Eventually, after lots of trial and error, I found the few animals that can survive when grafted to lightwood. You can't graft the whole thing either; otherwise, the animal becomes stressed and dies quickly.'

'So you're the brains behind all of this?' asked Abreeth, grinning at the thought of her besting Yonex and Borchin.

'It's a group effort, but yes, I'd like to think I was the one that got... how would you say, the boulder rolling. I'm not sure Borchin would have ever gotten this far on his own, nor Yonex for that matter,' smiled Grenda.

'Those two stone heads!' jibed Abreeth playfully. 'Why they're lucky to have someone like you in their lives, in fact, we all are,' he continued, softening his tone and stepping close, moving some loose strands of hair behind her ear. Grenda's breath quickened as Abreeth looked into her eyes and took her hand in his.

'It must get lonely out here all by yourself,' whispered Abreeth, his body only a fingers width from hers.

'I'm not lonely now,' Grenda replied, her body closing the gap and pressing against his. She smelled of honey and flowers, her lips flushed and plump, perfect for kissing.

Leaning in, Abreeth slid his hand to the small of her back and pulled her closer as she sighed and closed her eyes in anticipation.

'Right, what's for dinner, then? I'm starving!' declared Dwin noisily as he stomped into the kitchen. The moment lost, Abreeth and Grenda hurriedly found things to busy themselves with.

'Dwin, be a peach and set the table, would you? We're having rabbit and what's left of my potato crop after a cheeky possum got into them last week.'

'Those possums are still getting into your potatoes?' asked Dwin.

'I keep telling you Mother, you should trap them, and you know,' he made a motion of slicing his finger across his throat.

'I know, I know,' said Grenda, 'but I just can't bring myself to harm them. They're ever so cute, and besides, I grow enough to let them have a few now and then.'

'You're too kind to them if you ask me,' mumbled Dwin, making his way to the table with plates and cups.

The three of them enjoyed a wonderful meal and some more wine by the fire in the comfortable surrounds of Grenda's cottage. They talked into the night telling stories of friends and family, and how surprised Borchin and Yonex would be to see Grenda come back with them. There were laughs and a few tears throughout the night as they all swapped stories and anecdotes. Abreeth couldn't remember a time when he felt more content; in fact, he wished the night could go on forever.

———

By the time a fingernail of the first sun peeked over the horizon the next morning Abreeth, Grenda, Dwin, the hound Murphy and the three donkeys were well on their way through the forest on the outskirts of Grenda's cottage. Grenda looked slightly odd in Abreeth's breeches and tunic but somehow still managed to look beautiful with a woollen shawl wrapped around her shoulders and her hair in a neat ponytail. The cold had flushed her cheeks red and the song she hummed merrily reminded Abreeth of home, even though he hadn't had a fixed abode for several years.

The miles came and went as they made good time, not stopping for lunch but rather riding and eating. That night they camped close to the road in a clearing with a small stream happily bubbling nearby which they used to water the donkeys and make warming tea in the cold of the evening.

The following days they travelled through several villages with whispers of trouble floating on the wind like pollen in spring air. They heard nothing detailed, just murmurs and mystery with a tone that kept the trio on edge throughout the day. It wasn't until they got to the village before the town of Aprenta they realised something was wrong.

'What are all those people doing in the street?' asked Dwin.

'I don't know,' replied Abreeth, shielding his eyes from the suns to better see the large group gathered in the middle of the road. They were shouting and gesticulating in an angry manner.

'I think you two should stay here and let me investigate,' said Abreeth, dismounting his donkey and walking towards the bickering crowd, moving his cloak aside, giving himself easier access to the short sword he always carried when travelling.

Approaching the edge of the group, he saw a body lying in the middle of the cobblestones, a crossbow bolt embedded deep in his chest.

'What happened here?' Abreeth asked one of the villagers.

'Old Tom the blacksmith shot this fellow. Said he was acting all crazy and attacking his apprentice. Said he was working in his smith when he heard shouts and saw this one on top of young Walsh beating the insides out of him. Said he shouted at him to stop, but he just wouldn't listen, so he got a bolt in the chest for his trouble. Poor Walsh got his arm broke, and a few teeth knocked out,' said the villager.

'Thanks,' said Abreeth, turning on his heel and making his way back to Grenda and Dwin.

'Just a dispute between villagers, nothing to do with us. I'm sure the local magistrate will take care of it.'

They mounted their donkeys and as they passed the group, they heard them saying things like, 'He don't look local,' and 'What's that thing on his neck?'

The trio had travelled a further two hours when the smell of acrid smoke stung the back of their throats. It wasn't the familiar smell of cooking fires and hearths; this was something more.

'There must be a forest fire somewhere,' said Grenda.

'That glow doesn't look right.' said Abreeth, scrutinising the orange hue on the horizon, when suddenly it dawned on him. 'That's coming from Arpenta,' he said with a hint of urgency in his voice.

'Perhaps a house has caught fire?' Dwin offered.

'That's more than a house,' said Abreeth, 'It looks like the whole damn town is alight.'

Riding closer, the smoke grew thicker and particles of ash floated in the wind around them. Topping the hill that led to the skyport the trio witnessed a view of utter devastation before them. The entire town was alight and looked like it had been for some time.

'I don't understand,' said Abreeth, looking on in shock. 'How can the whole damn town be on fire?.'

'Uncle Borchin!' cried Dwin, giving his donkey a kick in the ribs.

'Dwin, wait!' yelled Abreeth, doing the same to catch up with him, grabbing the reins of his donkey to stop them both from going any further.

'We can't just go riding into town,' he said. 'We've no idea what's going on or what's happened. It could be a pyredrake attack or rebels or anything. I've never seen a whole town on fire like this before. We need to be careful.'

'He's right, Dwin,' said Grenda, a worried look on her face. 'We need to have our eyes peeled for trouble. I think we should hide the donkeys in that small grove over there and walk the rest of the way.'

'You two aren't going anywhere,' replied Abreeth forcefully. 'You need to stay here. Besides, I can travel faster alone.'

'Abreeth,' said Grenda, placing her hand gently on his arm, 'be careful.'

'Don't worry,' replied Abreeth, 'I'll be back in no time.'

Abreeth moved through a glade of trees and across a small stream, approaching the town making sure the suns were in his eyes, so any lookouts wouldn't see his silhouette against the setting orbs. The ash and dust kicked up by the firestorm in the middle of town made visibility difficult. Skulking around the edge of the village in the treeline, he hid behind bushes and shrubs to see if he could find out what was happening.

What he saw were burning buildings and little of anything else. There was no shouting or screaming. Not a single person had water or bucket. The only sounds he could hear was the roaring of flames and buildings collapsing into firey heaps throughout the village. It was as if everyone had set a torch to the town and left.

What the hell is going on? Abreeth wondered to himself as he warily left the treeline, sword drawn. Stepping slowly through the outskirts of town, he looked into the burnt-out shells of houses and businesses. As he passed the candlemaker's store, a noise caused him to stand rock still. Footsteps sounded in the distance at a light jog. He covered his face with his tunic to stop from coughing and giving away his position. Through narrowed eyes, he spied a figure slowly emerging from the smoke to trot right past him.

'Bloody goats,' he sighed, releasing both the grip on his sword and the breath from his lungs.

He jogged his way around the edge of town towards the skyports where he was hoping to see signs of life, a ship, or anything to indicate there was still somebody, anybody in a town. Arriving at Yonex's boatyard, all he could see was the burnt-out remnants of his large greenhouse. All the ships were gone.

'This makes no sense,' Abreeth said to himself. 'Where the hell is everyone?'

Abreeth walked to the centre of town in a daze.

'BORCHIN,' he yelled. 'YONEX. ANYBODY!'

Realising his bellows were futile, he decided to head back to Grenda and Dwin. Half a mile from the grove he heard Murphy barking and Dwin shouting. Getting closer, he could see a small fire lighting the outline of a man.

He was holding Grenda by the hair and pushing a murderous looking dagger against her ribs.

'LET HER GO. LET HER GO OR I'LL FUCKING KILL YOU!' screamed Dwin, holding up his dagger as Murphy barked threateningly by his side.

'It's you who's going to die, you little sprog,' the man hissed. 'You, the wench and that stupid fucking dog. Don't you see it's coming? It's coming for everyone.'

Abreeth stood in the shadows for a moment, taking in the scene before him. He knew when the time came, he would need to act quickly, with precision and great violence.

Grenda cried out, 'Dwin, put the knife down and just give him what he wants. What do you want?' she said through tears and a wavering voice.

'Redemption my lady. Redem...,' his voice cut off mid-sentence as Abreeth's short sword plunged deep through his body. A crimson pool widened on his chest where the sword tip appeared.

The man tensed and let out a guttural growl as Grenda grunted and lurched forward, both of them falling to the ground. Abreeth ran to Grenda, leaving his sword in the dying man. The attacker's knife had been driven deep into her liver and blood pulsed from the wound.

'MOTHER!' cried Dwin, falling to his knees beside her. Murphy pounced, taking the man's throat in his massive jaws, violently shaking the last remnants of life from his shuddering body.

'Oh gods, Grenda, I'm so sorry,' called Abreeth, taking off his tunic and bunching it to try to stop the bleeding.

'Dwin,' Grenda swallowed her words with difficulty, blood oozing from her mouth. 'Dwin, listen carefully.'

'Shhhh, try not to speak, Mother,' said Dwin, tears running down his cheeks.

'Dwin, your father is in Thade. His name is Edwick,' she coughed.

The pain in her face was evident, 'You have to go to Edwick, your father... Thade,' her voice faded, and she closed her eyes.

'Shhh, Mother, don't talk. It's going to be OK. You're going to be OK. Abe, she's going to be OK, isn't she?' pleaded Dwin. Squeezing his mother's hand, he looked at Abreeth with pleading desperation in his eyes.

Abreeth couldn't hold back the tears, no matter how hard he tried for the sake of Dwin. This was his doing. If he had returned earlier, or stabbed quicker or tried negotiating with the man, Grenda could still be alive. Now she laid cold and motionless in front of them. A wave of grief and guilt washed over him like heavy poison in his blood. His heart sank and his guts churned as he slumped to the ground, beaten and weighed down with remorse.

'Mother?' asked Dwin, slapping her hand several times. 'Mother, open your eyes. Please. Please open your eyes. Mother, please!' he cried, placing his forehead in her hands and sobbing uncontrollably.

8

FROM ASH AND PAIN RISES STRENGTH

'Father, there's a man in our field again,' said the young woman, casting her eyes through the front window. She often looked over the fields to watch the animals in their pens and the wheat and corn she, her younger sister and father, made a meagre living from, swaying in the cold winds of the outlands.

'Again? Are you sure it's not the scarecrow? I moved him this afternoon,' replied her father.

'No, it's a man. Look,' said nineteen-year-old Marsine, motioning her hand for her father to come to the window.

'Let's have a look,' said her father, groaning as he got up from his chair by the fire and walked to the window. He brushed the curtain to one side and rubbed the condensation from the glass to get a better look outside.

'Marsine, get my crossbow and some bolts please,' he said to his older daughter. 'Gabrielle, stay in the house and close the shutters.'

At nineteen years of age, Marsine had suffered through enough winters with meagre rations to know her father's tone was deadly serious. She ran to the storeroom to pick up the crossbow along with three bolts, more than enough to scare off the man who was no doubt trying to rob their crops. With growing regularity, Marsine and her father had to point a bolt at the chest of thieves stealing their corn. Just last week, a man tried to steal a pig from their pen, but the animal's squeals gave him away. Marsine's father was able to scare him off with some choice words, a large stick and a foot up the backside for his trouble.

Marsine put the crossbow on the floor, placed her foot in the cocking stirrup and pulled the string back until the latch clicked into place and the string stayed taught. Walking towards her father, she slid a bolt into place with practised ease.

'Here you go, Father,' she said, handing him the weapon.

'Thank you, my dear. Now, I suppose I should go and have a chat with this man. No one else will fight our battles, girls. The only people who have others to fight their battles are kings, and we're not kings, are we?'

'No, Father,' said both the girls in unison.

'Wouldn't want to be one either,' said Marsine's father, opening the door. 'Awful business being king.'

Gabrielle walked to the windows and closed the shutters as Marsine grabbed the only sword in the house and stood on the landing of their modest cottage, watching her father walk into the field, crossbow raised at the man's chest.

'They usually run by now,' Gabrielle's voice waivered as she stood by the door.

'I thought Father told you to stay inside?' said Marsine, gripping the pommel of the sword nervously.

'If I were king, I'd chop off the head of anyone who tried to steal corn,' said Gabrielle matter-of-factly.

'Really?' said Marsine. 'Right off?'

'Yep,' answered Gabrielle, 'right off, And I'd throw their head into a tree for the birds to peck at.'

'Well, remind me never to steal corn from your field should you ever become king,' said Marsine, smiling.

'I wouldn't chop your head off, silly,' said Gabrielle, rolling her eyes.

Both girls heard the click and snap of the crossbow releasing a bolt and threw their heads towards the field to see their father quickly loading another.

They could hear him shouting but couldn't make out the words. The wind snatched his words away like floodwaters in summer. The man slowly and deliberately walked forwards, which was unusual as their father was an incredible shot and rarely missed his target, particularly at such a short-range.

Managing to get another bolt loaded, their father fired it off directly into the man's chest. The shot threw the man back a step, but he continued walking forwards, unperturbed at the fact he had two crossbow bolts lodged deeply in his chest cavity. It was then the girls saw the others, surrounded by a hazy fog, walking through the fields.

'Daddy!' screamed Gabrielle as her father tried fighting off the man with little effect.

The others looked towards the cottage upon hearing the young girl's scream and changed direction to follow the sound, the smoke and haze following them despite the wind that cut through the night.

'Get inside Gabrielle,' commanded Marsine. 'They've set fire to the crops, they're not here to steal.'

'But what about Father?' cried Gabrielle.

'I said get inside,' snapped Marsine gravely, grabbing her little sister by the arm and roughly shoving her inside the house. She placed a plank of wood between slats on the inside of the door and shuttered the windows as she locked them.

The outlands were a rough place to live, and homes without the appropriate security soon found their belongings stolen. The Lavers Lawmen did their best to police the hundreds of villages located in the outlands but found it difficult to protect such a vast area with such few soldiers. More often than not, people were left on their own when it came to personal protection. Thieves, ratbags and scum flowed from the pyrelands over the great tundra to rape, steal and kidnap.

'Get below,' hissed Marsine as footsteps crunched on the gravel surrounding the cottage.

Gabrielle ran to the centre of the house and pulled up a cowskin rug hiding a hatch leading to the cottage's floor space. Marsine followed her sister into the cavity, pulled the cowskin over the hatch with a secretly attached string and slowly closed the hidden door-way. They soon heard the rattling of the door handle which quickly turned into a banging and then silence.

Marsine could just make out Gabrielle's face in the dark and musty crawlspace. It smelled of dust and cobwebs and both girls took shallow breaths, mostly out of fear, but also so they didn't breathe in the chalky, stale air too deeply. Bringing a finger to her lips, Marsine moved a little closer to her younger sister, who was covering her mouth and squeezing her eyes closed.

An ear-splitting crash exploded through the house as the front door splintered from a powerful kick.

'Little ones,' they heard a sing-song voice say, 'don't be afraid. We bring redemption. It comes for everyone.'

They heard several pairs of footsteps walking through rooms, turning over tables and moving furniture around. Small tendrils of dark fog wafted between the floorboards, hovering just above their heads. They lay as still as possible, but the fog grew thicker and drifted slowly towards them.

When one of the tendrils touched Marsine's shoulder, she shuddered as black despair consumed her reality. She wanted nothing more than to lay in the dirt and give up entirely. She didn't want to exist anymore. She embodied waste, futility and despair. She had never known a menace like this before, and it struck her like a blow to the face. She nearly let out a lamenting moan of anguish, but just as quickly as the effect took hold, it left her.

'They must have escaped,' they heard a voice say. 'Burn it down and check the fields.'

Marsine and Gabrielle could hear the intruders tossing shattered furniture and anything else that would burn into the fireplace. Above them, everything they owned met red-hot embers from the hearth that usually brought peace and warmth.

'What are we going to do?' coughed Gabrielle, wiping away her tears and holding a sleeve to her face. They'd had issues with thieves before, but nothing like this. No one had ever invaded their home. Their father had taken plenty of security precautions, like the trap door they used to escape, but their innocence led them to believe there would never come a day where they would need to use them.

Marsine shook off the despair and hopelessness the fog had injected, realising they needed to act quickly before the entire house went up in flames above them.

'Follow me,' motioned Marsine as she crawled to a small doorway that opened at the back of the house. Both girls tried not to cough or gasp as the smoke and heat intensified.

Spilling out of the hidden door, Marsine realised she was still holding her father's sword. As much as she didn't know how to use it properly, it was a small comfort knowing she at least had something to protect herself and her sister with.

Both girls ran into the fields surrounding the cottage, avoiding the men they could see scouring the property for them. They took cover in an irrigation ditch and ran, doubled over, to the forest's cover close to their lands.

'Whatever you do, don't scream,' whispered Marsine, taking her sister's hand as she led her into the darkness of the woods. They could hear shouts in the fields as the night sky turned orange from the flames that burned away their home, their livelihood and their future.

Finding a thicket of blackberry bushes to hide in, the girls collapsed, chests heaving. 'We can't leave Father,' whispered Gabrielle, wiping away her smoky, fearful tears.

'We can't look for him now, or they will find us and who knows what they're capable of?'

'But we can't leave Father behind,' said Gabrielle, almost sobbing now and raising her voice.

'Listen,' said Marsine harshly, 'we need to keep quiet; do you hear me? If we don't, we're as good as dead, and then we won't be able to help Father at all. You need to be strong. You can be strong for me, can't you?'

Gabrielle bobbed her head, trying to change her sharp intakes into calmer, slower breaths. After some hugs and whispered words from her big sister, she'd managed to calm herself.

————

The girls spent a cold and sleepless night in the bushes, listening fearfully to every rustle and snap in the forest and fields. A few hours before sunrise when the fires had burnt themselves out, leaving the smouldering remains of their entire world in the dirt, the girls finally managed to doze fitfully, embracing each other for warmth and comfort.

Woken by a deer crashing through the woods just after sunrise, Marsine chanced a peek from the cover of the blackberry bush.

'Cmon,' she said, scrambling from under the bush, standing stiffly in the cool of the morning, 'we need to find Father. But we have to be careful.'

Both girls were filthy, covered in ash and dirt with dark bags under their eyes and twigs in their hair. They walked into the empty fields, timid as newborn deer.

'There's nothing left,' whispered Gabrielle.

'Keep your eyes open for Father,' replied Marsine, walking cautiously to the remnants of their cottage. Ash and smoke still lingered above the remains of their home. All that was left was broken pottery, melted cutlery, soot and sadness.

Everything was gone. Their clothing. The patchwork Gabrielle loved to work on in the evenings by the fire. Their beds. Their clothes. Their entire life as they knew it was all taken by the flames.

'FATHER!' cried out Gabrielle, stopping in the field where they last saw him and looking at the ground.

'I've found some marks,' she called to her older sister.

Marsine stopped poking through the ashy remains of their home to stand by her sister, looking at the drag marks that led to the outskirts of their property. The girls followed the tracks for a distance until they disapeared at the edge of the field.

They looked for other signs, horse hooves, cart tracks, anything that gave them a clue to where their father might be, but it was futile. It was almost as if everyone in the field had simply disappeared.

'This is hopeless, we're never going to find him if we can't see any tracks,' Marsine said after hours of searching. 'Perhaps we should see old Bailey next door and see if he saw those people last night. Maybe he saw them taking Father somewhere. 'It's a long walk,' said Marsine, shielding her eyes from the afternoon suns. 'We'd better make a start.

The two girls trudged miles through burnt fields, kicking up dust and cinders as they walked. Late in the afternoon, they reached the edge of their property line, tired, thirsty and covered head to toe in grime and ash.

When they arrived at the small stream that bordered their father's lands, they fell to their knees, drank deeply, washed their faces and legs and rested briefly.

'They've burnt down old Bailey's place too,' Marsine pointed at the smoke rising from what used to be the cottage of their portly, elderly neighbour.

Gabrielle started to sob, her young cheeks spilling with tears. 'Why?' she cried. 'Why did they have to attack us and take Father? We didn't do anything to them. It's just not fair,' she wailed.

'Shhh,' Marsine pulled her sister's head into her chest and embraced her. 'It's going to be OK. We have each other.'

'Yes,' blubbered Gabrielle, 'but Daddy's gone and old Bailey too.'

'I know,' said Marsine, rubbing her sister's back to comfort her, 'this changes everything. We have nothing to eat, no shelter, and all the fields around us are burnt. We can't stay here.'

'But what about Father?' asked Gabrielle. 'We can't just give up trying to find him.'

'What other choice do we have? There are no tracks. We have no idea where he's gone or if he's still alive. Our home, our fields and all the animals are gone. There's nothing here for us, sister.' Marsine thought for a moment before saying, 'I think we should make for Wathermaske Village and decide what to do from there. Hopefully, the tavern owners remember Father and might be able to help us.'

'If there's a tavern left,' sniffed Gabrielle.

———

A few hours after trudging their way through fields and woods, they stumbled upon old Bailey's horse which had managed to escape and was grazing happily under a large oak tree. Luckily, old Bailey was a lazy man and hadn't taken the halter off his horse before he put her in the shelter for the night. The girls slowly approached the horse, taking her halter in exchange for a handful of grass.

'There's a good girl, have some grass,' cooed Gabrielle as she stood on tiptoe to rub the horse behind the ears.

'What should we name her?' she asked her older sister.

'Why don't you think of a name?' suggested Marsine, hoping it would distract her sister from their woesome situation. 'We should lead her for a while before we try to ride her. She will need to get used to us.'

'She's very friendly,' said Gabrielle, smiling.

'Yes, it looks like she's used to people,' answered Marsine, patting the grey mare as they walked.

'People!' cried Gabrielle, 'that's what we'll call her. People!'

'A horse named People? Don't you think that's a funny name for a horse?' asked her big sister.

'I think it's a beautiful name, and so does People. Don't you, People?' said Gabrielle, stroking the mare's nose with affection.

Marsine knew better than to argue and what did it matter, anyway? It was likely they would sell it at the first opportunity, so she let her sister call the horse her pet name.

Tired, hungry and dirty, the girls found an abandoned cottage just as the twin suns sank behind the mountains to the west.

'Stay here with People and let me look around,' said Marsine, cautiously scanning her eyes across the landscape for anything unusual. Holding her father's sword in both hands, she walked slowly towards the cottage. After a few minutes of looking around, she poked her head out of the doorway and called out to her sister, 'It's safe. Come in. You'll not believe what I've found.'

Marsine welcomed her sister into the cottage where almost all the furniture and belongings were still intact but for a fine layer of dust.

'There's a flintstone near the fire and I heard chickens out the back,' said Marsine excitedly. 'You know what that means?' she said, smiling.

'Eggs!' said Gabrielle, wide-eyed in happiness and hunger.

'That, or roast chicken,' said Marsine, licking her lips at the thought of a proper meal. 'You collect some firewood, and I'll see if there are any eggs. And if there isn't... well, sorry Mrs Hen.'

Luckily for the hens, one was sitting on a clutch of eggs which the girls gratefully collected. After washing one of the dusty pans in a nearby stream, they soon had a fire crackling away and eggs boiling for their dinner.

'I noticed some chamomile plants near the front of the cottage,' said Marsine, getting a kettle from the kitchen.

'Let's make some tea and stay here the night.'

'I like that idea,' said Gabrielle, 'I've had enough of walking for today. Perhaps tomorrow we could try riding People.'

Marsine snorted, 'That sounds ever so funny. Riding People!' she said, chuckling.

After eating their fill of eggs, both girls made their way through the fading twilight to the small stream happily bubbling through the land a few hundred feet from the cottage. They washed and filled the kettle for their tea and were making their way back to the cabin when Gabrielle stopped. 'Look at those pretty purple flowers. We should pick some,' she said.

'Stop!' cried Marsine, grabbing her younger sister by the back of her clothes to stop her running off. 'Gabrielle, that's wolfsbane. That stuff can knock out a grown man, even kill him.'

'Oh,' said Gabrielle, 'why would someone grow it near their house?' she asked.

'I'm not sure,' answered Marsine. 'It's likely a bird dropped seeds here. Whoever owned this cottage has been gone for a time. You go ahead Gabrielle. I'll be along in a minute. Put the kettle near the fire to start the water boiling.'

Marsine contemplated the wolfsbane in front of her. It was innocent in its beauty but deadly in its existence. With everything taken from her and only a sword she didn't know how to use, Marsine came to the conclusion her world had changed entirely. She would likely need to use every trick, weapon or deception she could conjure to protect herself and her sister. She knew from her extensive knowledge about herbs and plants, powdered wolfsbane can quickly knock out a grown man, even send him into an eternal slumber.

Having another form of protection might just come in handy for whatever she and her sister were going to face, so she carefully dug out the plant with the tip of her sword and carried it to the cottage. After her tea, Marsine picked another dirty pan from the kitchen, cleaned it and carefully placed it on the low coals to dry the wolfsbane.

After watching the fire for over an hour, she carefully used a well-worn mortar and pestle to grind the dried root into a powder to the great interest of her little sister.

'Don't get too close,' said Marsine, through a piece of cloth covering her face.

'Will we have to use that?' asked Gabrielle.

'I'm not going to lie to you,' began Marsine, 'but I'm not sure where we're going to end up or who we might meet along the way. There are evil people in the world Gabrielle. There are kind people too, but sometimes those evil people act with kindness. We only have Father's sword to protect ourselves with, and I'm not even very good at using it. This,' she said, pointing at the dried wolfsbane, 'is another weapon we can use. We have to rely on ourselves Gabrielle because no one else is going to fight our battles for us, are they?'

'The only people who have others fight their battles are kings, and we're not kings,' said Gabrielle, repeating her father's words.

'No,' said Marsine, 'we're not. Awful business being king.'

———

The girls spent a comfortable night in the cottage with full bellies and a warm fire to help them sleep. With nobody around to help them fix the broken roof, no crops in the fields and only a few skinny chickens for food, they knew they could not stay. The next morning they headed in the direction of the closest village with their horse, People, in tow. They met a handful of strangers along the way and heard news of other raids around the area. They found kindness in some who offered food and tea, and even got some warmer clothes from an older woman whose daughters had moved away a few years before, but she couldn't quite bring herself to get rid of their old clothes until now.

'Thank you,' said Marsine to the lady after being handed the clothes, 'you're too kind.'

'Think nothing of it, dear,' she said.

'Won't you come with us?' asked Marsine. 'You must get lonely living here by yourself, and it's getting more and more dangerous.'

'I've seen over seventy winters dear. I'm too old to go wandering. No, I'm happy here,' the old woman replied.

'You could ride on People,' said Gabrielle, pointing to the horse.

'Ha!' laughed the older woman, 'Me? On that thing? No, thank you very much. I'd rather face the menace from the west than get on that animal.'

'Why do you think those awful people from across the tundra are taking people and burning everything?' asked Gabrielle of the old woman.

The old woman thought for a moment before answering. 'I've heard the pyrelands are hard lands in which to live. All fire and mud. They've an evil kahn on their throne, and when the head of the snake is corrupt, the body has no choice but to follow. Who knows why they're taking people and burning everything? Perhaps his followers are all mad too?'

'We really must be going,' interrupted Marsine. 'We still have a long way to go before we get to the Wathermaske. Thank you for the clothes.'

'Safe travels, young ladies,' said the older lady as they made their way down the road.

'She was strange,' said Gabrielle after several minutes walking.

'Yes, she was a little strange, but she was also nice. I told you there are nice people in this world. She was one of them.'

'Do you think the king across the tundra is mad?'

'I don't know,' answered Marsine. 'Perhaps. It's so far away, and all we hear are stories.'

'Do you think Father is OK?' asked Gabrielle with round eyes.

'I'm sure he's fine,' she lied.

'We're never going to see him again, are we?' said Gabrielle, more statement than question.

'We need to prepare ourselves for that possibility,' replied Marsine, kicking a stone down the path and watching it disapear into the grass.

'We have to fight our own battles, don't we?' asked Gabrielle, looking up at her older sister.

'The only people who have others fight their battles are kings, and we're not kings,' said both the girls in unison.

———

It was late afternoon by the time the girls made their way into the main street of the small village of Wathermaske. Their tired bodies cast long shadows down the road. They trudged towards the tavern in the town's centre and gave People to the stable boy sitting on the front steps. Marsine took Gabrielle's hand and walked into the dark, smoky common room where a handful of patrons sat at tables drinking ale and murmuring. Walking to the bar, the two girls approached a man and woman cleaning plates and tankards. Marsine tried to straighten her wrinkled clothes to no effect.

'Hello, my name is Marsine Arnault, and this is my sister, Gabrielle,' said Marsine, introducing herself.

'Arnault,' mused the woman behind the bar, looking them up and down. 'You're Thomas Arnault's girls?'

'Yes,' said Marsine in surprise, 'You knew our Father?'

'Of course,' said the woman, putting a tankard down on the bar, 'and your mother too, before she passed. Dentri and I,' she said, pointing to the wiry man wiping plates and putting them into a cupboard, 'used to live on a farm not far from where your father settled. What do you mean *knew* your father? I saw him only two summers ago. Has something happened to him, lovey?'

Marsine found herself overcome by the past few days of horror. She'd kept herself together for the sake of her little sister, but now the enormity of their ordeal hit her like a blow to the face. She let out a sob and sank into a stool, laying her head upon the bar, crying out, 'He's gone. He was taken, and I don't know what to do.'

'Oh, lovey,' said the portly woman, walking around the bar to

Marsine and pulling the sobbing young woman's head to her considerable bosom. 'What do you mean he's gone?'

'Some men came in the night and burnt our house and fields then took Father. They tried to take us too, but we managed to run away. We went back to look for him, but there was no trace of him. No tracks, no signs, just nothing. We've no money, haven't eaten properly for days and I don't know what we're going to do,' wept Marsine.

Gabrielle walked to her older sister and took her hand to comfort her. Somehow she knew it was her turn to be strong at this moment. The woman gave Dentri a look, and he grabbed two bowls, filled them with broth, broke a loaf of bread in half and placed it on the table.

'Come and sit down, lovey,' said the woman, 'and you can tell me more about these men you saw. Before we do that, I think we need some introductions. This is Dentri,' said the woman, motioning to the man who simply smiled and nodded.

'He doesn't say much on account of him having no tongue. I'm Scarlet, but everyone calls me Scraps. I've met you before Marsine, but you probably don't remember as you were only a baby. And what was your name again, lovey?' Scraps asked looking at the younger of the two sisters.

'Gabrielle,' answered Gabrielle, 'and our horse is called People. We found him on old Bailey's property,' she continued through a mouthful of bread.

'I take it the same men who took your father also got old Bailey since you've got his horse?'

'Yes,' answered Marsine. 'After those men took Father, we walked to old Bailey's place. But he was gone too.'

'These people,' asked Scraps, 'did they have anything on the back of their necks?'

'I don't know. We didn't see them up close from where we hid,' answered Marsine.

'Did they happen to have fog, or smoke they used on you?' Scraps asked.

'I think so,' said Marsine, 'it was so hard to tell because they set our fields on fire, but when we were hiding under the house, a dark fog touched me. It was horrible.'

'And this fog, did it made you feel like you didn't want to live anymore? That all colour had drained from the world. That not existing was better than living?' Asked Scraps in a low voice.

'Yes,' whispered Marsine with a tear rolling down her cheek at the memory, 'how did you know?'

'Because I've felt that fog before,' said Scraps with a shudder, 'and so has Dentri. That's why we moved away years ago. This is not the first time this has happened. Farms being burnt, people being taken. One night about twenty years ago, we watched our neighbour's farm burn to the ground as men from the pyrelands herded them into wagons and took them away. They came to our house, but luckily we'd already hidden our children in a wood nearby. When they saw the children's clothes and toys, they demanded we tell them where they were, but we wouldn't, not even when they took Dentri's tongue. Their enchanter took out a device that made a finger of smoke like a worm floating in the air, and when it touched me, I wanted to give up completely and just give them everything. Luckily, some Lavers Lawmen were nearby, and they burst through the door just in time and cut them to pieces.' Scraps looked off into the distance, recalling the unpleasant memory. 'Is that what you saw, Marsine, a man with a device and a finger of black fog?'

'No,' replied Marsine, 'there were five men, and they had a cloud of fog around them. When they broke down our door, it was like the whole house was covered in fog. I could see it seeping through the floorboards.'

'A cloud, you say. By gods, they've gotten better at it since they last came at us with this bewitchment. They've learned to control it more over the years by the sounds of it.'

'But what is it... this fog?' asked Marsine.

'Some call it the Menace, others call it The Black or The Grey. From what I've heard, its something the soulsnitchers use to make people give up all hope so they can lock them up and take them back to the mines and work camps in the Pyrelands.'

'Do you think that's where Father has been taken? Back to the Pyrelands?' asked Gabrielle who had finished her meal and was listening intently.

'I'm sorry, lovey, but I think so. That's likely where he's been taken. I know you don't want to hear that, but you deserve to know the truth,' said Scraps.

Gabrielle dropped her shoulders and folded her arms. 'At least he might still be alive,' she whispered.

'So, what do you plan to do?' asked Scraps as Dentri cleared the bowls.

'I don't know. I thought we could go to Thade. Father spoke of a distant cousin there. I thought perhaps we could find them. I'm a quick learner and am sure I could get a job to help provide for the both of us,' said Marsine hopefully.

'No, no, no, that won't do at all,' said Scraps, getting up. 'You can't go off to a city like Thade with a half-baked plan in the hope some distant cousin will take you in. I have a proposition for you both. You may stay here tonight with a hot meal and a bath. In exchange, you will take some items to Thade for me. I have a brother there who owns a tavern. I have some items I need to get to him. I will also write you a letter of recommendation for a job as a barmaid. Do you know how to serve food and drink?'

'I've done it for our family so I can't imagine it's much different,' replied Marsine.

'Excellent,' said Scraps, 'Dentri will show you to your room and run you both a bath.'

'Thank you ever so much,' replied Marsine, feeling more grateful than she could articulate.

———

After a remarkably relaxing bath, both girls brushed each other's hair to the low rumble of voices growing louder as the tavern filled with evening clientele. The occasional raucous laugh and loud whooping from happy customers filled the air. The alluring smell of cooking, beer and people floated through the floorboards, reminding both girls they were still hungry, even after Scrap's and Dentri's kindness of bread and broth earlier that afternoon.

'It's a long way to Thade, isn't it?' asked Gabrielle.

'Yes, twenty days travel at least,' replied Marsine, stroking her sister's auburn hair to a bright sheen.

'How are we going to get there if we've not got any money?' asked her younger sister.

'I've been thinking about that,' replied Marsine, brushing the hair on the other side of her head. 'We're going to have to stop and work in villages and towns along the way... or... nevermind,' she said, looking away from her sister.

'Or what?' asked Gabrielle, turning to face her sister so she could look her in the face.

'I said nevermind,' replied Marsine, standing up.

'You can't treat me like a child forever, you know,' said Gabrielle angrily. 'It's not fair you get to make all the decisions about where we go, what we do and how we go about it,' she said flaring up.

'You're right,' said Marsine, sitting down beside her little sister, 'I sometimes forget you've been through just as much as I have. Losing Mother, then Father and now this,' she continued as she motioned around the room. 'Gabrielle, we may have to do some things on the way to Thade... unpleasant things.'

'What kind of unpleasant things?' asked Gabrielle, looking a little worried.

'I'd rather not say,' she said quietly.

'You promised!' cried Gabrielle.

'I did, didn't I. OK,' replied Marsine, deciding at that moment that if her little sister wanted to be treated more like an adult, it was time she learnt a harsh lesson about surviving in the world with no money, no family and a horse and sword as your only bargaining tools.

'We don't have anything to sell, other than Father's sword, and the horse.'

Gabrielle took a sharp intake of breath, 'We can't sell People,' she cried.

'Don't worry, we're not going to sell People, and I don't want to sell Father's sword either. It's the only thing we have left to remind us of him. I have another idea.'

The two girls put their heads together as Marsine laid out her plan.

9

SULFUR, SALT, SOOT AND SUFFERING

Nuri looked out the window at the black, choking smoke pluming from the belly of the far-off mountain. It looked like an angry swarm of thunderheads with lightning and death at its core. The hot, suffocating film killed everything it landed on, but given time, and rain, the volcanic dust moved into the valleys and plains close to her city, helping bring life and greenery to the surrounding lands, but only just. The city of Sember sat in the centre of a vast black and red plain resembling a scab picked too often. Black sands extended for miles around the city, pockets of gas and flames escaping the ground with regularity as fierce lava flows cut through the countryside, as if the gods had scraped their fingers through the very earth. This was home, her home. The only lands she'd ever known. Even though the harsh combination of geothermal activity, volcanic mountains and little rain made life in the Pyrelands demanding, she loved the perilous beauty of the kingdom of her childhood. Nuri was slender with cropped brown hair giving her a boyish, androgynous look. Her sharp features and black eyes often pierced into the very soul of any farmer, merchant or slave master that tried to fumble the numbers when it came to the delivery or price of goods, services, weapons and slaves to the Pyrelands.

She knew only the strong survived in the challenging conditions this land of mud, heat and fire provided. Looking over the small villages that dotted the lands, connected by raised walkways through swamplands and bubbling mud pits reeking of sulphur, she was thankful she'd never had to feel the cold of the kindoms to the east that her fellow Pyrelanders experienced when they struck out across the mighty tundra to raid for food, people and animals.

She had always been good with numbers, and her ability to estimate projected yields with great accuracy and gauge the success of raids and attacks based on the number of people, weather and the time of year, meant she was in the pyrekhan's group of trusted advisors. An enviable but precarious position.

'The slave bazzars are busy today,' Nuri commented to her Khan, looking over the extensive markets surrounding the city, their tents and banners the only thing adding colour to the bleak landscape.

'Trading in the human misery that runs this kingdom is an essential undertaking,' he replied absentmindedly picking at a healing scab on his arm.

The pyrekhan was tall in stature and sinewy in build, with a long face and high cheekbones framed by messy, black hair. He ruled with an iron fist and suffered no weakness or fragility from his subjects. His olive skin was covered in scars and cuts, for as tradition stated every time a pyrekhan ordered the death of a slave, peasant, advisor or spy, he was required to slice living flesh to enable evil spirits to escape the body of the one who muttered the order. He'd ordered the deaths of too many advisors of late. True loyalty was hard to come by and he had the scars to show.

Turning to a table adorned with food Nuri said, 'You need to eat, Khan, at least a little meat,' trying to convince her leader to eat.

'Food isn't something I require at the moment Nuri, don't you see? The gods have blessed me. They have placed a great burden on my people, but I realise now it's been a challenge all along. A challenge we have accepted with humility, and now, we are being rewarded. Nuri, this changes everything. This new weapon gives us an edge over our enemy. An edge that will enable us to take their lands and prosper as we've never known. How can anyone eat when possibilities like this present themselves?'

The pyrekhan was like ice and fire. There was no in-between with him. He was either gracious and playful, smart as a snake and quickly slid into the role of a leader that knew the truth of his words was without equal. Or he was joyless, cold and uncaring for both himself, his people and those closest around him.

She had become accustomed to the pyrekhan's temperament and quickly became an expert at recognising when he was in the mindset of a god or a devil. Today he played the role of a god.

'What you say is true, but no battle was ever won on an empty stomach. Here, eat,' she ordered, handing the khan a piece of roughly hewn meat from a haunch that lay near the fireplace.

The khan sat staring at a point on the wall, absently chewing his food, deep in thought. 'You know Nuri, with this weapon, I will take Thade,' he said. 'I have the numbers, the cunning and now a way through the walls. It's only a matter of time before I have both kingdoms within my grasp. For too long our pig iron and copper weapons didn't stand a chance against those in the east but now, we will take their lands, their mines and truly expand our kingdom and prosper.'

'With control of their farmlands, the city of Thade and its access to trade ships on The Brine, your rule will truly be endless,' said Nuri, cutting herself a slice of meat from the haunch on the table.

'First, we need to prepare. Nuri, bring me my crown.'

Nuri placed the crown of iron and bone on the pyrekhan's head, then buckled a cloak of dark fur around his neck. Today was a critical day for the khan as all of his warlords, captains, commanders and slave masters were gathered in his castle, and the mood was electric.

'Six generations this crown has been in my family and none have bested the Firmalands in battle,' said the Kahn, standing and straightening his cloak. 'They may have a larger army and better weaponry, but I have my spellcasters and now, this new weapon.'

Whispers of an advanced weapon, some new and exciting breakthrough had filtered through the villages and towns. There was talk of something that could rip through iron and rock like a hot knife through honeycomb.

Nuri had been helping the khan prepare for this meeting for several days now, he had not allowed anyone but her into his quarters. She was the only one he would allow near him when he spiralled into a fog of misery and hopelessness. Her aloof nature seemed to calm and soothe him no matter the depth of his sorrow. Her systematic, logical approach to any problem was both a cooling remedy to the passion of his fire and a candle of promise in the darkness of his misery.

Born in a village a few hundred miles from the city, she quickly proved herself expert in organising the family's finances. Her ability to solve and formulate complex calculations in her head meant she was soon the number keeper for the entire village, filling books and scrolls with transactions between merchants for debts owed and monies paid.

It was inevitable she would garner the attention of the pyrekhan and found herself working in his trusted circle by the age of fifteen. Those who did not perform felt the wrath of the khan and soon found themselves thrown into the devil's maw, a burning pit of fire and magma that had been bubbling for a thousand years.

Nuri had seen many meet their grisly end by the maw during her seven years advising the pyrekhan. She was acutely aware it was her deliberate and careful planning that kept her alive. She knew this meeting was of utmost importance to the khan and garnering support for expanding his kingdom, so she was fastidious in ensuring he was presented as a ruler should.

Tall and slender, he exuded a masculine charm that wasn't about brute strength or wealth. His was the confidence of a man who knew his life's work and wouldn't allow deviation from success, no matter the cost. There was danger in his dignity and audacity in his intentions which made those around him fear and respect him in equal measures.

Walking from his private quarters, Nuri and the khan ran through several last-minute preparations as they turned into the hallways towards the city's main keep. Nuri stood before two large doors, behind which she knew sat twenty of the khan's most trusted advisors. Opening them for her leader, the pyrekhan strode through the doors and all in the room rose respectfully, bowing their heads in supplication as he entered.

'My children!' the khan called, his arms gliding outwards in a sweeping motion as he entered the room. He stepped deftly to the head of the table and stood next to his black throne cast from obsidian with the addition of selenium oxide, which created rivulets of red running through the structure. Sculpted flames shot out from the mouths of creatures carved into the structure which in the firelight, gave them the appearance they were alive and made of brimstone.

'I'm so glad you've chosen to join me for today's little... performance. Trust me when I say, what I've got in store for you will not disappoint,' the pyrekhan said as he swept his cloak dramatically and sat on the thousand-year-old throne.

Nuri smiled to herself. This was one of the things she admired about the khan; his showmanship. Even if it did slide into the macabre from time to time. She never felt comfortable talking in front of groups of people. She was much happier to work in the shadows with numbers and lists. Digits and numerals were either right or wrong, unlike people who were messy, unpredictable and would smile and whisper sweet words as they slid a blade between your ribs.

'As you all know, I've been working closely with our alchemists and spellcasters to bring us a new type of weapon. It can reduce even the largest army to piles of meat and misery.'

'You've been talking about this for months,' said Wilsden, a trusted advisor who stood at six feet and wore a suit of leather armour covered with studs, 'but when do we get to use it against our enemies?' he demanded.

'Everybody here take note,' said the khan standing, making his way around the table. 'Wilsden has asked a fundamental question. When do we get to use it against our enemies?'

'You've said this weapon can cut through metal and stone. I don't see how that is possible. I've never seen a blade that could cut through stone,' said Wilsden.

'A blade, this weapon is not,' replied the khan, patting Wilsden on the shoulder as he continued around the table. 'You've not seen a weapon like this before. In fact, it's in this room with us right now.'

Everyone sitting at the table looked around in confusion, trying to find this mystery weapon.

'Enough of this, Khan,' said one of the older advisors. 'Show us what we all came here to see.'

'What you all came here to see my children is this,' said the khan, walking towards a bowl in the middle of the table filled with black powder. He took a handful and let it flow through his fingers. 'What I hold in my hands can crumble castles and crush our enemies in the blink of an eye,' he said.

Most at the table looked on in suspicion.

Nuri smiled to herself.

'How's a powder supposed to do that?' asked Anteros.

Nuri had never liked him. He had a sweaty face and rat-like eyes which she didn't trust.

'Anteros, I'm glad you asked,' said the khan with a sudden cold smile. 'Bring in the girl,' he shouted, making several members at the table jump.

A door at the side of the room flung open, and a girl in her twenties was forcefully shoved through it, causing her to stumble and fall hard on the cold, stone tiles. It was apparent she had been beaten, probably raped as she whimpered quietly through swollen eyes and bleeding lips, trembling on the floor.

Anteros stood up immediately and shouted, 'Don't believe a word this girl says! She's a liar and a whore!'

'My dear Anteros,' replied the khan cooly, 'please, take a seat. The girl has yet to speak a word.'

Anteros sat down slowly, looking nervously at the two burly soldiers who had positioned themselves on either side of his chair.

'A shame,' said the khan, walking purposefully towards the girl and gently helping her stand. 'You have quite the lovely face behind those bruises. I apologise if my gaolers got a little carried away. It's been months since they've had such a pretty plaything in their cells.'

The girl whimpered as her tears fell to the cold slate floor. She started to mumble apologies through her mangled lips.

'Shhhhh,' said the khan gently, 'there's no need to speak. You just need to nod or shake your head when I ask you a question, understood?' The girl nodded, her bottom lip trembling as she tried to cover her breasts with her ripped and dirty top.

'You know this man Anteros, don't you?' asked the khan.

The girl nodded.

'And you've only met him recently, haven't you?'

Again, the girl nodded.

'She's lying!' roared Anteros. 'Khan, you've known me for many years, you can't trust anything that spews from this back alley slut's mouth.'

The soldiers clasped his shoulders with an iron grip to keep him in his chair.

'Anteros gave you a scroll, didn't he?' continued the khan, ignoring the shouts from Anteros. The girl nodded again, pleading forgiveness in her eyes.

'And it was written in black ink, wasn't it?' Again, the girl nodded.

'Did you see what was written on that scroll?' asked the khan.

The girl shook her head with conviction.

'Liar!' screamed the khan, as the back of his hand stung her face, splitting her lip even more.

Tears and blood mixed on the stone floor as the girl blanched and stumbled from the blow. The khan seized a fistful of hair and yanked her broken and busted face close to his and hissed, 'If you didn't see what was written on that scroll, how did you know the ink was black, hmmm?'

The girl started sobbing, and her knees buckled. The khan let her dissolve into a sobbing mess on the floor.

'Anteros, would you care to enlighten us as to what was written in that letter and to whom it was addressed?' asked the khan to the nervous-looking man on the opposite side of the table.

'I've said it once,' growled Anteros, 'and I'll repeat it again. That girl is a whore and a liar, and I've no clue about any scroll.'

'Really?' said the khan. 'Well it just so happens someone else saw the scroll before this girl of yours here managed to destroy it.'

'Then it will be their word against mine, won't it?' scowled Anteros.

'So, you're saying there was a scroll now?' asked the khan, raising his eyebrows.

Anteros sat silently, staring at the khan, not trusting himself to answer such a loaded question.

'You see Anteros, I see everything in this kingdom. You don't get to be khan without knowing what's going on with your subjects and advisors. The person who also saw your scroll was the same person who swapped it for another identical scroll the morning this girl left to hand it to the Duke of Roda Codex in the Welkinpeaks. I have your original scroll right here,' said the khan, pulling out the scroll from his tunic with the personal seal of Anteros stamped into the wax seal. Seeing the scroll in the khan's hand, Anteros jumped from his chair and tried to run, but was roughly grabbed by the two soldiers standing next to him, sealing his guilt.

'Running won't do you any good, Anteros. What's done is done,' said the khan. 'Now it's a matter of what to do with you and the girl. Before we do that, I think everyone at the table deserves to know exactly what secrets you were selling to the enemy. Please, Anteros, enlighten them if you will,' the khan continued, sweeping his hand around the table towards the rest of the advisors.

Anteros sat in unwavering silence, glaring at the khan with daggers for eyes.

'Speechless all of a sudden?' asked the khan. 'Let me read out to those here what you've written, so they know the depths of your treachery.'

The khan broke the scroll seal, unrolled it on the table and placed two weights at the top and bottom. He then recited troop movements, numbers, slave counts in the mines and salt flats, and intentions of invasion. He showed those sitting at the table drawings of the city of Sember that included guard towers, watch change times and the exact position of the room they were now meeting in.

'One can only ponder what our enemies would do with such detailed information, Anteros?' said the khan, more as a statement than a question.

Anteros looked into his lap in dejection. In a low voice, he said, 'The gods will put a blight on you and our people for a thousand years, Khan. You've done nothing but drive this kingdom to the brink of insanity. Raids just to get enough food? We don't even have enough people to work your precious mines. Don't you see, I was trying to broker peace so we can prosper and avoid a war we all know we can't win.'

'So, you were presumptuous enough to assume what was best for the kingdom without telling the table or your king?' spat one of the advisors.

'I did what was best for the kingdom,' scowled Anteros, 'and if you fools can't see that, you're more shortsighted than I thought.'

'Enough of this,' said the khan. 'I grow weary of your insults and excuses. Typically, the Devil's Maw would see its fill for such treasonous baseborn as yourself, but today I'm willing to make an exception... well, more an example than an exception. I believe death by lava is too honourable a death for those who sell secrets,' continued the khan, his voice growing cold, 'and since you like declaring our intentions to our enemies, I'm going to give you the same courtesy, Anteros. I'm declaring my intention to ensure you never open that mouth of yours again.'

A burly guard threw a rope around Anteros and his chair, pulling him back harshly as two more soldiers wrapped a rope around his legs and forearms binding him securely to the chair. All the while, Anteros yelled and kicked wildly at them.

'Stop his caterwauling,' shouted the khan. 'It insults my ears.'

A guard nodded and took a thick metal rod leaning against the wall, ramming the middle of it into Anteros' mouth like a gag. Tying it to his head with ropes, he left a foot's length of rod protruding from each side of his mouth. Anteros had no choice but reduce his howling to a spitting mumble as he was dragged back from the table.

The khan strolled to a massive war hammer hanging from brackets driven into the rock at the back of the room. He placed his hand lovingly on the head of the hammer, feeling the cold metal. Closing his eyes and releasing his breath, he traced his fingers along the handle. Hefting the ornate hammer from its brackets, the khan sauntered to Anteros, dragging its head on the stone floor, filling the room with screeching unease.

'Anteros,' he said, stopping in front of him, 'this astonishing weapon belonged to my great, great grandfather. Did you know that? He called it Serenity after a girl he once loved but could never marry. He said she broke almost as many hearts as this hammer cleaved in battle. The last time it was used was over one hundred years ago in the battle of Stvor.'

Anteros was wide-eyed and struggling in his chair.

The khan leaned in close and whispered, 'Today I'm bringing her out of retirement.'

Anteros squealed and shook in his chair as the khan brought the hammer down upon the metal rod on one side of Anteros' mouth. His jaw broke with a crack that filled the room like a lightning strike. Anteros let out a high-pitched scream as blood and teeth fell to the floor around him.

The khan walked purposely to the other side of the blubbering Anteros, lifted the hammer again and struck the opposite side of the rod. Anteros' jaw hung from his face like a snapped sapling in a howling summer storm.

'A man without a mouth is no good for telling secrets,' said the khan. He let the hammer fall to the stone and turned towards his advisors, 'I think it's time we had a demonstration of what this powder can do. Guards, take our mouthless minstrel here to the corner of the room and bring the girl.'

The guards dragged Anteros to the corner of the room as the beaten, half-naked girl was tied to the chair with him. She tried to wriggle away from the blood and teeth in his lap, but strong hands held her down as ropes enveloped her like a serpent.

The khan walked to the head of the table and picked up a barrel about the height of a man's forearm and unstoppered a cork from the bottom of it, letting black powder spill on the floor. He stooped low and walked back a trail of powder to the corner of the room, placing the barrel under the chair where Anteros and the girl were tied.

'The black powder you see in that barrel is but a fraction of the stockpile I have available. In a moment you will see its true power. I'm sure you will be convinced of its advantage as a weapon of war. If you would all please stand and join me at this side of the table.'

Everyone at the table stood and walked to join the khan on the opposite side of the table.

'Guards, if you'd be so kind as to turn this table on its side?' asked the khan. Six guards looked at each other, not sure what to do until one of them shrugged and clasped the heavy table, waiting for the others to help. Slowly they turned the thick wooden table on its side with a thud, as dust billowed into the air, sparkling in the sunlight streaming from the windows.

'What you're about to see is like nothing you've witnessed before,' said the khan as he walked to the large fireplace, taking one of the torches from a bracket above the flames. 'You may wish to get behind the table in a moment,' he said, as he threw the torch into the trail of black powder.

Flames from the torch sputtered and spat until they took hold and burned their way towards the two unfortunates in the corner. The girl's eyes grew wide as she saw the flame move slowly towards her, spitting and dancing like a fire sprite. When the flame burned to within a few hands widths from the barrel, the khan instructed, 'Everybody get down and cover your ears.'

The barrel exploded with enough force to push the heavy wooden table into the advisors crouched behind it as stone, gore and splintered wood fell around them. When everyone stood, and the smoke finally cleared, sunlight flowed through a considerable-sized hole in the wall.

There was no sign of the two prisoners other than a mangled, bloody hand where the chair had been just seconds before.

10

HUNTING THE BINDER

Deadsun woke on his pallet and stretched the last lingerings of sleep from his body. It had been a strange few days, full of masked grief for his brother and the discovery of sinister happenings throughout his city. His men had been arresting many people with welltaker devices attached to their necks. Most of the Lavers Lawmen were now familiar with the devices, and all were aware of how they affected those who wore them. They, after all, were the ones who had to arrest and bring in these people for questioning.

The city's prisons were quickly filling. The king and his advisors were attempting to engineer a plan to deal with the influx of well-takers into the city. Law clearly stated that should someone take the life of another, execution would be their punishment. Still, many in the king's court argued those who had this device forced upon them weren't in control of their actions; therefore, shouldn't be held accountable.

There were cases of honest, good-natured citizens with no previous history of trouble, turning to murder and mayhem. One such case involved a bootmaker with several children, who, from all accounts, seemed a decent and kind man to all that knew him. He disappeared, only to turn up several days later on the other side of the city, arrested for killing a prostitute and breaking the arms of two bystanders who tried to stop his grisly, daylight murder.

'How could such a man do something like this, if not for his mind having been altered by these devices?' one of the courtiers argued.

It was a difficult point to counter, but the fact remained that people were getting hurt, and it was up to the Lavers Lawmen to stop them. They were to kill them if necessary, but capture, detention and questioning were preferable.

Deadsun had questioned twenty-three people with welltaker devices attached to their napes over the past few days, and they had all muttered the same thing: *'Darkness brings redemption.'* Several times he thought he saw a spark of humanity in their eyes, but it quickly vanished like smoke on the wind, and they returned to their soulless existence.

Dressing and preparing for the day, Deadsun weaved his way through the chilly morning streets to the city's keep and took the stairs two at a time. He was on his way to discuss the disruption in the city in greater detail with the king and his advisors. Everyone expected a lengthy assembly with multiple ideas, arguments and counter-arguments tabled for consideration.

Arriving early, he sat at the king's table, quietly discussing the device's role in the current troubles throughout the kingdom with the other advisors and several of his captains as they waited for the king. The low murmur of conversation ceased when the king and Bailur walked into the room, taking their seats at the head of the table.

'You've all been gathered here,' said the king in his deep timbre, 'to talk about these devices, these... welltakers. Some of you may be familiar with them; others are seeing them for the first time. Bailur, if you would be so kind as to implore to everyone the danger they pose to our kingdom?'

The king was known to be direct and get straight to the point.

That's one thing Deadsun loved about his leader. He didn't use flowery language or pontificate on points. He got to the heart of the matter and approached it face on, like a soldier.

Bailur stood to address the table. 'The device you each have before you is called a welltaker. Some of you may have seen a similar device used by the Acolytes of Stardark. Whilst they use these devices to expand and focus their minds, it seems this particular design has a different purpose. As far as we know, they're being made in the depths of the pyrelands and the khan is using them to control those he captures. They are being used to cause violent insanity to those he's binding. More than one hundred and fifty attacks in the past week can be directly attributed to these devices. So far we've lost dozens of people, and the citizens of the kingdom are starting to worry and talk.'

'What do you mean, talk?' asked Dobrim, an older courtier with grey in his whiskers, a patch of baldness on the back of his head and a large scar that ran from his left eye to the bottom of his jaw.

'The type of talk one would expect in taverns and docks, Dobrim,' answered Bailur. 'Laymen attribute the recent unrest to pyrespirits, despondent gods or celestial circumstance. Those of us sitting at this table know better. For the sake of harmony in the city, it should be kept that way. If the citizens wish to quibble and champion their theories about what's going on, we should not be stopping them. The less they know for sure, the better. Until we understand the pyrekhan's intentions with these devices, the appropriate strategy moving forward would be to keep people guessing, for now.'

'Why are we allowing them into the city in the first place?' asked Dobrim, packing tobacco into his pipe, shoving it into the chamber with a yellowed thumb.

'As you can appreciate, these devices are relatively small, therefore easy to smuggle into any city, town or village. We believe there is a band of trusted disciples of the khan that have made their way into Thade and Roda Codex, along with several other larger towns, and are attaching these devices to our citizens.'

'But, why?' asked one of the Laver Lawmen's younger captains. 'It just doesn't make any sense.'

'The pyrekhan can never win against the kingdom in a pitched battle, and he knows this, so we believe he's attempting to create unrest within the kingdom and exasperate our already tenuous positions due to colder weather and crop failures. He's doing this by turning our citizens against us with these devices. We've heard rumours. Those that kill and particularly those who die, under the influence of these devices, are heralded as heroes back in the pyrelands.'

'He can't fight fair, so he's fighting dirty,' rasped Dobrim through a puff of grey smoke.

'That certainly seems to be the case,' replied Bailur. 'If we're to stymie the flow of these devices, we need to find out who's smuggling them and identify the perpetrators binding them to our citizens. This, ladies and gentlemen, is where we turn to Deadsun.'

Bailur finished by giving a slight bow to Deadsun and taking a seat.

'As we know,' started Deadsun, 'these devices cause the wearer to become violent. To the point their own safety doesn't matter to them. We're likely not able to stop them coming into the city without searching every person that passes through our gates, which is impossible. But we can try to find those who are performing the binding. From what we know, you need lament – an elixir made from spurworm venom to complete the bind. This stuff is deadly, volatile and incredibly expensive. Even getting it on your skin means certain death, so it's unlikely whoever has come into the city to wreak their havoc with these devices travelled with lament in their baggage. They most likely purchased it here in the city. There are only four alchemists that sell lament within the walls of Thade, so our first port of call is to speak with those store owners and find out if any strangers have purchased the poison. With the Alchemy guilds being as incestuous as they are, we're hoping a stranger would have been noticed.'

'So what happens if we catch them?' asked Haleth, the advisor on wellbeing and medicinal requirements within the city. 'The people binding these... welltakers to our people, I mean.'

'Not if... when,' replied Deadsun. 'A long, very painful interrogation to draw as much information as possible, then death. We don't take kindly to traitors in this city, or anywhere in the kingdom for that matter.'

'Let's say we catch them. What do we hope to gain from the information they may or may not give?' asked Dobrim, puffing on his pipe.

'First, we need to establish how many of these devices are in the city. Then, we need to discover how many people are doing the binding. For all we know, it could just be one man or a whole team, but I can tell you this. If we don't find them and stamp out this scourge, they're just going to grow bolder, bind more of our citizens and wreak further havoc. The pyrekhan isn't known for his kindness towards those that don't do his bidding. An honourable execution if they're caught is far more pleasant than what lies in store for them, should they not follow orders from the khan.'

'What do you need to catch these bastards?' asked the weapons master for the keep.

'Men, peasant clothing and weapons that commoners would carry. I have a team of fifty men waiting for orders and I plan to spread them through the city in groups of five disguised as common folk to see if we can catch these curs in the act,' answered Deadsun.

'I've enough swords and daggers in the armoury for you,' replied the weapons master, 'but I'll say this. It's not often people want the plainer weapons,' he said with a chuckle.

'Mistress deHart?' said Deadsun, turning to the keep's seamstress. 'Do you think you have enough clothing to make fifty men look like commoners?'

The slim woman who wore her hair in a bun with a large knitting needle through the back of it looked up, 'No, no, no... I don't have that much,' she replied, 'but I can have my girls make you some. They won't win any accolades, but they will do the job.'

'Good. Hopefully, we won't need them for more than a couple of weeks. I plan to catch these traitors quickly.'

'Excellent,' finished Bailur, standing to indicate the meeting was wrapping up. 'Deadsun, I assume you have everything you need?'

'Yes,' he replied simply.

Bailur looked towards the king, waiting for his leave.

'This menace must not infiltrate my kingdom,' started the king. 'Our people have a hard enough time of it without this blasted pyrekhan making trouble for us. Find these traitors, Deadsun. I want them brought to justice.'

'We will find them my Lord, and when we do, they will be yours to do with what you see fit.'

'Good. Everyone is dismissed,' replied the king, the bags under his eyes giving away the burden of his concern for his city.

The assembly stood, talking amongst themselves as they exited through ornate wooden doors to their various vocations throughout the keep.

'Deadsun,' called the king. 'A word if you would?'

'Of course.'

'We need to quell this disquiet in the kingdom, and fast. These blasted devices are killing citizens and taking my people. I will not have it. Tell your captains there's a considerable reward from my personal coffers for the capture of the authors of these evil ploys.'

'Yes, my Lord. Consider it done,' replied Deadsun with a slight bow.

'I'm counting on you.'

'What was all that about?' asked Greeven as they made their way through the keep and into a busy courtyard, the morning suns barely cutting through the low, grey clouds to warm their faces.

Deadsun replied, 'The king is counting on us to find these men quickly. I shan't disappoint him. Greeven, I want you to assemble five of our best men. You and I will personally be overseeing this group. I want these traitors caught.'

'Then today we hunt brother!' cried Greeven, slapping his companion on the back. 'And this evening when their heads are atop pikes on the city walls, we shall find women and drink that are both cheap and wet to satisfy our desires.'

'And what would your mother have to say about that?' smiled Deadsun, happy to be out of the stuffy environment of courtier's meetings and king's tables.

'She'd toss me a silver and tell me to make a night of it,' laughed Greeven.

————

Deadsun and his captains assembled the fifty men needed for the welltaker operation. They gathered in groups in the keep's armoury to check weapons and clothe themselves in the garments made by Seamstress deHart.

'She's done a marvellous job given how little time she's had to put all this together,' commented Greeven, pulling a grey coloured tunic over his head and tying it with a sash of old fabric. He then strapped on a standard short sword and tucked a dagger into its sheath on the inside of his clothing to finish his ensemble. 'If people look closely, they will notice our soldier issued boots, but we've no time to get fifty pairs made so this will have to do,' he said as he held his arms out to show Deadsun and the other men his completed ensemble.

'You look right at home in the clothes of a commoner, almost like it made you happy,' laughed one of the captains, causing the men to chuckle.

'Careful, Alreed,' said Greeven, 'or I might just tap on the door of your sister in these clothes and give her something to be happy about.' A raucous peal erupted at his ribald retort.

'Ha!' tittered Alreed, 'with five sprogs at her ankles you'd be folding, washing and sweeping floors before you see her sheets.' Another howl erupted from the men.

'Five, you say,' answered Greeven. 'Well at least we know she likes to-'

'Enough of this now,' interrupted Deadsun, his commanding voice cut through the air like a blacksmith's hammer. 'There will be plenty of time for banter, after we catch these traitors.'

The men quickly returned to strapping on swords, choosing quarterstaffs, daggers and other standard arms from the array of weapons in the room.

When they were ready, Deadsun stood on a stool in front of the group. 'This is not an easy task that I ask of you,' he began, 'but we are men of the Lavers Law, who are ready to do the king's bidding. We will not back down. We will not fail. You have all been briefed and we know what we're looking for, so let's get out there and find these bastards.'

A collective cheer went up from the men in the room. Deadsun didn't like long speeches, and the Lavers Lawmen appreciated his direct words. A pre-prepared, stuffy address did nothing but eat into the time they could be using to track down those who wished the kingdom harm.

———

Deadsun, Greeven and five other soldiers dressed as commoners walked the streets for an hour, winding their way to the city's eastern quarter. Three of the city's four alchemist stores resided here and the group intended to approach these venues first. They wore hoods low over their faces, reducing the chance of being recognised whilst the men asked questions of the people they met and the stores they visited.

'Let's hope these alchemists can give us something to work with,' said Deadsun as they stood outside the first store.

Above the doorway, an ornate sign swung from wrought iron

brackets decorated with vines and flower carvings with the name 'Nominative Potio' painted white against the wood.

'Their guild isn't known for sharing secrets,' reminded Greeven as they walked up the stairs.

'Let's hope the owner is in a talkative mood today,' said Deadsun, pushing open the alchemist's door. It took a moment for their eyes to adjust to the dark, dusty interior of the store. Large windows covered with hangings, fabrics, maps and other paraphernalia of the dark arts dampened what little light filtered through. Looking around the dusty shelves, jars of herbs and collections of curiosities, Deadsun understood all too well the potential for evil contained within the shelves, should some conjurer or sorcerer decide to mix ingredients in just the right way.

He was reminded why he hated places such as this. He much preferred an enemy he could fight with sword and fist, in plain sight. The dark whispers and magic potions of mages and magicians seemed elusive and corrupt to his soldiers' morality.

The store owner stood behind a wooden counter, grinding ingredients in a mortar and pestle, his grey hair flowing over his shoulders. His dark robe stopped swaying as he paused to look up from his work. 'Good morning gentlemen, looking for something in particular?' he asked through his wispy grey beard.

Deadsun put a small silver coin on the counter. 'We're here to purchase information,' he stated simply.

The store owner continued his grinding. 'Well, that all depends on the type of information you're after, and if I wish to sell it, doesn't it?'

'We want to know if anyone has purchased lament from you recently,' stated Greeven.

'That's a very specialised product gentlemen,' said the store owner, still circling his hand around the mortar. 'Very rare. Expensive. What would the likes of you two want with someone who bought lament then?'

'Come on, let's go. He's wasting our time,' said Greeven, moving to grab the silver coin. Deadsun gently put his hand over Greeven's and looked at the old man.

'If we're the ones paying, it's us who will be asking the questions.'

'Right you are,' said the store owner, stopping his grinding and picking up the coin, biting it to ensure its quality. Once he was happy it was real silver, he deftly slid it into his pocket with practised hands and looked at them both with sunken, ice-blue eyes.

'A man, about two weeks ago, came into the store. Short. Rat-like little fellow with black hair and an impolite demeanour asking for lament. When I asked him what he was going to use it for he gave me some hogwash about his sister studying alchemy and herbal lore in the north that he often surprised with unusual items. I've dealt with enough customers in my years to know a liar when I see one, gentlemen. He wasn't a man of money, nor did he appear to have ever been in an alchemy store before. So I told him I had run out and wasn't due for a shipment for another three months. I know trouble when I see it lads and this man oozed dire tidings.'

'You say he was short with black hair. Was there anything else about him you remember?' asked Deadsun.

'Hmmm,' the elderly store owner scratched his beard, 'he had a cane with a black stained handle, but now that I think about it he didn't look like he needed it all that much. He walked fine out of the store. It was probably more for show than anything.'

'Did he ask any other questions or mention where he was staying in the city?' probed Greeven.

'Nothing else I can tell you, unfortunately. As soon as he realised I didn't have what he wanted, he left in quite the hurry.'

'Many thanks,' replied Deadsun as he turned to make his way out of the store.

'Oi,' called the store owner, 'what's this all about then?'

'You have your silver, and we have our information. That's all you need to know,' replied Deadsun, walking back into the midday sunshine.

———

Gathering his men around him, Deadsun said, 'We're looking for a man, short in stature with black hair, who carries a cane.'

'Where do you think we might find him?' asked one of his men.

'If you want to get your hands on a person to do evil things in dark corners without someone noticing, where would you go?' asked Greeven to the men.

The seven men all looked at each other and unanimously said, 'Thieves Run.'

Located in the southern section of the city, Thieves Run was known for its layabouts, pickpockets, drunkards and undesirables. You would not find a more dangerous street in any other city. If you needed someone killed, maimed, robbed or silenced, it was likely you'd find someone to do your bidding in Thieves Run for the low price of a few silvers. The gangs and criminals all had their head-quarters in or around Thieves Run. There was no loyalty amongst lifters and tricksters. Hence, it was not uncommon for some unfortu-nate to be dead in a ditch for several days before someone noticed and alerted the authorities. Most of the shady deals and cutthroat contracts took place in this quarter of the city, so it was likely Thieves Run would be the first place a person who wished ill on the city's residents would gravitate.

Deadsun placed his hood over his eyes once again and turned to his men, 'Fedden, Cervo, you two go to the other alchemist stores in this area and see what you can find out from the owners but don't act too suspiciously. We don't know how many of these bastards are in the city and where they may have eyes and ears. The rest of us are going to Thieves Run.'

Walking through the city, the men could see a change in the buildings, stores, and people. The commoners who ran the bakeries, candle shops and butchers gave way to dirty children begging for money and rowdy taverns where you were just as likely to receive a knife in the ribs as a mug of ale.

'I'm glad we're in the clothes of a commoner,' said Greeven from the corner of his mouth, eyeing off an unpleasant looking group of men who were arguing and grabbing at each other's shirt fronts.

'If we were in uniform, word would spread quicker than a fire in a woodworker's store,' replied Deadsun. 'Keep your eyes open, men and remember who we're looking for. I think it best we split up. You three take the left side of the road, Greeven and I will walk the right. Go into stores and taverns but don't make yourselves too obvious. We will meet at the end of the Run. There's a speaker's corner where priests often preach about the gods. We will gather there and discuss what we've found.'

The groups spent the next hour scrutinising side streets, talking with locals, and exploring stores and taverns. Occasionally the two groups would spy each other from across the cobblestone street and give each other a subtle shake of their heads. After going into countless stores and speaking with dozens of people, Deadsun and Greeven found themselves standing at a corner with a tavern called 'The Splendid Turkey' located directly across the way.

'That place looks almost clean,' said Greeven, tugging Deadsun's sleeve. 'Let's go in for a drink and rest our feet for a few minutes.'

'One drink. We have work to do,' replied Deadsun, inspecting the tavern occupants through the grimy windows.

Both men were greeted with the aroma of smoke, sweat, beer and meat as they entered. The few customers inside didn't give them a second look, either too drunk to worry or too engrossed in conversation to care. After the pair purchased drinks and sat at a booth, they discussed what they had seen so far.

'When was the last attack from someone with one of these welltakers?' asked Greeven.

'As far as we know, a few days ago. A young woman near the west gate killed a boy and his dog before our men were able to grab her.'

'And do we know who this young woman was?' inquired Greeven.

'It's challenging to get anything out of them once they've had a welltaker bound to them. It's not until someone notices they've gone missing that we can start to unravel who they are. There's only been a handful of people come forward looking for family members who have been bound with one of these devices. That's why I think most of them are coming from the poorer and more criminal sectors of the city. It seems no one cares if they're gone, or they don't wish to speak to the authorities.'

'Seems logical. I wonder if...,' Greeven stopped as he stared through the window intently. 'I think we have our man,' he said, sliding out of the booth.

'Wait,' said Deadsun, 'there's not a man alive in Thieves Run who would leave a full drink on the table. The last thing we want is to draw attention to ourselves.'

Both men downed their drinks and walked out of the tavern following their target. They spied a short man in a patchy black cloak striding down the cobblestones, a walking stick in his right hand.

'If ever there was a man that looked both out of place and right at home, it's him,' said Greeven.

Deadsun caught the attention of one of his captains waiting outside a store puffing a pipe. As their eyes met Deadsun nodded towards the short man walking away from them and the captain promptly tapped his pipe on his boot, put it in a fold in his tunic and rapped on the window of the store. His group walked down the opposite side of the street to keep pace as Deadsun and Greeven followed behind the man.

'For a man so short in stature, he's walking fast,' said Greeven, picking up his pace so they wouldn't lose him in the crowd.

'Yes, it seems our man has somewhere to be,' replied Deadsun.

Just then, a howl burst forth from a man in the middle of the street a few hundred yards back. He sliced a blood-covered dagger through the air at anyone who came near him. The crowd around him quickly panicked, and people started to yell, drawing swords and daggers of their own.

'Or somewhere to be away from,' replied Greeven as the hollering faded behind them.

As the short man came to the door of a large building, he looked around to see if anyone was following him. He knocked on the door quickly twice, followed by another three knocks in slow succession. He looked around one last time before he ducked into the building. Deadsun and Greeven moved from the alcove they had hidden in, drawing their swords as they arrived at the door, breathing quickly from their brisk walk up the alley. The door looked like any other throughout the kingdom, made of wood with two large hinges and a spy flap.

'What now?' asked Greeven.

'We get inside,' replied Deadsun, 'and quickly. Did you hear that knock? It didn't sound like a regular greeting.'

The other soldiers caught up and crouched several paces away from Deadsun and Greeven, waiting for their next move.

'Leave this to me,' said Greeven, rubbing his hands on the building's grimy walls and dirtying his face. He roughed his hair into a mess and walked to the door. Suddenly Greeven had a thought. 'Mokes,' he hissed to one of the soldiers, 'throw me your tobacco pouch.'

Mokes tossed his pouch as Deadsun and the other soldiers stood with their backs to the wall a few paces from the door.

Greeven rapped on the door with the same pattern the short man used a few moments ago, and a beady set of eyes evaluated him through the spy flap.

'What?'

'I've 'erd one of you ish looking for lament,' said Greeven, through slightly slurred words, looking every bit the part of a half-drunk criminal.

'Fuck off.'

The peep door slammed shut, and Greeven could hear muffled shouts with the words 'dirty', 'scum' and 'lament' escaping through the iron and wood.

Just as suddenly, the peep door opened again and a voice said, 'Who sent you?'

'No one. I was in the same alchemy shtore as the short man and 'erd him ashking for lament, wasn't I? Just sho happens I've some that needs sellin, cheap like,' replied Greeven, holding up the pouch of tobacco with a crooked smile.

'Wait there.'

The peep door shut and Greeven looked towards Deadsun, giving him a nod. They all gripped their swords and daggers, ready for whatever came next.

Greeven stepped back as he heard the metallic clunk and grind of the doors various mechanisms unlocking its bulk. When the heavy wood scraped along the floor, Greeven put all his strength into a kick that sent the door flying inwards. He felt the resistance of the door slamming into the face of the owner of the beady eyes. A sickening crunch preceded the sound of a body hitting the floor. Deadsun and Greeven looked at each other, nodded, then put all their weight into forcing the door open.

As they bullied their way in they saw a fat man slumped behind the door, holding blood-covered hands to his face as the short man ran down the hallway at full speed, cloak streaming behind him. Deadsun and Greeven took off after him, jumping over the small table he had thrown over to slow their pursuit. Deadsun sensed a flash of movement beside him as Greeven hurled his sword, hilt first, with all his might down the hallway. The heavy iron weapon sailed through the air like a spear and connected with the back of the short man's head, dropping him like a sack of spring potatoes.

'Good shot,' smiled Deadsun, slowing his pace and walking to the crumpled human heap at the end of the hallway.

'Thanks, I've been practising,' replied Greeven, shoving the short man with his foot and rolling him onto his back. His jet black hair was a mess and the deep pockmarks on his face told of illness as a child. His heavy leather cloak lay askew on the floor and he wore the largest copper necklace either of them had ever seen. It was rounded and circular with intricate patterns carved into the metal. There was a significant dent where the man's chin had slammed into it on his way to the floor, courtesy of Greeven's sword hilt.

Blurry, departed eyes stared back at them as a groan escaped the short man's mouth.

'On your feet,' growled Deadsun.

Greeven hauled the short man up and dragged him into the small grubby kitchen, dropping him onto an old wooden chair where he grabbed his shirt and delivered quick, sharp slaps as he called out, 'Rise and shine filth, we've got questions, and you're going to answer.'

As the short man's eyes focused, he realised what was happening and struggled under Greeven's iron grip.

'Easy,' said Greeven, shoving him roughly back into the chair, another soldier pointing his sword at his throat. The short man looked around the room with insolent eyes.

'You hurt my friend,' he spat.

'Your friend,' replied Deadsun, 'is the least of your worries at this moment. Check his pockets.'

All manner of items spilled out of the man's pockets including a dagger with a gem-encrusted hilt, a small wooden box, several scraps of paper, a pipe made from wood and horn, a golden ring with an eagle on it and some silver and copper coins.

'I'm assuming since your friend opened the door for us,' asked Deadsun as he poked at the items on the table, 'you were indeed inside the alchemy store Nominative Potio asking for lament? Perhaps to bind these to our citizens?' he continued as several well-takers poured from the wooden box in his hand.

'I'm a binder, it's true,' replied the short man simply, rubbing the back of his head.

'A binder? Not the name I was thinking of,' said Greeven as he sat in a chair next to the short man, cleaning dirt from under his nails with a dagger.

'So you admit to binding these devices to our people?' asked Deadsun.

'I just told you I was a binder. All of us know the risk. We will be caught eventually; in fact, I'm surprised it took you this long to catch me. I thought the men of the Lavers Law were supposed to be intelligent?'

'Who said we were Lavers Law?' asked Greeven, a little annoyed that this intruder already knew so much about them.

'Oh, come now,' said the short man incredulously, 'beneath those common clothes and bland swords the rigidity and training of soldiers of the city are plain to see.'

'You said all of us know the risk,' said Deadsun, ignoring the jibe. 'How many of you are there?'

The short man let out a throaty chuckle that turned into a laugh, 'You've seen nothing yet. An endless wave of misery will visit your city, and only then will you know redemption.'

'Here's what's going to happen,' said Deadsun, walking around to the other side of the table.

He placed several welltakers along the edge of the table as he spoke, 'We will take you and your friend to our city's dungeon, where our best torturer is waiting for you to arrive. He has a certain... let's say, affection for what he does, and he's very, very good at it. Isn't he, Greeven?'

Greeven looked up from inspecting his nails, 'Oh, he's quite the monster amongst men. I have a feeling he will be looking forward to getting to know you very, very intimately, short man.'

Deadsun continued, 'After your bones have been broken, your skin peeled and you've felt what will seem like an eternity of racking pain you didn't know was possible, you will know the real meaning of the term endless wave of misery as you squeal and bleed like a pig at slaughter.'

'Mmmmm, crackling,' said Greeven as he plunged his dagger into the tabletop.

The short man sighed and looked up at the ceiling, 'I knew this day would come,' he said, moving his eyes across the table to Deadsun. 'I'm aware you and your men are simply doing your job. As was I. I've prepared for this day and promise you I will go willingly. You may do with me as you wish. I ask but one, small favour. Before I face my judgement, will you allow me to enjoy one last pipe? I doubt I will have an opportunity in your dungeons to take my last draw from something that's brought me so much comfort over the years. As a man, not a prisoner, or an enemy, I ask, allow me this small indulgence before we go?'

Deadsun thought, weighing up the pros and cons of allowing the short man one last pipe. He could see no reason to deny him lighting some tobacco for the last time. Whilst he personally didn't care for it, he knew the enjoyment it gave his men when out on patrol or after long, cold shifts on the city's walls.

'I'll allow it,' replied Deadsun.

'We'll even give you the tobacco,' said Greeven, pulling out the pouch he borrowed before kicking in the door and throwing it on the table.

'My thanks,' said the short man, slowly reaching for his pipe and the pouch, showing his hands, indicating no funny business.

'Tell me short man,' asked Greeven, moving his chair towards the wall behind him and leaning it back, 'why is the pyrekhan doing this?'

'Simple,' replied the short man as he shoved a wad of tobacco into his pipe. 'For the expansion of his empire.'

'But why this?' continued Greeven, circling his hands at the wrist. 'Why run around a city turning its citizens crazy? Surely it's easier to pitch a battle or lead us into a trap?'

'I make no assumptions on the khan's plans. I just follow orders. A taper for my pipe?' the short man asked politely.

One of the soldiers looked to Deadsun, who gave a subtle nod.

'Your twin cities... thankyou,' said the short man as the soldier handed him a lit taper, 'isolate and erupt. Roda Codex is the first to go,' he continued, lighting his pipe and watching the flame dance on the taper. The men in the room hadn't noticed that he opened a hidden cap in his necklace just a moment earlier, pulling out a small piece of cord made from fireweed dipped in animal fat and highly flammable tree sap.

'Isolate and erupt, what the hell does that mea…,'

BOOM!

The walls shook from the violent explosion as the room quickly filled with smoke, screams and chaos. The two soldiers standing next to the short man died instantly, Greeven tumbled backwards from his chair as Deadsun flew into the hallway from the force.

Ears ringing and coughing through the acrid dust and smoke, Deadsun pulled himself groggily from the floor. The soldiers couldn't have known the short man's necklace contained black powder, nails, and balls of pig iron. It exploded with enough force to remove the short man's head from his shoulders and destroy a good portion of the kitchen.

Deadsun stumbled back to the kitchen and took in a scene of utter chaos. Greeven lay unconscious on the floor, cuts and scratches all over his face and body. There was so much blood in the room he could taste the metal. Grabbing Greeven under the arms, Deadsun lifted his limp body, dragging him down the hallway and away from the carnage.

———

Deadsun saw to it that Greeven, now awake but badly injured, was safely in the infirmary and comfortable, before walking doggedly back to his quarters. Finally, after one of the longest days he'd had in recent memory, Deadsun sat on his pallet, ears still ringing like a swarm of angry hornets. He rolled the walking cane of the short man over and over in his fingers, amazed it wasn't destroyed in the explosion.

How had the short man created such an explosion? Indeed it was magic of some sort, but neither he nor any of the city's mages or magicians had ever heard of a spell or concoction that could create such havoc. Fragments of the necklace had been found scorched, burnt and mangled throughout the kitchen. The smell of salt and urine filled the air and caught at the back of their throats but gave no clues.

He'd caught one of the binders, but he'd not been able to get him back to the keep for interrogation. None of this would have happened if he'd tied the short man's arms behind his back or not allowed him that last pipe. He was responsible for the death of two of his men and his second in command's serious injuries. The thought struck him that perhaps he was too late in bringing these binders to justice, just like he was too late to see his brother alive.

'Dammit!' he swore, rising from his pallet and pacing the room. 'What was in that blasted necklace? And why did he have this useless bloody cane?' he questioned himself angrily. It had been a long, exhausting day, and his anger was quickly getting the better of him. The more he tried to calm himself, the more clouded his judgement became and the harder it was for him to think clearly. It was not often he let his emotions get the better of him, but in the confines of his quarters, he occasionally allowed his anger or sorrow to flow unfettered.

'Dammit, dammit, DAMMIT!' he roared, swinging the cane through the air, striking the floor with the handle causing it to snap off and fly to the corner of the room.

Black powder, as dark as his mood, started flowing from the inside of the cane and gathering in a pile on the floor.

11

RUSH IN THE MIDDLE OF
A MEAL

Abreeth and Dwin spent several hours breaking cold ground with sticks and hands to lay Grenda down into eternal slumber beneath the frozen loam. Dwin sat silent, staring at the mound for an age before laying beside it and weeping. When his eyelids finally closed, he found an uneasy peace with Murphy resting at his side. Abreeth spread a cloak over him, causing him to stir, then rest his head into the crook of his arm, drifting off into forlorn darkness once more.

Abreeth had only known Grenda for a short time, but the attractive, bubbly woman had made a remarkable impression on him. Not only did she help him discover some semblance of understanding about his powers, but she also made him feel welcomed in a way very few others had. She was kind, loving and knowledgeable.

Now she was dead because of his actions.

He went over the scene, again and again, pondering what he could have done differently. Everything he imagined had him arrive slightly early or late, move to the left a little more, grab the man's hand before he managed to plunge his dagger into her lithe body. Every alternative he could conjure ended with Grenda still alive. But that was not his reality. Her body lay under the ground, quickly growing cold. Soon she would start to decompose, and just like the plants and trees she loved so much, she would be at one with the earth once again.

Abreeth knelt beside the mound, hand laid upon the dirt, eyes closed. Collecting his thoughts, he tried to think through what he had learned in Grenda's cottage. Concentrating on the coolness of the soil, the single grains of dirt against his fingertips and the small, jagged rocks touching his skin, he focused his mind as he slowed his breathing. Feeling a sensation like nothing he'd experienced before, he could feel himself, or at least his mind, seeping into the dirt below his hand. He sensed the earth, teeming with life and the body which lay just below the surface. Abreeth could feel the organisms, bugs, worms, seeds and creatures living below the soil. Overwhelmed, he snatched his hand away and sat back, confused, amazed and exhausted at the same time.

'I can't believe she's gone', whispered Dwin.

'Sorry. Did I wake you?' asked Abreeth.

'No, and don't be,' replied Dwin. 'I keep dreaming she's going to walk through those trees any minute and tell us it was all a nightmare, but we're living the nightmare, aren't we?'

'Go back to sleep, Dwin. I'll keep watch. We have a long trip ahead of us tomorrow.'

'I don't know what's worse. Knowing she's gone or dreaming she's alive and then waking up,' said Dwin, staring blankly at the mound in front of him.

'I know. I'm sorry,' stated Abreeth.

'Abe?'

'Yes, Dwin?'

'What are we going to do? Everyone's missing or dead.'

'We're going to do what your mother asked of us. We're going to go to Thade and find your father. First, we get to Roda Codex, then make our way through The Columns and then onto Thade, where we will find Edwick. Then, I don't know after that.'

'Mother always told me he died when I was young.'

'I'm sure she had her reasons,' replied Abreeth, trying to move the conversation away from another cause of pain for the young teenager. 'When we get to Roda Codex, we can find somewhere nice to stay. Get some good food, maybe even an ale or two. I promise I won't tell your...,' Abreeth stopped himself as he realised what he was about to say. 'I'm... I'm sorry, I didn't mean...,'

'That's OK. I'm going to sleep now,' said Dwin, rolling over and covering his head with the cloak. Abreeth swore inwardly at his stupidity.

Abreeth spent the next few hours staring into the fire and listening for signs of movement beyond the firelight. His thoughts wandered to Arpenta, and its destruction. The faint glow of the remains of the town still visible on the horizon. He couldn't make sense of it. The entire village was gone, all the people, all the boats and buildings, everything. Replaced with fire, ash and ruin. How could a whole village burn and its inhabitants just disappear? So many questions swirled around in his mind he wasn't sure which thread to pull at first.

Standing and stretching, he looked at the stars as he walked to clear his mind and warm his body. He found himself moving towards the man he had killed. Both he and Dwin were so focused on giving Grenda an appropriate burial he hadn't searched the man's body for clues.

'Might as well look him over,' he said to himself as he rolled the man onto his back, hollow eyes staring into the sky and a large jagged wound where his throat used to be. Abreeth patted him down to see if there were any clues or valuable items in his pockets. He found a few coppers and a woman's necklace – probably stolen.

Abreeth felt the back of the man's pants for pouches or parchment, then patted his way towards his head, running his fingers over the back of his tunic when he stopped just below his neck, for he felt something hard and boney.

'Strange,' he commented as he pulled down the neck of the

man's tunic to investigate. He couldn't quite comprehend what he was looking at. It looked to him like a piece of jewellery, but it had grown into the man's neck, the skin around it healed and scarred. Teardrop in shape with a piece of black crystal in the middle, it seemed an odd place to have such an adornment and a strange way to wear it. Something about it seemed oddly familiar yet strangely alien. The urge to touch the device crystallised in his mind before he realised, he was reaching out his finger.

His mind jumped from his skull and into the dead man lying face down in front of him. He could sense the coldness of his eternal silence, the blood in his veins starting to harden along with a grey fog that overran his mind before he died, still lingering within his fading lifeforce. The device seemed to draw him in, like an evil sprite, that promised fortune and prosperity, but also corrupt with a menace that floated on the edge of dominion and disaster. Snatching his hand away, he stood abruptly and walked to the fire to keep watch whilst Dwin slept. He didn't like what he felt when he touched that device and was more than happy to leave it and the dead man well alone.

The next morning Dwin and Abreeth packed up their belongings into the already full saddlebags for the week-long journey to Roda Codex. They stood next to Grenda's grave for one last time with their heads bowed.

'Come, Dwin, I know it's difficult, but we should go.'

Dwin knelt, placing a single flower on top of the mound with a shaking hand and whispered, 'Goodbye, Mother.' Closing his eyes and wrenching his hand from the last connection he would have with her, he stood and looked at Abreeth. 'Let's go', he said simply.

The first day they spent in companionable silence, only stopping to water the donkeys or to stretch their legs. They saw no one on the roads, which was unusual, but figured they would see people in the next village, which they expected to reach in the late afternoon of the next day. That night they set up camp near a natural spring beside the road and dined on roasted rabbit, caught and skinned by Abreeth. The well-worn fire pit and logs for seats indicated this was a popular spot for travellers when navigating their way between the Arpenta Skyport and the next village. Lying beside the fire, both young men stared at the blinking lights that pierced the blackness of the sky.

'Where do you think we go when we die?' asked Dwin.

Abreeth was suddenly aware of how little they had spoken that day, as Dwin's voice shook him from his thoughts. 'Hmmm,' replied Abreeth, 'no one knows, do they? Some say you travel to the other realm, where your spirit plays in the gardens of the gods. I've heard some people talk about being in a world of light or dark where you find eternal happiness or infinite pain depending on the person you are in this life.'

'But where do *you* think we go?' pressed Dwin.

Thinking back to his experience kneeling beside Grenda's grave, feeling the life force drain from her and the dead man, he replied, 'I don't think we go anywhere, Dwin. I think when we die, our bodies go into the ground or get eaten or burnt and return to the world. I think there's an energy in our bodies that goes back into nature when we don't need it anymore. Some of us might help trees grow or feed a bear or a pyredrake if we're unlucky enough.'

'I like the idea that Mother is helping a tree grow. I think she'd like that,' replied Dwin.

'I think you're right. She would have liked that.'

Both stared at the stars, then Abreeth let out a large yawn.

'I'll take the first watch,' said Dwin. 'You've been up for the past day. You need some sleep.'

Abreeth replied, 'Wake me when the moon reaches the high point, or if you hear something.'

'I will. Get some sleep, Abe.'

Abreeth rolled his exhausted body onto its side and shoved a tunic under his head, drifting off almost immediately to much-needed slumber.

———

'You should have woken me,' yawned Abreeth, stretching and rubbing the sleep from his eyes in the early morning suns.

'I couldn't sleep. Besides, you needed the rest. We should get to Midane village this afternoon. I can have a good night's rest then,' replied Dwin, handing him a strip of leftover rabbit for breakfast.

'Thanks. We had better break camp and get moving,' said Abreeth, standing.

'Everything's packed and ready to go,' replied Dwin. 'I'm surprised I didn't wake you with all the shuffling and rummaging.'

'You're surprised!' said Abreeth, looking around at the tidy camp, banked fire and three donkeys fully packed and ready to go. 'You've done a great job here, Dwin.'

The two travellers walked the roads towards Midane village, where they ate a hearty broth of meat and vegetables, washed down with a large tankard of ale and gained a wonderful night's sleep in comfortable beds stuffed with freshly cut straw. They strode out of the village the next morning, ready to travel, with a good night's sleep under their belt.

In the taverns and towns along the road to Roda Codex, they heard similar stories to their own. Men returning from hunting parties or the mountains to their villages in ruins, burnt and smouldering, not a soul in the vicinity, and no explanation of where they may have gone. Many were making their way to Roda Codex. Others were travelling to check in on other family members located in the vast mountainous regions of the Welkinpeaks. There were rumours that war may be brewing, but the people of the highskies didn't give it much credence as they were protected from everyone and everything that afflicted the land dwellers of the Firmalands below.

The cavernous structures called The Columns were a barrier

between the firmalands and the floating mountains of the Welkin-peaks. The Columns were leftover from the creation of the world. A time when gods walked the lands and swam in the oceans. When gods could pluck stars from the sky, and the very building blocks of life were harnessed to do their bidding. Many died trying to find their way through the caves and tunnels of The Columns in the early days. It took three hundred years before a team managed to find a path up into the Welkinpeaks. Half-starved and pale from the weeks spent wandering the dark caverns, they were the first to explore the wild beauty of the floating mountains in the Welkinpeaks. The caves had now been thoroughly explored, save for the deepest hollows where anyone courageous or foolish enough to navigate was never seen again. Dark and dangerous, the shadows of The Columns were not for the faint of heart.

'What do we do when we reach Roda Codex?' asked Dwin, taking a bite from one of the apples they had purchased from a young farmer a few leagues back.

'We keep our heads down and our mouths shut. Being in the city is very different from village life, Dwin. We need to have our wits about us, lest someone shank us and steal our belongings. Don't trust anyone. Especially if they're friendly.'

'It can't be that bad, can it?' asked Dwin in surprise.

'Trust me,' replied Abreeth, 'a city is no place to let your guard down, not even for a minute. The moment you do, that's when you're robbed, stabbed or knocked to the ground and your coin pouch slipped from your belt before you even know it's gone. I'm serious, Dwin. We need to look out for each other and trust no one.'

'OK. Trust no one. I promise.'

'And you'd best be hiding that dagger. It's likely to be used against you,' said Abreeth.

'I'd like to see them try,' laughed Dwin.

'Believe me. You wouldn't.'

The two rode for several hours before Dwin asked, 'Didn't you say you knew a girl in Roda Codex? Are you hoping to see her when we get there?'

'I hope not,' replied Abreeth. 'The way we left things wasn't... desirable.'

'What do you mean? Did you break her heart or something?'

'Let's just say it was never going to work. A girl like that and a man like me just wasn't ever going to be a possibility, so I did us both a favour when I left the city.'

'Is that when you came to Arpenta to work for Uncle Borchin?' asked Dwin.

'Soon after, yes,' replied Abreeth, looking into the distance, the mention of his former flame bringing back vexatious memories.

'I wonder what happened to Uncle Borchin? Do you think he's still alive?' Dwin's tone turned weighty at the mention of his uncle.

'When I looked around the village, I couldn't see any craft in the skyports, so I think some people at least escaped from whatever happened there. Knowing your uncle, he probably grabbed as many people as he could at the first sign of trouble and sailed them to safety.' Abreeth couldn't get the sight of the village in ashes from his mind. The empty streets and charred remains of buildings he'd grown to know over the past year rolled around in his head like an itch he couldn't scratch. He was comforted by the thought some may have escaped with their lives, even if everything they owned lay in collapsed, smoking ruins.

'I'd like to think that too. What happened, Abe? Why would anyone want to burn down Arpenta?'

'I don't know Dwin. It doesn't make a lot of sense. We need keen ears and sharp eyes in the city. I get a feeling something is happening in the kingdom, Dwin. I don't know what it is, but something doesn't feel right. Burnt towns, people going missing and all these travellers on the road. Something's brewing Dwin, and we need to make sure we get as far away from it as possible.'

'Abe?'

'Yes, Dwin.'

'Thank you,' Dwin said, his voice breaking slightly.

'That's OK, but for what?'

'For being here. With me. For trying to save my mother. For showing me things on the cloudcutters when we were hunting. For everything. I've never told you this before, but I sometimes imagine you're my older brother.'

'As far as little brothers go, I could do a lot worse,' laughed Abreeth. 'We're going to be OK as long as we stick together.'

As their donkeys plodded along the dusty road, the pair crested a hill that swept down onto open lands with green fields and homes dotted neatly throughout the landscape. Wisps of smoke wandered into the sky from chimneys of the houses in the distance. Further away, grey stone buildings crept towards the suns like fingers of stone clawing at the sky. In the middle of the sprawling urban centre was a structure so large Dwin couldn't comprehend it at first. Driving its way skyward, a massive column that touched the low clouds overlooked the entire city. From its top ran hundreds of wires like a maypole used by giants from childhood stories.

'Look, Dwin,' said Abreeth, pointing his gloved hand, 'Roda Codex.'

'I've never seen anything so big!' exclaimed Dwin, eyes wide with wonder.

'Then it's good you see this place before Thade. I've heard it's twice as big as Roda Codex, perhaps bigger,' said Abreeth, smiling at his young companion's marvel.

'I don't think I can imagine anything bigger than this,' replied Dwin.

'If we pick up our pace, we can make it to the Eastern gate before nightfall. They close the city gates after dark, so we need to move,' said Abreeth, poking his heels into the ribs of his donkey, causing a snort of annoyance from the beast.

Just as the suns kissed the tops of mountains, casting long shadows on the road, they arrived at the Eastern gate.

'Name and business?' a bored-looking soldier asked through a stifled yawn.

'Abreeth Earthwind, and this is Dwin... Earthwind. We're here to visit our relatives and also to sell these donkeys,' replied Abreeth.

'Earthwind, eh? Any relation to Mandrigral Earthwind? Owns the leatherworks in the Bishtark Quarter,' asked the soldier.

'No, I'm sorry,' answered Abreeth, 'I've not heard of him.'

'Lucky,' said the soldier, looking him up and down. 'He owes me money. Next!' And with that, Abreeth and Dwin entered the city of Roda Codex.

Abreeth wrapped his cloak around his shoulders and pulled down his hood as Dwin looked around in amazement at the buildings, people and animals of the crowded streets.

'Dwin,' hissed Abreeth, 'pull your hood down and for the sake of the old gods, stop looking around so much. You're making it much too obvious you've never been to a city before.'

'Sorry,' replied Dwin, pulling down his hood, 'there's just so much to look at.'

'We'll have plenty of time to explore tomorrow. We're here for at least a couple of days. Let's just get some food and find a place to stay without drawing too much attention to ourselves. Watch out for gangs of pickpockets, they often hang around the city gates'

'Fine,' said Dwin, grumbling.

'Need someone to watch your donkeys, sir?' asked a dirty young boy, who had seen no more than six or seven summers. His broad smile and innocent eyes focused on Dwin.

'Oh, no, thank you,' replied Dwin politely.

'You've got a lot of stuff here sir, I can watch it for you, for a price,' said the boy, skipping towards the spare donkey and its saddlebags.

'Oi, you. Fuck off before I slice your ears off and feed them to our dog,' growled Abreeth, swinging a leg down from his donkey.

The young boy spat at him and ran, yelling, 'The black be upon you,' as he sped away from the swipe Abreeth tried to level at his head.

'See,' said Abreeth in irritation, 'not even a few moments into the city, and we're being targeted by a bafflepincher.'

'A bafflepincher?' asked Dwin.

Abreeth sighed, now realising just how young and naive his travelling partner was. 'A bafflepincher is a young child, usually about seven or eight. Sometimes they work in pairs and talk to you all friendly-like, asking lots of questions. All the while, they're sizing up your belongings to see what they can steal or keep a mental list they can take back to their gang. If you're dumb enough to carry anything of value into the city without protection, they'll slice your neck and drain you for a few rounds of gold.'

'Oh,' said Dwin, suddenly embarrassed to realise they were likely being watched.

'Luckily, we've got nothing of value, but we'd best stay sharp all the same. Come, the rooms I have in mind are just down this road,' said Abreeth, 'we should walk the rest of the way.'

Both of them slid from their donkeys, noticing how travel-sore their muscles were and how numb their backsides had become from the hours of riding. The smell of cooking intertwined with animals and humanity clung to the air like a late afternoon fog. Their stomachs growled as they rememberd they hadn't had a hot meal in several days and hadn't slept in a proper bed for at least twice that.

After gathering their belongings and giving the livery boy a copper to stable their donkeys, Dwin and Abreeth hauled their belongings to their accommodation for the night. An old wood and stone building loomed before them, with whitewashed walls and a thatched roof. The building's ground level housed the tavern where they served food, ale, wine, and gratitude to anyone willing to toss a few coppers across the bar for their services. Upstairs housed small rooms with comfortable beds for weary travellers and visiting merchants.

The pair pushed through the front door and into the main

hallway and could hear the murmur of conversation behind the tavern doors as the smell of cooked meat, fresh bread and beer assaulted their senses. Abreeth headed to the counter operated by an older woman, hair in a bun, wearing a colourful woollen shawl perched on a stool, clicking knitting needles together with surprising speed given her advanced age.

'One room or two?' she asked, looking up from the paused needles in her hands.

'One please,' replied Abreeth, 'and could we have some hot water brought to our room? We've been on the road for some time.'

'That'll be two coppers extra,' said the old woman.

'Two coppers!' cried Dwin, 'For water?'

'Hush, brother,' Abreeth winced.

Turning back to smile at the old lady, he said in his most charming voice, 'Two coppers is fine,' as he placed payment for the room and water on the bench.

'Number sixteen. Up the stairs. Turn left, fourth door on your right,' replied the old woman as she plucked an ancient-looking key from a rack of similar door openers dangling behind her.

As she put it into Abreeth's outstretched hand, she held onto the key and said very matter-of-factly, 'No trouble, no fights, no dogs or weapons in the common room. Got it?'

'Of course,' replied Abreeth.

The older woman let go of the key and sat back on her stool to continue with her knitting, the sound of click-clacking following them up the stairs as they headed towards their room.

After they arranged their belongings in the small but comfortable room and washing the road from their travel-weary bodies, the pair tramped their way down the stairs to get themselves a hot meal, a cold ale and hopefully some news from strangers.

As Abreeth opened the door, an increase in the volume of conversation and the smell of hot, fresh food and ale-soaked floor and tables met his nose and ears.

'I don't know about you,' said Abreeth as they strode towards the bar, 'but I'm looking forward to a hot meal and a long sleep.'

In the common room were a group of rough-looking, battle-hardened mercenaries sitting in the corner playing dice. At another table were a group of older men arguing about the price of spurworm skins with other small groups scattered throughout the tables. A large tabby cat sprawled on a rug in front of a welcoming fire in the corner, a young girl rubbing its belly.

'What'll it be boys?" asked the young man behind the bar, his dark hair slicked back and a towel slung across his shoulder. "We've got a beef stew and a haunch of venison roasting in the kitchens.'

'Two ales and two bowls of stew please,' asked Abreeth.

'Two brews and stews coming up,' replied the barman, reaching for two tankards from under the bar. 'Where you boys from then? Haven't seen you here before?'

'We've travelled from Arpenta,' replied Abreeth to the friendly barkeep.

'Or what's left of it,' added Dwin.

'Arpenta... hmm, that's a skyport to the north, isn't it? What do you mean what's left of it then?' asked the barkeep as he slid two tankards of ale in front of them both.

'Well, it was a skyport until someone set it alight,' said Abreeth, taking a long draw from his ale.

'Firebug in the village, then?' asked the barkeeper, grabbing two piping-hot bowls of stew from the counter that led to the kitchen. They were placed there by a large cook with a greasy apron, sweat stains under his arms and a scowl on his face that made him look like he hated everyone and everything just for existing. Abreeth hoped his rancour didn't make its way into the stew.

'More than that,' said Abreeth sadly, ladling his stew to cool it. 'The entire village was gone. Every building was razed by fire.'

'By fire, you say,' said the young barkeep, leaning into the bar in front of him. 'You know, you're the fifth traveller this week that's told me his village has been destroyed.'

Leaning over to look past Abreeth and Dwin, who were now tucking into their stew with gusto, the friendly barkeep called to another patron sitting in a group a few tables away.

'Hey Kain, I say Kain. Weren't you speaking to a man from one of those skyports that got destroyed a few days ago?'

A man in a heavy woollen pullover looked towards the bar and adjusted the leather greaves on his arms that were easily the size of Dwin's legs. 'Aye, that's right. He was a captain, I think. Hunted spurworms. Said he was from up north, now what was his name? Bochan, Borkin. Something like that.'

Abreeth stopped his spoon halfway to his mouth and turned his head to face the massive man sitting a few tables away.

'It wasn't Borchin by chance, was it?' he asked.

'Aye, that's it! Borchin. Big fella, long red beard. Didn't drink a drop of ale but played the dice like he was born with 'em in his hand.'

Abreeth jumped from his seat and lept towards the man sitting at the table without thinking. Suddenly three other large and scary looking fellows were on their feet, coiled like snakes and ready to strike.

Abreeth put both his hands up in supplication and stammered, 'I'm sorry. I don't mean any trouble, please. This boy, his uncle was our captain on a cloudcutter that ran out of the skyport Arpenta, whose name was Borchin. Going from your description, it sounds very much like his uncle, who we thought dead.'

'Did he say where he was going?' asked Dwin hopefully.

The large man rubbed his chin, looking at Dwin, then back to Abreeth. 'As it happens, he did mention where he was going,' said Kain with a mischievous grin, 'and I'm wondering what that piece of information is worth to you both?'

Abreeth scowled, 'Look, his mother died a little over a week ago. Are you going to deny him the chance to see his only living relative for the sake of a few coppers?'

'Yes,' replied Kain, looking around at his three other companions and grinning. 'Yes, I am... and I'm thinking ten coppers should do it.'

Dwin jumped up from his stool, 'Why you no good son-of-a...!'

Abreeth spun and grabbed Dwin as the bartender yelled they would be out on the street if there was trouble.

Kain adjusted his leather greaves again and chuckled at Dwin. 'I like this one. He's got some fight in him. Fine. Two coppers is a fair price,' he finished by holding out his large calloused hand.

Abreeth fished out two coins and placed them in his palm.

'He was getting a crew together over by the eastern port on the far side of the city. Tried to get us to come with him. Said he was headed south, into the spurlands. I said no, thanks. There's nothing but savages, spurworms and suffering down there.'

'We have to get over there before he leaves,' said Abreeth, turning Dwin around and shoving him towards the door.

'It won't do you no good,' shouted Kain after them. 'He said he was sailing out tonight. You've likely missed him by now.'

12

FESTIVE TRICKERY WITH TOXIC TIPPLES

'Are you clear about what to do?' Marsine asked her sister.

'Yes! We've been through it a dozen times,' cried Gabrielle, rolling her eyes and shooing her sister out the door. 'You go downstairs, pick one out, then get him upstairs. If they're not asleep a few minutes after they're in the door, I hit them on the head with that pitcher. But not too hard.'

'Men's heads are harder than their stubbornness. You won't hurt them with a tap on the back of their skull,' replied Marsine.

'Go!' said Gabrielle, pointing at the door.

'OK, OK, I'm going,' said Marsine, excitement and anxiety in equal measures pulsing through her chest.

Standing at the top of the stairs she fingered the small packet of dried wolfsbane in her pocket. With a breath of preparation, she pulled her top down slightly and pushed her breasts together to accentuate them as she made her way downstairs to the common room.

On any given night there were dozens of locals and travelling merchants eating a meal, catching up with friends or sampling some of the fine wines and ales The Lofty Cockerel had to offer. Tonight was no different.

Pipe smoke, song and laughter drifted through the room along with a familiar song about a farmer who owned a pig that thought it was a dog. Marsine smiled to herself as several bawdy men joined the chorus. As she glided to the bar, she couldn't help but feel several pairs of hungry eyes drinking in her loveliness.

Good, let them envy what they can't have.

'Well don't you look ravishing tonight!' commented Scraps as she looked the nubile nineteen year old up and down. Marsine's red dress was cinched at the waist, giving her an hourglass figure and her auburn hair framed her pale face and ruby lips.

'Thank you, Scraps,' replied Marsine. 'Could I have a cup of water please?'

'Water! Not very often, a customer at this bar asks for water lovey! Sure I can't get you something stronger?'

'No, thank you, just the water please.'

Scraps shrugged her shoulders, filled a tankard and slid it across the bar to the young woman. Sipping the cool water, Marsine turned in her seat and looked around the room to see who had travelled to their little part of the world that night.

Towards the far end of the room, a group of farmers discussed their latest crops with gesticulating hands, ideas and interruptions. Near the window, a young couple deep in conversation whispered sweet lovings into each other's ears. A few tables over a group of sell-swords, rough and worn from being outdoors, sat with drinks and quiet conversation. In the far corner was a plump, soft-looking man with a younger companion who had striking blue eyes and a shy demeanour. In the corner opposite were a group of men singing and laughing, several empty tankards of ale on their table and a young teen boy with a broad grin and an angelic voice playing the lute.

She sat for a while listening to the sounds and songs of the inn. Now and then she would hear snippets of conversations. The group of singing men had moved on to an old drinking song that told of wineskins that never emptied, skies that never turned dark and a woman whose beauty couldn't be looked upon without bringing any man who saw her to his knees.

Marsine was looking into the bottom of her tankard for several minutes, taking in the talk of the tavern when she felt a light touch on her arm and distant words she didn't hear.

'I'm sorry?' she asked.

'Would you like to dance?' One of the sellswords said a little too loudly, glassy-eyed and a sly smile on his face.

'Oh, no thank you,' replied Marsine politely.

'C'mon, a young lass like you should be having fun on a night like tonight,' he said, sliding his hand around her waist and squeezing her.

Marsine tried her best to smile graciously and gently pushed his hand away. 'I'm not very good at dancing,' she lied.

'Don't be like that, pretty one,' said the man, forcefully taking her hand and trying to pull her from the stool. It was at this point a large man with a salt-and-pepper beard and a chest like a barrel roared 'PORGE! The lass said no, man.'

Grabbing him by the scruff of his neck, the large man pushed Porge back into the crowd of sellswords who shoved a tankard into his hand and laughed at his misfortune.

'My sincere apologies m'lady. Porge forgets himself AND HIS WIFE,' he shouted over his shoulder at the group. Looking back at her, he said, 'He won't bother you again or HE'LL HAVE ME TO DEAL WITH.' Again, shouted over his shoulder.

With a bow, the large man walked back to his group and slapped Porge on the back of the head. A new round of raucous laughter erupted.

Marsine studied the table where the large plump man and his younger companion were sitting. The younger man looked at her, but he quickly lowered his gaze when their eyes met.

Marsine smiled and kept looking to see the young man tilt his eyes towards her and smile before the plump man drew his attention away with conversation once again. After a time, the young man got up and made his way towards the bathrooms, smiling shyly at Marsine as he walked past her.

'Scraps,' said Marsine as she spun around in her stool to face the portly woman. 'Who's that young man who just walked past?'

'Don't know,' replied Scraps wiping down the bar with a rag. 'Never seen him before lovey, but the man he's with is a spice merchant from the north. Goes by the name of Tubert. Came in yesterday with two carts full of pepper, herbs, tea and some new spice he's found from the north that tastes like mint but is more bitter. Don't much like the taste of it myself. I buy my pepper from him when he comes through every year, although this year he didn't have much to sell me on account of the cold hurting everyone's crops, even up north. He must be doing OK, though. He has fine horses and paid for his rooms with silver pieces. I should have charged him double given the price he charged for his pepper. But listen to me rabbiting on while your drink is empty. Can I get you another, lovely?'

'No, thank you. This Tubert sounds like an interesting character. I think I would like to chat with him to see what news I can get from the north.'

'Suit yourself,' replied Scraps, 'but you're likely to be bored to death with stories about the price of basil and wormwood or how chervil and pepper are getting harder to find because of the cold.'

When the younger man came back, she floated slowly to the table. 'And that dear Stahl is why you can't find pepper north of the Thorn River. It's to be expected really for I ...,' The plump man cut off his sentence as he noticed his young friend completely ignoring him and instead looking at the stunning young woman with auburn hair and flushed cheeks standing beside their table.

'Good evening m'lady,' said the plump man, his large jowls shaking as he spoke.

'Good evening to you,' said Marsine gracefully. 'I'm awfully sorry to interrupt, but I couldn't help notice this amazing garment you had on and I simply had to come over and ask you about it.'

As she spoke, she fingered the sleeve of Tubert's tunic. Even though she was exaggerating to play to his sensibilities, the stocky man's top was beautifully made and by far the most elegant and expensive piece of apparel at the inn that night.

'Why thank you. Now here, young Stahl, is a woman of fine taste. Sit, sit and let us talk a while,' smiled the plump man. 'Let us make some introductions first. This is my manservant, Stahl.'

Marsine sat and held out her hand for the young man to kiss. He smiled and kissed her hand then turned to the plump man and said, 'Tubert, I really wish you wouldn't call me that.'

'Oh, don't be so sour, Stahl,' teased the older man. 'My name is Tubert. A merchant of fine spices, herbs and other delicacies. From tip to toe around the kingdom I go. If it grows from the ground I will make sure it's found,' he spoke in a well-rehearsed manner. Stahl rolled his eyes and groaned. Tubert continued, ignoring his young friend. 'And who do we have the pleasure of sharing our table with on this fine evening?' asked Tubert, his large friendly face broadening into a smile that had no doubt robbed many an innkeeper with his overpriced wares.

'Marsine.'

'Marsine. A fine name for a fine young lady. I can't have you sitting at my table without a drink.' Tubert turned in his seat and motioned for Scraps to bring over three tankards of ale.

'Now, Marsine. What brings you to The Lofty Cockerel this fine evening?' asked Tubert, leaning in and giving Marsine his full attention.

'I'm on my way to Thade, and this inn happens to be on the way.'

'Thade?' said Stahl, surprised. 'You're a long way from home.'

'Yes. It's quite a journey for a young woman all alone,' replied Marsine, pouting her lips a little. 'I'm what you would call, a teacher of sorts,' she lied, making up the story on the spot. 'I teach men how to make sure their wives are happy and won't stray too far,' she said, gently touching her hair with her fingers.

'I'm not sure I follow?' replied Tubert. 'What exactly is it that you teach them?'

'Well I can't tell you that, or I'd give away all of my secrets,' replied Marsine with a wink.

At that moment Scraps arrived with the ale and placed a tankard in front of each of them, 'Got this batch from the hop master last week, nice little drop my loveys. Enjoy.' Scraps turned on her heel and was soon back behind the bar.

'Here's to new friends,' said Marsine, raising her drink.

'Indeed,' replied Tubert as they all clinked tankards together.

'You mentioned you deal with spices from the north. I would love to hear what news you have from our northern cousins,' said Marsine, taking a sip of her ale and steering the conversation.

'Things are dire indeed, particularly in the way of crops, but that could be said of anywhere these past few years. Farmers are finding it increasingly difficult as the summers are shorter and the winters colder.' Tubert lowered his voice and leaned in over the table, 'Combine that with strange disappearances in many of the towns. People are going missing and towns being put to the torch by raiders. People are starting to talk.' Tubert took a sip of his ale and leaned in even closer, 'They're questioning the king's hold on the kingdom. Many aren't convinced he's able to give the protection he once promised. Many in the north feel abandoned, and there's talk of breaking off into their own kingdom. Of course, it's all falsehood and gossip, but there's chatter. Everyone knows the north wouldn't last a year without the help of Thade, but there is agitation and fear in the air from our northern cousins. Typically I travel alone. Have done for years, but not this year. My manservant Stahl here is both companion and protector on my travels.'

'I really wish you wouldn't call me that,' said Stahl coolly.

'We're headed towards Thade for a little way, perhaps we could travel together for some time?' enquired Tubert.

'That would be lovely,' replied Marsine seeing Stahl's eyes light up. 'I must say it's such a pleasure to meet honest and friendly fellow travellers. I simply must return the favour of your kindness and offer you another drink.'

Before Tubert or Stahl could decline, Marsine lept from her seat and made her way to the bar, subtly retrieving the small packet of wolfsbane from a pocket as she walked.

'What can I get you, lovey?' asked Scraps with a smile.

'I was wondering if you might do me a kindness?'

'Go on,' said Scraps, pausing her work to look at the young woman.

'I would dearly like to get another three tankards of ale as I'm currently negotiating some business with Tubert and Stahl over there,' Marsine motioned to the two men chatting cheerfully, 'but I won't be able to pay you until tomorrow.'

'What kind of business?' asked Scraps with a raised eyebrow.

'I'd prefer not to say.'

'Who am I to stop a woman making her way in the world,' replied Scraps, giving Marsine a wink. 'Besides, I know you'll be good for it. Three ales, coming right up.'

Marsine could feel her face growing red with anticipation as Scraps poured the ales and she hid her hands under the bar, opening the small packet of wolfsbane. Her mind raced as she had only planned on talking with one man to execute her plan, but the only likely target present that night was Tubert, and he had a companion with him.

Scraps put the drinks on a tray and began to pick it up with practised ease.

'Wait,' said Marsine, 'if I'm to get a job as a server in Thade, I need the practice.' Taking the tray, she almost dropped it as she was trying to keep the packet in her hand hidden.

'Are you alright, lovey?' asked Scraps.

'Yes, fine. It's just, this is all very new to me,' said Marsine, moving the tray to one hand as she made her way carefully and slowly across the room. Tubert and Stahl seemed to be engrossed in conversation, so she took the opportunity to quickly pour the wolfsbane into one of the tankards.

Standing in front of the table, she looked at both men and weighed up her options. Tubert or Stahl. She made a snap decision to give the potion to Tubert as he was a bigger man, and would likely be able to handle the effects of it a little better. If she gave it to the younger, lighter Stahl, it could potentially kill him, whereas Tubert was more likely to pass out. For how long, she wasn't sure.

'Gentlemen, your drinks,' Marsine said politely, putting the spiked tankard in front of Tubert. As the night wore on Marsine could feel the effects of the multiple drinks they consumed and found herself laughing at Tubert's jokes, whilst becoming increasingly flirtatious with Stahl, who was more than happy to receive the attention of the stunning young woman. After yet another round of drinks, Marsine was feeling more than boisterous. She turned to Stahl and said, 'Dance with me?'

'But lady Marsine, there's no music,' he replied.

The group of men who were singing earlier had reduced in numbers, and were now relaxing and smoking their pipes. 'I can fix that,' slurred Marsine, standing up, sloshing ale from her cup as she swept her arms towards the group and shouted, 'Gentlemen, a toast for your singing and a kiss for you all should you sing me a song to dance to!'

The group of men raised their tankards and cheered, taking up the offer and singing a jig, which was a favourite in this area of the kingdom.

'I think it's time for me to retire for the night,' announced Tubert, standing along with Stahl. 'I'm afraid I'm not feeling well. I look forward to speaking with you again tomorrow, Marsine, perhaps at breakfast?'

'That would be lovely,' said Marsine, loudly throwing her hands around Tubert's broad shoulders and planting a warm kiss on his large, soft cheek.

Holding out her hand, she turned and said, 'Come, Stahl, you promised.' The next thing she knew, she was whirling and spinning in the middle of the room with Stahl and a group of other men, dancing the night away. Even Scraps put her cleaning cloth down and joined in the festivities. As the song ended, a cheer went up from the crowd, Marsine approached the group of delighted men and kissed them all on the cheek as promised.

Exhausted from their good-natured frolicking, both Marsine and Stahl collapsed in their chairs, gasping for breath and laughing with each other.

'You're quite the dancer,' breathed Stahl heavily.

'You're not so bad yourself,' replied Marsine, sliding her arm around his shoulders and whispering, 'I'm so hot, let's go outside and get some fresh air.' Before Stahl could object, Marsine grabbed his hand once again and led him outside with the shout of last drinks echoing across the room as they left.

―――――――

'The stars look beautiful tonight,' sighed Marsine as they stood in the middle of the street.

'See there,' pointed Stahl towards a constellation of particularly bright stars, 'thousands of years ago four brothers lost their wives on the same day. One of them drowned in a flood, another in a forest fire, the earth swallowed another and the other, so overcome by guilt for being the only one left alive, hung herself from a tree.'

'Oh, that's just awful!' cried Marsine, pulling Stahl closer.

'The brothers built four bonfires that very night, and their grief was so burdensome they threw themselves into them.'

'Legend says they rose to the heavens to form those four stars,' Stahl continued, pointing to the four main stars of the constellation, 'and you see that line of smaller stars running through the cross, that's their wives. It's said they shine down upon us for eternity, to remind us of the bonds of true love.'

Marsine turned and looked dreamily into Stahl's eyes, asking, 'Do you think there's a star out there for you?'

'I think she's right in front of me,' replied Stahl as he slipped his arms around her waist, pulling her closer.

Marsine's breath quickened as she closed her eyes and Stahl's warm lips pressed against hers in the cold of the night.

Hungry, they explored each other, hot tongues and cool skin under the stars.

'Perhaps we should go somewhere a little more... private,' whispered Stahl into Marsine's ear. Marsine was flushed with drink and desire.

'Let's go to my room,' she whispered, nibbling his ear.

'That sounds like a wonderful idea,' replied Stahl, taking her hand.

When they reached the top of the stairs, he turned and grasped her around the waist, making her squeal in delight. Kissing her passionately, he picked her up and stumbled down the hallway.

'This door,' exhaled Marsine breathily, shivers of excitement tingling across her skin. It took several attempts to find the keyhole, amongst giggles and shushes, from a smiling Stahl. They finally tumbled through the door and kissed with the hunger of youth who've drunk too much in troubled times.

Moving Stahl to the foot of her bed Marsine slurred, 'Wait there.' She playfully slunk to the head of the bed, pulling her dress from her shoulders as she moved. She whispered, 'Do you like what you see?'

'Keep going,' Stahl croaked, the bulge in his pants growing larger.

Marsine's fingers slid her dress to her waist, the cold air caressing her body. Turning to face Stahl, she ran her fingers across her breasts and sighed heavily in anticipation. It had been over a year since she had been with a boy.

Standing naked, she cherished the feeling of anticipation, imagining Stahl's hard body on top of her. Her nipples hardened, partly because of the cold, mostly because of the promise of a night of lovemaking.

DING!

Stahl's body crumpled to the floor like a sack of flour thrown from a cart.

'Gabrielle!' Marsine shouted.

Her little sister stood over Stahl's body breathing heavily with excitement, a dented metal pitcher in her hand.

'I think I might have hit him a little too hard.'

The plan Marsine had discussed with her sister, and subsequently completely forgotten, came flooding back to her.

'Fuck.'

13

AN INVASION OF ONE

The khan had been in his quarters for two days. He had refused food or water, and angrily shouted anyone from the room who tried to deliver sustenance.

Nuri had given him some time to stew in his misery. He tipped from a motivated, charismatic leader to a tormented shell of a man, and no one knew when he was likely to swing from one or the other. The demonstration of the black powder was a great success. The smoke hadn't even settled in the room before the pyrekhan's advisors congratulated him on his new weapon of war. But the days after were a different story altogether.

Nuri entered his quarters to see him in front of the fire, two large wounds on his chest from the jewel-encrusted dagger he held in his hand. The evil spirits pyrelanders believed inhibited the body would only leave through a blood penance after someone took a life. The consequence of this ritual was often the precursor to the khan slipping into one of his black moods.

'Khan,' said Nuri quietly, 'you wanted to see me?'

The khan rubbed ashes into his wounds, both wincing at, and revelling in the pain.

'Nuri, come in. Please, sit.' Nuri sat crossed-legged on the floor, obediently facing the khan.

'Nuri, you know I had to do it. Anteros and the girl?'

'Of course. Not only did it send a message to our advisors about the risk of treachery, it also demonstrated our powder perfectly. Two birds, one stone as they say,' replied Nuri calmly.

'Yes, that is what they say, isn't it?' sighed the khan. 'Nuri, I need to ask something of you. You're not going to like it, but I don't trust anyone else,' he continued, staring into the fire. 'Will you help me Nuri?'

'Of course, my Khan. Name it, and it will be done,' replied Nuri, bowing her head in supplication.

'I need a set of eyes in Thade. I could send one of my other advisors, but they don't have the knack of numbers like you do. I need to know what we're up against when I pitch my forces against the king and his army. I must know where to put my powder, and how many barrels we might need to break through the city walls. You're the only one I put my trust in to give me such information.'

'Strategically, I would agree, I am the right choice. But wouldn't you prefer to send somebody with a little more military knowledge? Someone like Wilsden or Rellik?'

'This is a new chapter in our history, Nuri. A new beginning for us and, gods willing, the final chapter for our enemies. This is too important a mission to put in the hands of any of those yes-men and hotheads that call themselves advisors. I need your eyes and your logic. Your calm rationale and sound judgement are what's needed at this important turning point. We are writing the scrolls of history. I can't make the mistake of giving that capacity to someone like Anteros. I put my full trust in you Nuri, do you know why?'

Nuri sat, playing over several options for an answer. When she looked at the khan, she smiled and said, 'I have some ideas.'

'You've never once asked me for anything. Everyone, every single person in my retinue, has asked me for favours, be it a position in our leadership, land in a certain pastorage or to look away when a relative or friend is convicted of a minor crime. Not once have you asked me for anything. You've always wanted what's best for the kingdom and have executed your duties without question.'

'It makes sense that should the Pyrelands prosper, so will I.'

'You see! That cold leviathan logic of yours is what I need in Thade right now,' said the khan.

'What about the Welkinpeaks? asked Nuri. 'If we try to take Thade, they will be sure to send troops through The Columns for support.'

'The Welkinpeaks are in hand. They will soon be cut off and useless. Unable to help the Frimalands below them. What I need you to do is find a way into Thade and report back to me. There's a manifest over there,' said the khan, pointing to a piece of parchment on a table. 'On its pages is the information you require. Study it well, Nuri, for you can't take it with you.' he said. 'Nuri, everything I do, I do for the Pyrelands. I know I can be cruel, but it's a necessary kindness for our kingdom's prosperity.'

'I know this, Khan, ' replied Nuri softly. 'A wolf pack will eat their own should one of them die whilst hunting. For the betterment of the pack, they never waste an opportunity. Or so I've heard. I've only ever seen a wolf in tapestries and pictures.'

'You may chance upon one on your way to Thade,' replied the khan.

'That would be an opportunity I would prefer to experience from a distance.'

The pyrekahn smiled, then stood as if the pain from a thousand injuries pierced his bones at once. 'Ready your things, Nuri. I need you to leave tomorrow and make good time to Thade.'

'On your order, my Khan.'

Nuri left the room, her mind reeling. Shots of concern blasted their way through her psyche, wrapped in the electricity of excitement and adventure. Was this punishment, or opportunity? Was this mission folly or fortune? She had never left the Pyrelands. She'd been by the khan's side since coming into his service as a teenager. It was exhilarating and frightening to think that she would be in an enemy city preparing for her countrymen to invade in a little over a moon cycle.

———

The tundra's dry grass bent and cracked beneath Nuri's feet as the cold, thin air turned breath to clouds of mist. She had travelled two full days to arrive at the great expanse's edge, which divided the Pyrelands from the Firmalands. Even though it was noon, the cold penetrated her leather clothing through any nook or cranny it could weasel its way through.

She stood before a large sandsailer, designed to use the ever-present winds of the tundra to navigate the hundreds of miles to their sworn enemy's borders. On the horizon, she could see several craft making their way to the Firmalands, or returning home from successful raids.

Scattered against the edge of the tundra, dozens of other sand-silers waited, ready to transport people back and forth across the frozen expanse. Some were in different phases of repair or disarray, their owners preparing for the next trip or fixing broken masts and torn sails. The wood and bone wheels made criss-cross patterns in the sand and ice, slicing scars in this remote and barren landscape.

Lines of fresh captives, stolen from the Firmalands, were being herded towards holding stations, built close to the edge of the tundra. Little more than makeshift cages made of wood and animal bones, they didn't need to be strong, there was nowhere else to go, and the welltakers attached to the backs of their necks kept them compliant.

'You Nuri?' asked a tall, wiry man with sun-darkened skin. His hair was entwined with ribbon and leather and tied back into a messy ponytail. A piece of flat bone with a thin horizontal cut through the middle hung from his neck.

'Yes,' she replied.

'Good, put these on. You're going to need them. We leave soon.' The man tossed her a bundle and walked back towards the sandsailer.

'Wait,' she called, 'what are these?'

'First time?'

'Yes.'

'This here's your headscarf. Wrap it around your head so the ice and sand don't cut your face to pieces. Those,' he said, pointing to the pair of goggles made from bone, 'are your eyekeepers. If you wish to protect your eyes, I suggest you put them on and get used to them until we're on the other side. I'm your pilot, the name's Omar. Listen to me, and you'll get across in one piece. Go against my orders, and you'll be off my ship, pyrekhan's advisor or not. Do that, and we'll get along fine. Got it?'

'On your orders, Omar,' Nuri nodded her head.

'Good. We're going to get along just fine.'

After loading cargo, weapons and people, Omar's ship was ready to set sail across the vast expanse of the tundra. Rolling slowly, Omar and his crew wrestled the lumbering ship into the strong winds, leaving a trail of dust and ice with rainbows glinting through the light of their wake.

Limited by the tiny slit in the bone headpiece, Nuri could see just enough to view where they were going. As they wheeled onto the tundra proper and opened the mainsails, she had to hold onto the side rails as they flew across the hard, frozen ground.

'How long?' shouted Nuri above the howling wind.

'With this gale, five, perhaps six hours,' shouted Omar. 'There's room below deck if you want to get out of the wind.'

'I'm fine here,' came her shouted reply.

She'd never moved so fast, and the cold winds were a pleasurable change to the hot, humid climate of the Pyrelands. Travelling at this speed was exhilarating. The wind whipped at her scarf and bit at her skin through her clothing. She could smell the fresh cold winds, the lingering hint of freedom and adventure, a heady perfume indeed. She let out an involuntary howl of pure joy and excitement. Omar smiled, keeping his hand on the tiller and tacking his vehicle west.

After spending an hour on the craft's top deck, the landscape became repetitive and the cold insufferable, so she decided to go below. Making her way down the stairs and through a wooden hatch, someone shouted, 'Close that damn hatch. You're letting all the cold air in!'

Nuri pulled the hatch shut and walked cautiously into the darkened room, careful not to step on the bodies strewn over the floor of the small hold. In the centre of the room burned a small lantern, swinging wildly from a cross-beam. The light it threw swayed and moved as the sandsailer trundled and bumped over the tundra.

Sitting on one of the provided mats, Nuri took off her eyekeepers and blew into her hands, rubbing them together. Looking carefully around the small room she realised no one was talking or even looking at each other. Some sat with their heads down, away in their thoughts. Others slept.

Everyone in the hold was there for their own goals, and none seemed interested in finding out from the other their reason for being there. *Good*, Nuri thought to herself, *anonymity will be a warm cloak I shall wrap myself in when I arrive. It's better no-one knows who I am or what plans I have.*

The bump and groove of the craft had a mesmerising effect, and Nuri drifted off, head bobbing up and down to the motion of the landscape and the wheels' rhythm. Deciding it would be wise to get some sleep, she laid on her sleeping mat and quickly dozed into half-slumber.

———

Nuri's eyes flew open as she was mid-air. Arms and screams tumbled around the hold like rocks down a mountain as the ship lurched sideways, sliding and grinding to a screeching halt in the sand.

Omar opened the hatch and yelled, 'Everybody out. We've got a problem.'

'Damn right, we've got a fucking problem. You nearly killed us,' yelled a cloaked figure, extricating himself from a mass of bodies.

'Shut your damn mouth, or you can stay out here as a meal for the desert rats. I said everybody out.'

As she climbed out of the stricken ship into the light of the late afternoon suns, Nuri looked over the vast expanse of nothing which gave a view of the horizon in all directions. She moved towards Omar and his crew, surveying the damage on their craft.

'What happened?' she asked.

'I had to swerve to avoid hitting that fucking cloudcutter over there,' he replied, pointing at a wooden boat, broken in half a few hundred feet behind them.

Nuri looked at the strange craft and realised people were exiting from the bowels of the ship.

'Damn thing came from behind while the sun was in my eyes. Didn't see it till it crashed right in front of us, and now I've snapped a fucking axle,' he growled, kicking the side of his craft.

'We're going nowhere fast, folks,' he shouted to the group. 'Make camp and get a fire going. It's going to get very cold, very quick. There's spare wood in the hold, and if any of you bastards even think about using my ship for firewood, I'll slit your throat!' Omar gave his crew orders whilst several passengers worked together to dig a pit and light a fire.

'Those are cloudcutters from the Welkinpeaks,' stated Nuri to another passenger, as they scraped and dug a pit with their hands.

The young woman beside Nuri replied, 'Aye. From what I've heard, they're coming from Roda Codex. Seems we've been rounding people up into them and piloting them down to the tundra. When I say piloting them, it's more a controlled crash. My brother's a sand-sailer captain, and he's been ferrying prisoners back and forth for the past couple of weeks,' she said when she saw questions in Nuri's eyes. 'The name's Foni,' she said, extending her dirty hand.

'Nuri.'

'Greetings, Nuri,' she said, shaking hands. 'How did you come to find yourself out here? You on a raid?'

'Something like that,' said Nuri, keeping her answer deliberately vague.

'From what I've heard,' continued Foni, lowering her voice, 'the khan's building an army to take over the Firmalands. Got some new weapon or some such thing. All these extra raids and pickups from the middle of the tundra. You should see the lines of prisoners to-ing and fro-ing.'

'Where do you hear such things?' asked Nuri softly.

'Oh, you know, places,' she replied.

'Places? Like docks and bars?'

'Something like that,' replied the girl.

Nuri couldn't help but smile at her vague answer being used back against her.

A few hundred feet away, another cloudcutter crashed into the ground with a sickening crunch. Ice, wood and metal combined in a cacophany of mayhem as the cloudcutter carved a deep gouge into the earth, a wave of dirt and ice rolling and folding at the front as it ground slowly to a halt. The screams of desperate humanity trying to escape the mangled ruins of the ship sent a shiver down Nuri's back. Bodies lay on the ground, some dead from the force of the impact, others rising to their unstable feet. Nuri looked up to see the sky filled with more ships, some several hundred feet from the ground, others tiny specks above.

'There's hundreds of them,' exclaimed Nuri in surprise.

'Yep,' replied Foni looking at the sky, 'and I've heard it's been like this for weeks. The sandsailer pilots can hardly keep up with the numbers.'

Nuri realised why the khan didn't need to invade the Welkinpeaks. He was bringing the inhabitants of the Welkinpeaks to him. Not only that, in a dual insult to his enemies, he was using their own cloudcutters to do it.

He was using spellcasters to force villagers into these crafts and having them piloted to the tundra for transfer to work camps.

'Khan, you ingenious shrewd,' Nuri thought to herself, as she admired his bold plan taking shape throughout the skies of the tundra before her.

'The axle's firewood and the spare's broken too,' Omar called to the group. 'We're going to have to wait for another crew to wheel past. Shouldn't be too long, perhaps an hour or two. In the meantime, let's get that fire going and watch out for these bloody float boats dropping everywhere.'

Over the next few hours, the group huddled around the small fire as Omar periodically climbed atop his stricken ship to scrutinise the tundra with his eyeglass, only to swear and climb down again.

Finally, he came to the fire and announced he'd seen a trail reflecting in the late afternoon suns. Hopefully, it would be one of his crews with a spare axle.

Everyone huddled around the fire, feeling the drop in temperature as the suns set. They all watched the icy dust cloud grow bigger until a small craft finally took shape.

Omar stood on the outskirts and welcomed the craft into their camp. It was tiny and looked as though it would only fit two people in it, three at a pinch. The hull was stuck together by a combination of detailed woodwork and frugally placed tar seals making it sleek and fast. The pilot exited his craft and greeted Omar, talking with him for a short time before they both came over to the fire. The pilot was young with dark hair and a permanent scowl on his face.

Squatting, he blew and rubbed his gloved fingers together, letting the heat from the fire seep into his digits.

'This here's Pera,' said Omar, as Pera looked around the group huddled by the fire and simply nodded. 'He's not in my crew but says there are two of my guys a few hours behind him, so we shouldn't have too much longer to wait for that spare axle. Once we fix it, we can be on our way again.'

'How come you're out here by yourself?' a young man from the group asked.

'Got a pickup,' replied Pera.

'A pickup, at night? That's unusual, isn't it?'

'That's none of your fucking business, is it?' replied Pera with a snarl.

'Ok,' replied the young man in supplication, 'was just trying to be friendly.'

'How bout you try keeping your mouth shut,' said Pera, looking at the young man with a dead stare, causing him to find his lap incredibly fascinating.

'Pera isn't much of a talker,' said Omar, 'and it's mighty cold on the tundra in the evenings. Cold enough to put a chill into even the most cheerful, so how about we all enjoy the fire and a swig of wine.'

Omar produced a small skin of wine from a bag he wore around his shoulder and handed it to Pera. 'Take a swig to help take the chill from your bones.'

'And maybe your temperament,' mumbled the young man.

Pera looked at him with fierce eyes, 'What did you say?'

'N... nothing,' he managed to squeak out as he got up, finding somewhere else to be.

The group sat in uncomfortable silence as Pera drank deeply from the wineskin, almost emptying it. Omar looked as though he was about to stop him, but then thought better of it.

'Any of you have food?' asked Omar, looking around at the group.

The group all looked at each other, no one wanting to speak first.

'What about big-mouth over there?' Pera asked, pointing a knife he suddenly produced from the folds in his jacket. 'Does he have some food? Perhaps I'll have a little chat with him.'

'Wait,' said Nuri, as Pera stood, flipping the knife menacingly in his hands. 'I have some loufbread in my bag. I'll get some for you. It's inside.'

'That stuff tastes like the insides of a rotten dog,' spat Pera, 'but it's better than nothing, I guess. What are you waiting for? Go. Get it,' he snapped, prompting Nuri to climb into the overturned craft and reluctantly find her bag.

She returned and held out the cloth-wrapped bread. Pera snatched it from her hand without thanks and started eating it and drinking from the wineskin once again.

Everyone was uncomfortable and quiet in the presence of such a man. He had a sharp intensity like a coiled spring, ready to snap at any second. After eating his fill and throwing the leftover bread in the fire, Pera stood and pointed at Nuri.

'You, get your stuff, we're leaving.'

'Me?' said Nuri in surprise. 'I'm not going anywhere with you.'

Pera sighed and turned to the captain, 'Omar, tell your serf here to move it.'

'I'm no serf,' Nuri spat.

Omar took her by the arm and led her away from the fire. Speaking quietly, he said, 'I've been made aware of the pace in which the khan wishes you to accomplish your mission. Should it be found that I didn't do everything in my power to expedite you across this tundra, well... you know how the khan gets. Even with a new axle, it's going to take hours to fit. Nuri, I know Pera is an unsavoury type, but it's in yours and the Pyrelands' best interests that we get you across the tundra and into the kingdom as quickly as possible, and he's your best chance at doing that.'

Thinking for a moment, Nuri replied, 'What you say makes sense, but I feel uneasy about... him,' she said, flicking her head towards Pera, now picking his teeth with his knife.

'I've often found that given the right motivation, men like Pera stick to the plan,' said Omar with a smile as he rolled a gold coin across his knuckles.

Before Nuri had a chance to object, Omar shouted, 'Pera! Your cargo is ready.'

She found herself herded into the small sandsailer with Pera at the tiller and was soon flying across the tundra at surprising speed. For all of Pera's unpleasantness, he was an excellent pilot. They spoke not a word throughout the entire trip except for Pera saying, 'Quiet, we're close,' when the Ochota mountains loomed into view, signalling the start of the Firmalands.

There was a distinct change in temperature as the plain's winds died down, and the sandsailer slowed to a fast walking pace. Pera tacked his way back and forth across the ice and sand to pull up near an outcrop of rocks and, with expert grace, slid his craft between two large trees and dropped sail.

Pera tapped Nuri on the shoulder and put a finger to his lips. He stabbed his finger at a point of light half a mile away, obviously a guard fire of some sort.

Nuri's heart skipped a beat as she realised this was the most danger she'd ever experienced. Should she be caught smuggling her way into the kingdom on the outskirts of the Firmalands, it would be challenging to justify why she was there.

'Follow me and don't make a fucking sound, or I'll slit your throat and leave you for the wolves,' whispered Pera, his stale breath hovering in the air.

Nuri carefully extricated herself from the craft and shouldered her bag, being careful to make as little sound as possible. She'd made it across the tundra and was at the doorstep of the kingdom. The khan and his advisors had gone through many different scenarios with her before leaving, and she was confident in her mission.

Pera pointed to a barely visible track in the dim light of dusk and motioned for Nuri to walk.

After a few steps, she turned to notice Pera following her. He leaned in close and whispered, 'I'll take you to the first ridge. After that, you're on your own, serf.'

Nuri was glad when they finally made it there an hour later.

'Here's where we part ways, serf,' growled Pera.

'Thank you,' replied Nuri. 'I wish you well on your return journey.'

'What did you fucking say?' snarled Pera, moving closer to Nuri and standing over her.

'I... I said I wish you well,' stammered Nuri, turning to leave. Before her second step touched earth, an iron grip wrapped itself around her arm, making her wince. Spun roughly, she faced Pera, her heart beating a horse's gallop.

'You forget something?' smiled Pera, showing teeth that even in the moonlight were discoloured. 'My payment.'

'Payment?' stammered Nuri. 'Of course. A round of gold is hardly fair recompense. I have an additional silver piece I'm happy to pay.'

'I don't want your money,' laughed Pera, his hand still firmly grasped on her arm, his other slid between her legs. Nuri closed her eyes tightly and tried to move his hand away.

'I want your honeypot. I wondered since I saw you what was down there,' he sniggered, 'thought you might be a boy. It don't matter to me. I like 'em both.'

'Please,' whispered Nuri, a hint of desperation in her voice. 'Let me go. You're hurting me.'

'That's where you're wrong, serf,' said Pera, head tilted to the side, a maniacal smile across his face. 'This is hurting you.'

Pera swept Nuri's feet from under her with the practised ease of someone who occasions violence with impunity. Her face slammed into the ground with such force, her teeth rattled.

Gasping for breath, she tried to get up, but Pera's heavy, muscular body straddled hers. His hands made strong from years at the tiller, grabbed a clutch of hair and rammed her face into the dirt again, bringing tears of pain to her eyes. She tried gasping for breath but inhaled, choking dust and dirt instead.

'That's it, that's it,' Pera said, laughing. 'I like it when they struggle.'

Nuri could feel a hand under her garments, grasping and reaching between her legs. Rough fingers poked at her, entering her as she let out a cry and struggled even more.

'Oh,' said Pera in surprise, 'you're liking this, are you? Well then, let's keep going.'

'No!' shouted Nuri, bucking, writhing and trying to escape. She received dusty lungs and gritty eyes for her efforts.

'Oh, yes,' laughed Pera, 'it's like riding a feisty mare.'

Fists rained down on her head and face as she struggled and kicked to escape the iron grip of her captor. After several minutes, the fight slowly ebbed out of her. She was spent.

'You finished now?' asked Pera with contempt.

Nuri started to sob.

Leaning in close, he whispered in her ear, 'Good. Cause I'm just getting started.'

14

UP INTO THE UNDERGROUND

'Boomdust,' explained Deadsun, putting a small bowl of the black powder in front of Bailur and the king, 'is what killed our men yesterday.'

'I fail to see how this powder can make such a mess of things?' replied Bailur, stroking his chin.

'Watch this.' Deadsun took a readily prepared piece of parchment that had been folded and filled with boomdust. Cylindrical in shape and sealed with flammable tar, it had a wick of fireweed rolled in pitch sticking from its end.

Deadsun carved a hole into a cabbage with his dagger and placed the explosive package into the vegetable's guts, leaving the wick to stick out. Placing the head of tightly packed leaves into the corner of the room, he nodded at one of his men who took a taper from the fireplace and lit it, before hustling away with superstitious dread.

A loud crack filled the room along with particles of cabbage, which flew ten feet in every direction. The acrid smell of sulphur mixed with cabbage hung in the air as smoke and surprise dissipated across the room.

'The short man we caught had perhaps three times as much

boomdust in his necklace, and he managed to remove the head from his body, kill two of my men and put Greeven in the infirmary. Given enough of this stuff, who knows what the pyrekahn can do.'

'And this man, this short man, said that Roda Codex would be the first to go?' asked the king, pacing around the room.

'Isolate and erupt were his exact words,' answered Deadsun.

'If Roda Codex is cut off, we're in the position of facing the pyrekahn alone. Given this new weapon, the favour could very well be tipped in his balance,' said Bailur.

'Dammit,' swore the king, slamming the table with his fist. 'Well-takers, traitors and boomdust invading my city, causing harm to my people. I won't have it. Deadsun?'

'Yes, my Lord?'

'You are to go to Roda Codex. I'm well aware this short man could be playing us for dunces and sending us on a fool's errand, but I need to make sure the pyrekahn cannot isolate us from our brethren in the highskies.'

'Of course,' replied Deadsun, standing in preparation to leave.

'Take what men and materials you need. Leave nothing to chance,' said the king. He looked more worried than Deadsun could remember.

'Thank you, my Lord. On your leave?'

'Go. And safe travels,' replied the king.

Deadsun made hasty but logical preparations to leave that day. Greeven was still in the infirmary and wasn't fit for travel, so he chose to travel alone. Unhindered and unidentified, he could push his journey's pace and not slow his momentum for extra men or supplies. He briefed runners who ran ahead to prepare extra horses as he gathered belongings needed for a hard three-day ride to the bottom of The Columns. Shouldering his pack, Deadsun said goodbye to his captains and visited the infirmary on his way to the royal stables.

'I'm to go to Roda Codex,' said Deadsun to a bandaged and bruised Greeven.

'I've heard,' replied Greeven, shifting his weight to make himself more comfortable.

'Word travels fast. I'm sorry you won't be with me,' said Deadsun, placing his hand on Greeven's shoulder.

'Bah,' replied Greeven playfully, slapping his hand away. 'I was getting sick of you anyway. Who knows, I might even have your job before you get back.'

'Watch over the men and keep the city safe, brother,' said Deadsun, giving Greeven a nod as he stood in the doorway.

'Always. Be careful, brother. There are ill tidings on the wind.'

———

Three days of hard riding from suns up to suns down started to take its toll on Deadsun's body. He made the ride in record time, but his thighs and back were not happy about it. By the final day, his horse had a way of jolting his bones the way siege engines slam rocks into castle walls.

By mid-morning of the third day, The Columns loomed in the distance. Clawing into the sky, they shimmered large, as if made by gods. He stopped a mile before the entrance to The Columns and arranged his belongings in the satchel he wore. Pulling his cloak around his shoulders, he shivered even though it was only mid-morning.

The Columns stretched so high into the clouds they had blocked the sun for the past several miles. Waterfalls and streams cascaded from the vertical rock onto the Firmalands below, cooling the air and soaking everything within a mile of the mountainous structure. Everything around Deadsun glistened and shone like stars had fallen into the rock itself and rainbows refracted the suns light far above, making this a truly magical place.

Someone had laid crushed stone on the path, so the mist didn't make the pathway slippery, and it crunched below his horse's feet as he walked his mare to an opening in the canyon before him. Home to a glacier tens of thousands of years ago, the canyon's walls were smooth and high, making the crunch of hoof on gravel echo through the gorge.

Two men stood at the entrance of an impressive cave entrance carved into the side of the canyon. Their red, silken robes glistened in the misty light giving the appearance of movement where there was none. Their lithe, muscular bodies and weapons told Deadsun these were men who knew how to handle themselves.

These were the Archimedes, descendants of the first men who risked their lives to discover a way through The Columns thousands of years before. Their role was held sacred by both the Firmalands and the Welkinpeaks.

The Columns was the one place in the kingdom where rank, reputation or royalty made no difference. The Archimedes did not acknowledge class or blood. The order you entered was the order you kept. For a thousand years, they had dedicated their lives to ferry goods, merchants, soldiers, commoners and royalty through the caves and tunnels.

'Greetings,' said the man on the left as Deadsun approached. 'You wish to travel The Columns?'

'Yes,' Deadsun replied.

'The horse too?'

'No, just me. Someone will arrive within the day to take the horse. Here are the papers,' said Deadsun, unbuckling his bag and fishing out a scroll from it's depths.

'It's a pleasure to have you travel with us again, Commander. If you'd follow me, Meshrano here will take your horse,' he said, motioning to the other guard. The man to the right took the reins with capable hands and led the brown mare towards a stable tucked into a corner of the rock not far away.

'I am Platicevo. I will be your guide, Commander. I assume you have payment?'

'Yes, right here,' Deadsun replied, retrieving two gold coins from his pouch.

'Excellent. This way, please,' Platicevo replied, leading Deadsun into a room where three other people sat waiting. The room had a brazier burning in the corner, warming it to a pleasant temperature. The air filled with the smell of sweet tea, which bubbled away happily in a kettle hanging over the flames.

'Tea?' asked Platicevo of Deadsun.

'No, thanks. When do we leave?'

'Now we have five in our group, we can leave very soon.'

'Excellent,' replied Deadsun. 'I must get to Roda Codex as quickly as possible.'

'The Columns can be a highly perilous place for those that rush,' replied Platicevo. 'Please, take a seat. I will take only a little of your time before we depart.'

Deadsun sat, putting his satchel on the floor beside him and looked around the room. Seated next to him was a young man in his twenties who looked the part of a courtier or the son of some wealthy merchant. Next to him was a grim-faced dwarf, impatient looking, drumming short, fat fingers upon his knees.

In the corner was a woman in her mid thirties, with dark hair and a cape of green felt. From the look of her exquisitely made bow and quiver laid next to her bag, she was a huntress, and a good one. A bow that well made cost several month's wages. She looked at Deadsun with intelligent chocolate eyes. Hers was not a traditional beauty that many in the kingdom would fall for, like the court's princesses and royal ladies. This girl had confidence, and an air of resilience about her, like she knew how to handle herself in any situation that may arise.

'Now that we have our numbers, we can soon make our way to the Hoistpens, but before we do a few items that require your attention, please,' started Platicevo, his speech coming out in a well-rehearsed manner.

'Some of you have travelled The Columns before, others have not. Regardless of your familiarity with our ways and procedures, no one is to move away from the path. To do so will surely see you lost and then quickly, dead. Do not leave the group for any reason, is that clear?'

Everyone in the room nodded and the dwarf snorted, 'Spare us these proclamations, Archimedian, we are hardly tied to our mother's apron strings. Let us be on our way.'

'We travel for roughly ten hours, ensuring everyone can keep up with the pace,' continued Platicevo, emphasising the last few words as he looked at the dwarf, who humphed in disgust. He mumbled under his breath that his stature was no reflection of his pace. 'The slower you walk, the longer it takes. It makes no difference to me, but if you reduce our pace and keep other groups waiting, we are not responsible for what they may say or do. Let us leave.'

'Finally!' grumbled the dwarf, jumping from his chair and shouldered a bag almost as large as him. 'My kind have been living and travelling underground for eons before the Archimedians thought it fashionable.'

Deadsun and the huntress were the last to move, and they both paused when they reached the exit at the same time. 'He seems a jolly fellow,' said Deadsun, motioning his hand towards the dwarf.

'If you don't plan to, I might just shoot him if I have to listen to his moaning for the whole journey,' said the huntress dryly.

Deadsun chuckled, 'That would be a waste of a good arrow.'

'It would be, wouldn't it? I'm Kestral,' replied the huntress with a smile, holding out her slender hand.

'Deadsun,' he replied, taking her fingers and kissing them. 'A pleasure. After you.'

Kestral gave a mock curtsy and walked through the door as she and Deadsun caught up with the group in front of them. They walked towards the back of the large cavern that acted as a staging area for entry into The Columns. Platicevo stood at the entrance, arms crossed, waiting for them to catch up.

'Here, we enter into the first portal. This section of The Columns is a five hour march. Once we reach the first hoistpen, we'll be able to rest for a short period. There will be food and water at the first stop. If you feel like talking or asking questions, please don't.'

Platicevo set off at a brisk pace through the doorway and into the natural corridor. Deadsun ran his hands along the walls of the rock, feeling their smoothness. The small torches they carried made the passage unusually warm, and the earthy tinge of ancient rock filled the air. Now and then, a small shaft of light would filter through a crack or hole in the top of the cave, lighting up the side of the tunnel wall, but more often than not, the group walked in perpetual darkness except for the meagre light their torches threw.

For the next few hours the group walked in relative silence with the occasional cough or sneeze echoing through the caves. They were often forced to stop and duck into a side corridor as several Acrhemidians trundled past with carts of goods being hauled back and forth along the pathways. Platicevo explained that a large portion of their role was transporting goods through The Columns as well as people.

'Goods are easy,' he explained to the small group, 'they don't talk back or need toilet stops. That's why people cost more to guide.'

'I should have hidden inside a barrel,' gruffed the dwarf.

'It's not too late to put you in one,' replied Kestral.

'Enough,' said Platicevo. 'I will not have bickering in my group.'

Kestral looked at Deadsun and rolled her eyes, giving him a reason to smile and like her even more.

After hours of marching, the group finally made it to the first staging area, where hot tea and a fresh hock of meat was kept warm near the small fire. A group of young Archmedians prepared the beginnings of a meal for the small group.

'We rest here until we get word from above,' stated Platicevo.

'Do we know how long that will be?' asked Deadsun.

'We do our best to keep a tight schedule, but as you can appreciate, when dealing with people, timeframes can become elongated. I'm expecting a signal within the hour, so I suggest you eat up. We had a cart of meat arrive this morning, so it's fresh.'

'Speaking of carts,' asked the young man dressed like a wealthy merchant's son, 'what's in those carts we keep seeing being ferried back and forth along the paths?'

'All sorts of goods,' replied Platicevo. 'Weapons, gold, rare herbs and the like. We've even had a particularly large shipment of wine come through in the past several weeks. Thousands of barrels, in fact.'

'Wine!' exclaimed the dwarf. 'I'll take a cup.'

'There is to be no drinking whilst travelling through The Columns. We all need our wits about us. The last thing I need is to go galavanting after a drunken dwarf through tunnels untravelled,' scolded Platicevo.

'Bah,' he replied irritably, 'this day just keeps getting worse.'

Kestral returned with a plate of freshly carved meat and sat next to Deadsun. 'Eat something,' she said. 'You never know when they will get the signal for us to go.'

'How do they know when another group is above us?' asked the young merchant's son.

'First time, huh? They use a series of flags and pulleys. See over there?' Kestral pointed to a section of cloth attached to a wooden lever at the side of a large gate. 'When that flag waves, it means the crew above are ready. Then, we're all loaded into the hoistpens, and one of the servants pulls the lever to let the crew above know we're ready to go.'

'How do they get the hoistpens to move up and down?' asked the young man, intrigued with the system.

'Ah,' replied Kestral. 'Here's where the genius of the Acrhemedians comes in. They use natural waterfalls and a series of waterwheels.'

'And simple maths,' added Platicevo, walking towards the group. 'Where possible we organise our groups, so there's always more people above than below. This way, the heavier hoistpens lift the lighter ones. If we can't get the numbers right, we raise the cages using water wheels and counterweights.'

'Ingenious,' said the young man, surprised at the sophisticated engineering required to make such a system not only work, but be as safe and reliable as the Archemedians had made it.

'It's a simple system,' replied Platicevo, 'as many of the best solutions always are, like our series of flags here, they...'

Just at that moment, the flag on the end of the lever waved up and down. 'Ah, I see they're ready for us.' Platicevo turned to the group and said, 'It's now time to move into the hoistpens. Please gather your things and follow me.'

The group stuffed the remainder of their meals into their mouths and picked up their belongings, moving towards the cages as a sizable wooden gate was slid aside, wheels greased with animal fat.

The ride up to the next level of The Columns was smooth and slow. It took roughly an hour for the group to travel several hundred feet straight up into the belly of The Columns. Finally, they came to a stop and someone opened a similar wooden gate, allowing them to walk into a mirror image of the room below.

'Follow me,' snapped Platicevo as the group stepped out of the hoistpen. 'We've no time to dilly dally. We've much walking ahead of us.'

The next few hours lumbered past slowly as the group trudged through more caves and pathways, smaller, darker and hotter than the first level of The Columns. Finally, they arrived at the staging area for the next set of hoistpens after navigating hundreds of barrels stored along the pathway. A worker in red robes made his way towards Platicevo and quietly pointed to another plainclothes man seated in the corner whilst the group dropped their bags and found a place to rest.

'More wine?' asked the dwarf, pointing to the barrels after making himself comfortable.

'Yes,' replied Platicevo, 'and none of it is for you.'

'Surely the judge or rich captain ordering this won't miss one cup from a barrel,' jibed the dwarf as he popped the large cork from the top of a barrel.

'One drop, and you'll find yourself banned from travelling The Columns for life,' barked Platicevo. 'The merchant that sent this shipment also sent men to protect it, and one of them is sitting right over there,' he hissed, pointing to the man in the corner who was staring at the dwarf.

'Fine,' said the dwarf in supplication, 'if I can't drink it, a sniff will have to do.'

The man sitting in the corner stared at the dwarf with contempt painting his features.

'I don't like him,' whispered Kestral into Deadsun's ear. 'He has a hostile demeanour.'

'You picked up on that too,' replied Deadsun quietly.

'Hey,' said the dwarf loudly, 'this isn't bloody wine.'

Deadsun turned to see the dwarf pouring a handful of black powder back into the opening of the barrel. At that moment, the man sitting in the corner leapt up and paced quickly towards the dwarf. Previously hidden by the man's cloak, Deadsun noticed the copper necklace that seemed a little too large around his neck.

It took a second for Deadsun to register what he was seeing. The barrels of black powder, the man with the necklace. It struck him he'd seen the very same necklace on the short man they captured in Thade days previously.

His head swam as he tried to comprehend the explosive power of the barrels he saw before him. His body tensed and coiled like a spring as the man with the copper necklace approached. He struck the man with the necklace in his temple without thinking, dropping him to the floor like a sack of rocks.

It was at this exact moment that all hell broke loose.

15

JOURNEY TO THE DARKNESS
OF FREEDOM

'I'm sorry, lads, that ship left at noon today. They're a few hundred miles away by now with the north winds blowing this strong,' answered the bored-looking guard at the skydocks.

'Dammit,' swore Abreeth. 'Dammit, and curse all the old gods,' he shouted, kicking at nets sitting next to the wooden dock.

'Are there any other craft leaving in that direction?' asked Dwin hopefully.

'Not a chance,' replied the guard, 'that was the last of 'em. They said they were headed south. Had the strangest looking floatboat I've ever seen. Had wings on it. Everyone else has either left to hunt or check on family. There's something strange going on. Look around, lads. Never seen anything like it in fifteen years of working the docks. There's not a craft to be seen.'

The city's skydocks could hold over a thousand skycraft, but now, not even a one-person scull graced the berths.

'Thank you. We should be getting back,' answered Abreeth sadly.

The walk to the tavern was long and sombre. Both lads questioned why Borchin would want to venture south into the unpredictable and harsh Spurlands. Sure, there was a sky full of hunting to be had, but the pirates in the south were infamous in their savagery.

'He's headed to certain death in the Spurlands,' lamented Dwin.

'Have you ever known your uncle not to have a plan for everything he does?' asked Abreeth.

'No, but that doesn't mean he…'

'He's going to be fine, and besides, there's nothing to do about it now. We have to decide if we're going to hang around the docks in the hope some other craft arrives and then try to convince them to take us south, or go to Thade to find your father.'

Walking through the doors of the inn, Abreeth and Dwin found most of the patrons had left.

'I was wondering if you were going to come back?' said the barkeep. 'Here, I saved some stew for you.' He leaned in close as the two lads made their way to the bar and whispered, 'Even topped it up with some fresh stuff from the pot, but don't tell chef misery guts, OK?'

'Thank you. You didn't have to do that,' replied Abreeth.

'I know. But I can tell honest lads when I see them. Did you find who you were looking for?'

'No,' replied Dwin, 'he left at lunchtime today.'

'Shame,' replied the barkeeper, giving them both a tankard of water to wash down their stew. 'Family's the only people you can trust in this crazy city.'

Both Dwin and Abreeth ate their stew, even though they didn't feel hungry, thanked the barkeep for his kindness and made their way languidly up the stairs to their rooms.

The day's travel, as well as their expedition across the city had caught up with both of them. When they opened their door, Murphy leapt onto Dwin and licked his face, tail wagging.

'I've missed you too, boy,' said Dwin, giving him scratches behind the ears along with a handful of meat and a chunk of bread he'd saved from his meal.

Exhausted, they both fell into their beds.

———

'What's that noise?' groaned Dwin the next morning, yawning and pulling the blanket over his head.

'It sounds like a culling,' answered Abreeth, rubbing his eyes in the morning light that now streamed through the window.

'What in the old god's name is a culling, and why is it so loud?' complained Dwin through another half yawn.

Abreeth had to remind himself that Dwin had never been to a city, so the sound of thousands of people walking the streets in a state of excitement would be loud and unusual to him.

'You've never been told of a culling?' asked Abreeth.

'No. But I get the feeling I'm about to be.'

'Remember on the way into the city we saw that large spire in the middle of town?' asked Abreeth, propping himself up on his elbow.

'The one with all the wires attached to it?' Dwin replied.

'Yes, that one. Those wires have the spurs of spurworms attached to them at three feet intervals. Thousands of them. They keep their venom forever. Some spurs were put up hundreds of years ago and are still as lethal today as they were the day they were attached. They were originally put up to stop cloudcutters from the south attacking the city, but since the treaty of Setipar, the Spurlands haven't bothered us for at least a few decades. So now, when the prisons get too full, the city gathers a group of criminals in the city centre, mostly murderers, rapists and such, tie their feet and hands to stocks made of lightwood and let them float skywards. If they make it past the defences without being killed by a spur, they're pardoned.'

'How many make it through?' asked Dwin, his eyes wide with ghoulish curiosity.

'Almost none,' answered Abreeth. 'I've seen hundreds of cullings, and only three people have ever escaped the spurs.'

Dwin looked disappointed, 'I was hoping more people would get away.'

'Even if they get through, they have to hope someone in a cloudcutter is there to pick them up. Otherwise, they get swept away by the northwinds and end up as spurworm food or worse, dinner for a pyredrake.'

Dwin put his head back on his pillow and said, 'Imagine being eaten by a pyredrake. That would be horrible!'

'No less terrible than a spurworm!'

Abreeth rested for a moment collecting his thoughts and rubbing the wound on his shoulder.

'Dwin, I think we should head for The Columns today. I can't see any use in waiting around hoping another cloudcutter turns up at the skydocks. Even if they do, convincing them to take us south will be almost impossible.'

'I know. I just hate leaving the city, knowing we were so close to catching up with Uncle Borchin,' replied Dwin with a heavy sigh.

'Me too. I couldn't sleep last night thinking about it. The Columns are our best choice, even if our hearts tell us to wait and try to go south. Besides, it's what your mother asked us to do.' Abreeth was hoping the mention of Dwin's mother would help convince him.

'I miss her, Abe.'

'Me too Dwin. Come, let's get some breakfast.'

———

Both lads prepared for the journey through the city. Abreeth knew it would be slow going with a culling happening, so warned Dwin to keep a hand on his dagger and a keen eye on his coin purse now it was a little fuller from the sale of the donkeys. With their belongings in packs heaved onto their shoulders, the two young men and the large hound walked into the street. Crackling energy filled the air, with people rushing in the same direction towards the city centre.

'We should avoid going anywhere near the centre of town,' said Abreeth, as they were elbowed and nudged by the crowd.

'I wouldn't mind seeing what's going on,' said Dwin. 'Everyone seems to be pretty excited.'

'They do, don't they?'

'Excuse me,' Abreeth asked an older man, 'is there something other than a culling going on today?'

'The duke's being tried for treason. They found him sharing secrets with savages from the Pyrelands. Trying to broker some kind of peace deal apparently.'

'The duke!' exclaimed Abreeth. 'Treason?'

'That's what I said, isn't it?' replied the older man. 'If you want a good spot, you'd better get moving. Can't remember the last time this many people came out to watch a culling,' he said over his shoulder, picking up his shuffling pace.

'Is that the same duke who's daughter you...'

'Hush, Dwin,' hissed Abreeth. 'There are certain topics one should not speak of in a public place,' he said, looking around to make sure no busybody had eavesdropped on their conversation.

Dwin mumbled an apology into his chest and continued walking next to Abreeth.

———

In the middle of the city, a sizable wooden stage sprawled across the square like a morbid theatre show. Thousands had elbowed their way into the centre of the city to see the duke's trial by flight, and it seemed everyone from the lowliest stable boy to the wealthiest of merchants were all vying for a decent spot.

Abe, Dwin and his hound were only able to get to the teeming crowd's outer section. If they wanted to get closer, they would need to start pushing their way through, and Abreeth didn't like the idea of being so tightly packed into a crowd with all their belongings and a dog, so the edge of the group suited him just fine.

'See those box-like structures?' Abreeth asked Dwin. 'They're the stocks they put the prisoners in. They're tied to the gallows at the moment, but once the prisoners are locked in, they knock out a chock, and up they go.'

'Can they even move in one of those things?' asked Dwin, squinting his eyes to get a better look at the stocks.

'Not really. Their hands and feet a little, but that's about it.'

'That doesn't seem very fair,' exclaimed Dwin.

'That's the idea,' said Abreeth dryly. 'Look, they're bringing out the first prisoner.'

A roar went up from the crowd, followed by boos and howls as rotten fruit, stones and anything else the public could get their hands on was hurled at the accused.

'TRAITOR,' a woman screamed.

'DIE YOU LICKSPITTLE,' shouted someone else.

'That's the duke,' Abreeth shouted to Dwin over the din of the crowd. 'It appears as though he's not very popular at this time.'

'Yes, it looks that way, doesn't it?' shouted Dwin.

You wouldn't know the man shuffling to the stocks used to be a man of power. Dressed in a plain, simple tunic that fell loosely to his knees, he had messy hair, swollen lips and red eyes.

A man in a long, black overcoat stood at the front of the stage addressing the crowd. Abe and Dwin were so far back they couldn't hear what was being said other than occasionally catching the words 'treason', 'against the kingdom' and 'trial by flight' in the wind.

After the man in the coat had listed his crimes, the hammerman standing behind the duke lifted his large hammer and swung, releasing a chock. As the Duke slowly floated skywards, the crowd took up a cry of, 'Traitor! Traitor! Traitor!'

He didn't fight. He didn't struggle. The duke had overseen hundreds of cullings, and he knew the chances of coming out of this alive were virtually zero.

More prisoners were locked into their stocks and let loose to the will of the sky in quick succession. Soon there were no less than twenty people all floating towards certain death.

'They don't usually let them all go at once,' said Abreeth. 'This is really something.'

The crowd fell unusually silent as the duke crept closer to the deadly spurs. The morning breeze had turned him slightly, so his back was facing the sky, giving more places for spurs to touch. When the duke came within a few feet of the lethal spurs, the crowd held its breath and watched as he closed his eyes and waited for death.

A single arrow penetrated the sky in its flight skywards. Arching through the air with its bright red fletching, the razor-sharp broadhead struck the duke through the heart, killing him instantly and sparing him from the touch of the deadly spurs. Burning anger pulsed through the crowd as they realised the duke hadn't received the long, painful death a traitor deserved.

Abreeth heard smashing glass and ringing steel over the din and shouts of 'get him' as the archer of the offending arrow raced away from the bloodthirsty crowd.

'It's time for us to go,' said Abreeth, hurriedly grabbing Dwin by the elbow and leading him away.

'But you said we could watch three floaters,' objected Dwin, shaking his arm away from Abreeth's grip.

'Don't be a fool, Dwin. Feel the crowd. Look around. Trouble is brewing, and I plan on being as far away as possible when it boils over. We are leaving now.'

Abreeth pushed Dwin hard in the opposite direction, letting him know he wouldn't argue the point. More fights and shouting broke out all around them. Someone stumbled hard into Dwin, knocking him to the ground. Abreeth dragged him up and kept walking.

'We need to get out of here,' said Abreeth with a sense of urgency.

'I think that's a good idea,' replied Dwin, looking around at the rising panic and anger coursing through the crowd.

An ear-splitting explosion erupted close to where they were standing. A woman screamed, and shouts rose all-around. People panicked, crying and covering their ears as they started to run.

Dwin and Abreeth stole down an alley as more explosions ruptured the air behind them. They ran past people with horrific injuries, bleeding and moaning. Some attempted to drag the injured away from the chaos. Others ran and skidded on the cobblestones, slick with blood. Panic ran freely on the streets as the explosions threw meat and misery in all directions.

'What the hell's going on?' shouted Dwin, as blood-soaked citizens ran past the trio. Some, helping their friends or strangers hobble away, others simply running in blind confusion from the gruesome scene in the middle of the city.

'I don't know,' replied Abreeth. 'We go to The Columns now,' he ordered, arranging his bag and picking up his pace.

Soldiers and guards ran everywhere as both lads quick-marched to the city gates, only to find them closed. 'No one in or out until we find out what's going on,' said the guard.

'Dammit,' swore Abreeth, looking at the guards stationed in front of the closed gate. They had more than a hint of concern on their faces. When a city gets locked down, something serious is happening. When city guards look concerned, the public should be anxious.

'I know a place we can go until everything settles down,' said Abreeth as he walked a path that followed the city wall. He led them through a series of alleyways and along pathways until they came to a stream that bubbled happily in stark contrast to the unfolding chaos in the city. The brook was an oasis in the middle of pandemonium.

'Down here,' said Abreeth, leading Dwin and their hound down a path that circled back on itself and under the shelf of a cliff face that wasn't visible from the top of the banks.

'What is this place?' asked Dwin, looking at the wave-like formation of rock in front of him.

'It doesn't have a name. I just call it the hidehole.'

'The hidehole?' asked Dwin, confused.

'Up there,' said Abreeth, pointing to rough-hewn stairs that led to what looked like nothing.

'I can't see anything? It looks like that staircase leads to nowhere,' exclaimed Dwin.

'That's why it's called the hidehole,' smiled Abreeth. 'C'mon, follow me.'

All three of them picked their way up the large uneven steps, worn smooth from centuries of use by those in the know. Abreeth stopped a few feet from the opening and placed a finger to his lips. Both of them could see the flicker of firelight on the wall at the entrance. Abreeth drew his dagger from its sheath and stalked slowly to the opening of the cave. Sidling up to the entrance, he poked his head around the corner and glanced inside. He spied a hooded figure sitting close to the small hearth.

'What are you doing here?' called Abreeth. 'Show your face.'

Dwin jumped into the entrance beside Abreeth, his dagger drawn. 'Don't try anything stupid, or we'll slice you open,' he growled. Abreeth smiled at his machismo.

Both of them stood in the entrance waiting for the figure to jump up in surprise or look at them, but all they heard was sniffling and small sobs.

'I killed him,' is all they could hear through the sobs. 'He's dead, and it's my fault.'

Both Dwin and Abreeth looked at each other confused.

'Killed who?' asked Abreeth, moving cautiously towards the back of the small cave.

'My father!' cried the young woman as she turned to look at both of the boys.

'Prue?' said Abreeth in surprise.

'Abe, is that you? Is that really you?' said the young woman.

'Prue, what are you doing here? Are you OK?' asked Abreeth, falling to his knees beside her.

'Oh, Abe, it's you. It's really you,' she cried, throwing her arms around him and burying her face into his chest. Her blond hair was tangled and knotted and Abreeth couldn't help but notice the state of her clothing and the fact she smelled like she hadn't bathed for weeks.

'Wait, what's going on?' asked Dwin, thoroughly confused.

'Dwin, this is Prue Brynestad, daughter of the Duke of Roda Codex.'

'You mean the same duke we saw floating up towards those...,' Abreeth punched his arm and gave him a stern look.

'Ow... what did you do that for... oh, right... sorry,' Dwin replied as Prue started sobbing and fell into Abreeth's arms once more.

'Oh, Abe, he's dead, and it's all my fault,' she cried into his chest.

'C'mon, let's sit by the fire for a minute,' said Abereeth, stroking the young woman's hair.

Prue told them how soldiers arrived in the night to take her father away. She simply couldn't bring herself to believe her father could betray the kingdom. That was until she went to see him in the dank and foul dungeons of the city. As soon as she walked to his cell, she knew he was a man who'd sold his soul. She could read it in his eyes and hear it in the whispered apologies through the metal bars.

Her entire life had fallen to pieces shortly after her father's arrest. Stripped of all titles, land and income, she had become an outcast in her own city. Fear and condemnation soon started to fall in the direction of the duke's only daughter, so she did the only thing she could think of. She ran.

She had been hiding in empty warehouses, abandoned buildings and finally, this cave for the past few weeks. She was dirty, hungry and miserable, hiding and eating whatever scraps she could find.

She had one friend left in the city, but she wasn't able to meet with him given her current difficulties. He was a eunuch who managed the duke's servants and had a soft spot for Prue. He was the one who organised the single arrow to pierce the duke's heart on Prue's request. She couldn't stand the thought of her father going through an agonising death, even if he was guilty.

Abreeth and Dwin sat quietly, taking in the story of betrayal, loss and escape.

When Prue had finally finished her tale of woe Abreeth asked, 'So what are you going to do?'

'I don't know, Abe. I've lost everything. Everyone I love, everything I've ever owned, gone. All gone. All I have are the clothes on my back and this necklace my father gave me,' she said, looking into the fire, her hand absently touching the silver locket at her throat.

'Why don't you come with us?' asked Dwin. 'We're going to Thade to find my father.'

'Not with the city locked down, we aren't,' replied Abreeth.

'I suppose I could,' said Prue, lifting her head and thinking about the proposition. 'There's nothing left for me here,' she said softly, misty eyes reflecting the firelight.

'I'm not sure you're both hearing me properly,' said Abreeth, 'the city's in lockdown. We're not going anywhere until they figure out what's going on. That could be days, weeks even. Until then, we're stuck here.'

'Unless there's another way out,' said Prue in a small voice.

'Another way out?' asked Abreeth in surprise.

'Another way out,' repeated Prue. 'I know of a way out of the city that avoids all the guards and gates.'

'There's no such way,' said Abreeth confidently.

Prue's voice was almost a whisper, 'There is, but it's dark and perilous. We shall need our sharpest wits about us to navigate this path,' she replied.

'And you've used this secret passage before?' asked Abreeth, stoking the fire to raise the embers back to flames.

'Once, when I was very young.'

'This doesn't sound like much of a plan,' exclaimed Dwin, 'is there no other way?'

'Not unless you fancy fighting your way out through the gates,' Prue said.

'Alright,' agreed Abreeth, 'we'll leave when the suns no longer light the sky'.

———

Darkness fell over the city like a blanket. Multiple explosions rocked Roda Codex throughout the rest of the afternoon and the sounds of boots and war horses on cobblestones could still be heard, even from the relative safety of the hidehole.

'We're going to have to be careful. They're still looking for me,' whispered Prue as she led them down the stairway from the secret cave and along a path that followed the brook approaching a bridge.

Quietly, the group snuck underneath and sat down in waiting. Abreeth and Dwin huddled in close, as Prue whispered, 'We need to get over this bridge to the path on the other side of the brook. We should wait until the guards have done their pass.'

It wasn't long before they heard footsteps and talking in hushed tones. They all held their breath as the guards approached. 'And that's the thing. No one knows what it is,' said one guard.

'Sounds like witchcraft to me. People exploding and losing their heads. Gotta be the evil of some spell or spirit,' said his companion.

'I've 'erd they had the same thing happen in loads of villages. Lots of fires and explosions and such, but not people exploding, never people,' said the first guard.

'I don't like this at all. It stinks of spellcasters and...,' continued the second guard, their voices trailing off.

After a few minutes, Prue poked her head out from under the bridge and looked around. 'Quick, let's go,' she whispered as she scrambled up the bank and onto the bridge.

In the light of the lamps, Abreeth got to see Prue properly for the first time. She'd grown into a beautiful woman. Even beneath the grime and dirty clothes, he could see her dignified grace and womanly curves.

After crossing the bridge, they followed a pathway along the brook for a time until they came to the back of a large warehouse. The stream they'd been following ran directly through a tunnel that opened like a wound into the bowels of the building. Prue hitched up her skirt and waded into the water.

Abreeth followed her in and drew a sharp breath when the cold water soaked through his leather boots and trousers.

'I'm not going in there,' said Dwin, standing on the bank with his arms firmly crossed.

'Yes, you are,' replied Abreeth.

Prue stopped where she stood and turned around to face Dwin.

'I can't swim,' said Dwin, as if that settled the matter.

'Dwin,' said Prue softly, 'I promise the water will only ever get to your knees.'

'I don't care. I'm not going in. We'll just have to find another way out.'

'There is no other way out, Dwin, the city's in lockdown. Get yourself in this water before I-' Abreeth stopped when he felt Prue's hand upon his arm.

'Dwin,' she said, walking to him and clasping her hands in his, 'I know you're scared, I'm scared too.'

'I'm not scared,' said Dwin indignantly. 'I just can't swim, is all.'

'I know, I know,' replied Prue soothingly. 'I'm not a very good swimmer either. I don't like the water, but there's no other way out of here. I'm cold, Dwin, and the sooner we get out beyond the wall, the sooner we can make a fire and have something to eat. Do you know how to make a fire, Dwin?'

'Yes,' said Dwin suspiciously.

'And that dagger of yours,' continued Prue, 'do you know how to use that too?'

'Yes,' said Dwin, puffing out his adolescent chest a little.

'I don't have a dagger, Dwin, would you mind standing beside me as we walk so I know I will be protected? Then when we get out, you can make a fire for me. Will you do that for me, Dwin?' Prue asked, her eyes wide and her mouth slightly pouted.

'I... it's just... I'm not certain we...,' Dwin was stumbling over his words, and Prue took the opportunity to take his arm in hers and lead him into the water.

When he looked up at her, she smiled and said, 'You're going to need your knife, Dwin.'

'Oh yes, right,' he said, forgetting the cold of the water and rummaging in his tunic for his blade.

As they walked past Abreeth, Prue gave him a wink and walked with Dwin into the tunnel.

———

'You lied,' yelled Dwin as they emerged from the tunnels. It was an hour-long trip through the city's bowels, which saw them crawling on their bellies, ducking underwater in no more than three sections and fighting off all manner of rodents, bugs and unpleasant critters in the dank confines of the city's wastewater system.

'Shoosh,' laughed Abreeth through chattering teeth, 'we're still close to the city.'

'You said we wouldn't need to swim,' hissed Dwin, squeezing out the water from his clothes. Just at that moment, Murphy shook himself, spraying Dwin with a new layer of water and mud.

'Arrrrgh. Stupid dog!' he growled, stomping off.

Abreeth and Prue couldn't help but laugh at Dwin's misfortune. It had been a successful trip, but it wasn't a simple stroll through tunnels and troughs. It had taken both their powers of persuasion and finally the promise of a new sword when they got to Thade to finally get Dwin through the tunnels.

After reaching the forest on the city's outskirts, they built a small fire and crouched around it, figuring out their next move.

'The entrance to The Columns is a couple of hours walk from here,' said Abreeth, rubbing his hands over the flames. 'It's a few hours until daybreak, so I suggest we warm ourselves as much as we can, wolf something down and be on our way. We will warm up on the march.'

The trio ate some dried beef, shared a drink from their waterskin and kicked dirt on the fire, instantly regretting the loss of the comforting heat as they walked towards the entrance of The Columns.

16

A COLLECTIVE APPROACH TO DEALING WITH THE AFTERMATH

'No, no, no! This was NOT supposed to happen,' cried Marsine, covering her naked body with a blanket and rushing to Stahl's side. Blood slowly oozed from the wound on the back of his head, his body limp and lifeless on the cold, wooden floor.

'But you said...,' started Gabrielle.

'Yes, I know what I said,' snapped Marsine, rubbing her face and breathing deeply, trying to sober up, 'but things... changed.'

'Well, how was I supposed to know?' cried Gabrielle, defensively. 'It's not my fault. You told me to hit whoever you bought into the room.'

'I know it's not your fault. It's just... oh blast the old gods! What are we going to do?' Marsine could feel herself starting to panic as the fog of the evening's festivities quickly wore off.

'We could just leave,' said Gabrielle. 'Get all our stuff and go.'

'No, we can't do that. His body is in our room. They will know we had something to do with it. We have to move him somewhere.'

'Where?' asked Gabrielle. 'We can't just drag him into any old room.'

'That's it!' said Marsine, her mind becoming clearer. 'He came with a fat man called Tubert. He's the one I gave the wolfsbane to. He retired early. Now we just need to find his room. Check his pockets for keys,' said Marsine, hurriedly throwing on clothes.

'Found them,' said Gabrielle after a short search in his pockets. Looking at the large key, she said, 'There's a number on it; three-one.'

'OK, let's leave him here and find the room to make sure the fat man isn't awake. Come, let's go.'

They both crept down the hall, counting numbers on the doors as they went. Luckily room thirty one was only a few doors down, and no one stirred, given the late hour. Marsine put the key in the lock and turned it with a click as squeaky hinges made them both wince in the early morning silence. The room smelled of perfume, herbs and stale liquor. On the pallet laid Tubert, his face pressed into his pillow. Marsine looked around the room as Gabrielle closed the door behind them.

'Gabrielle, light that candle over there,' whispered Marsine.

A low light cast around the room, and the girls could see bags, clothes and appurtenances laid out neatly around the room.

'OK, here's what we do. We get Stahl, roll him onto a blanket and we drag him in here. Hopefully, when Tubert wakes, he will think he simply got drunk, fell and hit his head.'

'I don't think he's going to wake up,' said Gabrielle, moving the candle closer to Tubert's open, lifeless eyes. Shivering at the dead man's stare, she reluctantly shut his eyes for the last time. Gabrielle turned to her older sister. 'What about all this stuff?' she asked.

'What stuff?' said Marsine questioningly.

'This stuff,' she replied, moving her hand around the room. 'All this has to be worth something, surely? I mean, he looks rich, and he's not going to need it anymore.'

'Right,' said Marsine, remembering why they were doing all this in the first place. 'Let's just get Stahl into the room. Then we can go through their things to see what's worth taking. They have horses too.'

'Isn't what we're doing wrong? I'm not sure Father would approve?' said Gabrielle, a touch of guilt flooding her young, innocent sensibilities.

'Father isn't here, and we don't have time to think about that,' said Marsine matter-of-factly.

'I wish he were here with us,' said Gabrielle sadly, 'then we wouldn't have to do any of this.'

'Me too, but right now we have to focus. We have to get that man out of our room.'

———

'Pull,' hissed Marsine. Her calf muscles were burning and her fingers ached from gripping and pulling the blanket so hard.

'I am pulling,' wheezed Gabrielle. After fifteen minutes of tugging, dragging and grunting, they managed to wrestle Stahl's limp body into his room.

'Right,' huffed Marsine, bent over double, 'you check the fat man, and I'll go through the drawers.'

'Ew. Why do I have to check the fat man?' complained Gabrielle.

'Fine!' sighed Marsine. 'I'll check the fat man. You start going through the drawers and put anything you think is valuable on the bed.'

Soon the girls had several gold coins, three necklaces, two daggers, fifteen pouches of tobacco and several wonderfully made scarves, belts and tops that would fetch top prices anywhere in the kingdom.

'This is so pretty,' purred Gabrielle, caressing a silk scarf against her face, savouring the softness of its fabric.

'And these belts have real gems in them!' exclaimed Marsine.

The goods they managed to gather from the two prostrate men exceeded any riches they had ever managed to gather living on their farm. The girls put their haul into a pillowcase and quietly moved out of the room back to their chamber to discuss their next move.

'We need to leave tonight, before either of them is found,' said Marsine.

'But I'm so tired,' yawned Gabrielle.

'I know, but we need to get as far away as possible. The quicker we leave, the more distance we can put between us and two dead merchants.'

'Is People coming with us?' asked Gabrielle, perking up at the thought of their horse having some friends for the journey.

'Yes, People will come with us. Get your things packed... we leave in a few minutes.'

The sisters hurriedly packed the few belongings they had into bags and stole out of the tavern into the night, the cold air tickling their skin to goosebumps.

The stable at the back of the tavern smelled of horse and hay, and a small candle thrust its yellow tendrils of light into the darkness, guiding their way. Squinting as their eyes adjusted, the two girls went about the job of trying to figure out which of the several horses in the stable belonged to the two men they'd just killed and robbed. As they searched the stable, a figure materialised in the doorway, causing Gabrielle to squeak and hold her big sister close. Dentri, hammer in hand, walked into the stable menacingly but eased his stance when he saw the two girls. He stood with questions in his eyes his tongueless mouth couldn't ask.

'Dentri,' said Marsine in relief. 'Let me explain. We need to leave. Right now, in fact.'

Dentri stood still, looking Marsine over, trying to establish why they would need to flee in the middle of the night.

Feeling the need to fill the silence, Gabrielle blurted out, 'I didn't mean to hit him that hard, Dentri. You have to believe me. I only wanted to put him to sleep.' Gabrielle started crying. 'They're going to cut off my head when they catch me, aren't they?' she sobbed.

Marsine looked between her sister and the tongueless tavern

owner, confusion on his face. Marsine sighed. 'Dentri,' she said, walking towards him, 'we need to tell you about something. Something that happened in your tavern tonight.'

After Marsine had recounted the events of the night and explained they had no other choice because they were penniless and destitute, she looked at him with pleading eyes.

She could see him mulling over their story and working out what to do next. Marsine nodded in agreement as he held up his hand in a motion for them to wait, even though every fibre in her being was telling her to run. She owed it to Dentri and Scraps to at least allow them to deal with the fallout of their actions before they fled.

Several minutes later, Dentri returned with a sleepy-eyed Scraps, bird's nest hair and a fur wrapped around her shoulders. 'Hello, lovey. Gotten yourself into a pickle, I hear?' she said in between yawns.

'I'm so sorry to put this on you, Scraps. I didn't mean to cause any trouble,' said Marsine.

'Trouble! There's no trouble. As far as I can tell, both those buffoons drank a little too much, went to their room to sleep it off, left their door open and got robbed and killed in the middle of the night by bandits unknown, who also happened to take their horses. How their collection of overpriced herbs and spices made it into my basement is anyone's guess,' she said with a wink.

Dentri disappeared, coming back with two saddles that he harnessed to the dead men's horses. Marsine, overcome with emotion at the fact someone in this world was watching out for her and her sister cried as she embraced the older woman. 'Oh, Scraps, I don't know how to thank you!'

'You can start by getting yourself to Thade and giving this to my brother,' she replied, holding up a bag. 'His name is Avouris, but everyone calls him Avey. His tavern is called the Avouris Inn. Self-indulgent name if ever I've heard one. He's a good man and will give you a job. I've put a letter in there for him that will vouch for you and your sister. Now, you better get moving. Good luck, girls.'

With hope filling their hearts and gratitude in their tired smiles, Marsine and Gabrielle mounted their new steeds and rode into the night on the long road to Thade.

———

'Let's camp here for the rest of the day. I'm exhausted,' yawned Marsine as they led the horses into a grove off the path they had been following. Gabrielle's face, even though she was only twelve, had dark bags under her eyes, giving away her utter fatigue. She listlessly slid off her horse and curled into a ball on the ground, falling asleep almost instantly.

Marsine was struck by how young her sister looked at that moment. How much they'd been through in the past week. She placed a rolled-up tunic under her sibling's head and covered her with a blanket.

The late afternoon light from the dual suns was delightfully warm, but the weather would soon start to cool come evening. After unsaddling the horses and tying them on a long lead, Marsine gathered their belongings in a pile, ate some food Scraps had so kindly packed for them and rolled into a ball next to her sister to drift into much-needed sleep.

It was dark when both girls woke. The moon hung low in the night sky and cast a light grey lustre over their campground.

'How long before we get to Thade?' asked Gabrielle, warming herself next to the newly made fire.

'With the horses, we'll be able to make good time. I imagine we should be able to get there within a week or so,' said Marsine.

'What do you think it will be like? The city, I mean.'

'I don't know,' Marsine looked up at the moon. 'Noisy, smelly and lots of people, I suspect.'

'It sounds just like a tavern.'

'Yes, it does a little, doesn't it?' said Marsine, wrapping one of Tubert's expensive scarves a little tighter around her neck to ward off the cold. 'Let's relax here the rest of the night and break camp when the suns rise in a few hours.'

'I like that idea,' yawned Gabrielle, stretching out in front of the fire.

Marsine watched her younger sister staring off into the distance as the gentle breeze and warm fire lulled them both to relaxation. Marsine was just nodding off when her eyes tracked movement a few hundred feet away. In her sleepiness, she thought her mind was playing tricks. The moon crept from behind a cloud as the figure coalesced in the grey light, like a spectre from the underworld.

Staggering and exhausted, it was clear this walking shadow was injured and close to collapse.

'Gabrielle,' Marsine said urgently, 'someone's approaching.'

17

TEETH TO TEAR AND STEEL TO STAB

Nuri's eyes had swollen like a bee sting, her lips cracked and crusted with blood after her ordeal. She could still hear Pera's grunting as he finished inside her. His stink was on her clothes. The shame and raw fury that flowed through her body could fill the largest of lakes. The stabbing pains she'd felt in the first few hours of walking had turned to a dull throb between her legs.

Thoughts of revenge filled her mind as she slowly plodded the path towards Thade. She was sure, and given the right motivation, the khan would help in the pursuit of vengeance for the malice brought upon her by Pera. For now though, she needed to put aside those thoughts and continue towards Thade.

Finally, well into the second day of trudging along a well-worn path, she found a brook bubbling its way through a field. Clutching her almost empty waterskin, she found a secluded spot, stripped off her clothing and shivered as she slid into the icy water. The clear stream bit into her skin like an ice snake, but it was a relief to feel something, anything, after the past few days of numbing emptiness.

Shivering and wet, she walked to the bank to dry and dress,

thankful for the opportunity to wash away the deceit and defilement and warm herself by a fire.

Knowing the khan would be waiting to hear from her, she retrieved a small bowl from her bag and poured water into it she'd gathered from the brook. She collected and crushed herbs into her palm from a small box and tipped them into the bowl, reciting an incantation as she circled the outside of the bowl with a black crystal. Ripples formed on the surface as the water turned to black, and a face appeared.

'Ah, Nuri. The khan has been expecting you,' said the bearded man in the bowl, quickly disappearing.

A few minutes later, the khan's face materialised on the mirror-like surface.

'Nuri, what's wrong?' he said straight away, his voice sounding distant.

'Why would anything be wrong?' asked Nuri in surprise.

'Come now,' cooed the khan, 'I know when something ails you. It's written in your face as clear as a spellcaster's scroll. You have bruises, and your lips are cut and swollen.'

'It's behind me now,' replied Nuri, 'and something I plan to deal with on my return to the Pyrelands.'

'So I take it you've made it into the Firmalands? Excellent,' said the khan. 'Have you had any trouble from the locals?'

'Not from the locals. I plan to move forward with our strategy at the greatest possible speed,' she replied.

'It was a pyerlander who did this to you? I shall have them dealt with,' replied the khan.

'That won't be necessary, my khan. Nothing will come between us completing this mission together,' said Nuri in supplication.

'Good,' replied the khan. 'I knew I could rely on you. I must go as I have business to attend, but know this. I'm counting on your success. Contact me again when you can.' And with that, the liquid in the bowl returned to its original, transparent state, and the khan disappeared.

———

After several hours of walking, Nuri topped a ridge to see smoke in the distance and farmlands surrounding a small village. The twin suns edged their way behind the mountains in the distance, cooling the air and elongating her shadow. 'Finally!' she said to herself, 'hot food and supplies.'

Walking into the town, she drank in the differences between villages in the Firmalands and those of the Pyrelands. Greenery was everywhere despite the cold. Pastures surrounded the small town, with animals giving them a supply of meat and milk through the winters. The buildings here looked nothing like the rough-hewn, simplistic lodgings of those in the Pyrelands.

These were made of stone, wood and had thatched roofing to keep out the cold winds and winter snows. Low walls made of rocks, cemented together with clay, outlined the different fields, some filled with animals, others with vegetables, apple trees, large swathes of wheat, barley and other grains. Compared to the crops that could be grown in the Pyrelands, these fields looked bountiful, even though in reality, they yielded less each year.

Stopping at the inn in the middle of the village, Nuri pushed open the doors to the common room warmed by a large fire in the corner. The smell of cooking made her stomach growl.

'Hello lovey, what can I get you?' asked the plump lady behind the bar. She wore her hair in a bun with a welcoming face and a cheerful smile.

'I need supplies and a hot meal if that's something you offer,' said Nuri, sitting at the bar.

'We've got a nice beef stew with potatoes and carrots and a mug of ale for five coppers,' the barkeep replied.

'Perfect,' said Nuri. 'One of those.'

'I'm Scraps,' said the lady, extending her hand and shaking Nuri's, 'and who do I have the pleasure of meeting for the first time?'

'Nuri,' she replied as she looked around the room. 'I very much like your building. It's... homely.'

'That's what we were going for, lovey. Many people use it as a home away from home, but to us, it is home. Has been for over fifteen years now. Are you staying overnight or just passing through?' asked Scraps as she slopped a tankard of ale on the bar. 'We've got safe rooms that lock and no questions asked,' she continued, looking over Nuri's black eye and cut lips.

'Not staying. Just here to top up supplies and then back on the road,' replied Nuri.

'Lots of folks heading to the city lately,' replied Scraps. 'We keep hearing stories about people missing and villages put to the torch by those filthy swine over the tundra,' she spat, shaking her head.

'Yes, I've heard,' replied Nuri, trying not to balk at the hatred this woman held for her people, when only a moment ago she seemed like the loveliest person she'd met on her journey so far.

'They keep coming back, year after year,' Scraps continued, 'taking and raping everything we've worked so hard to build. Oh, will you listen to me, prattling on like an old fish wife? You must be hungry,' stated Scraps, turning to the bench that led through to the kitchen where a bowl of steaming meat and vegetables had arrived on the counter.

'I've always wanted to cut my hair short like that,' smiled Scraps as Nuri tucked into her hot meal.

'I find it a convenience to have it this way,' she replied through mouthfuls of her first hot meal in days.

'It looks good with your impish face. I'd just look like a fat woman with bad hair!' chuckled Scraps. 'Now, you said something about supplies. We've just gotten a fresh supply of herbs and teas early this morning. What is it you'll be needing?'

———

Nuri walked well into the evening with a weighted pack and the full moon lighting the road for several miles ahead. As she walked, Nuri reflected on life in the Firmalands. Some things seemed familiar, but many aspects also appeared vastly different. People lived a simple life that didn't seem to be touched by the tendrils of their king. Not like the Pyrelands where the khan oversees every harvest, every crop and every merchant that makes or imports goods.

There was a life, a spark in the people she'd met so far. It made her both uncomfortable and excited at the same time.

She'd lived with the khan for so long she'd forgotten what it was like to exist on her own terms. Even though she was still doing the khan's bidding, she realised she was the freest she'd ever been. She decided where she stopped, how far she walked, what she ate and with whom she interacted. How easy would it be to disappear in this kingdom? Start a new life. A life of freedom and choices.

She quickly dismissed the idea as a flight of fancy. 'Don't be irresponsible, Nuri,' she said to herself as she followed the moonlit path. 'The khan would find you, eventually. He would never let you go without a fight. Imagine his disappointment. You're the one that's constructed this position within his enclave. Why would you do something to jeopardise that?'

The khan could be cruel and malicious at times, but there was also a vulnerability to him that very few had seen, except for Nuri. It was this fire and ice, this rage and misery that fed her excitement. She enjoyed it, wanted it, needed it even. Her presence was the only one he would tolerate when he was in the depths of his darkness, and no matter how frenzied his fury, he never laid a finger on her in anger.

She felt protected in his presence but also incredibly vulnerable. This dichotomy of feelings made her feel alive in her world of numbers, crop yields, merchant traffic and payments.

Stopping to take a swig from her waterskin Nuri looked up at the very same stars she would have been seeing in her homeland. Even though they looked the same, she couldn't help but feel something different about them. It dawned on her that perhaps it was her that had changed and not the tiny, shimmering specks that pierced the darkness.

That's when she heard it. A low, ominous growl emanating from the forest to her right. She stopped in her tracks, cold sweat running down the back of her neck. Turning her head slowly, she observed a massive wolf crouching just off the path in the undergrowth.

Its grey and brown fur blended into the surrounding forest perfectly, no doubt why she didn't see the animal until it was too late. Its fangs flashed white in the moonlight, saliva glistening as its mouth curled into a low, guttural snarl.

She'd lived with dogs in the village where she grew up. They were constantly roaming the city streets and could be easily kicked or shouted at, should they get too rowdy. A forest wolf was an entirely different beast.

Where the village's skinny street hounds might get away with hunting a chicken or rabbit, if they were lucky, a forest wolf could bring down a fully grown stag and rip out its throat. As if sensing her fear, the wolf let out another throaty rumble, its hackles raised as it inched forward.

Nuri slowly reached for her blade – her only protection, and backed slowly away from the animal. As she focused on the intense yellow eyes in front of her, she heard another growl from the path in front, where a second wolf silently appeared with yet another smaller wolf off to its side.

Slowing her breathing, she felt the panic inside her start to rise. She looked at the trees around her, hoping to scale their trunks, but those she could reach had no low branches to climb, and the ones that did were too far away.

'I understand this is your forest,' she said slowly, her voice shaking, 'and I wish no trouble for you or your pack. I have a rabbit I caught earlier,' she continued, moving her arm towards the gutted rabbit hanging from her pack. 'I'm happy to leave it with you.'

The response was another low rumble. Nuri could feel her heart against her chest, pounding like a blacksmith's hammer on soft metal. She was about to cut the cord holding the rabbit when the large female wolf on the pathway sprang forward with lightning speed.

'Fuck,' she spat, turning to run as fast as she could.

She'd managed three strides before a snarling, biting weight knocked her to the ground. Everything happened quickly as fur, teeth, dirt, and carnage kicked up around her. Luckily her bag took the brunt of the initial attack, and she could feel the wolf shaking and pulling at it.

She blindly kicked and slashed with her knife as one animal grabbed hold of her leg, the other biting down hard on her forearm. A scream escaped her lips, joining in with the snarls and yips of her three attackers.

Panic set in, and Nuri started stabbing wildly at the wolf that was shaking her arm in its powerful jaws. She plunged the blade to the hilt into the wolf's throat, a yelp of pain her reward followed by hot blood spilling over her skin.

Flipping over and scrabbling back, she could see the largest wolf with the rabbit from her pack in his mouth. Baring his teeth, he looked at the wolf Nuri had stabbed, blood pooling from its body in the moonlight.

The smaller wolf loped to its dead packmate. Whining, it nudged at its fur. With one of his pack down, the lead wolf decided it wasn't worth continuing the attack on an enemy that delivered such a quick death to his beta.

Nuri breathed hard, staring at the lead wolf as well as keeping an eye on the smaller grey female pacing back and forth beside its dead packmate. After several moments of contemplation, he turned and stole back into the forest, silent as a whisper, the other wolf melting into the darkness with him.

Nuri held her bleeding arm to her body, the pain of the bite rising as shock set in. Shaking uncontrollably, she reached into her bag for a scarf to wrap around her arm. She winced as she stood, her legs trembling and tears in her eyes.

She knew she would need to continue until she reached safety. If she rested, the significance of her injuries would make it almost impossible to continue. 'Pull yourself together, Nuri,' she said to herself. 'You have to keep going until you find someone or get to the next village; otherwise, shock will set in, then you will die in the cold, alone.'

Stumbling forward, she held her injured arm to her chest and limped into the night. She didn't stop or rest, not trusting herself to get moving again if she did.

She'd been walking for what felt like hours when the moon dipped low on the horizon, throwing yellow light across the landscape. She knew she was getting close to collapse. Her legs were filled with iron, and she was stumbling more often than not. Her arm throbbed with each heartbeat now, and her shoe had become slippery with blood from the tear in her calf.

She'd told herself 'just one more hill' ten hills ago. It would be so easy to lie down on the side of the road and give in to the darkness that beckoned her. She was close to giving up. Sweet and seductive, it ran through her mind willing her to surrender to its shadows, but a light cut through its calling.

At first, she thought she might be seeing things, but as she stumbled closer, she could make out a campfire and two figures. At this point, her exhaustion and pain overrode any caution she should display walking into a stranger's camp and she continued closer as the figures stood and said something that seemed distant and muted. The last thing she remembered as she fell into their camp was being glad it was two young women with red hair.

18

VOLATILE CARGO HIDDEN IN PLAIN SIGHT

'THERE WILL BE NO VIOLENCE IN THE COLUMNS,' shouted Platicevo, incredulity and spittle flying from his mouth as a line of veins throbbed darkly on the side of his face.

'What a shot,' laughed the dwarf. 'He never knew what hit him!'

'That's enough from you,' spat Platicevo. 'And you,' turning to Deadsun, 'I expected better from the Commander of the Lavers Lawmen.'

'Do you have any idea how much danger we're in?' replied Deadsun calmly.

'Danger!' cried Platicevo. 'The only danger I can see is the good graces we will lose when our customer learns of your unacceptable violence towards his guard.'

'Your *customer* is a traitor to the kingdom and has put the entire Welkinpeaks in jeopardy,' replied Deadsun with cold fury.

'Those are strong words, Commander,' started Platicevo. 'I would assume you have proof backing your claim and if you want to...,'

'GET THAT FUCKING FLAME BACK NOW!' roared Deadsun, making everyone in the vicinity jump along with the young Archemedian walking towards them with a lit torch. He looked at Placetivo, then at Deadsun, not sure what to do.

'You're Deadsun, the Commander of the Lavers Lawmen?' cried the dwarf. 'I had a cousin that worked with your ilk back when the Pyre wars were...,'

'Not now, dwarf,' interrupted Deadsun. 'That black powder you thought was wine,' he continued, addressing everyone in the area, 'it's called boomdust and explodes with a force you simply can not imagine. A man we managed to catch had a necklace just like this one, except we didn't know it was filled with nails, metal and black powder before he lit it. It was enough to take his head right off, kill two of my men and destroy the entire kitchen we caught him in.'

'Right off?' asked the dwarf.

'Right off as in, all that was left of him was on the walls,' replied Deadsun, 'and that was just one small necklace. Platicevo, how many barrels of this stuff do you have in the columns?'

Platicevo thought for a moment and said quietly, 'Seven hundred and forty-two.'

Deadsun visibly blanched, 'Gods!'

'On this level,' continued Platicevo.

'What?'

'Seven hundred and forty-two barrels on this level,' reiterated Platicevo.

'And how many on the other levels?' said Deadsun slowly, as if delaying his question would somehow ease his growing discontent.

'The same again on the level above and half again on the level above that.'

'Thousands of barrels,' whispered Deadsun, 'that's enough to destroy the entire Columns and a good proportion of Roda Codex.'

'Wait, wait, wait,' said Platicevo. 'Boomdust, destroying Roda Codex? I... I don't understand?'

Deadsun popped the cork on one of the barrels and put his hand inside, grabbing a handful of the black powder. 'This,' he said, pouring it through his fingers, 'is boomdust. It's a new weapon the pyrekahn has developed, and it looks like he's shipping it up into the Welkinpeaks. I would bet a decade's wages he's planning to cause trouble with it. Big trouble.'

'This is like no weapon I've ever seen,' exclaimed the dwarf, inspecting the powder through the hole in the top of the barrel.

'That's right,' replied Deadsun. 'Nobody's seen the likes of it. Even a tiny amount explodes with enormous force. Thousands of barrels, well, that would be like...,' he trailed off.

'Like a volcano and an earthquake wrapped in every hammer strike past and future,' said the young man who looked like a wealthy merchant's son. 'I've had word from my uncle; a merchant, who trades in many skyports. Entire villages in the Welkinpeaks have been destroyed by fire and explosions. Whole villages have been levelled, and the people – all gone. Lots of his men said it was witchcraft. Some thought it was the gods, but if this stuff is as explosive as you say it is, that would explain such dire tidings.

'How many of these barrels have made it through The Columns and into the Welkinpeaks, Platicevo?' asked Deadsun.

'This is roughly half the shipment,' said Platicevo, watching Deadsun rub his temples. 'The last half.'

'You're telling me thousands of barrels have already made it through here and up into the Welkinpeaks?'

'That's what I'm telling you,' replied Platicevo.

'OK, everybody listen, here's what's going to happen,' said Deadsun, gathering his things.

'You have no authority here, Commander, if you think for a minute that...,' Deadsun grabbed the Archimedean by the throat and pushed him against the cave wall, growling, 'You gave up your command when you let through thousands of these city-eating barrels.'

Slipping the dagger from his belt, Deadsun pushed it into the terrified guide's crotch, causing him to squeal. 'If you know what's good for you, you will listen and listen well.' Waiting for him to nod,

Deadsun loosened his grip, and the red-robed Archimedian sucked in a deep breath as he slumped against the wall.

'All movement of people and goods through The Columns stops immediately,' said Deadsun coldly. 'You!' he snapped at the red-robed helper, making him jump. 'Send word to your fellow guides and guards that all activity in The Columns stops now. If they don't wish to follow orders, they will be judged in front of the king and by history. Is that clear?'

The young guard nodded, a terrified look on his face.

'What are you fucking waiting for boy? MOVE.' Deadsun barked. The young man turned on his heel, ran to the flag communication systems on the walls, and started messaging the other levels.

Kestral put down her bow and bag to rummage through the folds and pockets of the unconscious man with the copper necklace. 'What are we going to do with this one?' she asked, tossing his belongings into a pile.

'Dwarf, get that rope over there. We need to tie his hands and feet so he can't cause any more trouble,' said Deadsun.

'Horst.'

'I'm sorry?' asked Deadsun.

'Horst,' repeated the dwarf. 'If we're all going to die in this godforsaken cave together, I would rather you call me by my name.'

'No one dies on my watch, Horst. Rope... now,' said Deadsun, rolling the unconscious man over and placing his limp hands behind his back.

'We need to move these barrels out of The Columns,' started Deadsun.

'Thousands of barrels, that could take weeks,' said Kestral.

'Is there a way of destroying these barrels without making a mess of The Columns and ourselves?' asked Horst.

'Not that we know of as yet,' replied Deadsun. 'We only learnt of this powder less than a moon ago. One of these barrels alone would be enough to destroy this entire cave and everyone in it.'

'The chutes.' Everyone turned to see Placitevo standing against the wall, his robes straightened and the red from his face all but gone.

'The what?' asked Horst.

'The chutes,' repeated the Archamedian, 'is a channel filled with water that runs from the level above right down to the Firmalands in almost a straight line, like a waterfall inside The Columns. It runs on a slight angle, so we're able to send certain goods to the Firmalands with great speed. We use it only in emergencies if goods or people need to expedite their journey quickly.'

'You're telling us there's a quicker way through The Columns, and you don't offer it?' asked Kestral, her thin lips barely hiding her annoyance.

'That is exactly what I'm telling you,' replied Placitevo, lifting his chin and puffing his chest slightly, 'and we don't offer it as most people don't live to see the exit. The last person to go through the chutes was three years ago, and he barely made it out alive.'

'These chutes,' asked Deadsun, 'are they large enough to safely carry these barrels to the bottom of The Columns?'

'Certainly,' answered Platicevo, 'at their narrowest, it fits four men across.'

'And the entrance to these chutes?' asked Deadsun.

'Ah,' stumbled Placetivo, 'that could be a slight problem.'

Deadsun stared at the Archimedean, lowered his voice and asked, 'How much of a slight problem?'

'Two years ago, the Achamedian council decided in their great wisdom that the chutes should be sealed. I strongly disagreed with this decision as I could see their value, but the council closed all the entrances and sealed them with a fawelock.'

'Dammit!' swore Deadsun, kicking a plume of dust in frustration, fists balled and teeth clenched.

'A fawelock! I didn't think they still existed?' exclaimed Horst.

'Wait, what's a fawelock?' asked Kestral.

'A fawelock, my dear lady,' began Horst, 'is a lock that requires a combination of the four elementals; fire, air, water and earth, to be added in the correct order for it to open. Given there are four elements, there are two hundred and fifty-six different combinations,' he finished, smiling at his abundant knowledge of locksmithery.

'And how is it you know so much about fawelocks then, dwarf?' asked Deadsun.

'I've been breaking into long-abandoned caves and treasure troves long before your mother even knew the touch of a boy,' chided Horst.

'So you should have no issue cracking it then?' he replied dryly.

'Except,' squeaked Placetivo.

'None whatsoever,' laughed Horst.

'Except.'

'I could do it in my sleep.'

'Except.'

'Oh, do spit it out, man,' grumbled Horst, 'you sound like my cousin Dretar who was dropped on his head as a baby.'

'Except,' said Placetivo quietly, 'this is a double fawelock, and only three people know the combination, none of which are anywhere near The Columns.'

Horst blinked for a moment as he stared at the Acrhemedian. 'I don't understand,' he finally replied.

'The exits to the chutes are closed off with double fawelocks on every level,' Placetivo explained, 'and the council members that know the combination are thousands of miles away.'

'Well, what bloody use is having an escape route if you can't fucking open it?' demanded Horst hotly, 'and why by the old gods' arse trumpets would you put two damned locks on there?'

Placetivo stood stock still staring at his feet. All the fight and leadership he had previously mustered all but evaporated.

'OK,' said Deadsun pacing back and forth, 'so that doubles the difficulty in getting through the door. Horst, how long would you need to crack a double lock?'

'I don't think you understand, laddie. It's not that easy.'

'Why?' asked Deadsun, catching the slight hint of desperation in his voice and taking a breath to calm himself for the answer.

'It's not double the combinations. If two locks work in conjunction with each other, that's eight different points for the combination to work. That means there's...,' Horst screwed up his face in concentration and continued, 'sixteen million, seven hundred and seventy-seven thousand, two hundred and sixteen possible combinations.'

'Fuck,' swore Deadsun.

'Old gods be damned,' said Horst, wonder in his eyes and disbelief in his voice.

'I don't like where this is headed,' said Kestral. 'Is there any way to get around these locks, perhaps using some of this black powder?'

'We can't chance it,' replied Deadsun. 'One errant spark, and we will set off a chain reaction that will blow the entire place apart.'

'We've word from above,' said the young guard operating the flag system. 'Another group is coming down.'

'That's our cue to head to the next level,' said Placetivo, getting some of his previous bravado back.

'No one goes anywhere until we figure out what to do with these damned barrels,' commanded Deadsun.

Placetivo was going to say something but stopped himself. Thinking better of it he stated, 'As you wish, Commander.'

'They're on their way now,' the young guard announced.

Suddenly, a colossal rumbling shook the cave and threw everyone to their hands and knees. Dirt, dust and debris fell from the ceiling.

'What was that?' shouted Kestral.

'I don't know, but it didn't sound good,' replied Deadsun, white chalky dust settling over the group hiding their blood drained faces.

19

THUNDER AND DEATH IN A BARREL

Buckled over and heaving for breath, Abreeth, Dwin, Prue, Murphy the hound and their Achemedian guide all looked at each other, rattled by the sound of the explosion. Terror crept into their eyes as they came to the same realisation.

It had begun.

Abreeth cradled the deep cut on his arm, wincing as he applied pressure to stop the bleeding. Dwin was holding Murphy around his neck, wet lines sparkling from his eyes in the light thrown from the lantern in the shaking hoistpen.

'Thunder and death,' Prue whispered.

'He's d... d... destroyed the hot gates.' Tumbling on his words, the Archimedean guide was as white as the dust that lined his face, 'That river of fire will make its way through every level now.'

'How long do we have?' asked Prue.

'Three hours. Four if we're lucky,' he replied.

'Then we're fucked,' swore Abreeth.

'I don't want to die, Abe,' choked Dwin, fresh tears rolling down his cheeks.

———

Their trip into The Columns didn't start like this. After sliding and swimming their way through the guts of Roda Codex, the small group walked without issue for the first few days through The Columns, their young Archemedian guide snaking his way through the cave system.

The trouble started on the third day when a fifth member joined the group. A wealthy merchant had hired him to watch over a large shipment of wine making its way through The Columns. He had dark hair and a metal tooth that matched the colour of his oversized necklace. His air of arrogance got on Abreeth's nerves straight away. He acted as if his was the most critical job in the world.

He cornered Prue on more than one occasion, stroking her hair and offering to 'service her needs' to the point she rarely left Abreeth's side. Abreeth didn't like this man, not just for his uncouth manner but also the way he didn't get phased by anything. Not even the threat of Abreeth caving in what was left of his teeth if he spoke to Prue again.

'You're nothing but a worm under my boot, boy,' he laughed, spittle flying from his lips as he snarled. 'You think I'm afraid of you? I've seen the darkness. I've seen redemption, and it doesn't come in the form of a lickspittle like you.'

'Just stay away from us if you know what's good for you,' Abreeth finally said.

There was something amiss with him. Everything about him was different, from his dress, to his accent, to that stupid oversized necklace he wore around his scrawny neck.

Each time they rested for more than a few hours, he would stretch himself out and sleep like a babe with a belly full of milk. His snoring kept even the deepest of sleepers from getting proper rest. Abreeth laid on his sleeping roll thinking of ways he might be able to lose this uncouth invader or slide a knife into his throat as he slept, but every scenario he ran through seemed outlandish, ungentlemanly or ended up with the Achremedian guard finding out and banning them from ever travelling The Columns again.

Their guide had been very thorough in explaining the rules of The Columns. Should anyone deviate from the group or do anything they deemed unlawful, they could say goodbye to this mode of travel via a lifetime ban.

Mealtimes were exceedingly uncomfortable. The dark-haired invader, Abreeth had dubbed Wormface, always stared at Prue as he ate.

The worst part was Wormface deftly walked the line between rudeness and outright offence. Abreeth often felt he should say something but worried he would seem petty for doing so.

Wormface would often find a reason – any reason, to be in close quarters with Prue and deliberately rub himself against her. She would try to move away, but he would often stop her path until he saw Abreeth making his way towards her. It was a cat and mouse game that Wormface seemed to enjoy, and Abreeth endured with gritted teeth and clenched fists.

Well into the fourth day of travel, things started to heat up, literally.

'Why is it so hot?' exclaimed Prue, mopping the stinging sweat from her forehead with a cotton sleeve.

'We're getting towards the middle of The Columns. This is where the lava flows start to appear,' said their guide with practised ease.

'Lava flows?' asked Dwin.

'Brimstone, molt, redrock, ichor. It has many names, but it all comes from the same place deep below the ground. There are several sections of The Columns that have such flows cutting through it like a hot river. We're coming up to a flow in the next few hours. That's why it's getting so warm. This way, please. Keep up.'

The tunnel narrowed as they peeled off layers and wiped brows. Wormface stopped just before a single file section of the tunnel, positioning himself so that anyone going past would have to brush against him. It was obvious who he was waiting for, hot breath and bulging breeches, eager for the chance to smear his filth on the only female in the group.

Abreeth walked quickly past Prue, planting both feet firmly in front of Wormface. 'You heard the guide, keep up,' he said, roughly leading him into the narrow space of the tunnel by his elbow.

'Get your filthy hands off me, bootlicker. I'm simply waiting to make sure everyone gets through safely,' he said, violently yanking his arm from Abreeth's grip.

'You first,' Abreeth hissed through gritted teeth, his hand on the helm of his dagger. 'I insist.'

'If you wish to dance, my sweet little sycophant, it's best you know the steps.'

Both men stood eye to eye, each one waiting for the other to take the first step in a move they both knew would lead to blades and blood.

'Boys, stop this now,' flared Prue, slapping both of them on the chest with the back of her knuckles. 'Bloody men, always thinking with their swords,' she mumbled as she walked past them and down the tunnel.

Wormface was the first to snap out of the dance that almost was, and quickly jammed his body into the small space behind Prue, looking over his shoulder and scoffing at Abreeth.

'Let's see how well he dances with three inches of iron in his belly,' muttered Abreeth.

'And Murphy at his throat,' added Dwin. He'd been watching Wormface's behaviour towards the only two people he had in this world and was just as unhappy about it as Abreeth. Wormface kept a wide berth of the boy and his hound. Every time he went near them, a low rumble sounded in Murphy's throat, and Wormface suddenly found somewhere else to be. The first time Wormface got too close, Murphy strained against the leather lead in Dwin's hand, saliva and yellow teeth gnashing inches from his face. 'I'll stuff that flea-ridden cur in a sack and throw it in a flow,' he spat.

'I don't trust anyone Murphy dislikes,' Dwin revealed to Abreeth later that day as they stole a quick meal before going down another level in the hoistpens. Abreeth fully agreed with his friend and Murphy's instincts.

By the time they crossed the third bridge, the novelty of walking over a river of molten lava had worn thin. Dripping with sweat, thirsty and exhausted, they stopped before the last bridge to the next hoistpen, which had the widest span of them all.

Their crossing would take much longer now, thanks to Worm-face. He needed to move a trolley of thirty-two barrels of wine stored in a side room.

'This will delay our pace. We must not dally in this section of The Columns. The air here is not pure and will take its toll on anyone who lingers,' complained the young guide.

'I realise this Archemedian, but I have my orders and let me remind you my master has paid a considerable sum to your council to move his goods through your system.'

'And this system runs by making sure we, as guides, keep our groups moving so we can both be in hoistpens going up and down at the same time,' reminded the guide.

'If it makes you feel any better,' cooed Wormface, 'I shall let you move ahead of me, and I will wait for the next group if I slow your pace too much. I'm sure your kowtower here won't mind, will you?'

Abreeth ignored the jibe.

'All I ask is that you help me wheel the trolley to the bridge, and I will take care of the rest.'

'Gladly, if it means we get to see the back of him and that stupid necklace of his,' Abreeth whispered to Prue, who smiled, then caught herself and frowned at Abreeth in mock reprimand.

Struggling against the weight of the trolley, Wormface called out to Abreeth, 'Come, my little apple-polisher, if you're to see the last of me, you can help me with this load.'

'Not man enough to handle it yourself, I see,' needled Abreeth.

The trolley wheels meandered through the dirt of the cave floor, which made for slow going in the thick, hot air. Abreeth was doing his best to ignore the goading of Wormface by concentrating on the barrels in front of him. His hands could feel the wood and iron that held them together. He hadn't practised reaching out to anything with the Bind for several days as they'd been either on the run, navigating tunnels below the city of Roda Codex or making their way through The Columns.

He'd sat when they'd occasionally stopped, hands to the floor of the caves letting his mind wander into the rock and earth around him. This grew tedious as there was nothing but blackness and silence in the stones below.

Nothing like the feeling he had when he reached out at Grenda's grave, the tiny beings in the ground, the life slowly fading from her body all there before him as if in a scroll in his mind. More to drown out Wormface than anything else, he cleared his mind and tried to feel the wine inside the barrels. Perhaps there was some life left in the grapes, berries and yeasts used. Ignoring the burning in his chest from exertion and the fumes from the brimstone, he cleared his mind and placed a palm against the wood.

Black. Dry. Not wine.

'This will be far enough, Bootlicker,' commanded Wormface.

Abreeth blinked, not sure what to make of what he had just seen.

'Deaf as well as dumb now, my little lapdog?'

Abreeth walked past Wormface silently, wrinkles on his forehead, stroking his chin.

'Have it your way, lackey. Good riddance,' said Wormface as he continued to push the trolley.

The pair were met with a ragged gash in the floor two hundred feet across. In its depths, a raging torrent of molten rock flowed like the blood of the fire god Taw himself.

The only way the Archemedians could keep the bridges that spanned these flows from burning was by diverting water from the underground rivers to an ingenious aqueduct system, showering the bridges with a constant water flow. This kept the wood from burning and the iron from bending, but made it slippery and dangerous.

The group stood before the bridge, waiting for Wormface and Abreeth to manhandle the trolley into place.

'It looks like this is where we part ways. I wish I could say it's been a pleasure,' said Abreeth.

'Oh, the pleasure's been all mine,' said Wormface, bowing and taking Prue's hand. His kiss lingering a little too long to be cordial.

'Come, we mustn't stay in this place,' called their guide from the bridge's start, 'please watch your step as we cross.'

Walking into the tunnel on the far side, Abreeth looked back to notice Wormface's crooked smile. 'Something's wrong,' he said to himself.

The hairs on the back of his neck and the stone in his gut were a signal. Like when some wine-riddled inebriate seeking provocation walks into a crowded tavern and shoulders the biggest man there. Everyone feels the anticipation and trepidation rippling through the air, a murky lament with tones of impending trouble.

Five minutes into the tunnel, Abreeth pulled Dwin and Prue aside and said, 'I'm going back to check on Wormface. Something's wrong.'

'Oh, Abe, let it go. That awful man and his silly necklace are behind us now. Let's just get through The Columns and leave him be,' sighed Prue.

'I'm with Abe on this one,' agreed Dwin. 'I get the feeling he's up to something.'

'Fine! But don't take too long. I don't wish to remain idle in this hot, stuffy place longer than necessary!' With that, Prue turned on her fed up heels and took off down the tunnel with Dwin and Murphy close behind.

Keeping to the shadows, Abreeth crept to the edge of the cavern and poked his head around the entrance. Wormface was almost over the bridge, pushing the trolley, slipping and swearing his way to the edge. Abreeth watched as he changed direction and headed to the far end of the cavern. Slowly, he wheeled the laden trolley to the very edge of the river of fire and stopped.

'Why's he putting the trolley over there and not wheeling it through the tunnel?' Abreeth thought to himself.

Abreeth saw Wormface take a barrel from the top of the trolley, where he unstoppered the bung and tipped it over on its side.

'His merchant master isn't going to be happy,' thought Abreeth. 'Why would he pour perfectly good wine on the...,' Then it struck him. That wasn't wine at all. What should have been fine ruby elixir was a black powder spilling on the cavern floor.

Black. Dry. Not wine. Thoughts flashed through his mind.

Wormface worked quickly, making a pile of the black powder at the base of the trolley and dragging the barrel backwards, creating a coal-coloured trail as he went. Finally, when he was a hundred feet away, he stood with his back towards Abreeth, rummaging through his pockets.

Abreeth took several steps forward and Wormface whipped around at the sound of his footsteps.

'I thought you were carting wine?' asked Abreeth.

'I thought you'd fucked off?' spat Wormface.

Wormface placed the tinder and flint in his hands on the ground slowly, never taking his eyes from Abreeth. Sliding his dagger from his belt he spun it in his hands, it's blade glinting in the red glow of the lava-filled cavern.

'I've been waiting to dance with you since we first met. Let's see how graceful you are with your guts on the floor you knavish, shag-eared mouldwarp,' snarled Wormface.

Both men circled each other – Wormface with his blade, Abreeth with his shortsword. Abreeth tried to pivot so Wormface's back was towards the lava-filled canyon, but his opponent was having none of it.

'What's in those barrels?' hissed Abreeth as he lunged, testing Wormface out.

Gracefully moving like a king's court dancer, Wormface spun and struck out at Abreeth with his dagger. Abreeth only just got his shortsword up in time to block the blow.

'I suppose it doesn't matter now as we will all find redemption soon,' said Wormface, slicing his dagger through the air once more. He altered his position and gripped his blade in the traditional knife fighting stance as he continued, 'Those barrels are full of thunder and death. Quite fitting that this black powder is going to help you meet the eternal dark.'

Wormface suddenly rolled backwards like a circus tumbler, but when he came to his feet, he lunged forward, catching Abreeth off guard and slicing his arm with a deep gash. Abreeth grunted and gritted his teeth. He was well trained in swordsmanship, but it had been many months since he'd faced off against an opponent with this level of skill. He'd gotten rusty.

'It seems your hands don't dance as well as your mouth, you greasy crotch pole,' smiled Wormface.

'What do you mean, thunder and death?' said Abreeth, taking another swipe, missing Wormface's throat by a hair's breadth.

Wormface giggled like a schoolgirl, taking a step back. 'Boom,' he snapped, rolling backwards once more.

Abreeth wasn't stupid enough to fall for the same move twice. Taking two quick steps on the diagonal, he brought his sword down with all his force as Wormface lunged once more. Steel bit flesh, and Wormface squealed like an impaled pig holding his injured arm to his chest. Blood quickly covered his tunic, bone and muscle visible from the sword bite on his forearm. Hanging limp and useless, his hand dropped the dagger, and his face turned white. Wormface was staring at him with clear eyes where usually they were dark.

'Run,' Wormface whispered. 'If you value your life, run.'

Wormface's eyes glazed over with a dark covering as they went back to the gaze Abreeth had grown to hate. He spun on his heels and stumbled towards the trolley at the edge of the canyon, took one last look at Abreeth and smiled.

'Boom,' he giggled as he pushed both himself and the trolley over the edge into the roiling stream of brimstone below. Abreeth didn't

know what thunder and death were supposed to mean, but he didn't
intend to stay around to find out.

———

Abreeth came screaming down the tunnel, Dwin, Prue and their
guide were just entering the hoistpens as the explosion rocked the
tunnel behind them. Abreeth dived into the contraption, shouting
something about thunder and death.

'Doesn't this thing go any faster?' Abreeth demanded.

'This is as fast as I dare go for fear of snapping the ropes,' replied
their guide, working the pulleys and levers of their transport with
clumsy hands.

They tumbled out of the hoistpens as soon as it stopped at the
lower level, met by another group covered in dust and looking as
confused and scared as they felt. There was a muscular man with
dark hair in what looked like military-issued clothing walking
towards them.

'What the hell was that explosion?' he demanded.

'Thunder and death unless we get out of here,' replied Abreeth.
'We have to leave now.' Noticing the man lying on the ground, hands
tied, he asked, 'Why is it always these fuckers with the big necklaces
that are causing problems?'

20

A TRIO TRIP TO THE COLUMNS

Nuri awoke to the sensation of nuzzling behind her. As her mind raised itself from slumber, she became aware of a snuffling, heavy breathing, hot and wet on her back. She rolled over and came face to face with a large snout above an enormous set of teeth.

Fully awake in seconds, she clambered backwards as best she could with her injuries. She kicked up puffs of dust, half crawling, half scrabbling away from the horse sniffing and snorting around her.

'Oh, you're awake. Don't be scared, that's just People. He's our horse,' said Gabrielle, giving People a handful of grass and shooing him away. 'I'm Gabrielle and this is my sister Marsine,' she said pointing to her older sister stiring a pot of tea by the fire.

'How long?' croaked Nuri.

'How long have we had People? We found him on our way here. We're going to Thade,' bumbled Gabrielle.

'I think she means how long has she been asleep,' offered Marsine, walking from the campfire to kneel beside Nuri. 'It's been two days since you stumbled into our camp. How are you feeling?'

Nuri rubbed her leg. Her clothes were still bloodstained, but her arm and leg had been cleaned and bandaged. 'Like a pack of wolves attacked me,' replied Nuri.

Gabrielle's eyes grew wide as she asked, 'Is that what happened to you? We thought it was something like that. Marsine said a bear, and I said dogs, but wolves!'

'I apologise,' Marsine cooed, 'my sister could talk even with her face in a bowl full of porridge. Let me take a look at that arm.' Marsine deftly unwrapped Nuri's bandages and removed the leaves and herbal salve she'd applied to keep the sepsis at bay. 'I knew it was some type of animal wound, so I've done my best to make sure it doesn't fester. It will be sore for a while, but I don't think you will lose any use of your arm. So wolves, huh?'

'Yes,' replied Nuri, 'Three of them.'

'Three wolves! How did you get away? I bet you stuck them with that pretty dagger of yours, or did you hit them with a rock, or maybe you...'

'Gabrielle!' snapped Marsine, 'that's enough. The poor woman has just woken up. Don't bombard her with questions.'

'Sorry,' said Gabrielle, drawing lines in the dirt with her finger.

'What's your name?' asked Marsine

'Nuri.'

'Well, I'm pleased to meet you, Nuri. You must be hungry, yes?'

Finally fully awake and suddenly feeling the effects of two days without eating, Nuri realised she was ravenous.

'Thank you... for taking care... of me,' Nuri said between mouthfuls of vegetable stew and flatbread. 'I don't know... how much longer I would have lasted... if I didn't find the both of you.'

'You're lucky you stumbled into our camp when you did,' said Marsine. 'I've seen a few animal bites in my time and yours is one of the worst, but we've cleaned it up and I think you'll be OK.'

'I am in your debt,' replied Nuri thankfully.

'Nonsense,' Marsine's eyes crinkled at the sides, smiling with the glow of a healer, 'it's the least I could do.'

'You mentioned Thade?'

'Yes, we're travelling there, or at least we were until you fell into our camp,' replied Marsine.

'Sorry about that.'

'You were lucky you found us. Another day with those injuries and that arm would have started to fester,' said Marsine, applying a new salve and wrapping Nuri's arm in a fresh bandage. 'You probably don't have the energy to walk very far. Still, we have three horses, so we can ride as long as you can stay upright in the saddle.'

'Ride?' replied Nuri, eyeing off the horses in the clearing. 'On those?'

'Well, we aren't going to ride each other, silly!' laughed Gabrielle.

'I take it you're not a fan of horses?' asked Marsine.

'It's not that,' Nuri replied, 'it's just... I've never ridden one.'

'Don't they have horses where you come from?' asked Gabrielle, all pigtails and inquiry.

Nuri thought about how to answer this question. Horses were commonplace in the Firmalands but in the Pyrelands horses were a rare beast indeed. If she gave too much away, these two girls might realise she wasn't from the kingdom and become suspect.

'My family was very poor. We couldn't afford horses. I don't like to talk about it much,' Nuri replied softly.

'Did your family get taken by Pyremen too?' asked Gabrielle, her voice lowering to a whisper.

'I'm alone,' was Nuri's simple reply.

'Well, not anymore. You have us, and our horses,' smiled Gabrielle.

'You should travel with us to Thade,' suggested Marsine. 'We could use the company. And besides, it's dangerous to travel alone.'

Nuri thought for a moment. 'I should like that very much,' she replied.

'It's settled. We will camp here another night so you can gather your strength. We can leave on the morrow,' exclaimed Marsine, standing to stoke the fire with fresh wood.

———

'What's that?' exclaimed Gabrielle, wide-eyed in wonder as she looked at the mammoth column of rock spearing its way into the clouds like broken teeth biting the sky. The twin suns were high, shining straight down on the mountainous column as shimmering rainbows glinted in the noon sunslight from waterfalls that fell from the edges of the rock.

'That's The Columns,' replied Marsine. 'Father told me about them.'

'They're beautiful,' sighed Nuri, her breath taken aback by the sheer size and magnificence of the natural wonder.

'Look,' cried Gabrielle. 'Pyredrakes!' Specks floated through the clouds, massive wings outstretched, soaring on the winds of the highskies. 'They look like big lizards with wings,' said Gabrielle in wonder.

'They're exquisite,' whispered Nuri, 'like nothing I've ever seen.'

'Hopefully, we can get a better look at them. The road we follow goes close, look,' said Marsine, pointing at the winding snake of dirt rambling its way across the landscape like a drunkard. Small bridges crisscrossed the multitude of rivers and streams that flowed from The Columns. Rain and snow from the Welkinpeaks carved their way down The Columns and into the waterways, which the girls would be crossing all afternoon.

As the suns crept behind the massive pillar of rock, the three travellers dug out their overcoats and gloves. The cooling shade and constant mist drifting from the waters cascaded out from the pillar of rock, touching everything within a few miles of the natural stone structure. The continuous flow of water and mist-fed plant life and animals for miles around, and lush pockets of shrubs and trees scattered themselves throughout the rolling green plains. The only thing that looked dead in this place was the track, but even then, patches of wildflowers grew in the path where cartwheels didn't roll.

Marsine had to stop Gabrielle from stooping over every few

hundred yards to pick a new type of flower. The horses strained to move away from the road to eat the soft, fresh grass that carpeted the hills around them.

'This looks a perfect spot to spend the night,' said Marsine, stopping at a well-kept campsite stocked with wood, long grass for bedding and a small inlet with a beach entrance, perfect for collecting water and washing.

'I can see us being very comfortable here,' said Nuri, unpacking her things.

Marsine took charge and said, 'Gabrielle, you collect some water. Nuri, you get the fire started. I'll set some snares to see if we can catch ourselves some dinner. I saw some fat rabbits in a thicket about a half a mile back.'

Nuri was more than happy to leave the rabbit hunting to Marsine. Her bones ached from her injuries and a day of riding. She was tired, hungry and glad to be making a fire as the shadow from The Columns oozed their way into her marrow, like lava eats a village.

'Where did you learn to cook like this? This rabbit is delicious,' asked Nuri between mouthfuls. It had only taken Marsine an hour to snare two fat rabbits. She also found some wild herbs and tubers that added body to the delicious stew she prepared for their evening meal.

'Our mother died when I was very young, so it was up to me to do most of the cooking in the house,' replied Marsine.

'I helped too,' added Gabrielle indignantly.

'Yes, you helped too,' replied Marsine, 'and from what I can remember, I was always chasing you out of the kitchen for pilfering my scones!'

Gabrielle looked at Nuri, holding her stomach with both hands and exclaimed, 'She made the best scones! Oh, how I miss them!'

Nuri smiled and scooped another spoonful of meat and vegetables from her bowl.

'What about your parents,' asked Marsine, 'are they still alive?'

'Not any more,' lied Nuri. 'They were both killed in a rebel raid near the borderlands.'

'Oh, that's awful. Is that why you're going to Thade?'

'Partly. I seek advice from the acolytes of Stardark who reside within the city of Thade.'

'Stardark mages can put false thoughts in peoples heads,' offered Gabrielle through a mouthful of food.

'That's flim-flam and hokum little sister.'

'It's true,' countered Gabrielle. 'Old-man Streed said a Stardark mage travelled through his village when he was a boy. Everyone gathered around to hear news from Thade. Old-man Streed tried to steal a dagger from his bag while the villagers were questioning him, but somehow the mage knew what he was doing. He weaved his dark magic and made him think spiders were crawling all over his skin. He showed me the scars where he scratched himself to get them all off. What do you want with that lot anyway?' the young girl asked Nuri.

'I have some strands of memories I would like to get a clearer picture of.'

'And the Stardark acolytes can help?' asked Marsine.

'Something like that,' replied Nuri, standing. 'Would anyone like some more stew?' she asked, scooping more from the pot keeping warm by the fire. Not wanting to push the conversation further, both girls held out their bowls, and they ate in friendly silence for a time, the crackle and spit of burning wood their only company.

Lazing around the fire with cups of hot tea, the three girls started to wind down for the night when a low rumble shook the ground and startled birds awake in nearby trees.

'What was that?' cried Gabrielle.

'Shhhhhh,' hushed Marsine, straining her ears.

Nuri had her ear to the ground to try and gauge from which direction the sound was coming. She had felt tremors like this back in the Pyrelands. They often signalled an eruption by one of the many volcanoes that peppered the landscape, but there were no volcanoes here, which felt different yet familiar. Short and sharp with the ring of death.

'Marsine, I'm scared,' said Gabrielle, moving closer to her sister.

'I'm sure it was nothing,' said Marsine. 'Let's all get some rest. We have a big day of travelling tomorrow. You two get ready for bed, and I'll wash these dishes in the river.'

'I'll help,' offered Nuri, looking for an excuse to stretch her legs.

The water took her breath away as she plunged her hands into the shallow banks, grabbing handfuls of sand to scrub the evening dishes clean. Her fingers ached, but the cold was refreshing.

Once the dishes were clean, she rubbed her hands together and stretched her back to look skywards at the stars. Now that she was away from the fire, her eyes adjusted to the dark. The stars glittered like flakes of gold in a stream.

About to make a start back to camp, her eyes caught a glimpse of light coming from The Columns, there was something oddly familiar about the red glow that flowed, almost like water from the edge of the mammoth pillars. As she watched she was sure she could see it getting bigger, soon it looked like an enchanted waterfall cascading from the rock.

'Gabrielle. Come here for a moment,' Marsine called to her sister. All three girls stood at the inlet and looked. 'What do you make of that?' she asked, pointing at the constant flow of red liquid spilling into the sky.

'Lava,' said Nuri simply. 'That's a lava flow.'

'I've heard there was lava inside The Columns,' replied Marsine. 'I never thought I would see it flowing out like that though!'

'Flows like that happen from time to time,' answered Nuri, 'especially if there's a fissure or a build-up of pressure. That's probably the rumble we heard before. That lava flow is pushing its way out the side of the rock.'

'Oh,' replied Marsine, gathering up the dishes. 'I'm sure it's nothing to worry about. Let's get some sleep.'

21

AN ELEMENTAL PUZZLE

Abreeth, Dwin, Prue, Murphy and their guide stood before Deadsun and his group, still breathless and shaking.

'You've seen someone with a necklace like this before?' asked Deadsun of Abreeth.

'That explosion we just heard, a worm-faced little shit like this was the one that caused it,' replied Abreeth, pointing at the still unconscious man lying bound on the floor.

'Look, I'd love to stop and chat with you about jewellery and such, but if we don't get the hell out of here, we're all going to die,' continued Abreeth.

'Placetivo,' cried the young guide. 'They've destroyed the Hotgates!'

Everyone turned to Placetivo for answers, but all they found was shock and turmoil written in the lines of his face.

'Hotgates?' asked Deadsun.

Placetivo was staring at the wall, a glaze over his eyes, mumbling to himself.

'PLACETIVO!' roared Deadsun. 'Hotgates, what are they?'

'They're... they... it's where we divert the Brimstone. We can't control the flow. Just divert it away from holes leading to other levels. Oh, by the old gods, we're doomed! I suggest you all pray and make peace with your gods because, in a matter of hours, these halls will be filled with molten rock,' he said, knees buckling as he stumbled to the floor on all fours.

As if foreshadowing their blistering and gruesome demise, there came a loud crack followed by rumbling from above, causing another covering of dust to float from the cave ceiling.

Deadsun kneeled in front of the ashen-faced Placetivo. 'Placetivo, I need you to think. The hoistpens have been destroyed, so we can't go back out the way we came. It's not likely we're going to crack the fawelocks on the doors of the chutes, is there any other way, any way at all that we might use to get out from here?'

A calmness came over the older Archemedian's face. 'Commander,' he said softly, 'I've walked these tunnels for 46 winters. I know every nook and cranny of this place, and there's not a single thing we can do. These halls will be our tomb.'

'Not if I've got anything to do with it,' growled Horst, grabbing a barrel of boomdust and hefting it on his shoulder.

'And where do you think you're going with that?' asked Kestral, standing in his way.

'To blow a fucking hole in that fawelock, and if you don't get out of my way, I'm at the right height to give you a nasty bite in a place your lover might ask questions about,' Horst retorted.

Kestral stood with her mouth open, as if not quite able to believe what this bearded, grumpy, short man had just said to her. Despite the seriousness of the situation, Deadsun had a grin on his face.

'What's a fawelock?' asked Abreeth.

'A lock based on the four elements that's about to be blown to bits,' huffed Horst, sidestepping the tall huntress and swaggering down the tunnel, barrel on his shoulder.

Abreeth looked at his hands, remembering the conversations and discoveries in Grenda's cottage and thought to himself, 'It's worth a shot.'

Abreeth rushed to stand in front of the dwarf.

'I don't think we've met. My name is Abe,' he said, extending his hand.

'I don't give a fuck what your name is laddie, as long as you get out of my way,' growled the dwarf.

'Horst!' snapped Deadsun. 'If you light that barrel, we all die.'

'We're all dead anyway,' he hissed. 'We might as well go out with a fucking bang.'

'Horst, your name's Horst?' stumbled Abreeth, trying to get the dwarf's attention again.

'Aye laddie, you're a fucking sharp one, aren't you? Now, this is the last time I'm going to ask nicely. Get... out... of... my... way.'

'Horst, I promise you I will let you blow up that lock, but please, let me look at it first before you do,' pleaded Abreeth.

'And what do you think you're going to be able to do with it then, laddie?' scoffed Horst. 'Get your hound to dig under it?'

Abreeth ignored the barb and asked, 'This fawelock, you said it's locked using parts of the four elements – fire, air, water and earth, right?'

'Yes, now make your point laddie and make it quick, my patience is wearing thin for these games,' Horst answered.

'I have a... way with elements that might be able to help us,' said Abreeth.

'A way?' laughed Horst. 'We're going to need more than 'a way' to help us get out of this mess. My bet is on this boomdust. Now move.'

'Wait, wait!' cried Abreeth, not thinking and just acting. He took his waterskin and poured water into his hand, but rather than running through his fingers, it formed a ball and hovered above his skin, roiling and moving like a river caught inside a bubble.

'He's a fawesooth!' whispered Placetivo.

'I don't care what he is. It's going to take more than tavern trickery and water balls to get us out of here,' said Horst, making his way towards the exit.

'Wait!' shouted Placetivo, recovering from his previous shock and pointing at Abreeth. 'You. Come with me.'

Placetivo and Abreeth walked past the dwarf towards the exit, Deadsun and Kestral right behind them.

'I don't care what sorcery you think he has, Archemedian,' shouted Horst, bundling himself behind them. 'I'm still bringing this barrel with me!'

They stood before a door more intricate than any Abreeth had seen in all his travels. Hewn from solid ironwood, two feet thick with creatures conjured from the darkest nightmares carved across its face. The door was in four sections; top, bottom, left and right. The middle of each section was home to two spheres carved from the wood of the door itself. Runnels led to seats at the corners of each door, perfectly matched to the size of the spheres.

'Behind this door is the chutes,' said Placetivo. 'We just need to get the right combination to open the door.'

'What happens if we get the combination wrong?' asked Abreeth.

'As far as I know, nothing.'

'As far as you know?' growled Horst, stroking his beard. 'A fat lot of good that will do us when the ceiling caves in or a wraith shoots out from the bloody thing.'

'There are far greater ways to protect something of value than a fawelock, my short-statured friend,' replied Placetivo calmly, regaining some of his composure. 'Each section represents an element. Eight spheres placed in the right combination at the edges of the door will clear the way.'

'Do you think you can open it?' Deadsun asked Abreeth.

'Only one way to find out,' said Abreeth, shrugging his shoulders.

'I don't want to put any pressure on you laddie,' said Horst, hoisting himself atop his barrel, 'but if you can't open this door, we're all fucked, and I for one don't fancy spending my last few hours thinking about how I'm soon to become a well-done roast.'

'If Abe here can't open it, perhaps we could light your barrel?' Kestral offered.

'Aye, now we're talking,' Horst answered, a broad smile running across his features.

'With you atop it when we do,' she continued.

Horst poked out his tongue and crossed his legs to get comfortable.

Abreeth took a deep breath and placed his hands on the door, feeling the wood, iron and fire that bent both tree and metal to the will of its maker. As soon as his hands touched wood, he sensed the magic-infused throughout the entire door. The hairs on the back of his neck stood on end, and he tried to slow his breathing and concentrate.

Closing his eyes, he put his hands over the spheres, feeling them in his fingers, sensing the power and trace within each one. Choosing just one of the spheres, he felt it grow warm in his fingers and behind his eyes, he saw patterns of red flame.

Opening his eyes, he smiled widely and announced, 'This one's fire... the one I'm touching is fire.'

'That's right,' said Pacetivo. 'As is signified by the symbol upon it, flame for fire, droplet for water, tree for earth, and so on.' Abreeth grinned sheepishly, trying to hide his embarrassment.

'Are you sure you know what you're doing, laddie?' asked Horst, chuckling. 'Because from where I'm sitting, it doesn't seem that...'

'Leave him alone, dwarf,' said Deadsun. 'If he has a chance of opening this door without lighting up the entire tunnel system, I, for one, want to see him try it. Now be quiet and let him concentrate.'

Abreeth placed his hands back on the door, reaching, finding, trying to discover. Fingers felt the wood and runnels, lingering in the grooves to trace the magic and matter that joined sphere to seat. All he needed was a taste, a hint, something to tell him which direction to move. He could feel the wood. The tree it came from flashed in his mind. Deep forest, dark, wood, bark, the smell of wet earth. Elvin blades cutting the phloem, carving it, felling it, animals rushing from the crash.

His fingers moved to the first seat, searching, seeking when he heard a noise. Quiet at first, almost indistinguishable, but the silence of the tunnels helped him hear it over the breathing of his companions. A faint roar, a shell to his ear. Water. Ice. Rain. Behind his eyes, he could see undulating waves moving in his mind, then rain and rivers. Opening his eyes, he searched the spheres, found one with a droplet symbol on it, and moved it into place.

Once again, he closed his eyes and moved his hands along the runnels to the next seat, feeling the carving, the magic, the trace. His hair stood on end like young love whispered down his nape, coolness on his skin through the heat. Opening his eyes and rubbing his arms to remove the goosebumps, he moved the sphere with the symbol of air to its seat.

Five more spheres he moved until he came to the last one. Looking at his companions, he said, 'There is only one place this one can go. Let's hope I've got it right.'

Holding their breath as he moved the sphere, the group watched Abreeth snap the last sphere into place and step back.

Nothing.

No movement. Not a sound.

Nothing but stale breath and disappointment.

'Well,' stretched Horst, jumping down from his barrel, 'you did your best laddie, but now it's...,'

CLICK

Everyone froze and looked at the door as the eight seats began to glow. Runnels filled with glowing red, green, blue and white light and seeped their way to the middle of the door, colours swirling and fusing as they met.

'He did it!' cried Horst. 'The bastard did it!'

They all stood back as the door slowly swung on its hinges and they were greeted by the noise within. The roar of water and frigid gushing air let them know the chutes lay just beyond the threshold of the door in the darkness beyond.

'Well done, Abe,' said Deadsun, slapping him on the back.

'Thanks,' he replied, a broad grin plastered across his face. 'I didn't catch your name?'

'Deadsun. This is Kestral. Horst you've met and Placetivo here is our guide,' Deadsun answered, holding out his hand.

'I wish we could have met under happier circumstances, but it's nice to meet you all,' said Abreeth, taking Deadsun's calloused hand in his.

'Introductions later,' said Horst. 'Let's get the others and get out of...' The grinding crack of rock giving way made all of them cover their ears and stumble.

Along the tunnels, dust kicked up from the floor and floated down from the ceiling. Then, through the haze, they saw it, slow and dire like oil on water. The red glow was unmistakable, and they felt the heat instantly, even through the freezing air from the chutes.

Slowly making its way down the tunnel several hundred feet from the door, lava oozed and slinked towards them, eating everything in its path.

'Stay here!' roared Deadsun, taking off down the tunnel. 'I'll get the others!'

———

Deadsun erupted into the waiting chamber like a bursting dam wall, closely followed by Abreeth shouting amid the chaos, 'GET UP... WE LEAVE... NOW!' they shouted.

Inside the pandemonium of the shaking dusty tunnels, the waiting group didn't need to be told twice. Legs pumping, coughing and scared, the tunnels seemed to shrink, feeling more like a coffin with every step. Arms flying, feet stumbling, the group collided their way towards the door of the chutes.

Through the dust, they could see Placetivo, Kestral and Horst shouting and gesticulating their hands wildly. A few hundred feet from the door, they felt it before they saw it.

Red and angry. Slow flowing death with the heat of a thousand suns.

Deadsun was first to the door, heaving for breath as he turned to ensure everyone had followed.

'What... do... we... do?' gasped Abreeth.

'The chutes,' pointed Placetivo. 'Feet first and take a breath where you can.'

The heat was intense as the oozing coulee crept ever closer to the entrance. Water droplets flying out from the chutes turned instantly to steam, adding to the chaos in the tunnel. One by one, they ran straight into the gaping maw of fast-flowing water. Even Murphy the hound didn't have time to come to a halt, following Dwin right into the water and disappearing.

The lava was twenty feet from the door now. Placetvio and Deadsun had to stand behind it to shield themselves from the heat. Kestral had jumped, Prue following directly after her. The youthful merchant and young Acrhemedian guide were still hobbling down the tunnel, helping each other after they'd stumbled and one had rolled his ankle.

'HURRY!' shouted Deadsun.

Looking up, they could see the lava a few feet away from the door and tried to double their pace, but it did nothing but trip them up again. Eyes wide, they looked up as the lava flow crept around the door.

'We have to go now, or we die!' shouted Deadsun to Placetivo, throwing his arms over his eyes to shield them from the heat.

The two injured men were still twenty feet from the entrance and hobbling as fast as they could. Placetivo looked at them, knowing they stood no chance of getting to the door in time.

'I'm sorry,' he cried. Not able to stand the heat any longer, he jumped into the torrent.

The lava crept past the door, continuing its destruction of The Columns and towards the two men, now stumbling back the way they came, trying to cheat the river of death that would inevitably seize them.

22

RAIN OF TERROR

The air around them was fresh and cold, the open spaces adding to the chill. The warmth from the fire was comforting, like steaming tea on a rainy day. The three girls slept soundly, snug coverings wrapped around them, a blanket of stars as their roof. Comfortable, warm and rested, they slept; colourful, pleasant thoughts of tomorrow playing in their dreams.

Nuri was the first to wake, eyes opening to the sound of birds. Still sleepy, it didn't quite register that birds weren't supposed to fly at night. Rolling over, she felt a tremor from below, which made her sit up and shield her eyes from the fire.

A white-tailed deer ran through their camp, jumping over the fire and startling Nuri. Letting out a frightened cry, she woke the others.

'What's wrong?' asked Marsine, rubbing her eyes.

'I don't know,' replied Nuri, 'the animals are acting strangely.'

'The animals should be in bed,' yawned Gabrielle, rearranging her pigtails to a more comfortable position and closing her eyes again.

'Listen,' said Nuri, 'can you hear that?'

All three girls strained their ears to hear what they thought was shouting and splashing.

————

The sting from the water was biting and painful, like frozen hands plunged into hot water. Gasping for breath every chance he had, Abreeth slid and tumbled through the frigid waters of the chutes. Complete darkness, fear and chaos, his only companions. Water just above freezing. The snowy, mountainous runoffs from the Welkinpeaks adding to their gelidity. Numb and half-drowned, he plummeted ever downwards, staying alive the only thought crashing through his mind.

Murphy was the first to exit the chutes, eyes shut, body limp and lifeless. Dogs don't fare well in waterfalls. Close behind, still gasping for breath, Abreeth hadn't quite registered he was out and alive. Looking up, he saw the stars, making him scramble to try and stay afloat.

The moon escaped the clutches of a cloud, illuminating the figures behind him. He let out a gurgling shout.

'Dwin,' he coughed and bubbled as his head fell below the waterline.

'Abe,' shouted Dwin, trying to stay above the water. 'I can't see you, Abe.'

'Swim towards that fire,' came a shout from behind them.

What was left of the group eventually found solid ground beneath their feet. Rasping for breath and retching water, they crawled onto the banks of an inlet and collapsed.

————

The dim light from the fire fell over a group of people crawling their way out of the water, heaving and coughing on the banks.

'Gods are you OK?' asked Marsine, running towards them. 'What are you doing in the water at night? It's freezing.'

A young boy and two men crawled onto the banks. More shouting and splashing came from the darkness beyond them.

'We... have... to get... away,' shivered a large muscular man with black hair plastered to his face.

'You need to get out of this water first,' said Marsine, helping him up, his legs trembling from both shock and cold. 'Nuri, Gabrielle... help those other two. We need to get them warmed up.'

'You d... d... don't... und... d... derstand,' stammered the muscular man through blue lips.

A groan from the water made Marsine turn to see a tall, slender woman dressed in green dragging herself onto the banks.

'What is going on? Where are you all coming from?'

Pointing the muscular man towards the campfire, she went back to the bank to help the trim woman from the water.

Shaking and disoriented, the group staggered up the bank towards the fire. The large muscular man was the first to the small hearth. Grabbing a large branch and picking it up like a torch, he walked away from the camp, still dripping and shivering.

'Hey,' cried Marsine, 'where are you going?'

The others, still soaked, walked right past the fire, following their companion whilst trying to drag Nuri and Gabrielle with them.

The slender woman at Marsine's side stuttered, 'We... have... to... g... g... get... away,' attempting to drag Marsine along with her.

Reefing her arms from the woman's grasp, she shouted, 'Now wait just a damn minute. We aren't going anywhere until you tell us what the hell's going on.'

'Listen,' said the muscular man, 'we c... c... can't... stay here.'

'And why not?' demanded Marsine.

In answer, a blazing light with the strength of a thousand suns lit the entire sky on fire. It was as if every lightning bolt from past and future had joined forces to illuminate the land. Those facing the light covered their eyes from the billowing flames, everything aglow like flaming suns.

It took several seconds for the shockwave to hit them, throwing them all to the dirt like a kick from a horse. It was as if the gods themselves had hammered the earth with lightning as the crack and boom of the explosion hurled a sonic boom, that could have been heard as far away as the city of Thade, ricocheting through the air.

Those that had rubbed the dust from their eyes gathered their senses through ringing ears and could do nothing but stare, slack jawed at the billowing plume of angry heat and fire that erupted its way skywards from what used to be The Columns.

The group stood spellbound by the horrific beauty of the rippling fireball tearing across the sky.

When Marsine was a little girl, she sat under a tree at her fathers' farm and was startled by a sound from above. She heard the crashing of branches in the small tree she was using for shade. Looking towards the sound, she saw a hawk with a dove in its clutches, its feathers askew in its needle-like claws. She could see the wide-eyed terror which left the dove unable to move. She now felt an affinity with that dove as she looked into the burning sky.

There was no precedent for the sheer scale of destruction in front of her. Comprehension of this event was left to instinct. A boulder twice the size of a horse flew past the group crushing everything in its path. Rocks and debris rained down, a storm of stones, malice, dust and gravel showering them with torment.

Shaken from their stupor, the group all ran in the same direction, away. The chaos, noise and heat meant everyone was in charge of their own fate. The air tasted electric, the crackle and hiss of lightning inside the explosion adding to the pandemonium.

Marsine looked for her sister as she ran parallel to the river. Another blast of lightning lit up the sky and highlighted a body floating face down in the muddy water. She heard her sister scream through the darkness and peeled off towards the sound. Dust and ash hammered down around them, choking the air and filling their lungs with dust and chaos.

She heard another scream, and she ran towards a shape on the ground, hardly stopping to drag her to her feet. Another flash, and she caught a glimpse of her younger sister's face covered in blood. A group of trees to their right was flattened by another large rock, rolling and crashing away.

The shower of rocks and earth seemed to dissipate just enough for the group to shout for each other and assemble into some semblance of cohesion. The large muscular man had dropped his torch, no longer needing it as the sky was still burning. The younger man was limping and helping the slender woman holding her arm, sticking out at an unnatural angle.

'Is everyone OK?' asked the muscular man.

'Alive,' said one.

Others simply coughed or nodded their heads in answer. A horse whinnied in the distance.

'People!' cried Gabrielle to her sister, the blood from the gash in her head still running freely down her face.

'Forget the horses,' said Marsine. 'We need to fix you up. Is everyone else OK?' She started taking stock of the group, seeing to wounds and trying to be helpful.

Dwin came stumbling into sight, covered in dust but still in one piece. 'What happened?' he asked. 'Did the world just end?'

'Here,' Marsine said to him, 'hold this cloth on Gabrielle's head.'

Gabrielle looked up at Dwin and smiled.

'Hello,' she said.

'Hi,' replied Dwin shyly.

In the distance, they could hear someone swearing and cursing like a sailor fresh off the brine. The large muscular man and his younger companion both looked at each other.

'Horst,' they said in unison, starting towards the sound.

They found the dwarf a few hundred feet away, stuck in a tree.

How he got there is anyone's guess. After helping him down, they started shouting, 'Pruuuuue! Placeeeeetivoooo!'

————

They had been searching for over an hour when they heard it. It started as a low rumble but gradually grew louder. Cracks and groans weaved their way into the night as parts of The Columns gave way. Sections the size of cities fell to the ground, followed by a deafening boom and crunch, making speech impossible. Already exhausted, the group had to once again run for their lives away from a hail of stones, earth and rocks still burning from the explosion. Within minutes a cloud of pulverised rock dust enveloped everything and everyone. Visibility was zero, and figuring out a direction was entirely impossible.

Disorientated and choking, the group ran in any direction they thought was the right way. Tripping and scrambling over rocks and fallen trees, they tried to find refuge any place they could. Marsine and Gabrielle had managed to stay together, huddled behind a large boulder.

Kestral dragged herself behind the stump of a large tree, arm dangling uselessly by her side, the pain temporarily masked by her fear.

Dwin hid behind a tree a few feet away, for all he knew in this chaos, he was entirely alone.

Deadsun, Abreeth and Horst huddled behind a large, overturned tree, covering their heads from the falling detritus.

Still settling into their new state of disarray, The Columns continued throwing out more grey pall across the land for the next several minutes.

Still burning.

Still moving.

Still dying.

———

Abreeth was the first to find Nuri. Blue and still, she lay face down on the banks of the muddy river. She looked like she was sleeping if you ignored the dirt and mud covering her face and body. She was slender, with short hair and an elvish face. Not beautiful, but by no means ugly, and her face looked peaceful in the rising morning suns.

'Hey!' shouted Abreeth, shaking her. 'Hey, can you hear me? Wake up.'

Horst picked up her feet and started pumping her legs up and down.

'What are you doing?' asked Deadsun.

'Old sailors trick,' he answered. 'Helps get the water from the lungs.'

'Water,' said Abreeth. He'd put his hand on Nuri's chest before he'd realised what he was doing. If you asked him, he wouldn't have been able to tell you why he did it.

Closing his eyes and feeling into her body, he could sense the water in her lungs, the dirt and mud in her throat. The sensation of movement flowed through his hands as he moved the water and earth up her windpipe and into her mouth.

Her eyes shot open and she coughed a spray of water and mud as she heaved air into her starved lungs. She'd faced death and dodged its grasp, and the first set of eyes she saw when returning from the brink were Abreeth's.

If you were to ask anyone in that small group years later, what happened on the longest night of their lives, every single one of them would answer the same. It came to be known as 'The Shift.'

That night signified more than just the shifting of rocks and earth. The world had altered explosively, and a power shift had developed in the kingdom. It would take weeks to solidify, but things had changed in Fawe, and the destruction of The Columns was just the beginning of a creeping evil.

23
THE SCALES ARE TIPPED

High in the mountains at Point Terrene Elkstone stood, shielding his eyes from the setting suns to stare into the distance. It had been weeks since Deadsun and Greeven left, in haste, from the lonely outpost. He had packed his belongings, as tomorrow he would be saying his goodbyes to the men that gaurded the Firmalands from the rising darkness in the west.

A warm bed, a soft woman, a hot meal and a cold ale were the first four things he intended to indulge in when he got back to his posting in the city. For now, at least, his last night on the mountainous outposts was his focus.

'Looks like another dust storm,' he said to his young second in charge, 'let the men know they should cover the water buckets and close their tents tonight.'

'Yes, captain.'

'And ask the quartermaster if there's any wine. The men deserve a tipple. Damned if I'm suffering through another blasted dust storm with a parched throat, especially on my last night here.'

'Aye, captain. I'll see to it straight away.'

'Bloody dust storms, getting worse every year,' Elkstone grumbled to himself as he walked the perimeter of the lookout, chatting with his men. He was in the middle of a conversation with one of his lieutenants about incoming supplies when one of his men called out.

'Captain, I think you should come and look at this.'

His long strides marched him to the telescope mounted on a tripod that overlooked the vast Tundra, separating his camp and kingdom from the Pyrelands.

'Look, sir,' said the soldier, motioning to the copper framed spyglass.

'Looks like a dust storm to me?' replied Elkstone.

'That's what I thought at first too, sir, but look through the glass.'

Pressing his eye up to the spyglass, Elkstone swore, 'Gods be damned. Alert the men and start the signal fires.'

'The signal fires?' asked the soldier. 'We don't even know what it is.'

'I know damn well what it is. I said to alert the men and start the fires. NOW!'

———

The Pyrekhan stood at the head of his fleet, adorned in black leather, which hugged his slender, muscular frame. The late afternoon suns were warm against his skin and his dark hair was whipping in the wind.

The news of his success in crippling The Columns had touched his ears, and now was the time to strike for Thade. By this time tomorrow, his forces would be over the Ochota mountains and a week's march from their ultimate target, Thade.

Victory would be his legacy, his shining glory.

A new crown.

A new throne.

The absolute rule of both kingdoms and death to those who resisted.

'They're going to know we come,' the khan said to his captain.

'Their outposts will be overwhelmed easily and we'll mop up any runners,' he replied.

'This will be a war the likes of which they've never seen,' the pyrekhan said coldly.

With several hundred sandsailers in his fleet, the pyrekahn was moving across the Tundra with thousands of men, weapons and beasts, all bringing with them the promise of destruction.

A lookout cried from above, 'Fires on the peaks!'

Pacing to the front of the craft, the khan looked at the mountains before him, a large bonfire raging on its central peak, smaller signal fires spluttering to life before his eyes.

'They're expecting us,' growled the captain, the lines on his face as deep as the ruts from the wheels of his sandsailer.

'With an army of this size, they were always going to see us, but the element of surprise is not required when we have our powder,' said the pyrekhan.

'It's a good day to expand the kingdom,' replied the captain.

'Kingdom,' scoffed the khan. 'This is the start of an empire. Ready the troops, we're close.'

The glint of copper weapons, shields and armour in the approaching cloud was unmistakable. Elkstone knew instantly the vast pall of dust was no storm but a massive army crossing the tundra. He realised that he and his men would be in a fight for their very lives in a matter of hours. With an army of that size coming over the range, they would likely need to fight a rearguard action and lay traps as they retreated.

'I don't care if they've only just gotten back. Get those runners back to the city, now!' he shouted to a slow lieutenant, somewhat limited in his ability to realise the seriousness of the situation.

'We have an hour to prepare men, two if we're lucky.'

The camp was abuzz with activity. Men ran to their posts. Others handed out weapons or helped their fellow brothers in arms strap on armour, greaves and gauntlets. The massive bonfire at the peak of the range roared like a tavern fire in the fading light.

Looking at the mountains further afield, Elkstone could see other posts lighting their warning fires. It would be a matter of minutes before the city knew trouble was brewing. These fires hadn't burned in over a hundred years. The last time their light threw flame and warning into the skies, the two kingdoms fought the battle of Svort. The old pyrekahn was unsuccessful in his war against the kingdom then, and this new khan would suffer the same fate if Elkstone had anything to do with it.

'Be prepared. The khan's forces are likely to push a vanguard up the main paths of the range, and the sneaky bastards will likely test our flanks and try to encircle us,' yelled Elkstone, helping his men get into position.

'Finally, you're here,' he said, as a group ran into the middle of the main force, a bulky device in their hands.

'I'm sorry sir, it took some time to get all the pieces together.'

'No matter, you're here now. There's another five like this?' asked Elkstone.

'Yes sir, all spaced out as you said.'

'Good,' Elkstone replied. 'Set it up and be ready with the javelins.'

The men assembled the bulky ballista, ready to hurl lethal javelins amassed in a pile next to the deadly weapon.

After the battle of Svort, the king of Thade ordered a series of permanent outposts and camps along the range, the last bastion of his kingdom. All manner of defensive positions had been built. Boulders held by chocks that could smash enemy fighters should they be foolhardy enough to attempt an attack. There were mounted crossbows with rotating barrels able to throw dozens of bolts a minute positioned a few hundred yards apart.

If the enemy wanted a fight, they would be facing boulders, bolts, arrows and free men protecting their homelands. A dangerous combination for any invading army to face. The outposts in these mountains housed some of the hardiest warriors in the kingdom. The brutal cold and remote locations meant the men who guarded these ranges were conditioned and ready to fight.

Making last-minute preparations, the men checked javelins and ballista strings, arrows and blades before they settled down to that part of war every soldier despised, waiting. In the fading light, every shadow became a threat. Each rustle beyond the soldiers' posts was someone wanting to kill them. Was that the glint of moonlight on sword, or a restless mind playing tricks?

The night bled into the woods like a stab wound, dark, thick and deadly. Every man on the line looked into the trees, waiting, hoping and saying a silent prayer.

'Keep your eyes sharp,' said Elkstone. 'They're out there somewhere lads.'

For the past hour, they'd heard the sounds of troops and movement in the woods, but none had shown their face or made an attack. The men were getting restless. Some of the more experienced soldiers sat and smoked their pipes or played cards.

'No use in getting yourself tied into knots, son,' said an older pikeman to his younger companion. 'If you overthink what's about to happen, you'll drive yourself batty before the battle's even started.'

Movement sounded just beyond the treeline. Eyes and ears sharpened as grips on blade and bow tightened in anticipation of the assault they all knew was coming.

Then they heard it. A slinking glissade approaching them.

'Hold.'

A rolling, sliding, glide sounding from the undergrowth.

'Hold.'

Something big.

'Hold.'

Something almost silent.

'Wait until you see the whites of their eyes.'

Something long.

Something black.

Something with reptilian eyes.

'Are those fucking snakes?' came a cry.

'FIRE!'

———

The waiting was over. No warcry or charging soldiers. Just chaos and confusion as Elkstone's men aimed at the glistening, black coils sliding through their lines of pikes and poles.

Hundreds of snakes as thick as a man and a hundred feet long coiled their way up the mountain towards the waiting men. Many were shot by arrow and bolt before they made it to the defensive lines making them screech and hiss, but most managed to break through the line.

Dozens of men screamed as they were crushed by coils of pure muscle or punctured by fangs as big as daggers. Bedlam reigned as men and reptiles fought against one another. Fang against fist. Scale against sword.

Elkstone saw the beasts had ropes with barrels attached to them, like a newlyweds carriage dragging shoes.

'What kind of bloody game is the khan playing?' he thought to himself as the last of the writhing snakes were cut down by his men.

'Can't fight his own battles, got to send bloody beasts,' he heard one of his men grumble, staggering past to replace pikes broken by the immense reptiles.

Bloody and battered but still standing, the men took stock of their losses. Elkstone took a knee next to one of the dead snakes, examining the barrels tied to its tail. Half filled with black powder; the rest spilt all around.

In the light of the still blazing signal fire, he saw more barrels and trails of powder leading back to the treeline where the enemy was no doubt waiting just out of bowshot. That's when he saw it.

A line of flickering light beat back the night. It filled the woods, highlighting hundreds of men holding torches, more still lurking in the shadows.

'Be ready, men, they make to charge,' he yelled. The soldiers around him steeled themselves for the next onslaught.

Looking into the darkness, he heard a whistle from a distance as the enemy threw their torches to the ground. Elkstone could swear he saw the men turn and start walking away, but that made no sense. With his numbers thinned and the men tired after battling the snakes, if ever there was a time to take advantage of their position and charge, it was now.

Everything in his soldiers' training told him to be ready for hoards of men shouting and running through the woods, yet all was silence and shadows. Squinting and looking through the dark, Elkstone could see the torches were getting closer, moving towards them, steady in pace and orderly in line.

'What kind of sorcery is this?' he said, the men around him swaying nervously.

'What should we do, sir?' asked one of his men.

'Wait,' he said. 'We wait until we can see an enemy we can kill, then we fight.'

The flames had grown in both size and speed, hundreds of lines of fire burned their way towards them, hissing and cracking as they raced forward. Sliding towards them like firesnakes, the men watched as the spitting pyres coursed up the hillside towards them.

When the flames reached the first dead snake, the barrels attached to it exploded, sounding like a thousand boulders hefted from a quarry at once.

Fire and light flashed into the night, showering the men with shrapnel and dirt. It was mere seconds before the next group of barrels exploded, and then more again, and again, until it seemed like the entire mountain was hauled skywards.

Elkstone turned to run from the barrels closest to him, but the last thing he remembered was being hurled into the air by unseen hands and forces unnatural.

———

Elkstone tried opening his eyes, but they were stuck together. Distant voices arrived in his ears, a sound from afar, the ringing taking centre stage. He tried his eyes again, and one popped open, the bloody, dried seal opening like cracked earth before a spade. Blinking to clear his vision, he saw utter devastation around him. Many of the stories about the old gods he'd heard in churches talked of a fiery place where evil reigns and eternal pain is constant. This is what he saw around him now.

Trying to move, he found someone had bound him to the base of a tree. His arms stuck fast by his side.

'This ones awake,' he heard an unfamiliar voice say.

He saw bodies lying all around, hunks of meat and bone scattered the battlements. The enemy had broken their line. Pyreland soldiers wandered through the camp, picking at corpses – swords and armour their prize.

A silhouette walked through a gap in the flames, tall, muscular and sinewy.

Elkstone's throat was dry, he tried to swallow, but the ash and dust in the air choked his throat.

'Water,' he croaked to the figure in front of him.

'Oh, you won't be alive long enough to be needing that,' said the figure, who had now squatted in front of him. 'Do you know who I am?'

'Fuck you,' wheezed Elkstone, his throat all broken glass and gravel. He would have spat in this stranger's face if he could have.

'That's no way to speak to your future king,' said the pyrekahn, spinning a knife on the tip of his finger. 'Now, be a good fellow and tell me how many troops Thade has inside its walls.'

'I said, fuck you.'

'You have fight in you. I like that,' said the pyrekahn. 'This will be the last time I ask. How many troops reside in Thade?' He put the point of his knife against Elkstone's chest.

'I'll die before I tell you,' seethed Elkstone through gritted teeth.

'Then die you shall,' replied the pyrekahn as he eased the blade between Elkstone's ribs. Elkstone's eyes grew wide with pain as his life pumped out of the hole in his chest and onto the forest floor, a crimson carpet to match the rest of the camp.

The pyrekahn stood and surveyed the outpost his men and beasts had quickly overrun.

'To Thade and victory,' he cried, his men howling in response like a wolfpack surrounding a fresh kill.

24

DISCOVERIES IN THE AFTERMATH

As the rising dual suns threw light over the landscape, the level of destruction to The Columns became apparent to the injured, exhausted group. There was still a haze in the air, making them cough and rub their watering eyes. It would take days for the rock dust and smoke to clear, and weeks before the damage to The Columns became fully known to the two kingdoms.

The group searched through the rubble for survivors in the cold, long dawn. Minutes became hours along the dusty, freezing banks of the muddy creeks that sprung from The Columns, all whilst the rumble and crack of unstable rock split the air with alarming regularity.

'A broken arm, a gash to the head, a sprained ankle and lots of cuts and bruises,' said Abreeth. 'I'd say the gods were looking out for us.'

'They weren't looking out for them,' countered Horst, pointing at the three mounds of dirt near their makeshift camp.

'We should say some words for Prue and Placetivo,' said Deadsun.

'And Murphy,' added Dwin sadly.

'And Murphy,' Deadsun agreed.

They'd found Prue a mile downriver. Her blue, limp body drifted face down on the bank of the muddy waters. A section of her torn dress stuck on the branch of a tree.

A rockslide had crushed Placetivo. The only evidence they found was a torn piece of his robe and a bloody, mangled hand lying in the dirt. The rest of him was ground to a pulp by the tumbling rocks, red stains and smears of meat, the only indication of his previous existence.

Murphy was harder to find. His brown fur blended into the muddy waters, but Dwin refused to give up and searched until he found his faithful friend broken and bent on the banks of the frigid waters.

Marsine had trouble holding back the tears when Dwin ran into the water to hold Murphy's head in his lap, sobbing and telling him he was sorry he couldn't save him.

The group spent the morning burying the dead, tending to injuries, setting Kestral's broken arm and recounting to the three girls how The Columns become a smoking mess.

'I don't understand?' said Marsine. 'If the pyrekahn wanted to take over the kingdom, why would he destroy The Columns?'

'Simple,' replied Deadsun. 'To isolate Thade. It stops us from getting reinforcements, weapons or goods from the Welkinpeaks. With Roda Codex effectively cut off, we're on our own against his armies which he's no doubt massing for an invasion.'

'War?' questioned Abreeth. 'You think it will come to that?'

'I don't see any other logical conclusion to destroying The Columns,' replied Deadsun.

'That black powder explains how he destroyed entire villages in the Welkinpeaks too,' said Abreeth.

'This powder changes everything. I have to get back to Thade as soon as possible,' said Deadsun. 'We leave in an hour. Those of you who wish to travel with me may do so but know this. I will not stop or slow if you fall behind. I have a duty to the kingdom, and that duty lies in Thade.'

'I want to help,' said Abreeth. 'Tell me what I can do.'

'The best thing you can do is keep up and help me get to Thade. Once we're in the city, we'll need every man we can get.'

Nuri sat on the edge of the group, listening to the conversation. She couldn't believe her luck. By a sheer turn of fate, she'd found herself in a group with the Commander of the Lavers Lawmen, the very troops which protected the city the pyrekahn wanted her to infiltrate. She had grown to like Marsine and Gabrielle but was still conscious of her mission and its purpose. It would sting to betray them, especially after they'd shown her such kindness, but in the expansion of the pyrekahn's kingdom, people were bound to get hurt. As they say, 'you can't make feasts without killing beasts.'

She would do all she could for them when the khan took over the city. She would likely sit as a trusted advisor for the khan in the halls of Thade when he won, but for now, she needed to find out all she could and grow the bond and trust between herself and this new group.

'Deadsun,' said Nuri, walking towards him, 'I would also like to help. I have a certain acumen for numbers and calculations. Please use my skills in any way you see fit.'

'Thank you, Nuri,' he replied. 'The kingdom appreciates your loyalty.'

As she bowed, she smiled to herself.

———

The horses were nowhere to be found, so the group was forced to march. Whatever they could find of their belongings, they slung over their shoulders. Deadsun set a steady pace, and soon everyone had settled into a rhythm as their feet ate up the miles.

Several hours into their march they started seeing streams of people making their way towards The Columns to see what had happened. Some scoffed and snorted at the idea someone could destroy the colossal stone structure, but they would find out the truth soon enough.

When they walked into the first village, people couldn't help but stare. A more haggard and dishevelled group they'd never seen. Villagers were more than happy to help them any way they could, and they soon found themselves being offered water to drink and wash, food to eat and clean clothes to dress in.

Many in the village had heard the explosion and ran outside during the night to see the sky on fire. They needed no further convincing when Deadsun told them to prepare themselves for war in the coming days.

Sitting in the shade eating the villagers' food and wearing their clothes, it began to dawn on the small group just what they'd been through in the past twenty-four hours.

Deadsun looked at Abreeth and his young companion Dwin, Kestral's broken arm, Horst with his fiery red hair and grumbling nature and Nuri, Marsine and Gabrielle, who'd helped drag them out of the water.

Quite the eclectic group, he thought to himself. If you'd told him a week ago he'd be sitting under the shade of a birch tree chatting with a group like this, he would have marked you unstable and had you thrown in the drunk cage for the night. Yet here he was.

In the short time he'd known him, he'd grown to like Abreeth. He was young, smart as a whip and prepared to help without question. His young companion Dwin seemed a good lad also. Nuri was an interesting one, quiet, with a way of talking that quickly cut to the bone of the matter. Deadsun liked that, but there was also something about her. Perhaps it was her slight accent he couldn't pick or the way she presented herself. She was very different from most of the women he'd met in his life, from her short hair and ambiguous features to her male clothing and the way she spoke. There was something peculiar about her that he couldn't quite put his finger on.

Deadsun turned his eyes to Marsine, a beautiful young woman with flowing aurburn hair and a pretty younger sister that would no doubt grow up to be every bit as gorgeous as her older sibling. He'd been too preoccupied when stumbling out of the river to notice her beauty in the firelight. But now, having cleaned off the dust and muck and dressed in a borrowed kirtle that hugged her shape in all the right places, he was aware that Marsine was one of the most beautiful women he'd ever laid his eyes upon.

'Pretty, isn't she?' said Abreeth, sitting down next to Deadsun.

'Very,' he replied. 'I have a soft spot for red hair.'

'I can see why,' Abreeth replied, appreciating the figure and face of the pretty young woman. Marsine looked over at the two men and flashed them a winning smile. They both waved, grinning like idiots.

Tearing his eyes away from Marsine, Deadsun said, 'You know I never got to say thank you.'

'For what?' asked Abreeth.

'For saving us all. Without you opening that fawelock, we never would have made it out of The Columns alive.'

'Gods, that seems like weeks ago,' said Abreeth, leaning back against the tree. 'Can I ask you something?'

'Sure,' Deadsun replied.

'What happens when we get to Thade? I mean, if the khan's got this powder, what's stopping him from using it against us? City walls are no good if they've been blown to bits,' said Abreeth, taking another sip from the waterskin.

'I've been thinking deeply about that,' replied Deadsun. 'We're going to have to set up extra defences to make sure he can't get that powder anywhere near the walls or our gates.'

'That's a lot of men,' said Abreeth. 'Are there enough soldiers in the city?'

'We have seven thousand in the city at any given time. I will pull in all the other outposts, which will bump us up to ten thousand, plus any men that volunteer or come in from the villages.'

Both men continued to talk about possibilities and potential for an attack as they ate, not realising one in their group had turned an ear to listen, making mental notes as she ate.

Abreeth noticed Nuri sitting by herself and excused himself from Deadsun to sit next to her.

'Nuri, right?' he said, smiling and extending his hand. Nuri took it and chanced a small smile.

'Your young friend called you Abe if I'm not mistaken. I am in your debt for saving me, Abe,' replied Nuri. 'I'm sorry you lost some of your group in the explosion,' she continued.

'We're lucky this many of us got out alive. How are you feeling?' Abe asked, offering the waterskin.

'My chest still burns,' Nuri replied, taking a swig from the water-skin, 'and my throat feels like I've swallowed iron shavings and broken glass.'

'Well, I'm glad you're alive,' he replied.

'I have no memory about what happened,' she said, handing him back the waterskin. 'The last thing I remember is the explosion, then being thrown into the river. I came back from the black, and I was looking at you.'

Abreeth was just about to answer when Deadsun shouted, 'OK, we must leave. Let's get our gear and move out.'

———

Soon the group were marching again, strengthened by their short rest, food and clean clothes. One of the villagers had offered them a donkey for the younger members of their entourage when the pace became too much. Kestral grudgingly used the beast of burden when she stumbled more often than not. Her arm was still painful, and her pale face and fever showed her level of discomfort, but she took it all on without complaint.

Horst, despite his size, kept pace with the group – led them even, as the countryside crept past mile after mile. They even saw a group of horses grazing in the distance, one with similar colourings to People. Even if it wasn't their horse, Gabrielle and Marsine convinced themselves it was People, roaming freely in the countryside with his own kind.

Abreeth took the opportunity to hang back and catch up with the three girls on a particularly shady section of road.

Smiling at Nuri as he kept stride beside her, he said, 'I couldn't help but notice your wounds. Do you mind if I ask what happened?'

Gabrielle sprang to life at the question and answered, 'She fought and killed a whole pack of wolves with her bare hands. Big ones too! Tell him Nuri, tell him how you killed those horrible beasts.'

'Wolves!' said Abreeth, amazed. 'A pack of wolves attacked you?'

'Three wolves, to be exact,' replied Nuri.

'You should have seen her when she stumbled into our camp,' started Gabrielle again, twirling a pigtail in her hand. 'All covered in blood and almost dead. We helped her. My sister Marsine is great at healing. You have nice hair, you know?'

Abreeth couldn't help but chuckle.

'Please excuse my sister,' said Marsine before her little sister could wind up again, 'she's very excitable, and sometimes her mouth opens before her mind catches up.'

'I quite liked your story,' smiled Abreeth to the young girl. Gabrielle poked her tongue out at her older sister and said, 'See, Abe likes my story.'

'It seems you have a wound of your own,' replied Nuri pointing to the bandage on Abreeth's arm, hiding the deep cut he received at the hands of Wormface.

'Occupational hazard,' he replied, smiling.

'I saw what you did to Nuri on the riverbank,' said Gabrielle, 'are you a warlock or something?'

'Gabrielle, that's not something we call our friends,' reprimanded Marsine. 'You're not, though… are you?'

'No,' chuckled Abreeth, 'nothing like that. Let's just say I have a way with the elements.'

'You're a fawesooth,' declared Nuri calmly.

'A what?' asked both girls at once.

'A fawesooth,' replied Nuri. 'Someone that can control elements like fire, air, water and earth. That's how you got all the mud and water from my lungs.'

'I don't know much about fawesooths,' said Abreeth apprehensively, 'but it seems I can control elements. But not very well mind you.'

'Enough to save Nuri's life,' said Gabrielle.

'I don't understand it or know much about it,' continued Abreeth. 'Dwin's mother told me a little about it, but I didn't get to spend much time learning as we've been on the run ever since she was killed.'

'Did men from the Pyrelands try to take your family too?' asked Marsine.

'They destroyed our entire village with that powder,' replied Abreeth, 'and murdered Dwin's mother.'

'They took our father too,' replied Gabrielle with sorrowful eyes. She looked ahead at Dwin, walking at the head of the group with Horst and Deadsun. Both around the same age, both without parents.

'How is it you know about the Bind, Nuri?' asked Abreeth.

Nuri knew all about the Bind because the high priests of the Pyrelands used a form of it to keep the people they enslaved for the khan's salt and sulphur mines in check. The high priests had discovered that elements entwined with people's basic and primal drives. When they attached a Welltaker to a prisoner, they used the natural elements to control them.

Earth for feeding. Hungry slaves are working slaves.

Fire for fighting. Slaves can supplement an army.

Air for fleeing and water for fucking. By controlling base urges, the khan was able to command them entirely.

'I like to read,' replied Nuri simply, not wanting to give anything away.

Abreeth was someone whom she wished to become closer with. He could turn out to be very useful in the expansion of the Pyrelands.

25

BRING FORTH THE LOCUSTS OF WAR

There was a single tavern in the village of Wathermaske, owned by a married couple who had seen their fair share of hardships and difficulties over the years. They created themselves a marvellous little business over the years serving drinks and dinners whilst lodging beasts and bodies.

The fact the village sat at the base of the Ochota mountains hadn't bothered them. They'd lived in the outlands all their lives and were used to raiders and Pyreland rebels invading from time to time. Rebels hadn't made it to the village, at least not in the past few decades, which is why, when a local burst through their doors that morning shouting warnings of an invading army, they thought he was crazy. It wasn't until Scraps was dragged forcibly out by the young man they realised something was terribly wrong.

'Listen here, lovey. I'd appreciate it if you take your hands off me,' snorted Scraps, pulling her hand from the nervous young man who had burst through their doors only minutes before yelling about an invading army.

Dentri was in the middle of tapping a cask of beer and didn't appreciate being herded out the door, but made no sound as it was difficult to speak without a tongue.

'I'm telling you, they've lit the signal fires, and I've seen men on the march,' replied the young man, pushing both of them out the door and into the morning light.

'Old gods be buggered,' exclaimed Scraps, eyeing the rising smoke from the signal fires, still burning bright in the morning sun. 'They don't light those fires for nothing.'

'I told you it was serious,' cried the young man. 'What do we do, Scraps?'

'I've heard the rumours, but thought it was just tavern talk from drunken dolts. If they've lit those fires, a serious force is coming this way.'

Dentri tapped his wife on the shoulder and walked two of his fingers across his palm.

'For those that have horses, yes,' she said.

She turned to the young man and said, 'Tell anyone with a horse or beast to make their way to Thade. Tell them to grab what they can and run, or they're likely to be corrupted by the khan's dark mages.'

'What if they don't have horses?'

'Hide or fight,' replied Scraps as she turned heel and hustled back into the tavern, Dentri close behind.

Puffs of dust trailed the young man's heels as he ran to warn the rest of the village.

———

An army on the move has a particular sound and smell to it. Dust follows them wherever they go, and the aroma of men, beasts, metal and leather hang in the air like fog before dawn. There's a low rumble to an army on the move. The background noise of boots on the ground interspersed with shouts and clangs of steel on copper intertwined with barking dogs and braying beasts gives it away. If you'd not heard it before, you wouldn't be mistaken in thinking a storm was on its way. The rumble and boom is easily confused for a squall from the heavens.

With most of the village already on the road, those who remained heard the army before seeing any sign of armour, arrow, or sword. Those that stayed behind hid themselves and their children the best they could.

Some ran to the forest just beyond the town. Others hid in barns or the cellars below their homes, hoping the soldiers would see an empty house and keep moving.

Scraps and Dentri knew better. They'd dealt with the pyrekhan's dark mages before and knew they had a way of drawing people out of their homes with black magic. It seems they'd gotten better at it over the years too. Just over a week ago, two young girls with fiery auburn hair told them about the mages and soulsnitchers who attacked them and used a new type of menace to try and lure them into the dark. They were lucky to get away.

Scraps just hoped their secret room would hide them well enough to avoid detection. In the cellar of their tavern was a fireplace that heated the baths. If you were to sweep the ash and wood away, one would notice a hidden trapdoor into a large room below the cellar where Scraps, Dentri and several other villagers hid.

———

The pyrekhan's army was the largest ever raised in the history of the Pyrelands or the lands of Fawe. For the past five years, he'd been putting in place a series of orders to kidnap, steal or coerce at steel-point people from beyond his lands.

The past few weeks had seen many villages from the Welkin-peaks razed and the inhabitants bound with welltakers to do his bidding. They would make the perfect arrow fodder for running his barrels of boomdust to the walls of the city of Thade.

There was a kind of poetic justice in using the kingdom's own people to breach the walls and finally take the crown. Rows upon rows of soldiers with crude copper and iron weapons marched through fields and roads as they spilled over the Ochota mountains and into the Firmalands. Copper scales decorated their leather armour, and their long hair had been tied back in ponytails, feathers and animal fur adorning the backs of their heads.

The men of the Pyrelands were not muscular like the men of the kingdom. They were hardy and had the stamina of a workhorse, bred for exploitation and conflict. All manner of beasts pulled wagons and carts filled to spilling with barrels of black powder.

The army raided and ate its way through multiple villages and farms, burning buildings and binding anyone they found with welltakers. If they found a house or barn filled with a family, the dark mages used their fog to eliminate any semblance of resistance. Prisoners were effortlessly bound and controlled this way. This is how the pyrekhan raised his army so easily. So quickly. So effectively.

Many of his soldiers were Pyreland-born and didn't require a welltaker to ensure submission to his rule. Still, many of his army were conscripts, taken from the kingdom and hammered into submission by his soul stealers and dark mages. Now those very same mages travelled with the military, bringing their Vinculums, the rounded bowls filled with liquid and magic used to control bound slaves. This was how a few dozen mages managed thousands of captives in the khan's conscripted army. Some marched through the very homes and farms they had been snatched from but didn't register this indignity or seem to care. Their only thought was of moving forward, doing the dark mages bidding.

When it was time to stop, they would work together to make camp and prepare food. When it was time to fight, a wave of bloodlust and rage was implanted by the mages, which then fused into the minds of the stolen men and women.

———

Scraps lit a candle, shrinking away the inky dark of the hidden room beneath the cellar of their tavern. A low rumble, felt more than heard, emanating through the ground provoked concern on the faces of the small group hiding with her and her husband. Dust floated from the ceiling, glittering in the candlelight like an omen of things to come – dust, fire and fear. A small child whimpered, his mother holding a finger to his lips and gently stroking his hair. The sound of breaking glass and boots on floorboards made everyone jump, and the small child began to sob.

'Shut that child up, or we're all going to be found,' hissed Scraps to the young mother. Holding her child tight, she frantically tried to calm him, whispering and humming in his ear. Everyone in the room held their breath as they heard orders from above given to search the tavern. The small group huddled and looked at each other, eyes wide, darting left and right.

No one in the village knew this room existed. Scraps and Dentri had it made several years before, and it was a place they could go to in times of trouble and doubled as a storeroom for any items they didn't want others knowing about.

Many things had been left in rooms over the years – swords, scrolls, even the odd body. This room was evidence of all the back-room dealings and stolen goods they'd happened to come across.

Dentri moved several jars of tea and spices they had secured from a rotund tea merchant that met an untimely end in one of their rooms just a week ago and snatched several knives from the back of the shelf. Working hard not to make a sound, he handed one to Scraps and the others in the room, holding his finger to his lips as he did.

It seemed they were in the room for an age, holding their breath and waiting for the sounds of men to fade away. Scraping furniture and crashing tables could be heard above. Scraps sat, seething in silence, thinking about what those bastards were doing to her tavern.

Steeling herself for a long wait, Scraps was the first one to see a snaking tendril of vapour make its way into the room from the doorway above. Searching and swirling, it slid down into the small space like a hungry snake in a rabbit's warren.

Cold, black and soulless.

The young boy whimpered at the sight of it. His mother tried calming him, rocking him back and forth in her lap. It was almost as if the tendril heard the boy's whimper causing it to pause, listening for the location of its next victim. Scraps gave the young mother a pleading look as she held the nervous child against her, hoping he would be quiet for the next few minutes.

The tendril moved closer to Scraps, and she scampered back, avoiding its touch. Then, slithering like some serpentine diablo, it touched the floor and wound its way towards the group. A high pitched scream burst from the young boy.

'Fuck,' swore Scraps.

The tendril darted towards them, thrashing and whipping itself around the room like a vicious storm. It was the last thing the small group saw before their minds went dark.

————

And so it went with every village the locusts of war devoured. Every man, woman and child old enough to carry weapons, prepare food or comfort the men after a day's plundering was taken and used. All others were put to death.

A trail of dead – children and frail alike, washed behind the khan's army would be known in years to come as The Ending. Those who had yet to live never had the opportunity to, and those too old to be useful had their skulls crushed and necks cut – no more thought given to them than an animal in the slaughter yard.

Village and town fell alike. Small bands of Lavers Lawmen tried to sabotage their progress through the kingdom by burning bridges and setting traps, but ultimately it would not stop the inevitable onslaught of the khan's army.

Three days march into the Fawelands, the khan's army had swollen to almost fifteen thousand, more than double the armed guards, soldiers and men in the city of Thade. The khan had more men, his dark mages and the black powder on his side.

It seemed the gods had the khan in their favour.

26
QUESTIONS UNDER STARLIGHT

Grass to the side of the well-worn road crunched under the group's leather boots in the cold of the morning and the wagons rolled following ruts made from a thousand years of travel to and from the city.

After seeing the signal fires lit, the king of the Firmalands sent a garrison of men on horseback to round up and direct citizens of the outlying towns to the city. The captains had briefed Deadsun of the situation, not that he couldn't have guessed when he saw the signal fires burning brightly on the mountain tops. Half the kingdom saw the peaks of the Ochota mountains aflame and the fireworks that followed the khan's invasion.

Deadsun knew the khan had used his boomdust to devastating effects in the mountains that night and mourned quietly at the inevitable death of his men on those lonely peaks.

War was coming to Thade.

Deadsun secured several horses and a horse-drawn cart to expedite his trip to the city. They all took turns between riding or being jostled about in the cart. The closer they ventured to Thade, the more citizens fleeing the impending war joined them along the roads.

'Abe, how long before we get to Thade?' asked Dwin, shifting his weight to get more comfortable. Two days of riding and travelling in a wagon had a way of making one's buttocks numb beyond all comfort.

'Deadsun said we should arrive in the city tomorrow,' he replied.

'Good,' said Marsine, plaiting her sister's hair. 'I don't know how much longer I can sit in this thing AND be at the rear end of that horse.'

'It beats walking, Lassie,' said Horst, his low timbre echoing over the creak and groan of the cart, 'and the arse end of a horse is better than the pointy end of an army when we're outside the protection of the city's walls.'

'We travel at quite a pace?' stated Nuri, sitting next to Deadsun on the buckboard.

'I have to get back to my city as soon as I can,' he replied. 'The khan is coming. You've seen the smoke from the villages he's ravaged. By my best estimates, he's three to four days behind us, which means we will have little time to prepare.'

'I understand,' replied Nuri. 'It makes sense you wish to get back to your city. Can I ask you something, Deadsun?'

'Certainly,' he replied.

'What becomes of us when we arrive?'

'We pull together as a kingdom and fight the khan and his army,' replied the commander.

'No, I mean us. Our group. We've all grown quite close these past few days, given what we've been through. I'd hate to think we all go our separate ways once we reach Thade,' she added. 'Is there any way we could stay together?'

'I've already thought that through,' replied Deadsun, looking over his shoulder at Marsine. The sunlight bounced off her auburn hair in the afternoon sun, and Deadsun found it challenging to keep his eyes away from her.

'I will speak with the king's steward when we arrive to ensure we all stay in the keep. I might even have use for you. If you're as good with numbers as you say you are, we're going to need help with weapons counts and food rationing should the khan lay siege to the city.'

'Perhaps there's a way we could speak with the khan, come to some agreement?' Nuri asked, prodding Deadsun to uncover his motivations.

Snorting with derision, Deadsun replied, 'I wish that were the case, Nuri, but you don't know men like this. I do. They're driven by greed and power and will stop at nothing until they have it.'

'You're right,' said Nuri quietly. 'I don't know men like the khan, and I can see that you love your city and will protect it at all costs. I will leave you to your thoughts, Commander.' With that, she sat in silence, thinking to herself, *If only he knew.*

————

They travelled long into the night, only stopping when the moon had passed well into its third quarter.

'We'll rest for a few hours before sunrise and continue in the morning. Cold camp, no fires,' said Deadsun, dismounting and rolling out his sleeping roll. He spoke with the few guards travelling with the group to organise watches and laid down to rest.

The rest of the group tumbled out of the wagon, revelling in the softness of grass after days in a rigid wagon bed. Exhausted, most fell asleep almost instantly, except Horst, who seemed to have no trouble falling asleep in the back of the wagon, despite the persistent bump and dance of wheel on rut and rock. His loud snoring had kept any chance of sleeping in the wagon at bay for the past several hours, but now the group had an opportunity to move away from the noisy dwarf, their minds and bodies rested easily.

Sleep escaped Nuri as her thoughts floated into the night sky to join with the shooting stars, making her eyes flicker to the different corners of the sky. She had grown to know Marsine and Gabrielle well, perhaps even class them as friends in the short time she'd known them. They'd saved her from certain death when she stumbled into their camp in the middle of the night.

Abreeth had saved her life on the muddy banks of the frigid waters below The Columns just days later. Deadsun had his charms as a leader. Kestral, she didn't care for, but her broken arm kept her in the corner of the wagon, eyes glazed in pain at every bump. Even the dwarf she thought fondly of, though loud, obnoxious and seemed to let his anger get the better of him. As she tried to get comfortable, her injuries still scabbed and raw, she thought about the days ahead and her primary mission.

It was foolish to get too close to these people, she thought to herself. Once the khan breached the walls, she was bound by loyalty to betray them. She'd spent years with the khan under his protection and tutelage, yet she felt a strange affinity to this small group.

They weren't scheming against her or thinking of her utility; they simply wanted to help her. They'd saved her life twice. If this was how the people of the kingdom cared for each other, did they deserve a war waged upon them?

'Can't sleep?' whispered Abereeth rolling over and looking at her.

'I think sleep escaped me a few hours ago.'

'I know how you feel,' he replied.'You know, when I was a child, my father always used to tell me to relax one muscle with every breath, but that's a bit difficult when you have a rock in your back. Mind if I lay over near you?'

Nuri looked at the empty ground around her and answered, 'It isn't my ground so I have no place to deny anyone to lay upon it.'

Abreeth groaned as he lay beside Nuri, wrapping his blanket around him to get warm.

'It's a strange time we find ourselves in,' sighed Abreeth, looking up at the stars.

'In what way?' asked Nuri.

'Well, just a few weeks ago, I was working on a cloudcutter catching spurworms. I've seen my home burned to the ground, an explosion I didn't think possible and worst of all, I've lost people I've grown fond of on the way. It seems everyone around me ends up dying.'

'Dwin's still alive,' offered Nuri.

'You're right,' said Abreeth, 'and I need to do everything in my power to make sure he stays that way. His father lives in Thade. Hopefully, he will take him in after all this is over.'

Nuri felt a pang of guilt for a moment, knowing both Dwin and Abreeth would likely be killed in the coming war or bound as slaves to do the khan's bidding and that Dwin would likely never meet his father.

'How did you find yourself to be here with us?' asked Abreeth.

Nuri kept her story short and with few details, telling Abreeth only the main points. Poor family, father died young, going to Thade for a better life, etc.

'Want to see something?' asked Abreeth after Nuri had told her tale.

'That depends on what it is,' she replied.

Abreeth rolled away and rummaged through his bag. When he moved back, he was holding a feather.

'What do you plan to do with that?' asked Nuri suspiciously.

'Just watch,' was Abreeth's simple reply.

Sitting up and gathering his blanket around him, he held his hand out into the moonlight. Then, concentrating hard, he placed the feather in the palm of his hand where it hovered and spun slowly on its axis.

Nuri's eyes grew wide. 'A trick, surely? You have a hair or something holding it up.'

'I assure you it's no trick,' smiled Abreeth. Then, focusing more, he made the feather spin faster.

'You can control the feather?' asked Nuri.

'Not the feather. It's the air around the feather I can move. When I concentrate hard, I can feel the air around it like it's touching me, or I'm touching it. But, to be honest, I still don't understand what it all means.'

'What else can you control?' asked Nuri.

'I'm not sure control is the right word,' he laughed. 'Not yet, but I'm getting better. When we visited Dwin's mother, she talked about the Bind and how it's everything and nothing at the same time.' Abreeth continued trying to explain the Bind to Nuri but tied himself into knots.

'I've heard The Bind flows through everything in the lands. Rocks, dirt, animals... us even, and the four base elements tie into our four base instincts,' Nuri continued.

'I've heard about the four elements, but not the instincts,' said Abreeth.

'Fighting, fleeing, feeding and fucking,' said Nuri.

Abreeth chuckled. 'That makes a lot of sense,' he said. 'Everyone does those things. Even the animals.'

'Especially the animals,' offered Nuri.

Abreeth yawned, 'We should try to get some sleep. Good night, Nuri.'

'Good night, Abreeth.'

'Abe... call me Abe.'

'Good night, Abe.'

Nuri laid listening to the regular breathing of the young man lying next to her, thinking about his abilities and their conversation. Never had she felt so free to talk without thinking carefully about her words or plan three steps ahead.

Even with the khan – especially with the khan, she had to curb her true thoughts and consider what she said. She'd done it for so long it had become the natural state in which she communicated, but her conversation with Abreeth just now had opened a portal in her mind that she was afraid once opened would be a challenge to close.

She had not known freedom of the kind available in the kingdom. Everyone here had been pleasant towards her, unlike her life in the Pyrelands. She couldn't even trust her countrymen, as was proven that fateful night she entered the mountains with Pera.

She'd only been in the kingdom for a little over a week, and she was already questioning her loyalty to the khan. She told herself not to be so naive and that once the khan's army broke through the city walls, the years of sacrifice and planning alongside him would be worth it.

Closing her eyes, she tried to catch what little sleep she could before they set off for the city the following day.

27
PENTALOVE BEFORE THE PUSH

The mage pulled his cloak around him in the early morning fog as he pushed through the flaps in the khan's tent and woke him gently.

'It's Nuri, your eminence; she is sending a message,' he said, bowing low.

Rubbing the sleep from his eyes, the khan rose and strode from his sparsely decorated tent into the fresh morning air. His breath escaped in vapours as he entered the mage's tent and stood next to the Vinculum in the middle of the room.

'Nuri, what news?' he asked of the hazy face in the pool of water.

'Your powder has decimated The Columns,' she started.

'Good. This is very, very good,' the khan said, smiling.

'And I find myself in a group with the Commander of the Lavers Lawmen.'

'Excellent,' replied the khan. 'Can you talk openly?'

'I've moved away from the camp to pass morning water. I will need to go soon so as not to arouse suspicion. There's something else, Khan.'

'Something else! My dear, what you've achieved so far is nothing short of remarkable! What else can you possibly tell me?' asked the khan.

'There's a man in our group. A binder, not of lives and base instincts like our mages, but of fire, air, water and earth,' whispered Nuri.

'Keep him close. And the commander too. Go back to your camp, we will speak again soon.'

'Yes, my Khan,' replied Nuri.

'And Nuri?'

'Yes,' she answered.

'Play the game, continue the path, and you will have rewards beyond your dreams when I rule both kingdoms,' said her master.

'As you wish, my Khan,' Nuri replied.

'Now go, before others question your absence.'

Looking towards his mage the khan whispered, 'A binder of earth and fire. Tell me, Eisgarn, have you ever heard of such a thing?'

The mage in his black robe and grey beard rubbed his chin with bony fingers for a moment before stating, 'There's mention of binders in some of the old Fawe prophecies. They mention binding only briefly, not like the Pribram scrolls that helped us develop the welltakers. From what I remember, it talks about elements like fire and water but doesn't specifically talk about being able to bind them.'

'And what does it mean for us, this binder being able to control elements like this?' mused the khan.

'Depends on his ability. I've not heard of anyone being able to bind elements. There are stories, but from thousands of years ago. You have to go far, far north even to start hearing fables of people binding water and earth and such. Even then, they were tales to scare children. This could be good for us, or extremely bad. Only the gods know.'

'You mages and your riddles. I don't know why I pay you so handsomely sometimes,' grumbled the khan.

'Because we've helped build you an army, Khan, and we keep that army in check for you.'

'Yes, yes, I know all that. Now leave me in peace to think,' he said with a wave of his hand.

'As you wish, Khan,' replied the mage, shuffling out of the tent, leaving the khan with his thoughts.

Pondering this new development, he felt a surge of potential at the idea of capturing someone who could control the elements. His mages had worked tirelessly over the past decade, perfecting the binding of souls to his whims. They discovered slaves could be easily controlled and moulded to the bidding of their master. A little magic, a touch of fire and crystal, and you could cast one or several hundred into a rage. Likewise, water kept them forlorn and easy to manipulate. Earth was by far his favourite element. It brought forth reproduction, new life and unadulterated fucking.

Bursting from his tent, coiled tight in anticipation, he walked to the mage's sleeping quarters a few tents down and opened the flap to see the old wizard seated on his pallet smoking his pipe.

'Eisgarn, I want you to go to the women's camp, fetch me five of the prettiest maidens and go to work on them with some earth,' ordered the khan.

'As you wish, Khan,' said the wizened older man, groaning as he stood. 'Only five today?'

'Waging this war has left me a little... drained of my stamina,' replied the khan.

'Five it is then. I will have them brought to your tent and make a start with the casting.'

'Good,' replied the khan. 'And make sure they're whole this time. The one with a missing leg is not the type of surprise I want again, even if she had a pretty face. I'm a man of specific tastes and calibre, Eisgarn. You should know this by now.'

'As you wish, Khan. Only whole maidens. I will make the preparations.'

It didn't take long for Eisgarn to return with five half-naked girls.

A generous fire in the centre of the tent spat and crackled as the khan sprawled languidly on the furs of his pallet, chest bare, scars glowing white in the firelight. Sitting up and inspecting the girls from his bed, the corner of his mouth rose in delight.

'Very good, Eisgarn, very good indeed.'

'Thank you, Khan. They breed them pretty in the kingdom. I will go to my quarters to begin the casting.'

'No,' insisted the khan. 'Cast them here, I enjoy watching you work.'

'As you wish,' said the older mage.

Pouring water into the Vinculum, he pulled out his dagger and pricked the tip of his finger, letting several drops of blood fall into the water. Closing his eyes and putting his hands together, he started a low thrum in the back of his throat, chanting and moving around the pool of discoloured water.

Soon, a slight diffusion of light shimmered just above the liquid, which had now turned the colour of night. A creeping fog slowly rose, hovering just above the water, blue and black like a new bruise.

The mage looked up from his work at the khan and half-naked girls bathed in blue light. Taking a breath, he looked once again into the void of blue and black as thousands of small grey whisps emerged through the fog, each one representing a welltaker bound soul made from the same crystal held in his hand.

Slowly, he moved his fists into the fog, the light giving his hands a faint hue as he dipped his fingers in the water and spread them through it. The wisps moved and danced until he finally found the five grey wisps he was looking for.

'Good... good,' the old mage mumbled as he released his hands and hovered them just above the liquid. Kneeling, he plucked a chunk of earth from the floor and crumbled it into his hands, rubbing them together like a soldier readying for battle. Cupping his hands around the wisps and moving them together, the mage looked at the girls who had stiffened at the mage's surrogate touch.

Chanting with closed eyes, he clapped his hands over the circle, a shower of dirt and dust floating through the spectral light.

Instantly the girls' demeanour changed. Pupils dilated with pink hue cheeks, one of the women let out a mewl of intense delight as she spied the khan. Walking to the edge of the bed, she ran circles with her fingers around her nipples. The other girls were in various states of undress when the mage asked, 'Will that be all, Khan?'

'Yes, Eisgarn, you serve me well,' he replied, never taking his eyes from the naked form in front of him.

As he tried to leave, one of the young women stood in front of him. Tweaking her left nipple, she inserted two fingers slowly in her mouth, wet, slippery, inviting. The old mage tried to sidestep the maiden, but she moved in front of him again, fingers running down to the velvet of her mound and spreading her lips apart, letting out a soft moan of wanting.

'You've got the wrong man, my pet,' said the mage, turning her by the shoulders and pushing her towards the khan. A squeal of delight escaped her lips as she bounded to his bed, throwing herself onto the furs with gusto.

'Don't know how he does it,' chuckled the mage to himself, shaking his head as he walked back to his tent for a nice cup of tea, a draw of his pipe and a good night's sleep.

28

KING AND KEEP

As Deadsun and his group travelled closer to the city, the roads became leaden with human traffic. Luckily, several guards who travelled with them ranged ahead to move merchants and those seeking the city's safety from their path.

Deadsun drove at a hard pace. In the distance, he could see the familiar shape of the city's buildings on the horizon. The smell of salt from the Brine drifted through the air like the craft that sailed it, urging him to pick up the pace.

Time was a precious commodity when preparing for war, and this was something Deadsun did not have. The acrid columns of smoke behind them were a clear indication that war was coming to Thade, and soon.

'We will be at the city gates by noon,' Deadsun said to the group. 'Kestral, are you well?'

Kestral nodded meekly from the back of the wagon, pale and exhausted from the countless jolts and bumps. Then, looking at Deadsun through grey eyes, she hissed, 'Get me off this cursed wagon, and I will be forever thankful.'

'I will ensure you get the best treatment from our infirmary when we arrive,' replied Deadsun.

Kestral tried to smile, but the wagon hit another bump, causing a sharp intake of breath from the huntress.

'A broken arm is better than a broken heart, lassie,' said Horst. 'Have I told you the story of Lady Eversor and her...'

'YES,' groaned the group.

'We've heard nothing but your stories for the past three days,' replied Kestral through gritted teeth.

'I quite like your stories. Especially the one about the kitten and the pyredrake,' said Gabrielle, smiling at the dwarf.

'Why thank you, m'lady,' replied Horst, tipping a non-existent cap to the young girl, narrowing his eyes at Kestral.

Deadsun smiled to himself. Over the past week, this group had come to mean a lot to him – even the dwarf.

Familiar with overcoming hardships and pushing through diffi-cult times with his men, it had been a long time since he'd spent this much time with a group of 'commoners.' He'd made a promise to himself to attempt to keep his new friends as safe as possible in the coming days of war. Unfortunately, hard-won lessons taught him it was likely he wouldn't be able to keep everyone safe, but he was determined to try nonetheless.

Lost in thought, Deadsun felt a deft touch on his shoulder. He turned to see Marsine's demure smile framed by her soft red hair.

'I was wondering if you could show me those tricks with the horse again?' she asked softly.

'Of course,' he replied instantly, trying hard to hide his delight.

Marsine slid into the saddle in front of Deadsun; his right arm wrapped protectively around her waist. She wiggled backwards, placing her hand on Deadsun's muscular forearm. The horse peeled off into a canter through the field, leaving a track through the long grass.

―――――

'Those two are getting cosy,' chuckled Abreeth.

'Like the kitten and the dragon,' sighed Gabrielle, looking fondly at her sister and the muscular commander keeping her safe.

'He forgets himself,' growled Kestral, holding her arm and gritting her teeth as the wagon swayed.

'How so?' asked Abreeth.

'We are about to go to war,' said the huntress, a determined look on her face. 'We've all seen the smoke behind us and heard the explosions. The pyrekahn's army is just days behind us, and the city's commander is gambolling around like some teenage boy with his red-haired hussy.'

'Hey,' said Gabrielle sharply, 'that's my sister.'

'Please excuse her,' said Horst in a low voice, looking straight at Kestral as he spoke. 'She's had a long and painful journey these past few days and knows not what she says.'

Kestral grumbled, closed her eyes and tried, unsuccessfully, to get more comfortable.

'I think it's the perfect time to fall in love,' said Abreeth.

Everyone looked at him like he'd grown a second head.

'Think about it. A man with something real to defend, like love, will walk over fire and broken glass to protect it. I'm sure Deadsun loves his city and the men he commands, but a new love like this one? Love puts fire in a man's belly better than any devotion to city, stone or soldiers ever can.'

'I think Abe is right,' added Nuri. 'Love does have that effect on many people.'

'Aye, but it can also addle your brain,' replied Horst. 'As much as it loathes me to say it, I think Kestral is right. We must prepare for war, and we need all the men we can gather. It's going to be an excellent fight,' he added enthusiastically.

'If we don't get blown to bits first,' said Abreeth.

'I'd like to ride with Marsine,' blurted out Dwin, who had been quiet the whole conversation.

Everyone looked at the teenager, who quickly turned red as a freshly peeled beet when he realised he'd said out loud what he meant to keep in his head. Even Kestral managed a smile as the rest of the group laughed heartily at Dwin's embarrassment.

———

'Good... very good,' mused Deadsun, shielding his eyes from the midday suns. Thousands of citizens were digging lines of trenches and ramming sharpened wooden stakes into the ground a few feet apart for hundreds of yards around the city walls.

'It's been over a hundred years since war visited our walls, but we still know how to defend a city,' said Deadsun proudly to the group. They all stood in the wagon to get a better look at the goings-on around them.

'These are good defences, Commander,' said Horst, 'but do you think they will be enough?'

'They're going to have to be,' replied Deadsun, a determined look on his face. A tent stood a few hundred feet from the entrance, and several guards stood to attention as Deadsun rode into view.

'Commander, we're glad you're home,' said one of the captains, shaking his hand vigorously.

'It's good to be back,' replied Deadsun, clasping the man by the shoulder. 'I see preparations are going well. This is new,' he remarked, pointing to a large wooden wheel laying horizontally in the middle of the road.

'Yes, sir. Greeven's idea. Those chains on the wheel are attached to beasts behind the walls. They pull back these platforms along tracks. Underneath are ditches filled with spearheads and such. Got to be strong enough to pierce their cavalry sir, when they eventually come.'

'Excellent. I expect word of my arrival has reached the keep?' Deadsun asked, but already knew the answer.

'Yes, sir, the king is waiting for you.'

'Excellent. Keep up the good work,' Deadsun replied.

The captain stood a little taller in the midday suns.

———

The group walked towards the gates, marvelling at the large platforms made of solid hardwood beams lashed and nailed together. Under the platform, they spied ugly looking spearheads, barbs and other crude pieces of sharpened metal.

As they approached the gate, a lone figure limped from behind the guardhouse, arm in a sling and cuts on his face.

'I thought I'd finally gotten rid of you when I heard The Columns were destroyed,' smiled Greeven.

'Brother,' said Deadsun fondly, embracing his second in charge in a massive bear hug.

'The arm, the arm!' hissed Greeven.

'It's good to see you up and about,' said Deadsun. 'I've been wondering how you were healing. Come, I want you to meet some new friends.'

After Deadsun made the introductions, Greeven stood beside Kestral, inspecting her arm.

'That needs tending to,' he said. 'Come with me, and I will take you to the infirmary. I'm going there anyway to get some bandages changed.'

'Gladly,' she said, walking wearily beside him. 'Anything to get away from that damned wagon.'

'The rest of you, follow me,' said Deadsun in a commanding tone.

Something about being back in the city helped him slip back into the role of commander and leader. The heat of the midday suns poked through the clouds, warming their backs as the group walked through the outer reaches of the city. Along the roads, they passed taverns and stores, guards and markets, shops and sellswords. All had a quickness to their step like they needed to be somewhere hours ago and a look in their eye that wasn't quite fear but certainly wasn't calm. There was a slight disquiet in the air. Bad omens and dark perils were on their way, and the citizens of Thade knew it was coming.

Many of the experienced soldiers were acutely aware that the city was going to change in the next few days, possibly forever. First, there would be foreboding, seeing the khan's army marching towards the city, eating everything in its path. Then, there would be the uneasy stillness as the city watched to see what the king and his advisors would do. A truce, perhaps? Or would they all be fighting for their lives?

Then would come the fear of the first attack, then relief that the waiting had ceased. And after that? Well, that depended on a mixture of luck, skill and the will of the gods.

The first to greet them as they arrived at the keep's walls was Bailur, the king's steward.

'Deadsun, I'm so pleased to learn you weren't hurt in the attack on The Columns. I see you've brought company,' he purred, gliding towards the commander and his group. 'Allow me to introduce myself. Bailur, the king's steward and confidant at your service.' He bowed low and long, like one used to a life of servitude, but his dress gave away he was no stranger to power and politics.

'Introductions can come later, Bailur,' grunted Deadsun, 'we have business with the king.'

Smiling at the group and sweeping his arms towards the main stairs of the keep, Bailur stated, 'Our commander always gets right to the point. It's one of the things I like about him. We need men like him in our city, especially in times so troubled.'

'The king, Bailur,' said Deadsun impatiently.

'Of course, please follow me,' he replied.

Horst leaned over to Abreeth and said with a hand over his mouth, 'That pompous arse has more wind than an old maid after a month of cabbage soup.' Abreeth stifled a laugh as they walked up the marble steps and into the large keep in the centre of the city. Each massive block of stone used in the walls around the impressive building was polished smooth. Soldiers were stationed atop the walls at intervals with large mounted crossbows pointed towards the ground.

Entering the keep through two massive solid wooden doors, the group saw a hubbub of courtiers, servants, errand boys and all manner of staff buzzing through the hallways and doorways.

Deadsun took the lead and walked them all through a maze of tunnels, gardens and archways until they finally stood in front of a pair of elaborate double doors. He turned to the group huddling together at the entrance and said, 'We're about to go into the main dining area, which will now be the war-room. Be quiet and don't say anything unless asked.'

'Why are you looking at me when you say that?' cried Horst.

'I mean it, dwarf. I will be giving a full report to the king. I expect you all to give your accounts when asked and nothing more. Am I clear?' asked Deadsun. A few mumbles and nodding of heads came from the overwhelmed group.

Deadsun narrowed his eyes. 'Good enough,' he said. 'Bailur, if you'd be so kind as to show us in?'

Opening the double doors with a flourish, Bailur announced Deadsun and his fellow travellers to an important looking group and a tall, handsome man with salt and pepper whiskers and a golden crown atop his long flowing hair. Looking up, a glint of relief shone through in his deep blue eyes and a broad, but worried smile wandered across his weathered face.

'Deadsun,' he exclaimed, pushing his chair back with a scrape on stone. Making his way around the table full of maps, quills and parchment, he rumbled in his deep baritone. 'When I heard about The Columns, I had feared the worst. Oh, do get up off that knee and embrace your king.'

Deadsun rose from bended knee and embraced his king in a bear hug, given as much as received.

'I have much news to share,' said Deadsun.

'And many preparations to make,' replied the king. 'Come, sit. You and your friends must be hungry and travel weary. We'll share food, wine and news. All of you, please join us. I'm sure you all have value to add to Deadsun's account.'

For the next two hours, the group gave their account of travelling to and through The Columns as they drank and ate at the king's table.

29

A WOLF AT THE WALLS

'I wish those birds would be quiet,' yawned Marsine, pulling the covers to her chin in the cold rooms of the keep. They slept late, as they were up well into the night, talking about what may happen in the following days. It was mostly the sisters that talked. Nuri seemed unusually quiet, even for her. The only real thing Nuri contributed to the conversation was to say she'd heard the pyrekahn was kind to women and children, and should the city fall, she was sure they would be looked after.

'Is there nothing we can do to help?' asked Gabrielle, getting up and poking the fire with a stoker to help it catch some new wood she'd just added.

'The king said we need to stay in the keep,' said Marsine, brushing her hair as she sat on a wooden stool in the corner, 'and I, for one, am happy to stay safe behind these walls whilst the pyrekhan's army stands outside our gates.'

'The king just wants to keep us out of the way,' complained Gabrielle.

'Do you blame him?' asked Marsine. 'You saw what that black powder did to The Columns. We're much safer here in the keep.'

Nuri stood up and started pacing the room.

'Is everything OK?' asked Marsine, walking to her friend and placing a concerned hand on her shoulder.

'Yes, fine... it's just...' Nuri turned and walked to the window.

'It's just what, Nuri, what's wrong?' enquired Marsine. 'You've not been yourself of late.'

'Both of you need to promise me something,' Nuri said, staring over the city, streets all but abandoned.

'Of course. What is it?' asked Marsine, looking at her younger sister, confusion on her face. Gabrielle shrugged her shoulders and sat back down on her bed.

Turning to both of them with misty eyes, she said, 'When the khan breaks through these walls, and he will, promise me you will hide and then run from the city the first chance you get.'

'Nuri, you're speaking as if we've already lost the battle. It hasn't even begun. Thade has stood against attackers for thousands of years,' said Marsine, holding Nuri by the shoulders.

'Promise me you will hide,' said Nuri, a tear leaving a glistening trail down her cheek.

'Nuri, is there something you know that we don't?' asked Marsine. 'Why are you so sure the pyrekahn will prevail?'

'I have to go,' said Nuri, tearing herself away from the gentle grip of her friend.

'Go where?' questioned Marsine.

But it was no use. Nuri grabbed her cloak and walked quickly through the door.

'Nuri, wait!' cried Gabrielle from the bed.

Nuri stopped with her hand on the door handle, staring at her feet, breathing deeply. She turned slowly, looking at the two sisters with pleading eyes. 'Promise me,' she said. And then she was gone.

———

The sound of ravens flying overhead caused Horst and Abreeth to look up from their breakfast. In the silhouette of the doorway, they saw the outline of Dwin, puffed up and standing tall.

Tearing a leg from a chicken and chewing with gusto Abreeth asked, 'And where do you think you're going with that?'

Dwin looked at the short sword he'd managed to convince the keep's armourer to give him and then back at Abreeth and Horst. 'I'm going to use it against the khan's forces,' said Dwin, sitting at the table and helping himself to a plate, 'if it comes to that.'

Abreeth smiled at Horst, who raised his eyebrows. He poured Dwin a tankard of ale from the pitcher on the table and passed it to his friend. 'Really?' he asked, 'and where do you plan to use this sword of yours?'

'Right here in the keep,' said Dwin, taking a long draw from his tankard, 'hopefully, with you both beside me?' he asked.

'Good,' said Abreeth, 'I'd hate to think you've grand ideas battling at the wall with the rest of us.'

'So you're going to the wall?' asked Dwin sadly.

'Everyone capable of shooting a bow or swinging a sword is needed, laddie,' replied Horst.

Dwin was about to speak, but Abreeth cut him off and said, 'Everyone of age, that is. So yes, we're both going to the wall.'

Dwin dropped his shoulders and looked at his plate. Abreeth realised he'd grown so much in the past month. Looking at him now in his oversized greaves and too large sword, Abreeth easily forgot he was still only a boy on the cusp of manhood.

'Besides,' said Abreeth, 'you're needed here to help protect the women and children. That's an important job.'

'Yes,' replied Dwin, throwing a chicken bone on his plate, 'with all the old men and boys.'

'Don't be too quick to want the taste of battle, laddie,' said Horst. 'There's no shame in helping to protect those who can't protect themselves. Everyone has a role to play today, and before the day is done, I'm sure you'll have had your share of excitement.'

'Perhaps,' said Dwin, 'but we've all come so far together. I want to be beside you when the arrows start flying.'

'Trust me,' said Abreeth, standing from the table, 'it's much better you're here. Besides, someone needs to keep an eye on Marsine whilst Deadsun's away,' he said with a wink. A chicken bone flew past Abreeth's head as he and Horst left the table.

'Keep practising that aim, laddie, and one day you might make it to the wall to sling arrows,' smiled Horst as he and Abreeth departed the common room.

30
PREPARATIONS AND TREACHERY

The two groups scrutinised each other as they approached. Vanguards looking for any sign of weakness. Deadsun and the king strode at the head of the group, every soldier on the wall held notched arrows with itchy bow fingers.

The khan and his men walked forward with their chins held high, sauntering with the confidence only men with nothing to lose can display. The king was a tall man, but the pyrekahn stood a full head taller and walked directly to him, eyes boring through him the last few feet. The two leaders looked at each other, waiting for the other to speak first. Finally, after several moments of awkward silence, the king spoke.

'You bring an army to my gates, Khan. I can only presume you wish to do my city and its people harm?' he rumbled.

The khan walked along the line of soldiers that flanked the king, looking them up and down.

'Enough of your games, Khan,' said the king impatiently. 'What say you?'

The khan ambled back to the king, sucking his teeth and putting his hand on the bottom of the king's tunic feeling the expensive cloth between his fingertips. The soldiers beside the king pointed their pikes in the direction of the khan. The king held up his hand to calm them.

'You may not have heard of it, but there is an animal called the firegale,' started the khan. 'It's only a small animal – about the size of a raven, with golden coloured feathers. The firegale is the only animal known to be able to escape the clutches of a Pyredrake. You see, when a Pyredrake knows it is about to die, it will burn itself from the inside out, taking its prey to a fiery death with it. When it turns its own body into doomed cinders, the firegale's feathers protect it, and it prevails,' continued the khan, picking dirt from around his fingernails and looking at the king once more.

'Whilst we appreciate the biology lesson Khan, I think we'd all prefer you get to the point,' said Deadsun through clenched teeth.

'You must be the commander. A simple soldier would have neither the presumption nor the guile to speak on behalf of their king,' replied the khan, standing in front of Deadsun, who now stared directly into the khan's piercing blue eyes. 'What say you, King? Should we listen to your commander here and... get to the point?'

'What do you want, Khan?' the king asked simply.

'It's very simple. I want one thing and one thing only,' replied the khan.

'And that is?' asked the king.

'Fealty.'

The soldiers surrounding the king all laughed and chuckled to themselves.

'Fealty, or?' asked the king.

Now it was the khan's turn to chuckle, 'There is no or,' he said, turning to his captains. 'I don't recall saying or. Did you hear me say that?' he asked. His captains smiled and shook their heads.

'No Khan, no mention of or.'

'You see, King, I am the firegale and I will prevail. You have a city full of citizens, and there's only one action you can take to save them.'

'Go on,' said the king.

'Bend the knee,' commanded the khan.

The king clenched his jaw as his breath became sharp. Deadsun drew his sword, causing every soldier in the two groups to do the same. He calmly stepped forward and lodged his sword into the ground, tip first at the khan's feet.

'This sword is named Kilbride. It has taken more lives than days you've been alive, and I promise you this, Khan. This steel will be the last thing you see at the end of your, what's soon to be, short and miserable life if you do not leave our lands.'

The khan scoffed in Deadsun's face. 'Oh, I'm not going anywhere. Not only are you surrounded, but you're alone. You have no support from the Welkinpeaks,' he said smiling, running a long finger over the hilt of the sword wedged into the ground.

'In fact,' he continued, 'I suspect within the next two moons you will be begging for your pathetic lives in the dying embers of your stinking city.'

With that, the khan pushed Kilbride over. Its hilt fell into the dust as he spun his heel and strode back towards his army.

———

Abreeth and Horst insisted they stand beside the gates, to be as close to Deadsun as possible, when they heard the vanguard was to talk with the khan.

'Well?' asked Horst as the group walked back through the city gates, 'What's it to be?'

Deadsun narrowed his eyes and looked at the men around him and answered, 'We go to war.'

Horst laughed excitedly, slapping Abreeth on the back. 'A fight for the ages this will no doubt be. They're going to tell stories about this for a thousand years, laddie.'

Abreeth's mouth was dry as tinder, and a large river stone had suddenly appeared in his stomach. As much as he wanted to share in Horst's enthusiasm for battle, he was also acutely aware of how outnumbered they were, and the khan had that cursed black powder.

Deadsun rubbed the stubble on his face and took a deep breath, lines below his tired eyes creasing. 'Sound the battle horns,' he said with a grim look. Four massive Alphorns, all made from a single piece of mahogany, sounded in harmony above the city gates.

The king raised his voice and addressed the crowd as everyone came to a standstill. 'It's been over one hundred years since our city has heard the call of these horns. Our city defeated the old khan then, and our city will defeat this new khan now. We will stand united, as a people, as a city. As men. As BROTHERS!'

A roar went up from the thousands of men that gathered at the city gates and walls. Soon the whole city had heard they were to go to war. There was much to do.

'What do you need from us?' asked Abreeth in the commotion.

'I need you two to go back to the keep and tell Marsine, her sister and Nuri that we are going to war. I'm not going to be able to see them for days. Also, I need you to give this to Bailur, and then I need you both back here as quickly as you can,' Deadsun pushed a scroll into Abreeth's hand.

'Tell Marsine that I... that... I hope, with all my soul, to see her very soon,' he said. 'And give her this,' he took the leather strap with a stone carved into the shape of a bird in flight from his neck and placed it in Abreeth's hand.

'I will,' said Abreeth, taking the necklace and squeezing Deadsun's arm as the commander turned to prepare his city for war.

'Deadsun?' Abreeth called.

The commander looked back, stern determination on his face as Abreeth stated, 'I can think of no one better to lead us to victory.'

Deadsun nodded and walked back to his men.

'He's drunk deeply from the fountain of fondness for that girl,' smiled Horst with a twinkle in his eye as they walked towards the keep.

Their journey was fast, as there were no crowds to block their path. Abreeth and Horst found more houses and businesses had nailed boards atop their windows and doors overnight. People on the street had the same look a deer gets when it spots a bear from a distance. Cautious. Wary. Ready to run.

'Do we stand a chance?' asked Abreeth to the dwarf.

'There's always a chance, laddie. It just depends on what you want that chance to be.'

'I'm not sure I understand?' replied Abreeth as they side-stepped an older woman pushing a cart, with what seemed like everything she owned inside it.

'Think about all the people who die before they have a chance to be born. All those that die in the cot as a child. Think about the people who pass into the dark when a bad winter hits, and there's not enough food to feed their families. Every one of those people has no chance to do something different. No chance to choose a different path. But we do.'

Horst stopped and looked up at Abreeth, his hand resting on the axe at his hip.

'No one knows what path lies ahead of them, laddie. Not even the gods. There's a chance we will die in battle, it's true. But there's also a chance we will prevail. No one knows which way the dice will roll in the game of life. That's what makes it so interesting!'

'You could just say you don't know,' smiled Abreeth.

'Bah,' laughed Horst, slapping Abreeth on the arm. 'What's the fun in that laddie? All I know is that today, we're to be part of history.'

Abreeth wondered how someone could face death and greet it with a smile.

———

Nuri had been pacing the halls of the keep for the past few hours, unable to stay still for more than a few minutes. She'd been avoiding Marsine and her younger sister Gabrielle, even though she knew they had been looking for her. There was a feeling in her stomach like someone had turned her guts inside out and upside down.

Running through every scenario in her mind didn't seem to help her come to any sort of decision about what to do. If she did the khan's bidding, she betrayed Deadsun, Abreeth, Marsine and Gabrielle. She knew in her heart that none of them deserved to die at the hands of the khan. They were innocents wrapped up in the game of war.

She also couldn't rid herself of the ingrained contempt she harboured towards the kingdom. It was something she'd had drummed into her since birth. But since travelling here and seeing the people and places, she realised everything she'd learned throughout her life was mostly wrong. These people weren't the overlord neighbours that kept the Pyrelands in servitude.

'Can I help you?' asked a serving boy walking past.

'No, thank you,' she replied. 'Is everyone so damned polite around here?' she mumbled to herself as she continued down the hallway and back to her quarters.

She listened outside of the door before going into the empty room. Walking towards her bed, she knelt to retrieve an elegantly carved box about the size of an apple from her bag. Sitting on the bed, she stared at the box in her hands, fingering the grooves in the wood as she contemplated her position. She knew that once she opened it, there was no turning back.

———

Horst and Abreeth made their way to the girls' quarters and knocked gently on the door as it swung open to display Nuri shoving belongings in her bag.

'Nuri,' said Abreeth, 'do you know where Marsine and Gabrielle are?'

'I'm not sure, but I think I saw them on the front stairs of the keep earlier. Has there been any word from the khan? Has he sent a vanguard?' asked Nuri.

'He has.'

'And?' she asked.

'We go to war,' replied Abreeth.

Nuri's jaw tightened as she nodded. 'Then may the gods have mercy on us all.'

'I need to give something to Marsine. Do you know where she is?'

Nuri shook her head

Abreeth and Horst started back down the hallway but Nuri ran to the door and called Abreeth's name, making him turn.

'May I have a word with you?' she asked.

'Of course.'

'Alone?' said Nuri, looking sternly at the dwarf.

'Hmmph, I know when I'm not wanted,' scowled Horst, turning on his heel and walking down the hallway. 'I'll meet you at the stairs, Abe,' he called as he turned the corner.

Nuri stepped close to Abreeth. 'I wanted... to apologise,' she said softly.

'Apologise? For what?' asked Abreeth.

'For this.' She leaned forward and kissed him softly. Her hand slid behind his neck, lips lingering as their eyes locked. Pulling away, she looked at the ground.

'Nuri, you don't need to apologise for kissing me,' exclaimed Abreeth.

'That's not what I'm sorry for,' she replied, wiping her mouth with a cloth.

Abreeth felt his chest tighten as the hallway started to spin. The last thing he remembered was Nuri standing over him.

'I'm sorry for what's about to happen.'

31

THE MIGHTY ROAR OF WAR

'It's been a full two circles of the suns since they've arrived, yet they've not attacked! Also, where the hell is Abreeth? Has anyone found him yet?' growled Deadsun, growing weary of waiting for the khan to roll the dice in the game of war.

'We've searched the keep twice, Commander, and it appears the woman Nuri is also missing,' answered one of his soldiers.

'He'll turn up,' said Horst cheerfully between bites of a chicken leg. 'You know what it's like when you're young and full of fire. He's probably just getting some time alone with her, is all.'

'That's what I'm worried about,' replied Deadsun. 'The khan is likely to attack at any moment, and he's off getting his prong wet.'

Deadsun threw a stone off the edge of the city wall into one of the trenches below. All last night and the previous day, they'd heard the sound of axes in the forest. When they looked out from the walls, they could see the trees shaking in the distance as they fell. Small groups would occasionally emerge from the treeline to stop just beyond bowshot, only to return to the forest once more.

'What game are they playing at?' asked Greeven, feeling well enough to make the climb up the stairs to the walls.

'I don't know, brother, but I don't like it. They're preparing for an attack. I can smell it. But what are they planning?'

'They're likely planning on using as much of that black powder they can get their hands on,' grunted Horst, throwing his chicken bone over the wall and watching it spin through the air onto the frosty ground below.

'Well, we've got every archer in the city on the walls, and thousands, probably tens of thousands of arrows, both flame and spearhead to stop them before they can make it to the walls. If they send runners carrying barrels, we will stop them.'

'And if their runners outnumber our arrows?' asked Horst, shielding his eyes from the suns as he looked at the forest where the khan's army lay in waiting.

'Then we fight for our freedom or die behind our shields,' said Deadsun coldly.

'A runner approaches,' came a shout from the wall. Deadsun walked to the edge of the wall to see a middle-aged man standing in front of the city gates.

'State your businesses,' called Deadsun in a booming voice.

'I speak for the khan,' called the man in reply.

His stained leather pants and worn tunic looked almost clean compared to his filthy face and bird's nest hair. Over his clothing, he wore makeshift armour of bone and sticks, string and leather.

'His graciousness is giving you one last opportunity to swear fealty. He states if you embrace the darkness, it will bring redemption. You need only to bend the knee, and all this can be over.'

Greeven limped to Deadsun's side and whispered, 'I recognise that man. He's the tavern owner from Tirrena. We lodged there just months ago on patrol, remember?'

'I have it on good authority that you own a tavern not far from here,' called Deadsun, 'is that true?'

The man shook his head like he was fighting against his thoughts. 'My... no... that tavern's gone, and so is he. I speak for the khan. What say you?' called the man, now pacing back and forth, becoming more agitated by the minute.

'Tell your khan we decline his offer of fealty in the strongest possible terms,' replied Deadsun.

'He said you may answer this way,' said the man, untying the wooden armour from his body and leaving it in a pile at his feet.

'What's he doing?' whispered Greeven.

'Who knows?' answered Deadsun, as every soldier on the wall watched the man undress.

'The khan reminds you of his influence with this sacrifice,' said the man, pulling a blade of obsidian from a sheath at his back.

He inspected it like a rare and beautiful butterfly that had just landed in his palm. A look of wonder reached his face as he moved the blade in the sunslight turning the black, razor-sharp shank in his hand. With his left hand, he grasped an ear between his finger and thumb and sliced it off in three jagged jerks, throwing his flesh to the ground.

Taking the blade in his other bloodied hand, he cut off his second ear, all the while standing silent. When he took off his nose, a moan escaped his lips. Hardened soldiers looked on in horror as he sliced off his manhood and added it to the pile of dead flesh at his feet.

The man's small intestine had just started to fall from the slice in his belly when Deadsun looked at the archer standing next to him and commanded, 'Put a stop to this... now.'

The arrow buried itself to the fletching with a wet thump, like meat slapped on a butcher's board. The man dropped to the ground, his blood steaming in the cold morning air and pooling on the frost laden ground. Even the most seasoned soldiers quickly realised they were soon going to be fighting a battle like none they'd ever fought.

A battle horn sounded from the forest as the roar of the khan's army raised the hair on the back of every soldiers' neck. The city's defences exploded into activity with soldiers racing to their positions. Boys stoked coals in the braziers so archers had a steady fire with which to light their flame arrows.

Animals that had taken shelter close to the city quickly fled from the sound of the horn. A deer ran away from the tree line, attempting to leap over one of the trenches protecting the city only to impale itself on one of the pikes. Kicking and bleating, its life slowly ebbed from its body, adding a strange and haunting overtone to the noises coming from the forest beyond.

'PREPARE YOURSELVES!' roared Deadsun.

Along the wall, every man looked intently at the forest, guts churning, preparing for what was to come. Arrows were nocked. Crossbows were loaded. Ballistas were armed and ready.

'THEY COME!' cried a shout from lower down the wall.

The soldiers heard them before they could see them. Bodies black with ash encased in wooden armour, masks of bone and branch came screaming from the treeline towards the city gates. They ran like wild animals across the space between the forest and the defence trenches, teeth bared, eyes wild.

The first wave collided into a swarm of arrows dropping their bodies as they ran. Many tumbled into the trenches designed to protect the city, whilst others slid in slush and mud that quickly turned red. Only a few made it past the trenches, but they too were dropped by bolt and bow.

Three more waves of bound souls ran from the forest over the space of the next hour. Arrows, bolts and quarrels mowed down all of them.

'This is a massacre,' exclaimed Horst, overlooking the carnage. 'They don't have any weapons.'

Moans and screams came from those injured below. Deadsun watched as several men and women, arrows protruding from their bodies, dragged themselves into the trenches to die.

'He's filling the trenches,' said Deadsun quietly.

A soldier appeared before the commander, breathless from his dash along the wall.

'Sir. We have to put a stop to this. Many of the men are firing on their own people. Some have even seen their families in that lot. Surely the gods are punishing us?'

Deadsun grabbed the man by his tunic and pushed him against the wall. 'We will do no such thing,' he snarled. Raising his voice, he yelled, 'We are here to protect the city and protect the city we shall!'

The hundreds on the wall which had been firing clenched their jaws and rallied their courage to face whatever came next.

Deadsun pulled one of his captains aside and said, 'Get these men rotated and quickly. No one should have to fire on their kin more than once.'

'Yes, Commander.'

As the suns slowly meandered behind the mountains, more waves of bound souls ran towards the city, filling the trenches even more. Thousands of dead lay scattered in piles before the walls. Every injured body that was able, crawled or hobbled into the trenches, taking their final resting place amongst the dead, their life slowly ebbing from their wounds.

———

'Looks like they've settled in for the night,' said Greeven, rubbing his hands near the glowing coals.

'I wouldn't count on it, laddie,' replied Horst. 'From what I've seen, that bastard has all sorts of corrupt tricks up his sleeve.'

'The dwarf is right,' added Deadsun. 'I have a feeling this is just the beginning.'

A lull in the onslaught gave some much-needed respite. The stink of blood and misery hung low in the air as crows started to gather, despite the late hour. The strewn and mangled bodies would start to smell on the morrow when the tang and acrid stench of death would waft its way over the wall.

Cooking and quiet conversation filled the twilight as wrapped furs and smuggled drinks helped stave off the cold. Fires made shadows dance and flicker along the wall in the twilight. A frigid, lingering night of waiting and worry laid ahead. Just as Deadsun was about to sit down to eat, a yell came from the wall. 'They come! They come!'

Pushing his hunger aside, Deadsun looked into the darkness to see fires at the edge of the treeline. Blue in colour, like no fires he'd ever seen before, it took him a moment to realise the flames were moving towards them. Screeching and howling met their ears as hundreds of moving blazes dashed across the ground.

'Archers be ready,' roared Deadsun amidst the organised chaos on the wall.

Men threw down whatever they were doing to prepare themselves for the next onslaught.

'What have you got for us now, you rat bastard?' Deadsun murmured to himself as the ignited figures came into view.

Foxes, dogs, horses, hundreds of men and women, even some donkeys burned with a bright blue hue, throwing dark and magical light around them. Every figure carried a barrel on their back or had several strapped to their bodies. Even the dogs and foxes had small barrels tied to their sides.

'Fire!' thundered Deadsun. 'Aim for the barrels.'

As if to accentuate his command, a horse exploded one hundred feet from the city walls sending hoof, gore and guts into the air. Those close to the explosion were knocked to the ground, partly by the blast and partly by flying meat and muck.

The night sky lit up with arcs of flame sputtering through the darkness. Some struck their targets, dropping animals and men to the ground in a writhing heap. Others hit the ground harmlessly, wedging themselves into the cold earth. Those who aimed true hit the barrels of black powder which threw smoke, screams and slaughter into the air in a sickening display of carnage that even the most experienced soldiers found hard to comprehend.

When the smoke cleared the men on the wall discovered there were many more bound souls hidden in the darkness of the night, dressed all in black, ash and mud smeared on their faces and arms.

With barrels of powder strapped to their backs they picked their way thorugh the bodies towards the wall.

'Fire!' roared Deadsun. 'Do not let them get to the wall.' The twang and whistle of arrow and bowstring quickly filled the air.

'Kill them before they get to the wall,' came shouts from the captains. New archers were brought to the front as others couldn't pull their longbows back anymore. The stench of death hung over the city like a cloak of misery and dashed hopes to those fighting a desperate battle.

'How can we fight against those who are possessed?' came a cry from one of the archers, his draw arm limp from firing into the night.

'They die, just like any man when hit with an arrow,' shouted Greeven. 'Make yourself useful and fetch more arrows.'

Again and again, the archers fired arrows into man and beast running at the city. The number of living beings thrown at the city was incomprehensible, and defences would soon be overcome by sheer weight of numbers.

Before long, a pile of dead crowded the city gates, all of them with barrels of powder tied to their backs. Explosions were still echoing off the walls and causing chaos below, but it seemed a concentration of people and animals had broken through the onslaught and made it through to the gates. As they fell, they crawled to find a gap in the carnage to squeeze their arrow-riddled bodies before they died.

Once again another row of blue-tinged fires sprang to life at the edge of the forest.

'Brother, if this keeps up, we're going to be overrun,' hissed Greeven as he looked around at the exhausted men on the wall.

'We have no choice but to keep firing,' replied Deadsun. 'Men!' he yelled, 'hear me!'

Deadsun jumped upon a barrel, his voice echoing across the walls. 'They come to us again, but we are ready. We are prepared. We are willing. When the scribes write about this battle in the annals of history, they will tell stories of great men. You are those men. You are those stories. You are those brave enough to fight the evil at our walls. FOR KING. FOR VICTORY!'

Every man along the wall took up the cry, a new enthusiasm running through them.

'FOR KING. FOR VICTORY.'

Arrows flew in a torrent of renewed zeal. Burning beasts and slaves made their way into the pile of bodies and barrels strewn at the entrance of the city. Hundreds of barrels lay at the city gates, just waiting for a spark. Hot coals and flame showered the enemy below from a brazier that was knocked over in the fighting.

Six feet thick though they were, the city walls shook with the explosion. Men were thrown from the wall by the blast. Deadsun was beginning to realise he would not be able to keep his beloved Thade safe without significant cost. In the keep hangings fell, and windows shattered as the king cast a troubled eye over the city.

32

BOUND BUT NOT BROKEN

Dwin muttered to himself as he kicked stones down the damp and shadowy tunnels beneath the keep. They had become his stomping ground over the past few days, and the shadows matched his mood.

'I can't believe I've been relegated to babysitter!' he scowled. 'I'm almost fourteen. I should be on the wall with the men. Dwin, you're old enough to work on a cloudcutter and risk your life catching spurworms, but not old enough to be in the biggest battle this kingdom has ever seen,' he complained to himself, kicking a rat that dared scurry across his path, sending it flying with a squeak down the inky passage. 'At least the rats don't tell me what to do,' he lamented to no one in particular.

He took another turn in what seemed an endless series of passages and tunnels, some well lit, others dark and intimidating. He occasionally came across a guard or someone from the keep who didn't seem too bothered by a teenage boy wandering by himself in the belly of the biggest city in the kingdom. It's not like he could steal much.

The rooms in the tunnels were full of old books, parchments, locked trunks, weapons and armour that were so rusted and old, a long-dead king would shake his head, clicking his tongue at their condition. One saving grace of being down here was that he didn't have to listen to the roars and shouts of the raging battle on the wall.

He'd begged with the soldiers at the entrance of the keep to let him go and watch from a safe distance to no avail. He'd even tried to find a way up the spires of the keep to secure a window or vantage from which to watch the battle, but was always stopped by guards or some other person of authority. It seemed the rooms in the highest places of the keep had been delegated to kings, queens, their advisors and anyone else that wasn't him. He'd even tried to sneak by in a serving boy's outfit to take food to someone essential, but he'd grown so much in the past year none of the uniforms fit.

His favourite room had a collection of old tapestries and paintings displaying battles in great detail from the kingdom's history. Pyredrakes blew bellows of flame at soldiers brave enough to face them. Crowned kings sat in lavish courts with ladies wearing old fashioned dresses and men in strange-looking attire.

A candle in the corner threw light, creating stars of dust which floated in front of a painting he'd moved into the light. It was his favourite. A woman standing with her hound. Locks of curly blond hair framed her pretty face, and behind her were plants and flowers of all shapes and colours. The woman reminded him of his mother. Even the dog looked a little like Murphy if he squinted.

He'd lost his mother the day his village burned and a best friend the day The Columns exploded. The only person he had left was Abreeth, and he'd not seen him for days – in fact, he'd not seen anyone from the group he'd entered the city with for days. Leaving the room in a daydream, he walked straight into someone walking the halls.

'Nuri!' Dwin said, as surprised to see her as she was him.

'Dwin... I... I was just... how are you?'

'What are you doing in the tunnels? Shouldn't you be upstairs with Marsine and Gabrielle doing whatever it is that ladies do when there's a battle?'

Nuri laughed nervously, 'I'm not the type to sit around knitting when there's a kingdom on the brink.'

'Have you seen Abreeth? No one has heard from him for over two days now,' asked Dwin.

Nuri looked at her feet and replied, 'Sorry, Dwin, I haven't seen him. Sometimes people get fearful at the thought of going into battle. Perhaps he's found a quiet place in the city to wait until everything is safe?'

'Abreeth's no coward,' said Dwin angrily. 'He's a spearman on a cloudcutter. One of the most dangerous jobs in the kingdom. He wouldn't just go and hide when his friends needed him.'

'I don't know what to tell you, Dwin. I haven't seen him. I must go. Good luck,' said Nuri.

'Good luck?'

'Finding Abreeth, of course,' replied Nuri as she made her way in the opposite direction down the tunnel, just a little too briskly for his liking.

The way she looked back didn't sit right with him. Something in his gut told him she was acting unusual, very much like she didn't want him to follow her. So that's exactly what he did.

Soft as moss, his footsteps followed behind Nuri as she turned her way left and right through the tunnels with confidence. To Dwin, she looked like she knew where she wanted to go, but surely that couldn't be the case for someone new to the city and its keep?

Keeping far enough behind not to arouse suspicion, he balanced the fine line between maintaining his distance and allowing Nuri to take too many turns and slip away.

He was beginning to think he'd left too much space between them when he turned the corner and came to an empty corridor. Squinting to see if she'd dashed down the tunnel, he listened carefully in the darkness. All he heard was a faint, echoing drip in the distance. Cursing, he realised there were multiple tunnels ahead, and it was likely he'd lost her. Hurrying, he came to a junction. Left or right? Before he could make a decision, a noise from behind made him turn. A glancing, intense pain shot through the side of his head like lightning before darkness overcame him.

———

Consciousness slowly leaked back into Abreeth's mind. He heard the sound of water poured in a cup over his breathing. His head throbbed like he'd been celebrating with cheap wine and fistfights for a month. The smell of damp earth and stone filled his nostrils with the oily residue of a beeswax candle, recently lit.

Sensing movement behind him, he tried to move, discovering he was tied face down to a table. Testing his restraints, Abreeth realised he wasn't going anywhere, the cold draft on his bare back caused goose pimples to rise on his neck.

'There's no chance of escape, I'm afraid.'

'Nuri?' The memory of her kiss rushed back. Abreeth had no idea how long he'd been out. The poison she used was fast working and effective. He could be anywhere by now.

'Why are you doing this?' he croaked.

'Simple,' she said. 'Given the choice of being on the side that wins or the one that dies, which would you choose?'

'I don't understand?' said Abreeth.

'I'm making a choice,' said Nuri, walking around the table and stroking the hair from his eyes and placing a hand on his cheek. 'A choice that will help decide the fate of this city. Unfortunately for you, your fate is to be bound so you can find redemption.'

'Stop toying with him and bind him, then bring him to me,' came a voice that wafted through the room like it came from below the stones.

'Yes, my khan. I will have him to you as soon as I can,' came Nuri's reply.

Abreeth's eyes widened at those words. 'You fucking traitor,' he snarled, bucking and hammering his body against the table. 'You betrayed me. You betrayed all of us. You sold yourself to the khan.' In his struggles, Abreeth spied a body slumped in the corner tied with rope.

'Dwin!' he yelled. 'Dwin, can you hear me? Wake up.'

'Don't worry, he's alive,' said Nuri, opening a bag on the table next to Abreeth, 'for now.'

'You aren't going to get away with this,' breathed Abreeth through clenched teeth.

'That's where you're wrong, Abe, I already have. Our dark mages are controlling souls from your kingdom and sacrificing them against the walls as we speak. Soon the city will be flooded with our soldiers and...'

'Nuri, enough!' came the khan's voice from the corner of the room. 'Bind him and bring him to me.'

'Don't worry,' said Nuri, walking to a table in the corner, 'it will only hurt for a moment.'

Twisting his head, Abreeth could see Nuri taking an object from her bag and unwinding the needle-like tentacles from the internal mechanism. Ever so carefully, she opened a small box and took out a needle that glistened black in the candlelight and dipped it into a small vile.

'It's better if you don't struggle for this part,' she said.

Abreeth didn't listen. As the cold metal touched the back of his neck, he cried out and struggled. The poison Nuri had used on him had sapped most of his strength, and it wasn't long until he resigned himself to what was about to happen.

'I saved your life. We took you in. Are you going to betray Marsine as well? You wouldn't be here if not for us.'

'We must all make sacrifices, Abe. You may want to remain still,' was her reply.

Abreeth felt a slight pressure as Nuri jabbed the pin dipped in lament into the crystal placed on his back. The needles at each end of the welltaker whipped around as if they were alive, and he felt intense pain as they drove their pointed ends into his flesh and bore themselves into his body.

Abreeth's back arched as his leather bonds squeaked and popped. As his blood flowed through the device, he could feel the surge of menace and dark flow through his mind. The colour drained from his world as a despair that had hoarded itself behind the anguish and pain of a thousand years of bound souls burst forth from his screams.

'You finished now?' asked Nuri.

Abreeth groaned in a fog of pain and delusion.

'Good,' said Nuri, 'because we're just getting started.'

———

'Khan, I think you need to come and look at this,' said the mage, breathless from running.

'Might I remind you we're in the middle of a battle?' replied the khan, looking through a section of trees with his eyeglass.

'I would not be foolish enough to disturb you if I didn't think it was of great importance,' puffed his mage in reply.

'Fine,' said the khan, snapping his eyeglass away into its case, 'lead the way.'

The mage led the kahn back through rows of soldiers and bound slaves to his tent where his vinculum stood in its centre. Ornate carvings on the stone column showed demons and wraiths from the underworld eating and chasing humans. Inky, black liquid created a pool in the middle where thousands of tiny wisps, ruddy red in colour, moved around in groups. Seven other mages stood close, all working their dark magic at their own vinculums.

'As you know, each one of these wisps represents a bound soul,' said the mage.

'I dearly hope you didn't bring me here to educate me in the uses of the vinculum? It is a lesson I could do without at this moment,' said the khan dryly.

Ignoring the khan, the mage continued, 'When we fight, we add fire, and they turn red. If we want them to work, we add water, and they turn blue.'

'I know all this, mage,' said the khan impatiently. 'What is it that you felt so inclined to interrupt me in the middle of a battle to show me?'

'This,' he replied, pointing to a clump of red wisps, 'is that group of souls over there preparing for the next wave of attacks.' Moving his fingers around the liquid, a smaller group of red wisps appeared. 'That is the group attacking the city wall as we speak.'

'Go on,' replied the khan.

The mage dragged his fingers through the inky liquid and said, 'This is within the city. The keep, to be exact.'

They both stood looking at a single bright wisp floating in the vinculum, white as forgotten bone on the beach.

'I've never seen a soul represented in this way,' replied the mage. 'Red, green, blue and yellow. Those are the colours of the bound. Not white. This is an omen, Khan. This white soul is a harbinger of death. If darkness brings redemption, this light will bring perdition.'

Taken aback by the viciousness of the blow, the mage stumbled to his knees. The other mages looked up momentarily, but quickly returned to their work. Gripping him by the front of his gown, the khan dragged the mage to his feet. 'You will say no such thing ever again,' he hissed.

'We are about to win a great victory. I will not have it overshadowed by your infantile doubts and predictions. Get back to work.'

Rubbing his cheek and spitting out blood, the mage looked at the city with a hint of doubt in his eyes.

———

Nuri was dragging Abreeth down a dimly lit tunnel when he came to. Picking him up she jammed her shoulder under his armpit and led him through the darkened passageways.

'No!' he yelled, pushing her away, 'get away from me.'

Nuri stopped and stared. She'd seen hundreds, thousands of people bound and never had they spoken out of turn or shown any kind of defiance after the procedure. That was the whole concept of binding souls, to have complete control over every aspect of their being so they could do your bidding.

'What did you just say?' asked Nuri, not sure she'd heard him correctly.

'I said, get away from me,' Abreeth spat as his mind cleared. His body was recovering from the racking pain of being bound. Stumbling down the corridor in the opposite direction, he leaned against the wall for support. He could feel the stone against his hands like he'd never experienced. Every grain of compressed earth revealed itself to him in his mind. He reeled back from the overwhelming sensation of millions of tiny connections and elements active in his mind at once and again stumbled forward.

Nuri ran forward and grabbed Abreeth by the arm and spun him around, her eyes boring into his. 'You will come with me,' she said, looking for compliance in his demeanour.

Abreeth felt a menace and anger stir within him. He'd been betrayed, blown up, sliced open, seen his young charge's mother murdered and his town set ablaze, all in the past few weeks. The pent-up outrage roiled through his veins like an avalanche.

'I said NO!' he screamed as he pushed Nuri back with all his strength.

He could feel the air rush between them as she flew backwards fifteen feet into a wall, sagging unconscious on the ground.

Goose pimples rose over his body, and his perception of the air around him grew like battle rage. A yellow haze glowed like a sun on his hands. Chest rising, heart pounding, he fell to his knees and threw up.

33
TOWARDS THE BREACH

Bodies, bones and shattered hopes lay strewn across the cobblestone intermingled with the broken, tangled mess that used to be the city gates. Screams cut through the smoke as men lay dying and soldiers milled around in stunned silence.

Deadsun crawled out from the twisted wreckage of wood and weapons that covered him. Those working the ballista directly above the gates were not so lucky. They now joined the pile of mangled bodies and limbs where those indomitable wooden gates had once stood for centuries.

Wiping the dust and blood from his eyes, Deadsun ran downstairs to start fortifications of the gaping hole that now left the city as vulnerable as a bride on her wedding night. That's when he heard it – a chant floating from the forest which sent shivers down his spine. The khan's forces were preparing for their assault.

'You!' shouted Deadsun at a group of men milling around. 'Help me get what's left of those gates and move it onto that pile of bodies.'

A pile of dead soldiers, barrels and stone twice the height of a man lay at the city's entrance. Trying not to slip on the blood draining from the mass of corpses, the men helped manhandle sections of the city's gates, making a ramp to the top of the pile.

Pulling one of his captains aside, Deadsun ordered, 'Get as many troops as you can to the entrance. The khan will be throwing his soldiers at us now he's got a way into the city. This is where we make our stand.'

Within minutes two thousand soldiers gathered around the newest entrance to the city. If the khan desired access to Thade, his price for admission would be blood. Deadsun ran up the makeshift ramp to the top of the pile of bodies. From the ground, the destruction and chaos looked tenfold. Beasts and bodies of every kind lay dismembered for a hundred feet around.

'Only ten men can fit across this entrance,' yelled Deadsun to his troops, his voice hoarse from the dust and smoke. 'The khan's troops will have to bottleneck here to get through us. We stand here and fight. If one falls, another takes his place. If the khan wants this city, he will have to get through us first.'

A roar went up from the men, beating swords and shields together in reply. As if in response, screams and hollers came from the forest beyond the walls. The stark realisation dawned on everyone in the city that the next few hours would decide the fate of the Firmalands.

Deadsun ran atop the wall to command his troops once more, mentally preparing for what he knew would be hours of bloody fighting to the death. The khan had thrown thousands of bodies at the city wall, but they were all bound souls. Citizens of the Firmalands, people he'd kidnapped, all bound and put to use in his war efforts.

Now the khan had utilised his black powder to force an entrance into the city, Deadsun knew he would mobilise his army's full strength to wreak havoc. Thousands of warriors prepared themselves in the forest, chanting and beating their chests, no doubt sold on promises of land, steel and bound souls when they claimed victory. Grim, determined and outnumbered, the Lavers Lawmen of

Thade stood side by side with citizen-soldiers to fight for victory or death.

———

Abreeth wiped the vomit from his mouth and rose slowly. His body felt older than it should. The effects of controlling the air with his mind still swirled in his head like a summer storm. Shuffling over to Nuri, who lay still on the ground unconscious, he looked down at her and couldn't help but feel a combination of anger and pity.

'Oh, Nuri, how could you do this?' he said sadly. 'I thought we were friends... Dwin!' Abreeth cried, remembering his young charge. Turning, he ran to the room with Dwin still bound in the corner.

'Dwin, Dwin,' Abreeth shouted, shaking his friend. 'Dwin, wake up.'

'Mmmmrgh,' groaned Dwin in annoyance, 'let me sleep just a little longer.'

'Dwin, we have to go... c'mon,' said Abreeth, untying the teenager's bonds and scooping him into his arms.

Navigating the tunnels as best he could, Abreeth climbed every staircase that made its way upwards. Eventually, he found himself in a room he recognised and made his way to the keep's infirmary.

'Abreeth, what happened to Dwin?' cried Marsine, running down the hall. 'And what happened to you?'

Naked from the waist up, vomit on his pants and a welltaker attached to his neck, Abreeth only just realised what a mess he must look.

'Marsine,' sighed Abreeth, thankful to see a friendly face. 'Nuri betrayed us. She's with the khan. She poisoned and bound me, but it didn't work. She hurt Dwin too,' he said, the words spilling out.

'What?' said Marsine. 'I knew there was something strange about her.'

'She betrayed us, Marsine,' growled Abreeth, surprised at the acid he spat as he continued into the infirmary.

Marsine gasped when she saw the angry, red welltaker scoured into the back of Abreeth's neck. He placed Dwin down gently on a bed as a young girl dressed in yellow walked quickly to his side to tend to his injuries. By this time, Gabrielle had heard the noise and wandered into the infirmary to stand beside Dwin.

'Look after this boy like he was your brother, understand?' said Abreeth forcefully.

The nurse nodded.

Abreeth spun on his heel and made for the door but was stopped by a hand grabbing his sleeve.

'Abe, wait,' cried Marsine, 'you must tell me what's going on.'

'All those souls the khan has gathered up throughout the kingdom,' said Abreeth, shaking with rage at the thought, 'he plans to sacrifice them all to get through the city walls. I must tell Deadsun. We have to find the khan's dark mages. They hold the key to controlling them.'

'How?' asked Marsine.

'I don't know,' said Abreeth. 'I plan to figure that part out on the way.'

'I'm coming with you,' she said, taking his arm and supporting him down the hallway.

'I suppose I'll stay here and look after Dwin,' sighed Gabrielle to no one in particular.

By the time Abreeth and Marsine arrived at the gates, the first wave of the khan's soldiers had slammed into the defenders, pushing them back. Both of them were awestruck with the carnage at the entrance of the city. The gates that seemed impenetrable just a few days ago lay broken and shattered, just like the bodies and beasts that coloured the stones red with their cruor. The smell of burnt powder and acrid smoke hung low, stinging their nostrils.

'Abe, my boy. Where have you been?' hollered Horst when he saw him from the top of the wall.

'Horst! I must speak with Deadsun, have you seen him?' he called as they ran up the stairs. Marsine was white as a ghost from seeing the carnage of battle.

'Aye, laddie, he's right here!' said Horst.

Abreeth reached the top of the stairs with Marsine close behind.

'Marsine,' said Deadsun in surprise, 'you should not be here. It isn't safe. Abreeth, where have you been?'

'Nuri has betrayed us. The khan plans to use our people to...,' as Abreeth reached the edge of the wall, he saw the thousands of bodies strewn outside the city.

Right through the middle, the khan's troops had cut a line to ferry men and weapons. A wooden structure covered with hide created a protected path to the gaping hole in the city's defences.

'By the four gods,' stammered Abreeth, looking at the gruesome picture before him. Marsine gasped, turning her face into Deadsun's chest.

'We know,' said Deadsun quietly, putting his hand on her shoulder. 'The khan has used our people as beasts for this butchery.'

'There are so many,' said Abreeth, trying to comprehend the destruction of so many lives.

'We've been fighting as hard as we can,' said Deadsun, his arm wrapped protectively around Marsine. 'We're going to lose the city, Abe. It's only a matter of time. We're outnumbered three to one.'

'Surely there must be something we can do,' said Marsine softly over the screams and clashing of weapons that surrounded them.

'We will be able to keep them at bay for a few more hours, but we've already got nearly a thousand men dead or injured. The khan has at least five thousand well-trained soldiers at his disposal, probably more bound souls, and that blasted black powder. If we had men and weapons coming from the Welkinpeaks, we might stand a chance, but with The Columns destroyed, we're on our own.'

Abreeth couldn't believe what he was hearing. After everything they'd been through, everything they'd fought for. The chance of victory was quickly slipping through their fingers.

'No,' he said, 'I can't let myself believe that we're just going to give up.'

'No one said anything about giving up,' said Deadsun, 'we will make our last stand in the keep. If we're going to die, we will at least make the bastards work for it.'

Abreeth noticed how exhausted they all looked. They'd all been living off a few hours sleep. Abreeth and Dwin had been running for weeks, never knowing what would happen to them or which path they would take next. Throughout the entire time they'd been travelling, running, fighting, there'd always been hope their journey would take them to a better place, until now.

'So this is how it ends,' said Abreeth, 'the khan's army overwhelms us?'

'It's either that or surrender,' replied Deadsun.

A runner stopped at Deadsun's side and stated, 'Commander, the ballista has run out of javelins. Your orders?'

Deadsun sighed and ordered, 'Get whoever's manning down into the reserves at the gates. We need everyone who can swing a sword at the entrance.' Turning to Marsine, Deadsun held her shoulders in his hands and said seriously, 'You must go back to the keep. It's too dangerous for you here.'

'When will I see you again?' Marsine whispered.

Deadsun's answer was a kiss before running towards the gates yelling orders.

'Horst, there must be something we can do?' asked Abreeth, turning to the dwarf.

'I've been on the wall, laddie and Deadsun's right. I've fought in the northern wars and seen my share of battles and blood, but never have I seen slaughter to match the likes of this. Our hours are numbered. Make peace with your gods while you still can,' replied the dwarf.

Abreeth roared and kicked a brazier over, spilling the contents along the stone of the wall. Picking up a sword, he hurled it over the wall where it bounced off the hide-covered structure that protected the khan's troops.

'You lickspittle sons of dogs,' he thundered, 'hiding like fucking cowards!' He was so angry he picked up the brazier he'd knocked over and hurled it over the wall. As the ash and coals fell through the gaps in the iron, he could feel them against his skin, not burning him, but feeding his rage.

He closed his eyes and let the anger take over. The air around him swirled and bounced into a small whirlwind. Picking up speed and ferocity, the wind gathered up the coals strewn across the stones, now glowing red and angry.

Abreeth stood before this apparition of wind and fire, his hands glowing with this new magic that flowed through his veins. Sweeping his arms aside, Abreeth threw the blazing tornado over the wall, sending it crashing into the wooden structure below, causing screams and carnage as it tore through wood, hide and bodies.

Horst, Marsine and several others along the wall stood, their mouths agape and eyes wide, uncertain about what they'd just witnessed. Abreeth stood, letting the rage drain from his body, feeling as though he was looking at himself from afar but still inside his own body.

'You are a bloody fawesooth!' said Horst in disbelief.

'Look,' came a shout from the wall, 'in the distance!'

The dark shadows of a dozen massive pyredrakes materialised on the horizon, wings slowly cutting the air as they flew towards the city.

There's a funny thing that happens when panic takes hold of a crowd. It's like floodwaters smashing through a village. It would be folly to try and stop it, and almost impossible not to get swept away. Shrieks and howls of 'he has pyredrakes' and 'we're done for' echoed across the stones as men who'd just spent the past two days seeing absolute carnage looked panicked to the core by what slowly flew towards them.

34
REDEMPTION BY THE SWORD

Dismay ran through the men protecting the city like a virus. One thing that instills fear in even the bravest of soldiers is a battery of pyredrakes flying towards a city. Seeing this meant one thing and one thing only. Your home will suffer from fire and brimstone as these vicious creatures circle and spit death from above.

Some men ran, leaving their stations against orders. Others stood rooted to the ground, having never seen a pyredrake, let alone dozens of them. As the silhouettes coalesced to form a firmer vision of these beasts, a soldier yelled, 'There's something wrong.'

'Is that a fact?' replied his friend. 'Pyredrakes are about to attack us. That's what's fucking wrong!'

'No, look,' came his reply. 'I've seen pyredrakes before, and they don't look like that.'

Abreeth, Horst and Marsine walked to the edge of the wall to look into the distance. There seemed to be a lull in the fighting for a brief moment as even the khan's troops turned to look at the group of flying horrors gliding towards the city.

Abreeth saw the familiar shape of the cloudcutters he'd worked on for the past year, as the group banked to the left. His mind flashed back to several weeks ago when Yonex showed him the prototype of his winged boat.

'That crazy son of a bitch must have escaped,' said Abreeth, more to himself than anyone else.

'Who escaped?' asked Horst, looking at the boats, confusion on his face.

'It's a long story, but those are boats. Cloudcutters with wings attached to them. And they're on our side!' replied Abreeth.

'What are they carrying?' asked Marsine, awestruck as the cloudcutters loomed closer, their wings slowly gliding through the air, ropes floating behind them.

Abreeth whooped. 'Those are spurworms,' he cried, 'and if I know Borchin like I think I do, we're about to see something very spectacular.'

Deadsun ran back to the top of the wall and stood beside Abreeth, perplexed at the scene before them. 'What in the four gods is going on?' asked Deadsun.

'Wait and see,' said Abreeth, 'and get your men ready for an attack on the khan's troops.'

Sliding through the air, the lead ship picked up pace and carved off towards the city's entrance. Coloured red and with a carving of Taw, the air god at its helm, Abreeth recognised the craft instantly. Standing on the bow of the boat, his hair and beard streaming in the wind, was Borchin, smiling as the craft came to a gliding hover near the entrance of the gates. Borchin called, 'Ahoy, Abe! Is Dwin with you?' Abreeth was speechless. 'Well, don't just stand there with your pecker in your porridge,' called Borchin, obviously enjoying the look of disbelief on the face of every man along the wall.

Shaking himself from his stupor, Abreeth called, 'Yes, Dwin's fine. How did you... what are you... I don't...'

Borchin smiled wide and answered, 'We thought that since the Welkinpeaks couldn't send troops to help, we could introduce the next best thing to the khan's army.'

Climbing back to the helm of his craft, Borchin peeled his cloud-cutter away and flew in a lazy loop towards the back of the khan's troops, pulling two spurworms wrapped in nets behind him.

Sailing over the top of the khan's soldiers, Borchin opened the nets with military precision. Two writhing, very angry spurworms landed directly on the enemy troops. Screaming and howling erupted as the two massive worms thrashed and tore apart the wooden structure and the men beneath it. The khan, in his arrogance, had cleared bodies and debris, creating a direct line to the entrance of the city for his waiting troops. Thousands of Pyrelanders in a neat row, ripe for destruction.

Borchin directed his crew with the deft expertise of one who'd lived life at the helm as the men on the wall cheered and hooted at the scene unfolding before them.

Even larger than the first two, another pair of worms dropped at the head of the khan's troops, effectively cutting off movement forwards or backwards. Before long, there were dozens of spurworms wreaking havoc and death upon the khan's fighters.

Abreeth couldn't believe his eyes as the worms decimated the khan's soldiers in a matter of minutes. He'd resorted himself to fighting on for hours, making a last stand to the death in the keep. The city's redemption had come in the form of wings and worms.

One of the worms let out an ear-splitting screech and crashed against the walls, making all those on it stumble. Writhing and gnashing massive teeth, it rolled into the square at the entrance of the city, causing men and horses to scatter. Several men tried to attack it head-on but quickly had their limbs detached from their bodies for their efforts. Swords and spears hung from its skin like a pin cushion, the frontal attacks making no difference to its destructive power.

Abreeth ran to the edge of the wall where the shattered remains of a ballista lay strewn across the stone. Sifting through the rubble, he found what he was looking for and tested it in his hands. The javelin was heavier than the ones they used to hunt spurworms, but the razor-sharp tip would do the same job. Waiting for the worm to turn, so its ear was facing him, he took a calming breath and hurled the javelin in an arc towards the thrashing beast. The wet slap of metal hitting meat and a limp spurworm told him he'd hit the sweet spot as the creature became still.

A mighty cheer came up from the men in the courtyard as they ran to the city's entrance to watch the carnage of the khan's troops being torn apart by angry spurworms.

'What a throw, laddie!' cried Horst, slapping Abreeth on the back.

'Thanks,' replied Abreeth, 'it seems now we have the advantage.'

'Indeed we do,' agreed the dwarf. 'Deadsun, now is the time to attack the khan and his mages while we have the advantage.'

Deadsun turned to Abreeth and said, 'Can you get us on one of those boats? We're going hunting.'

———

Just as Horst suspected, the khan – upon seeing he was fighting a losing battle, had gathered his captains, mages and senior advisors and fled on horseback. The khan's stallions were no match for the winged cloudcutters that now gave chase. Lined with archers along the side of the craft, Borchin sailed over the top of the fleeing enemy. A hail of arrows made quick work of both men and horses. The few left able to run peeled off into a large copse of trees in the hope of finding cover.

'Can you get us onto the ground?' asked Deadsun.

'BRACE YOURSELVES!' hollered Borchin as he banked his ship and headed straight for the trees in which the khan and his men were hiding. Abreeth ran to the bow of the boat, holding the ropes used to attach the hunting harpoons and howled as the craft crashed through the trees, coming to a stop on the ground.

The khan and one of his mages burst from their hiding place, galloping to open ground. Without a second thought Abreeth grabbed a harpoon, its wood and metal a familiar comfort in his hands.

For a split second, his mind told him he would never make this throw. It was too far, even for an experienced spearman like him. Calming his breath, he hurled the harpoon with as much power as he could muster. It wasn't something he noticed in the moment, but the men on the craft saw the ripple and wave of manipulated air surrounding Abreeth's arm as he heaved the wood and metal spear at the escaping khan.

No mortal man could have made that throw. Men would tell stories in taverns and on talking posts for years to come about this extraordinary throw. As if lifted by the gods themselves, Abreeth's harpoon sailed through the air for hundreds of feet, straight as an arrow and lodged itself through the khan and his horse, causing them both to crash in a cloud of dust and failure.

Seeing his khan fall, his last standing mage looked at the stream of soldiers crawling over the sides of the grounded vessel and then back again to his khan, weighing up his options.

'Help me up, mage,' gurgled the injured khan, specks of blood misting from his mouth. 'Do not leave me,' he snarled. 'You will pay dearly if you turn that horse,' he said, wincing in pain.

'You have lost all power, Khan. It's over. I hope you find redemption in the death that approaches you.' Turning his horse, the mage rode off at a gallop. The khan yelled insults and promises of revenge as he disappeared into the distance.

Resting his head on the cool ground, the khan looked to the sky; a grey cloud in the shape of a Pyredrake floated across his gaze, making him chuckle at the irony as triumph, power and life ebbed from his grasp.

Deadsun was the first to reach him. 'Hello again, Khan,' he smiled.

'Get it over with, Commander,' wheezed the khan, holding the bloody tubes of his belly in with his good arm, the other hanging limply by his side.

'You've met Killbride before,' said Deadsun, placing his sword at the khan's throat. 'I told you this steel would be the last thing you see. Perhaps you now wish to swear fealty to *our* king?'

The khan gritted his teeth and spat at Deadsun, spraying blood up the blade.

'That won't be the last of your blood this sword sees today,' Deadsun replied as the blade sank into the khan's carotid artery slowly, like a first-time lover. Sharp and slow, it opened his neck. As his lifeforce pumped onto the ground in spurts, the khan gurgled his last word. 'Redemption.'

35

SAFE AT LAST

When Deadsun, Abreeth, Yonex, Horst and Borchin finally made it back to the city, they were given a hero's welcome as word the khan was dead and the war over had spread quickly. Riding through the city streets on horses they'd sequestered, Abreeth was busy catching up with Borchin and Yonex as they tried to navigate the crowd.

'So you left Roda Codex and went south in that tiny boat of Yonex's?' said Abreeth. 'I thought there was nothing but hot winds and savages in the highskies down there?'

'Aye, so did we until we met a Southman that kept pyredrakes. Said he had too many on his farm and was going to kill off a bunch of them. Tried to sell us the skins, but we were more interested in the wings. I sold everything I had to get five cloudcutters and headed south with him,' replied Borchin, moving in the saddle to take a flower and a kiss from a young woman in the crowd.

'Five?' asked Deadsun. 'How is it you came to have many more in your fleet then?'

'With villages in the Welkinpeaks being put to the flame and people missing, I knew the khan was up to something. Something big. So we took two of our new wingships and started poking around the kingdom, looking around from the highskies. We spotted the khan's army crossing the tundra and hundreds of stolen boats and cloudcutters that had crashed onto the plain. That's what he was doing, sending his men up into the Welkinpeaks to bind our people, and steal our cloudcutters. I knew we would need as much help as we could get, so I struck a deal with the Southmen.'

'What kind of deal?' asked Deadsun, raising an eyebrow.

'Let's just say I'll be needing to speak to the king about letting the Southmen salvage those boats on the tundra for helping save his city,' said Borchin with a smile.

'Bloody pirates,' jested Deadsun. 'You lot are worse than dwarves!'

'I heard that,' Horst exclaimed, 'and I expect you to buy me a mug of ale for that insult.'

Laughing, Deadsun replied, 'Friend, I'll buy you a whole keg for the way you fought on the wall.'

'Five gallons or ten?' asked Horst quickly.

'The king has thirty-gallon kegs in his larder,' replied Deadsun with a wink, as Horst's eyes grew wide with glee.

The king and his courtiers were waiting as the group dismounted at the steps of the keep. Deadsun walked to kneel in front of the king, holding the dead khan's crown in his hands above his head. The king looked at the large crowd gathered in the centre of the city and smiled as he took the pig iron, bone and dark crystal crown, raising it above his head and shouted, 'Victory!'

A roar exploded from the city like a waterfall, cascading over king and kin. Every weary soldier standing in front of their king felt a swell of relief. The head of the khan sat on a pike at the stairs of the keep for all to see and spit on. As bent and broken as his army's honour, his crown would be melted down and used to make medals for those who showed exceptional bravery during the fighting.

Immense funeral pyres spewed columns of greasy, black smoke that hung over the city for days. The flies and crows feasted on those waiting for cremation. Fallen soldiers and bound souls were returned to the earth reborn as ash and soot.

Blacksmiths beat their hammers and carpenters lovingly carved the wood of new, stronger gates as stonemasons repaired the damage the khan's boomdust caused to the walls. The city was saved and its citizens safe. Slowly they stopped hiding in their homes and restored their lives to some semblance of normal once more.

Enemy soldiers who were lucky enough to escape the violent attacks from the spurworms were either chased back over the mountains or thrown in the city's dungeons, where they would spend the rest of their short lives in damp, crowded conditions before their eventual execution.

The khan's mages all fled or were hunted and killed, the crystals in their vinculum's destroyed. When the dark gems shattered, every bound soul woke from their bindings to see the light once more.

Families were elated in reunion and devastated by loss in equal measure when their loved ones were discovered alive or found fallen. The kingdom could finally pick up the pieces from the devastation the khan and his army had caused. Now the danger had passed, villagers would soon return to their homes after a week-long celebration of feasting, drinking, and dancing.

———

The heady mix of roasted meats, woodsmoke and victory wafted through the keep's hall as the sound of laughter and song rose from the long tables. At the head sat the king, merry from a little too much wine. To his right sat Deadsun, who had finally been able to let his guard down and enjoy the festivities after the long days of mopping up the khan's fractured army. Putting the city back in order had been his priority, which meant little time for himself or his new love. But that would change soon. The ring in his pocket would make sure of that.

He stole a kiss from Marsine, who sat next to him, arms wrapped around his muscular bicep with the soft promise of a new lover. The wine flowed unreservedly, and stores from the larders had been given freely by the king to the hundreds within the hall and the thousands outside.

Abreeth sat next to Borchin and Dwin, deep in conversation as servants piled more plates of food in front of them. Filling up Abreeth's cup with ale, Borchin asked, 'And this Nuri girl, did they find her after you saved Dwin?'

'No,' came Abreeth's reply. 'She managed to escape... I suspect she's long gone by now. Probably headed back west to the Pyrelands.'

'Shame,' said Borchin, 'would've liked to have met the girl who bested you!'

Dwin snorted.

'Don't you laugh,' smiled Abreeth, 'she bested you also!'

'I, for one, am glad you're OK, ' said Gabrielle, misty-eyed from her seat next to Dwin.

'Thank you, Gabrielle,' replied Dwin, 'at least someone here cares about my wellbeing.'

'If we're to marry one day, I have to look after you,' she purred, sliding her hand into his.

Dwin coughed as he choked on a piece of chicken, much to the amusement of those at the table.

———

Later that evening, under the light of the moon, Deadsun and Abreeth sat on a balcony wrapped in furs as they spoke about what was to come next.

'Will you go back to the Welkinpeaks?' asked Deadsun.

'I don't know. Now that Borchin can get back up there, many more people will move between there and the Firmalands, including me. But for now, I plan to spend some time here and recuperate.'

'Good. It would be a shame to see you leave so soon,' replied

Deadsun.

Walking to the edge of the balcony and looking into the moon, he exclaimed, 'Those wingships are amazing. It opens up many opportunities for the kingdom.'

'That it does,' replied Abreeth as he took another sip of ale. 'We will be able to trade and hunt further afield than ever before.'

'We need good men in the city, Abe,' said Deadsun, turning to face his new friend. 'Stay. Work with me and help rebuild the city and the kingdom. I can make it worth your while.'

Abreeth smiled. 'The old me would have jumped at the chance to do something in the city of Thade,' he said. 'But so much has happened these past few weeks. I was never expecting to see Borchin again, so I thought I would be looking after Dwin until he was old enough to fend for himself. Now I find myself with this magic, these powers I know little about and don't know how to control. I don't know. It just seems like everything is so... up in the air at the moment.'

'I feel the same way,' replied Deadsun, sitting back down next to Abreeth. 'My head is swimming after the past few weeks.' Suddenly he turned and said, 'I plan to ask for Marsine's hand tomorrow.'

'Really?' said Abreeth in surprise. 'Good for you.'

'It feels right,' said Deadsun.

'Then you should do it. Do you have a ring?' Abreeth asked.

Deadsun pulled the ring he'd been keeping in his pocket the past few days and showed it to his friend. Turning the gold over in his fingers, Abreeth smiled. 'Well then, that settles it!'

'Settles what?' asked Deadsun.

'I have to stay. At least until the wedding,' Abreeth smiled.

'Good,' replied Deadsun simply.

Lacing his hand on Abreeth's shoulder, he said, 'Come, let us get another drink. We have much more celebrating to do.'

Very few slept that night, and many were still discussing a pathway forward for the kingdom as the twin suns threw their first sunbeams across a city full of hope and promise.

EPILOGUE

Fog shrouded the boatyards like a grey, sodden blanket, dampening the sounds of footsteps in the dim light. Ropes creaked, and waves slapped gently on the bows of sleeping ships, waiting for the suns to rise before heading back out to the Brine.

'Two silvers for passage,' said the captain of a swift trader to the hooded figure who'd arrived on his gangplank. 'Three if you don't want any questions.'

'Three silvers it is,' replied the passenger, handing him the coins.

'What should we call you?' asked the captain.

'I thought you said no questions?' replied Nuri as she slipped into the belly of the craft, ready to set sail on the morning tide.

To be continued...

ACKNOWLEDGMENTS

Whilst writing a novel is primarily a solitary endeavour involving long hours in front of a computer screen and staring out of windows alone with your thoughts, many hands touch a story before it becomes ink on a page or pixels on a screen.

To my wonderful wife, I can't thank you enough for the encouragement and support you've shown me over the past few years whilst I toiled away at this tome.

To my two children, who inspire me and bring light and wonder to my world, I thank you for listening to countless storylines and character ideas and for helping me build a better story.

A massive thank you to my beta readers, who pointed out plot holes and areas that needed improvement. In particular, I want to single out Alex, who has been my #1 fan from the beginning and has been on this journey with me over the past few years, reading my work with unbridled enthusiasm. Thanks, mate. Your words of encouragement and support mean the world to me.

I want to thank my publisher Sarah for taking a chance on me and her team at Serenade Publishing for helping me shape this book into its best possible version.

I also thank the fantastic musicians Heilung, Wardruna, Meshuggah and Gojira, who filled my ears with the soundscapes which helped feed my creativity and forge many of the scenes (in particular the battle scenes) in this novel.

And lastly, thank you coffee – without this magic bean juice, none of this would have been possible.

MORE FROM SERENADE PUBLISHING

Brigadier Station Series

By Sarah Williams:

The Brothers of Brigadier Station

The Sky over Brigadier Station

The Legacies of Brigadier Station

The Outback Governess (A Sweet Outback Novella)

Christmas at Brigadier Station (An Outback Christmas Novella)

Heart of the Hinterland Series

By Sarah Williams:

The Dairy Farmer's Daughter

Their Perfect Blend

Beyond the Barre

A Dying Second Sun

by Peter A. Dowse

Winner Winner Chicken Dinner

by Sarah Jackson

For more information visit:

www.serenadepublishing.com